Earth ANGEL

FRANKY GOMEZ

NEWMAN SPRINGS PUBLISHING
320 Broad Street
Red Bank, NJ 07701

First originally published by Newman Springs Publishing 2022

ISBN 978-1-68498-685-9 (Paperback)
ISBN 978-1-68498-686-6 (Digital)

Printed in the United States of America

Sunday

Isaiah continues his free fall. He is struggling to get his parachute around to his back. He must be careful to not lose the parachute against the powerful force of the wind rushing against his body. He contorts himself just enough to get the pack onto his back. He works to secure it and tightens the straps. During his maneuvering in the air, he gets himself turned to where he can now see the jet. It's hard for him to tell how far away it is, but he knows that it's dropping in elevation fast.

"They don't have parachutes," he softly says as he looks on. He has a large sense of guilt while he watches it in free fall. *I've got to get to the ground fast*, he thinks. He changes his mind; he decides to go help the angels instead of looking for the halo. So he straightens his body out, head toward the ground, and torpedoes down to the forest in the direction of the jet. He knows that he will reach the ground faster, but the danger is that he won't leave himself much space to deploy this chute. Adding to the difficulty is that he doesn't have any goggles, so he must keep his eyes closed as he torpedoes so not to get them dried out or damaged by other flying debris or bugs.

During his decent, he will have to continuously open his eyes and check his elevation relative to the tree line. He opens his eyes to check his altitude. He feels like he has reached a good altitude to release his parachute. He pulls the chute and gets the upward thrust against the canopy. He grabs the controls and begins to steer the chute. He turns his parachute back in the direction of the jet, which is now out of sight.

I hope that they survived the crash, he thinks to himself. He can see a faint dust of cloud coming out from the forest. He stares at the cloud of dust and smoke for a bit. He looks down to see how close he is to the tree line when a sound catches his attention. The sound is faint but familiar. He looks around, down below, and does not see anything. He gives his chute a quarter turn, and still, he sees nothing. The sound is getting clear and louder as it is getting closer to him. He does another quarter turn and can now see what helicopters. He counts what he can make out to be about nine choppers. Now that he can see what they are, the sound of blades cutting through the sky is more apparent to him. He knows who it is; he begins to curse and yell helplessly through the air. He grips the controls and begins to steer the parachute faster toward the jet and, now, the helicopters.

* * * * *

The devils reach the crash site. They hover above and drop their ropes into the trees, down to the jet. The ropes do not reach the ground.

"Get as low as you can," Ty orders the pilot. Even with the choppers as low as they can get, the ropes are short, approximately sixty feet.

"This is as low as we can get," the pilot says.

"All right, we are scaling down the trees," Ty tells the crew.

One by one the devils begin to rappel down the ropes then jump onto the trees. As they jump on the trees, they transform into beast mode. While in beast mode, they can scale down the trees with little effort. As the devils reach the ground, they move into position to surround the jet. They stay hidden from view so they can attack with the least amount of resistance as possible.

Ty reaches the ground first; Sara, unloading in a different area, reaches the ground second. The devils are traveling light as they are only carrying their weapons. They anticipated not having to spend much time on this mission. After several minutes of unloading, all the devils reach the ground. The helicopters move out of the area and return to the devil staging area.

On the ground, they continue to move intentionally around the jet, directed by Ty and Sara. The devils heavily outnumber the angels fourteen to one, and they hold the element of surprise, to some degree. Although they want to surprise the angels as much as possible, they expect the angels to be prepared for them. They are also counting on the angels to be unprepared and hurt after a crash landing, but knowing that the angels can move quick, they need to move quicker. Ty and Sara have their team in place, ready to attack.

* * * * *

Isaiah continues his decline in elevation toward the crash site, but he's still far from it. He runs out of sky and is about to reach the tree line. He diverts his eyes from the forest, as he enters, attempting to maneuver his way through the trees. Right away his chute begins to tear as it snags some tree branches. His attempt to avoid contact with the trees is short-lived as he gets whipped and hit by some limbs and branches. His canopy and suspension lines get caught on a larger branch, leaving him hanging about thirty feet from the ground. He swings a little before coming to a full stop. He looks around a couple of times and then lets out a big sigh. He puts is head back and looks up at the sky. He can feel the sun beaming down on his face as debris falls around him. He brings his head back and begins to try and get out of his harness. He moves with a deep sense of urgency as he wants to get back to his fellow angels.

Knowing that the devils are on their way makes him uneasy. He looks down around him to see what is below. He doesn't see anything concerning. He presses the release on his harness and detaches from the canopy. He drops and lands on his feet then onto this back and rolls over his head onto his hands and knees. He quickly adjusts and begins to orientate himself.

As he's not familiar with the forest, as most people won't be, the three-sixty view looks the same to him. Before he starts to run in the direction he thinks the jet is in, he checks his person to see what he may have on him. He is hoping for his phone, a knife—anything that may help him in any way—but he finds nothing. The angels are prepared for situations like this. Their parachutes are equipped with a pack that is attached to the harness, full of provisions. Unfortunately, Isaiah's pack is up thirty feet stuck in a tree. He looks up and stares at it. It will be difficult to get to, and he can't afford to spend that amount of time trying to retrieve it. He lets out another big sigh. He begins to run to the angels, in hopes that he can get to them in time.

* * * * *

With no reason to run, Vanessa and Uriah continue walking through the forest. Little by little, Vanessa begins to fall behind as she is deep in thought. She comes to a stop; Uriah continues to walk.

"Did we leave them to die?" Vanessa asks.

Uriah stops then looks back at her for a moment and begins to walk again. He is unsure how to respond to that question. Vanessa remains staring at Uriah walking away.

"Tell me we didn't leave them back there to die!" she shouts.

Uriah takes a couple more steps and then stops. He looks up to the sky then forward again.

"I don't know. It changes every minute for me. But I know this, if I were in their place, I would have told you to leave me as well. We have to get back so we can get help and come back for them. We have to keep going. We might be able to catch up to Rudy," he explains.

He continues to walk. Vanessa stays behind a moment to gather herself. She takes a deep breath, looks up at the sky, and then begins to walk again. They walk for a bit when Uriah hears water. He stops for a moment to confirm.

A river, he thinks. "Vanessa, I hear a…" She isn't behind him. He doesn't want to draw attention by yelling out her name, so he waits.

She comes into view. She is staring at the ground as she walks. She won't look up, so he looks around while he waits for her to catch up. He is cautious that there may be devils nearby. She finally looks up.

"You hear that?" he asks.

"Hear what?" she asks in return. She is in such a daydream that she doesn't realize that she is within hearing range of the river.

"It's water, a river, a creek. Either way, it's a good sign," he tells her.

They walk to the river.

"Now what?" she asks.

They look across the way and down both sides of the river.

"Which way should we go?" she asks.

"I don't know," he responds.

"Well, let's go this way for a bit." She points to their right. "And if we have to cross the river at some point, then we will," Vanessa suggests.

She begins to walk in that direction. Uriah stays back, staring across the river. After a half minute or so, he begins to follow. Not a minute passes when Vanessa sees Rudy's body.

"Uriah! It is Rudy!" she yells out.

Uriah runs to Vanessa, and together they run to his body.

Vanessa begins to cry. "Why?" she asks, kneeling next to Rudy's lifeless body.

A sound catches Uriah's attention. He looks around and sees two devils in the distant. They cannot see them. "SSHHH," he tells Vanessa.

"Why? He is dead," she points out.

"Up ahead, there are some devils. We just have to keep quiet," he tells her.

"Look at him," she says.

"I know, but we have to keep moving. The devils are still around, and by now, they know that Rudy didn't have the halo. They might even know that it was not in the jet at all. They are probably all over the forest. We have to get help. We will come back for him," he expresses.

"All right," she replies.

They wait and lie low around Rudy's corpse watching the devils.

"You know what, we head the other way then cross the river. I think we will be safer on that side," he tells her.

"Okay, let's go," she replies.

They wait a little longer. The devils turn away from their direction, allowing them to continue down the river in the opposite direction.

* * * * *

Isaiah continues to move through the forest. He stops for a moment to try and figure out where he is. He realizes that he has been running with tunnel vision, not really paying attention to where he is going. Not only does he not know where he is, he doesn't know how long he has been running or how far he is from the crash site, but something tells him to stop. He takes a moment to catch his breath. He looks around but sees nothing that will bring him any sense of direction or any indication that he is going toward the jet. He puts his left hand against a tree nearby.

He takes inventory of himself. He is tired and frustrated and slightly hungry. The concern for the angels suppresses his full hunger. He thinks about finding something to eat.

"I'm going to need some fuel," he says aloud.

He releases his hand from the tree and looks around more intently as he listens for anything that may help him. He hears nothing and sees nothing. He is frustrated and lost. He continues running in the same direction.

Hopefully, this next stretch will bring me some food or water or both, actually, he thinks to himself.

* * * * *

Sara returns to the jet. "You all check the jet for the halo," she instructs a group of devils.

The devils stare at one another.

"What is it? Why are you all just standing there?" she asks.

One of them decides to speak up. "We did that already. We didn't find anything," the devil tells Sara.

"Damn it," Sara expresses. She looks around in disgust. "Tell me that you guys took care of the angels?" she asks.

The devils look around at one another again.

"What is it now?" she asks.

The devils stay silent, longer this time. None of them want to respond.

"One of you better say something, now," she commands.

Finally, a different devil decides to answer. "They got away."

"Are you fucking kidding me?" she asks.

The devils remain silent. She walks around, thinking. "Which way did they go?" she asks.

A couple of devils point in the same direction.

"All of you, go after them, now. Do not come back until you find them," she instructs.

They all run into the forest.

One devil stops and turns around. "Sara," he says.

"What?" she yells out.

"Three soldiers already went after them," he tells her.

"Are they dead?" she asks.

"Who?" the devil replies.

"The fucking angels, you moron," she says with annoyance.

He stands silent for a moment. "I don't know."

"Go find out, you idiot," she says.

The devil runs off to catch up to the rest of the group.

"Everyone else, get out there and look for the halo!" she shouts out.

*　*　*　*　*

Uriah and Vanessa are moving slowing along the bank of the river. They stop for a break.

"I'm going to sit for a minute," Vanessa tells Uriah.

She finds a flat spot to lie down. She throws her arms above her head to open her chest up. Uriah finds a tree to lean up against, and then he hunches over and puts his hands on his knees. There is a whimper and sniffles coming from the ground. Vanessa moves her left arm over to cover her eyes. Her right arm moves to the top of her head. Her whimper becomes a full cry.

Uriah moves away from the tree and walks over to sit next to her. He rubs her left forearm. Her right hand grabs his. She turns toward him and crawls into his lap as her cry intensifies. Uriah continues to comfort her by rubbing her arms and back.

"They're all gone," she struggles to say.

Uriah doesn't know how to respond as he tries to hold back tears of his own.

"Why…why…I don't understand," she says after letting out a big breath.

Trying to stay strong for her, Uriah keeps the tears from running down his face.

"Why did this happen to us?" she asks.

He still has no response. He has the same questions and feelings as she does but isn't able to be as expressive. He is angrier more than anything. Vanessa puts her hand on the ground and sits up, separating herself from him.

"This is crazy. How did this happen?" she asks.

"I don't know. Something ain't right," he responds.

"What do you mean?" she asks with a strong curiosity.

"Just the way it all happened—it was almost perfect for the devils, too perfect," he says.

"I don't know what you mean," she says.

"Think about it: they knew our route, accurate on their hit. They only took one shot. Then they knew where to find us in a forest. Too perfect. They are not that good," he explains to Vanessa.

She moves off his thighs and lays back down on her back and throws her arms to the ground then above her head again. "So you think we were set up?" she asks.

"I don't know, but all of it together is, again, to perfect," he says. He gets to his feet.

"If what you think is true, then we are in even bigger trouble. You know what I'm saying?"

"Yeah, I do," he replies. Uriah walks toward the river and positions himself to get a drink of water. It's hot, and the sun is beaming down on him as there is no tree coverage near the water. He stands up and realizes how much sweat is covering his body. He wants to cool down and get the sweat off him. He looks around to make sure they are still safe then takes his shirt off, then his boots and socks.

The sound of the boots hitting the ground gets Vanessa's attention. She lifts her head up to see Uriah taking his pants off.

"What are you doing?" she asks.

"What does it look like. I have to cool down," he responds.

She lays her head back down, thinking, *That's not a bad idea.*

Uriah gets to his draws. "You might want to not look!" he shouts.

"Don't worry, I'm not," she replies.

Staring up into the trees, she can hear his body splash into the river. She is also sticky from sweat and will rinse off but doesn't want to add to the awkwardness that is already present. Her breathing has slowed, so she is feeling calmer. "Once you are done in there, it's my turn!" she yells from the ground.

"What?" Uriah yells back, not hearing what she said.

Knowing that it is now safe to look, she gets up into a seating position, holding herself up with her hands. "I said, once you are done there, it is my turn," she repeats to him.

"Cool, I'm almost done. The water isn't too bad, but there is still that initial shock when you enter," he tells her.

"I'm going to see if there is anything around that we might be able to eat."

"Don't be long. We have to keep moving," he tells her.

Uriah goes back underwater as she walks into the forest. When he resurfaces, he is closer to the bank. He positions himself to get out but then realizes he is going to get dirt stuck to parts of his body in doing so. He looks along the river on both sides to see if there is better place to get out. Seeing no better options, he gets out. He grabs his shirt and uses it to dry parts of his body. In this heat, anything that is wet will dry very quick. He gets his draws on, then his pants.

Vanessa returns. "I found some berries. I had a couple. We can pack some up before we move on," she tells him.

"Cool, nice work," he replies.

Vanessa walks close to the river and begins to undress. She gets down to her bra and panties.

Uriah looks up at her "What are you doing?" he asks.

"I'm waiting for you to finish so you can move away and not see me," she replies.

"Right," he says as he pulls his feet out of the water and uses his shirt to dry them off. He gets his boots on but doesn't lace them up. He will do it away from the river. He gets to his feet and turns away from her and the river.

"While you're in there, I'll take inventory of everything we have," he tells her.

"Good idea," she responds as she removes her bra and drops her panties. Unlike Uriah, she walks into the river then slowly submerges herself. She realizes that this is the more painful way to enter the river, and perhaps Uriah's method is more effective. It's too late, but she feels the instant refreshment of her body.

Uriah finishes with his boots. He begins to gather the little items they have between them. He lays them out on the ground. Vanessa makes her way back to the bank of the river.

"I'm coming out now," she warms him.

He turns his back again as he continues his task.

Before she gets out, she asks Uriah, "Hey, can you throw your shirt over here."

"What, why?" he asks hesitantly. "Are you out yet? Can I turn around?" he asks.

"No, not yet," she replies.

"Well, how am I supposed to see where to put it?" he asks.

"I mean no, I'm not out of the river yet. You can turn around," she clarifies.

He grabs his shirt and takes it to her pile of clothing. "Yellow, huh, cute," he says, referring to her panties.

"Quit being a perv," she says back.

"Relax, you're like my sister," he says in return.

He returns to his task, and Vanessa gets herself out of the river.

"So here is what we have: a bow with no arrows, two knives, and a sword," Uriah calls out.

Vanessa finishes getting dressed. She doesn't put all her clothes back on; she leaves off a T-shirt. She walks next to Uriah and checks out the inventory. "Okay, let's pack up and move. We'll stay on this river. At some point, we will hit a bridge or something," she suggests.

Uriah grabs his shirt and walks to the river.

"What are you doing?" she asks curiously.

"I'm going to rinse my shirt off. You know because it's dirty from being used as a floor mat, and then put it around my neck to keep myself cool," he tells her.

"Great idea. Here, do mine." She throws her shirt at him. "You gather our things. I'm going to fill this with berries. Follow me so we can eat some before we move on," she tells him. She walks into the forest while he rings out her shirt.

He walks over to gather their supplies. He puts the bow around his body and the knives into his belt. He looks around to make sure he has not forgotten anything. He makes his way through the forest until he finds Vanessa eating berries.

"I've filled the container with berries for later, and I've eaten enough for now," she tells him.

Uriah stuffs his mouth with berries while Vanessa gets her knife from his belt.

"You want me to carry anything else?" she asks him.

He shakes his head no at her. "I'm good for now. Let's roll," Uriah says. He stuffs his mouth one more time then fills his left hand with berries. He jogs to catch up to Vanessa. "These berries are not going to last us long. We need to get out of the forest fast," he tells her.

* * * * *

Isaiah has stopped running again. He is more fatigued, but worse, he is more frustrated. This time is no different than the last time he stopped. He has no sense of direction, and he is no closer to the other angels. He is now starving, and that is what distracts him most. He stands, looking around.

Trees, just trees, he thinks to himself.

He is feeling disheartened at the idea that he cannot be there for the angels. He walks around thinking about what he should do. *Do I spend more time trying to find the jet? Should I try to get home?* he asks himself.

The halo is now an afterthought. His focus has been on his friends, and considering he cannot find them, he now contemplates if he should focus on the halo or try and get home. After wrestling with his options, he determines that it's best if he tries to get home. He is fatigued and hungry and questions how helpful he would be to the angels at this point if he did find them. Several hours has passed, and many things could have happened in that time.

Getting home seems to be the most sensible plan, he thinks. With his mind set on home, he focuses his energy on finding a river. "All rivers lead to towns or people," he says aloud.

He knows that a river will be his best shot at getting out of the forest. He stands still to listen for the flow of a river. Hearing no river, he tries to read the contours of the forest floor to determine which direction is at a slop. The forest floor being relatively flat does not offer much help. He selects a direction that seems to be the most on a decline. As he walks, he can only hear birds and other wildlife. He stops to look up to the sky; he checks the position of the sun to gauge the time. As he checks for the time, his stomach reminds him that he is hungry. From this point on, the hunger will only get worse as he will have to expend extra energy trying to get out of the forest.

He continues to walk for a couple more hours. His pace is slower than a hiker's; he is hungry and tired. A new sound catches his attention. As he continues along his path, the sound becomes more apparent. "Water," he says.

He gets a sudden burst of energy from the prospect of a river. Not only will the river serve as a guide, but he can at least stay hydrated along the way. The sound is becoming clearer and clearer with every step. When he gets about twenty yards from the water, it becomes visible to him. He smiles big and races toward the river.

When he gets to the edge, he sees that it is a creek. He drops to his knees and cups his hands. He dips his hand cup and takes a drink. He only gets half into his mouth as the other half runs down his face. He can feel the water hit the bottom of his stomach. He takes two more drinks before he takes a break. His stomach is starting to feel full, but he has room for more. He continues to drink. The water sits heavy in his stomach, but at least, he doesn't have to worry about dehydration.

He gets to his feet. The dilemma for him now is deciding which way he should follow the river. He looks back and forth from one side to the other. One way does not show any signs of promise over the other. He looks up at the sun to gauge the time.

"This has to be my direction," he says as he looks over. Now that he has a direction, he decides to take time to cool down. He lies flat to submerge his head.

* * * * *

"Be careful, honey," Lupe calls out to her daughter.

"I'm right here next to her. What do you think is going to happen?" Brad asks his wife, mildly insulted.

"You're not always paying attention," she jokes at her husband.

"Mommy thinks I can't keep you safe," he tells his daughter, who has no concept of what he is talking about.

She looks up at him. "Seff," she says back.

"Yeah, that's right, honey, safe," he confirms.

She playfully splashes water at him when his phone rings. He checks to see who it is. "Hey, Nate, what's going on?" he asks. "Bradly, how are things?"

"Good, Lupe and I brought Lisa to the waterfront to play in the water," he tells him.

"Oh, that sounds wonderful. I'm sure she is enjoying that, especially in this weather," Nate says.

"Honey!" Lupe yells out.

Brad doesn't hear her. Lupe walks toward him as he looks up in her direction.

"It's Nate!" he yells over at his wife.

She points behind him at their daughter, who is walking away from him. He turns around and walks toward her.

"Don't worry about it. I'll get her," Lupe tells Brad.

"Thanks, sorry, honey," he says.

"Tell Nate I say hi," she requests.

"Lupe says hi," he relays.

"Well, hi to her as well. Tell her that I miss her and that you three need to come over for dinner really soon," he says.

"Will do, Nate. What can I help you with?" Brad asks.

"Right, well, have you heard from the angels returning from Bend?" Nate asks.

"Uh, no, I haven't."

"They should be back by now, right?" Nate confirms.

"I would think so." He checks the time. "Let me give them a call. I'll call you back in a bit," he tells Nate.

Brad paces around as he dials Rudy's number; it rings six times before it goes to voice mail. He thinks for a second. "I'll try Dom," he says aloud. He dials that number; it rings seven times before it too goes to voice mail. *All right, that is odd*, he thinks to himself. He looks up over at his family. "Let me try…" he says to himself. He pulls up Angela's number; he dials. The phone rings several times before it goes to voice mail. He hangs up.

"Ah, crap, I should have left messages, damn it," he says. He thinks for another moment then sighs. He looks at his phone again and dials a fourth number. He decides to call the warehouse. He begins walking toward his wife and daughter. An angel at the warehouse picks up.

"Hey, it's Brad, can you tell me if the jet from Bend has arrived?" he asks.

"No, it hasn't," the warehouse attendant tells him.

"It hasn't. Okay, can you track it?" Brad requests.

"Okay, gimme a second." The angel runs over to a computer to check. "Tracking now… Radar has it over a forest, maybe twenty-five minutes outside of Bend, but it's not moving," the attendant says.

"Not moving?" Brad says as he stops walking. "Listen, try to connect with the jet, got it?"

"Yes, sir," the angel replies.

Brad continues to walk toward his family. He calls Nate back. "Hey, Nate, I wasn't able to get ahold of anyone on the jet. Something isn't right," he tells him.

"What exactly does that mean?" Nate asks.

"We are not able to connect with the jet. We've located it, but it is not moving. It appears to be in a fixed location. So either landed or crashed. I'll let you know when I have something more definite," he says to Nate. He hangs up the phone.

He reaches his family. "Honey, I have to go," he tells his wife.

"Okay, will stay out here a little while longer," she decides.

"Okay, I will catch up to you guys later for dinner," he says as he kisses his daughter then wife. "I'll leave you the car. I'll take a cab," he adds.

He runs toward the street; he sticks his arm out to hail a cab. Several occupied cabs pass by before an empty one stops for him. "To the warehouse," he tells his driver.

* * * * *

Isaiah has been walking for several hours, and the evening is nearing, but it is still hot. He decides to sit for a moment to regain strength. He sees a boulder nearby and decides to use it as a seat. He looks around as his stomach continues to remind him of his hunger. He gets off the boulder and kneels next to the river for a drink. He knows that he has a couple of hours left of sunlight, so he will continue until he cannot see effectively.

He leans over for another drink then hears a noise. He looks up across the river then to each side. He hears the noise again and scans slowly across the way this time. A cub comes into view. It's making its way to the river to get a drink of its own. It brings a smile to Isaiah. A couple of seconds later, mama bear comes into view. He is mesmerized by the bears and briefly forgets that he's lost and looking to make it out of the forest.

He sits back on the boulder and watches. The cub explores the grounds as mama bear is close by standing guard. She goes for a drink of her own. Isaiah's reminded about how his good friend Christian's favorite animal is the bear. Isaiah likes bears, but they are not his favorite animal.

Mama bear finishes her drink and looks around. She spots Isaiah from across the way. She stares at him and then stands tall, letting out moans and grumbles as she waves her head back and forth.

"No worries, mama bear, I'm on your team." He is fascinated that she is communicating with him. He assumes she is telling him to move along. He continues to stare as she drops back on all fours. She stares at him a little longer before turning to her cub to tell him that it's time to move on.

The cub is enjoying his time in the water, so he ignores his mother's commands. Isaiah agrees with mama bear and decides it's time to go. He takes one more drink before he moves on.

* * * * *

Brad dials Hayley's number first. He catches her while she is out shopping for grocery. "Hey, Brad."

"Listen, Hayley, I need you to get to the warehouse ASAP."

"Um, okay. What's going on?" she asks.

"Something is going on with the jet. It hasn't returned. I'm on my way to the warehouse now," he replies.

"Well, I'll be a little bit. I'm leaving the grocery store," she informs him.

"Can't you come here first?" he asks.

"Brad, I've got perishables," she tells him.

"Right, of course, you do. Make it quick. I fear something has gone seriously wrong," he expresses to her.

"Got it. I'll be there as soon as I drop these groceries."

Brad hangs up. He dials Elise next. "Hey, Elise." He catches her while she is working out at home.

"What's up, Brad?" she answers.

"Elise, I need you to come in ASAP," he tells her.

"Okay, um, I can be there in an hour?" she tells him.

"Elise, this is urgent. The jet has not returned from Bend," he tells her.

"Hmm, that is serious. Okay, I will leave in ten minutes," she tells him.

"Good enough. I'll see you soon. We are meeting at the warehouse," he informs her.

"Got it. See you soon."

Brad dials Nate.

"Hey, Brad, you find out anything?"

"Well, no details. I can't get through to the jet, no one on the jet. We know they left Bend around ten this morning. They should have been back in town before noon. So something is definitely wrong. It's hard to say what. I'm on my way to the warehouse to find out more, and I'm having Elise and Hayley meet me there," Brad explains.

Nate lets out a loud, rough grunt. "This is very disturbing, Bradley. Nothing about this makes sense. I don't want to draw any conclusions yet. When you get to the warehouse, investigate all possibilities," Nate requests.

"Yeah, I will. I am almost there. I'll call you again after I send off the ladies." Brad hangs up with Nate as the car arrives at the warehouse.

* * * * *

Elise arrives at the warehouse first. She gets out of her car, with sunglasses on to block the bright sunshine. She stretches and sees Brad walking through the warehouse.

I should get in there, she thinks to herself.

She closes her door and walks toward the entrance. Brad looks up and sees her walking in. "I'll fill you in when Hayley gets here. For now, get your team together—get them here now. If you finish before Hayley gets here, get her team here also. Enough for recovery, search and rescue, battle—everything. I'll get with you soon," he instructs.

She pulls out her phone as she walks away. Brad returns to talk with a warehouse worker. Elise is in the middle of reaching out to Hayley's team when Hayley arrives. She makes eye contact with Elise. Elise waves at her. She walks over to Brad.

"I got here at quick as I could. Traffic was crazy. What's going on?" she asks.

"Glad you're here. Hang out for a sec. Find Elise. I'll get with you soon."

She walks over to Elise. "Warehouse. Great, see you soon," Elise says over the phone.

"Hey, lady," Elise says.

"Hey, what's going on? What are you doing? What are we doing here?" Hayley asks.

"Geez, got any more questions?" Elise asks as she giggles.

"Yeah, is there a gym here now?"

"What?" Hayley looks her up and down. "Oh, I was working out when Brad called," she explains.

"Hmm, I was grocery shopping."

"Well, Brad didn't tell me anything. He just sent me to you."

"Yeah, he hasn't told me either. He just told me to get our teams here. I've called mine. I started calling some of yours. I'll let you finish."

"Do you know what's up with the jet?" Hayley asks.

"No, but it should have arrived a couple of hours ago, so something is wrong."

"Ladies." Brad waves them over.

"Oh, here we go," Hayley says.

"I'll get right to it, ladies," Brad says with concern. "The jet was supposed to return sometime around noon today. Did not make it back. We can see where it is, but we have not been able to reach any of the angels. The jet appears to be downed in the forest outside of Bend. We don't know why, how, or when, so you two will go out there and find out what is going on. Be prepared for it all—mechanical failure, an attack, or a crash. Start gearing up for all possibilities. You get ahold of your teams?" he asks.

"Yeah, I've got mine on the way. We are finishing hers now," Elise responds.

"Okay, you have your mission. Any questions?" he asks.

The women stare at one another.

"Are we good?" Brad asks.

"Yeah, we are good," Hayley responds.

"Good, get your team here and leave ASAP. I'm going to see Nate," Brad instructs as he walks away.

"You get your people here. I'll get gear and equipment ready," Elise tells Hayley.

* * * * *

The devils are spread around the forest in search of the halo. They have been searching for all afternoon. They have been searching with no specific plan other than to walk, spread apart randomly. They have no point of reference, so they search blindly.

"What are we going to do if we can't find the halo?" a devil asks Ty.

They are walking about ten feet apart as they search through the forest. He doesn't know what they will do for sure, but he doesn't want to give any impression that he doesn't have things under control, so he gives a response. "That's not an option. We will find it. We won't leave until we do," he tells the devil.

"Right, we are wasting our time out here. There is no way we can find it like this," he tells Ty.

Ty agrees with the devil but will not admit it. "Just keep looking," he instructs the devil. He doesn't want to continue this conversation, so he begins to move away from the devil. He radios Sara but not until he's away from other ears. He looks around to confirm.

Feeling like he is far enough away, he radios his sister. "Sara." She doesn't answer the first time. "Sara," he calls again.

"What? What do you want?" she asks.

"Listen, you and I both know that we are not going to find the halo like this. This is a waste of time. We need to get out of here."

"Oh yeah, you want to go back right now and tell Jason what exactly?" she asks him.

He goes silent for a moment. "You have nothing, do you?" she says. "We tell him we didn't find it. It is what it is. It's lost in a fuckin forest. I'll bet you he can't find it!" he exclaims.

She laughs. "So what? You gonna go back and tell him to come out here and look for it himself?"

"No, sister, but there has to be a smarter way to do this, and that is what we tell him. Make him understand."

Sara laughs again. "Oh, brother, it's not often you speak reason, but I must say that I agree with you about this. Let's just do this until the angels show up. At least then we will have a legitimate reason for ending the search. Just keep on until then," she tells him.

"Yeah, I guess. This is still bullshit," he expresses.

* * * * *

Isaiah continues his trek through the forest. It's only been a couple of hours, but to him, it seems like it has been a couple of days. Still walking along the river, he stops for another drink. He takes a couple of drinks as he looks around and across the way. He is hungry, but for now, the water will have to do. He gets his fill and continues along the river. He walks for about ten minutes or so when something catches his attention, something across the river.

He stops and lowers his body to conceal himself behind a boulder. He watches intently; he sees bodies moving through the trees. He gets lower and begins to scoot closer to the river's edge. He is low but has nothing to provide him cover. He lies flat on his stomach and moves with an army crawl. He sees that they are devils. He watches earnestly as they canvas the area looking for the halo.

"What are they looking for? It has to be the halo," he says.

He sees two of the devils stop. He rests still, watching. The two devils come together near the river. Shortly thereafter, the other two devils join the two by the river. They look casual as they meet.

"What are they talking about?" Isaiah whispers.

He sees one of them get on the radio. He gets an odd feeling; it's a suspicious feeling that goes down his spine. He doesn't like that they are huddled near the river, so he begins to back away. He looks back to see where he is going. He looks forward again at the devils. With his eyes locked on the devils, he moves behind the boulder.

He gets to his knees then to his feet but stays low behind the boulder.

"He's moving!" a devil yells out.

Two devils jump into the river after him. He turns and begins to run straight away from the river, looking back several times. "What the fuck," he says, breathing heavily.

One of the devils in the river gets caught up in a current and gets swept downriver. The other devil stops and watches his partner go downriver as the other two on land watch as well.

Isaiah stops and looks back again. He doesn't see anyone behind him, but he can hear arrows whizzing by. He continues to run. *They must have seen me right away*, he thinks.

He is confident that he has lost them, but to make sure, he continues to run, turning parallel to the river.

* * * * *

All angels have arrived at the warehouse and are helping with final preparations. Elise and Hayley gather all the angels.

"Okay, guys, we've got a lot of work ahead of us," Hayley tells the group.

"Everyone needs to understand that we are hoping for a quick trip but plan for an extended stay, with a positive outcome either way," Elise says.

"I'm sure you have questions about what happened out there, but there aren't many answers we can offer right now. We know as much as you do. The jet isn't moving, and the team is not responding," Hayley tells the group.

"It can be a number of things. We will arrive, planning for and hoping that it is just some mechanical issues. We will get information from Brad as he learns it, but we can't really count on getting anything from him," Elise says.

"Does anyone have any questions about this mission?" Hayley asks.

Ariah raises her hand. "What about the devils? Do we think they will be out there? Are we expecting a fight out there?" she asks.

The knights look at one another.

"It's hard to know, but if they are and they're still out there, be ready for a fight," Hayley responds.

The angels look at one another with an understanding.

"Okay then, let's go get our people and our halo," Elise says.

The group breaks, and they run to the choppers. Serina stays back, staring at the ground. Hayley walks away, but Elise notices Serina standing there, looking at the ground.

"Serina, are you okay?"

She looks up at Elise.

"What's on your mind, Serina?"

"Um, I'm fine, just a little tired," she replies.

"Do you need to sit this one out?" Elise asks.

"No, no, no, I'm good. Let's do this."

"Okay then." Elise nods as she walks away.

Serina makes her way to the choppers. She begins to climb in when she notices that it's empty. She looks around, confused. She pokes her head out and looks at the other two choppers.

"Hey, why are you empty?" she asks the pilot.

"We will be returning with possible cargo," the pilot says.

"Got it." She hops down and goes to one of the other choppers. She is joined by Elise, who is signaling to the pilot that they are ready to go.

"Trying to get your own ride, huh?" Elise says.

They both laugh as they climb into the chopper together.

* * * * *

The devils have been searching the forest for the entire afternoon. The evening is approaching, and they have no idea if they are making progress of any kind. Ty is taking a break; he has taken several today. This is not the type of activity to which he is accustomed. As he sits and rests, Sara gets a call on her phone.

"Go ahead," she answers. She listens intently to the devil on the other end. "How long ago?" she asks. She hangs up. "Ty...Ty," she calls.

"What?" he responds. "Well, you're getting what you want."

"What do you mean?"

"I just got the call. The angels just left Portland, so it's time for us to get out of here. Call in the helicopters."

"Fuck yeah, it's about time," he says.

"Come get me," she tells him.

The helicopters move in to pick up the devils. Ty gets into his chopper and settles in. "Go get Sara," he tells the pilot.

They move on to pick up Sara, a mile away. She gets settled in.

"You know what your gonna tell Jason?" he asks.

"Hold on, brother, let me get settled and relax a little. It's been a busy day. I just want some quiet right now," she tells him.

"So you're going to sleep?" he asks.

"Just a quick nap. We'll talk later."

Midway home, Sara wakes from her siesta. "How far out are we?" she asks.

"We are about halfway there," the pilot replies.

"Damn, I was hoping to sleep the whole way," she says aloud. She looks around, unsatisfied at not getting a longer siesta.

"What are we gonna tell Jason?" Ty asks.

"Wow Ty, you are impatient. Why are you so concerned? Seems like your scared of what Jason is gonna do or say."

"I'm not afraid. I'm more curious. He is gonna be pissed, so I just want to know," he says.

"Well, it's nothing special, but first, we are just going to make him understand how difficult it was and is to look for a halo in a forest like that. Second, I'm going to suggest that we let the angels do all the work for us. If they find it, we will be ready to take it. Why waste our time searching like fools?" she says. "We will have to go back out there, but we won't have to do the dirty work," she adds.

"Hmm, you really think that he is gonna like that? I think it's a good plan, but I just don't think he will feel the same. Whatever, just as long as I don't have to go back out there," he responds.

"Just let me do all the talking. Your mouth is what would piss him off," she tells him.

* * * * *

Brad arrives at Nate's home. He makes a call before he gets out. He missed a call from his wife on his way over. He dials her back. "Hey, hon, sorry I missed your call. We have a situation with which I've been dealing. I just arrived at Nate's. I won't be long here and should be home in time for dinner."

"How serious is it?" she asks.

"The jet didn't return from Bend, so we are sending a team out there. We haven't heard from anyone on the jet."

"Oh dear. I do hope everyone is okay," she says.

"Me too. Let me get inside, and I'll be on my way home soon," he requests.

"Okay, honey, be safe," she says.

They exchange "I love you."

He gets out of the car and walks up to the door. He knocks.

Fernando answers the door.

"Hey, Fern."

"Hey, Brad, come on in. He is in the backyard," he tells Brad.

"Thanks, man. How you been?"

"I've been well, you know. Just here watching over the elders," he says.

Brad laughs as they walk through the house. "Good to hear, my friend. How is the wife?" Brad asks.

"She is also well. Spending a lot of her time painting," Fernando tells him.

"Oh good, that is really good. Glad to hear that she has gotten back into it. Give her my best, will you?"

"Of course. I'll leave you to it."

"Thanks, my friend."

Fernando leaves him to walk outside alone and returns to the front of the house. Brad walks into the backyard to find Nate grilling.

"Bradley."

"Hey, Nate."

"What is our status?" Nate asks.

"Still haven't been able to reach the jet. Hayley and Elise have a team together, and they should be in the air by now. I've got folks monitoring the jet and still trying to reach it. It's all we can do right now," he tells him.

Nate sighs, closes the grill, and walks away from it. "Yes, I suppose it is. You want to stay for dinner?"

"No, thanks. I've got to get home," Brad replies.

"Yes, of course," Nate says.

There is a pause. Brad is waiting, expecting Nate to speak about the situation they are in. He waits and waits. He finally decides to move the conversation along.

"So what's the next move, Nate?" Brad asks.

Nate grunts. "We wait to hear from the girls. We will know more from them, right?"

Brad tilts his head quizzically, wondering if it was necessary for him to stop by. "Well, I have many thoughts, but I don't want to jump to conclusions. It's not the fact that the jet is down, but more about not hearing from the angels. That tells me that something is terribly wrong. I can't shake this feeling that Jason is behind this," he tells Brad.

"Yeah, I feel the same way."

Erin walks into the backyard to deliver items. "Bradley, how are you, dear?" she asks.

"I'm well, Erin. How are you?" he asks.

"I am well. Wish I could say the same for this man. Are you staying for dinner?"

"Thank you, but no. I told Lupe that I would be home soon."

"Oh, how is Lupe? It's been far too long since seeing her last," she says.

"She is well, at home with Lisa."

"Oh, little Lisa. That little precious one. When can I see her?"

"Um, I will talk to her about coming by soon," he tells her.

"Good, good then. I will leave you to it. Good to see you," she says.

"You as well, Erin. Be well," he tells her.

"Listen, Bradley. I know you came here expecting more information from me, but I don't have a good feeling about the halo, and that has me bothered. Before I make any decisions, I want to know that the halo is still safe and secured. Be ready for anything and everything. I'm getting a lost vibe from the halo. Might be nothing. I'd like you to call Christian. Fill him in on what's happening, and have him ready to go," he instructs Brad.

"Yes, sir. Anyone else?" he asks.

"No, not now, but be ready to visit Jason."

*****

"We're here," Landon radios to tell Elise.

"Great, find us an accessible area," she instructs.

Kelly informs Hayley that they have arrived as well. Hayley's chopper gets into position and drops the rope. One by one, the angels drop into the forest. They drop into a space about twenty-five yards from the jet. The jet is visible from where they dropped. The first group of angels land, draw their weapons, and set up a perimeter. Hayley hits the ground and begins to coordinate an approach to the jet.

Once they have the plan, they move toward the jet.

"We've got dead devils out here," Lilly radios.

It's in that moment they are certain why the jet didn't make it back to Portland. At the jet, Hayley splits her group in half. She goes around one side of the jet; the other half takes the other. Her group reach the opening of the jet first and enter cautiously.

The angels in the second group get the opening shortly after the first group. The angels see Anna's body first. Hayley goes to her and signals to the other angels to sweep the jet as she checks on Anna.

Outside, the second helicopter drops Elise's team. Elise touches ground. Having most of the area covered and with Hayley at the jet, she delays in joining to ensure that a full perimeter is set up.

"You three shore up the perimeter, a full three-sixty, thirty yards out, twenty feet apart. Then close the perimeter at twenty feet. I'm positive there are devils watching us. If you spot one, don't react. Radio it in, got it?"

"Got it," they respond.

Having set up a perimeter, Elise makes her way to the jet. She walks in to find Hayley kneeling next to Anna's body. She walks up to Hayley.

"She's the only one in here," Hayley tells Elise.

"Elise, Hayley, you better get out here. I've got something. We found more angels," Serina says over the radio.

They look at each other. Hayley stands up, and they leave the jet urgently.

"Where are you?" Hayley asks.

"Start at the windows and come out at your three o'clock. Can't miss me. I can still see the jet."

They arrive at Serina's position.

"What do you got?" Elise asks.

"It's Angela and Dom," Serina says.

"Goddamn it," Elise shouts mildly. She kneels to them.

"Shit... Fuck," Hayley says.

Elise gets up from her kneeling position. "I think it's safe to assume they all came this way. They wouldn't split up, not out here," Serina offers.

"I agree," Elise says.

"How did this happen?" Hayley asks.

"Damn, she was so young," Elise adds.

"Okay, Hay Hay, I'll stay out hear and set up a sweep starting at the jet. I think Serina's right about this being a path they took away from the jet. You go back and focus on the inside of the jet," Elise suggests.

"Yep, will do," Hayley replies. She returns to the jet.

"Sweep completed," Aiden reports to Hayley.

"Thanks. Becky, you get on that black box."

"On it."

"Jed," Hayley calls him over. "You and Aiden prep Anna for extraction. Janie, call the choppers. Inform them that we have at least three bodies to extract right now."

"Got it."

Hayley looks around, trying to envision what happened. She has flashes of what she thinks the angels went through during the attack. Lilly walks up to her.

"This is hard, isn't it?" she asks Hayley.

"Yeah, it isn't right. I don't understand why the devils keep attacking us. They know the halo belongs with us," Hayley says.

"We don't attack them. This isn't right," Lilly agrees.

"I think all that is about to change," Hayley says in a soft voice.

Outside, Elise has a larger group of angels preparing to search. "There were eight angels on this jet. We have three. Right now, we are going to operate under the assumption that the other five are still alive. We will fan out starting at the jet. Let's start with a quarter mile out then turn back along a different path. We can't miss anything. Stay combat ready, everyone. I'm confident the devils are still close," Elise explains.

"Let's fucking do this. Let's find our people!" Ernesto yells out.

The groups take their place and begin to fan out.

"Hayley, we are heading out."

"Cool, we will take care of Dom and Angela soon," Hayley says.

"Cool, talk soon."

Hayley walks up to Aiden and Jed. "Once you have her taken care of, let's go outside. I'll show you where the other two are." She then walks over to Becky. "You got what you need for this?" she asks.

"Nope, got everything right here," Becky responds.

"Great, once it's out, get back to town and begin working on it. I'll send some other angels with you."

"Got it," Becky acknowledges.

* * * * *

Ty and Sara arrive at Jason's home. They knock on the front door, and the house guard answers.

"They are all in the party room," the guard tells them.

They head downstairs to the party room. They see Franco first, holding a billiards stick. He acknowledges them as they enter. They also see Jason, Crystal, Delaney, and other devils. No one else greets them; instead, they are met with a statement from Jason.

"I hope you have some good news for me, daemons," Jason says as he sits in his chair.

Crystal leans in to take a shot. The sound of billiard balls smacking fills the room temporarily. Ty and Sara look at each other.

"We have some good news, but not all good," Ty says first.

"We killed the angels, including Rudy," Sara says.

But we didn't get the halo," Ty adds.

Jason brings his hands together as he crosses his legs. "Explain to me how you failed to get me the halo," he asks.

"Well, we are confused about it also," he tells Jason. Jason gets a look of confusion on his face. "This is not surpr—"

"CONFUSED!" Jason yells with a stern tone to the daemons as he interrupts his wife. He uncrosses his legs and places his hands on the arms of the chairs as if he is going to get up. The room goes quiet for a moment. Instead of getting up from the chair, he leans back again.

"As I was going to say, I'm not surprised you two failed again," Crystal mentions.

In a lower tone Jason asks, "Tell me how you two are confused?"

Franco lines up for his shot. He focuses and steadies himself. He takes the shot, again the sound of billiard balls smacking fills the void of sound. Ty and Sara take a moment to watch Franco take the shot, buying them just a couple more seconds before they must explain what has happened. Ty looks at Sara then goes over the refrigerator; he opens the door and reaches for a beer.

"Oh yes, that beer is well deserved," Crystal says as he closes the door.

That statement prompts a devil to approach Ty and attempt to take the beer from him. Ty grips the beer and growls at the devil. The devil backs off a step.

"That is my beer, daemon, and I'm not convinced you have earned it!" Jason tells Ty.

Ty looks around then stares at Sara for a moment. He opens the refrigerator door again, staring at the devil as he returns the beer. The devil begins to back away. Ty closes the door with force, rattling some of the contents inside. He walks back to where he was previously standing and leans up against a wall.

Sara looks back at him and then proceeds to explain. "So we don't know where it is," Sara says.

"I don't understand why you daemons continue to fail," Crystal says as she lets out a sound of derision.

Both Ty and Sara look at each other and then at Crystal.

"We can't fail if it wasn't there," Ty responds with an annoyed tone.

Crystal gets up from her stool and leaves the room.

"Does the truth my wife speaks upset you?" Jason asks them.

"When—"

"No, sir," Sara responds, cutting Ty off. She knows that whatever her brother was about to say would only infuriate Jason even more than he already is. She also knows that Ty is getting increasingly

30

upset; she doesn't want this conversation to get any worse than it already is.

"I, too, am a little confused. I had confirmation that the halo was in that jet," Franco says confidently.

"We covered all of our bases. We don't continue to fuck up," Sara tells Franco.

"I don't care that you killed all the angels, which is your satisfaction. I want the halo," Jason tells them.

"Listen, the angels didn't have it on them. It wasn't in the jet. If you are positive that it was there before we hit it, then the only explanation is that it fell out of the jet after the explosion," Ty says.

Franco and Jason ponder the possibility. "Did you guys go looking for it in the forest?" Jason asks.

"We did for the entire afternoon, but it's the forest. Everything looks the same. We didn't know where to begin exactly, but we searched," Sara explains.

Jason stares at Sara for a moment. "I want you to return to the forest and take a deeper look," he instructs her.

"Yes, master," Sara responds.

"If what you theorize is true, then the halo is out there in the forest unclaimed," Franco says to the room.

"If that is true, the opportunity still presents itself. Do not fail me again," Jason tells her.

"I will not, master," she responds.

"I know you won't."

"I'll take a team out there myself. I don't need Ty out there," she says, attempting to spare her brother.

"That's fine. I've got a different plan for him," Jason says.

Franco gets off his stool and walks to the stairs gesturing for Sara to follow. They walk up the stairs and through the house passing Crystal along the way to the front door.

"It's super important to find this halo. Jason is not happy that you let this slip through. Get things ready. I'll catch up with you in a little while," he tells her.

"You're not coming with me?" she asks.

"No, not yet," he responds.

"Why not?" she asks.

"I've got to get back downstairs," he tells her.

She stares at him with suspicion. "What is going on, Franco?" she asks.

He smirks a little. "Don't worry, your brother will be fine," he reassures her.

She is not sure if she believes him; she trusts him, so that's what she's counting on. Franco opens the door for her. She walks out slowly.

"I'll be calling you soon," he tells her. He shuts the door. Franco returns downstairs to find Crystal has rejoined them.

"Nate must know by now," Jason says aloud.

"I agree. I think it's time to call others in, like the triplets," Franco suggests.

"I agree," Jason replies.

"Why do you feel the need to call them in. There are others that can help," Ty suggests.

"Considering your failures," Crystal says.

"It's not a bad idea to have additional help," Franco suggests.

Fury for Crystal builds in Ty's eyes.

"Why are you always talking shit? Your message was clear the first time," he says.

"Calm yourself, Ty, especially when talking to my wife," Jason demands as he gets up from his chair and walks to the fridge. "Ty, I'm troubled by you lately. I have never minded your over aggressiveness. In fact, I appreciate that about you. But lately you have been reckless." He opens the fridge and pulls a beer out. "I can't have you fucking shit up for us right now." He walks over to Ty and hands him the beer. "I'm going to have you collaborate with the triplets on this one."

"What does that mean?" Ty asks.

"It means that I can't trust you right now. You need to be baby-sat," Jason says.

"Are you kidding me? I'm the best you have!" Ty shouts.

"Not like this, you're not." Jason walks back to his seat. "That will be all for now," Jason tells Ty.

Ty chuckles a little and looks at Franco. "Fuck it, you're going to regret this. No one can do what I do." He laughs some more and walks out of the room.

Franco walks after Ty, and as he reaches the top of the stairs, he calls for Ty. "Wait, hold on, I'll walk you. Listen, lay low for a bit. I can still use you. I'll talk to him, but you've got to get your shit together. Don't make me look like a fool. Clean yourself up. I need you focused if I'm going to use you. Don't make me regret it."

Ty looks at Franco with a glare.

"I'll call you. We'll meet soon. Before we do, stop by the triplets and tell them to see Jason," Franco instructs.

Ty shakes his head as he walks out of the house.

* * * * *

Aiden and Jed finish prepping the bodies for pick up.

"Chopper is here," Janie tells the men.

Becky stands nearby waiting for them to finish. The chopper hovers above and sends down hooks for the angels.

"I'll go up," Jed tells the other two. He hooks himself in and goes up. He sends a basket down. They load Anna's body in first. Jed sends the basket down again. They send up Domingus's body then Angela's body. Jed returns to the forest floor. Janie hooks herself to it with Aiden's help.

"All right, see you soon," Janie tells Aiden.

"Yeah, be careful." She signals to the tech to lift her up.

"Our chopper is close," Becky tells the guys.

"Do I have everything?" Aiden asks himself.

They all do a self-check.

"Well, I've got the box, and that's all I really need," Becky says.

"I wonder if we are coming back out here?" Jed asks.

"Oh, for sure," Aiden says.

A movement among the trees catches Becky's attention. She doesn't react to it. She continues with the angels as if she didn't notice. She can tell it's a body. She sees it again, confirming what she thinks. "Guys, we are being watched or followed," she tells them as she looks at the ground.

They continue to act casual.

"On our left, a couple of trees back, a devil is watching us," she says.

They casually move back-to-back to cover a three-sixty view as they set their hands on their weapons. The chopper arrives above. A set of hooks lowers.

"Becky, go!" Jed says as he and Aiden set up protection.

Becky goes up.

"Aiden, you go," Jed says as the hooks lower again.

Aiden hooks himself up. As he rises, he draws his bow. "I can see him," he radios to Jed.

Aiden makes it in. The hooks come down a third time. Jed hooks himself up; he too draws his bow. As he rises, he begins to see the devil through the woods. He pulls his arrow back and releases, hitting the devil at the top of his head. Another devil nearby sees his friend fall to the ground. Jed gets into the chopper.

"I got him, but I doubt he's the only one out there," he says.

"Well, we knew they were watching us. That means they are still looking for something," Becky says.

* * * * *

There is a knock at the door. Elise walks over to open it as she rubs a towel through her hair.

"Hey," Hayley says as she enters.

"Hey," she replies as she returns to the bathroom.

"How long until you're ready?" Hayley asks.

"Oh, fifteen or so."

"Becky is ready for us with the black box."

"Oh, good."

"Have you called Brad?" Hayley asks.

"No, have you?"

"No, I figure we can call him after we know what the box tells us."

"Yeah, that's what I was thinking."

The ladies arrive at Becky's room.

"Okay, I've got most of the information here," she tells them.

She starts by telling them the time of day the jet was hit and how long it took them to hit the ground. She shows them the jets location at certain points of elevation. They measure the distance from the attack to ground impact. They begin to make a search radius on a paper map.

"Let's listen to some audio," Elise suggests.

As they listen, they can only hear Domingus and Vanessa up front.

"There is so much background noise we can't hear the others," Hayley says.

"Yeah, there is so much wind going through there," Becky responds.

"We aren't gonna get anything useful from this," Hayley says.

"Okay, let's work with what we've got," Elise tells them.

They determine that they must cover a six-square-mile area of forest.

"Damn, that's going to be tough. This is crazy," Hayley says.

They think for a moment.

"Look, I think we can cut this in half and just focus on this area." Hayley points to the map. "There is a river right here. You know they would look for a river to guide them out of the forest," Hayley points out.

"Yeah, that's a good call. We can definitely focus on the river right away," Elise adds.

"There's more. The jets tracking system was on," Becky tells them.

They remain still for a moment.

"What does that mean?" Elise asks.

"It means that the devils had a separate way to track the jet. The jet itself was not tracked, and that's why Dom or Vanessa were unaware," she explains.

"So that means…" Hayley says with surprise.

"Yup, they were tracking someone inside the jet," Elise finishes.

"Damn, that is not good," Hayley expresses.

"We have to let Brad know," Elise tells them.

They begin to walk away.

"Oh, wait!" Becky shouts.

They stop in their tracks and freeze. They slowly turn around.

"As we were leaving the forest, we saw at least one devil. We killed that one but fairly sure that wasn't the only one."

"No, definitely wasn't," Elise says.

"Well, that is good news. That means they are still looking for the halo," Hayley adds. The knights look at one another.

"Thanks, Becky," Elise says.

"Yup."

"Call us if you find out more," Hayley tells her.

* * * * *

Brad, Nate, and the other angels are at the warehouse waiting for the choppers to arrive.

"Have you heard from the girls yet?" Nate asks Brad.

"No, not yet. If I don't hear from them soon, I'll call them."

"Do we know how many angels we are expecting?" Nate asks as they see the choppers come into view.

"Three, sir. Here they are," Brad motions to some angels to rush some equipment out to the landing spots.

"Do you know who?" Nate asks.

"Janie called me on the way and told me it's Anna, Angela, and Dom, sir."

"Enough with the formalities, Bradley."

"I'm working on it, sir."

Nate closes his eyes in thought. The chopper lands. Nate opens his eyes. Angels rush to unload it. Nate and Brad walk up to the chopper and enter to view the bodies.

"Go ahead, I want to see," Nate requests.

An angel uncovers the faces of the three fallen angels.

"My angels," Nate says in a soft voice.

"Go ahead, you can take them," Brad commands the angels.

"Call the girls now. I want to know exactly what is going on. I want to know if we are expecting any other angels and if they have recovered the halo."

"Will do," Brad replies.

Nate remains in the chopper as Brad walks out to make the call. He dials Elise.

"Hey, Brad."

"Hey, Elise, the angels have arrived. Give me an update on everything else?" he asks.

"Okay, so we found those angels at the crash site. The other five are still unaccounted for, along with the halo. We have strong reason to believe the devils don't have it, because we found them out here watching us. We went through the black box and got information to help guide our search tomorrow. We searched today but came up empty. We have a search plan for tomorrow. Um, what else?" she asks.

"Okay, what's the story with the devils?"

"Uh, Becky told us that her, Aiden, and Jed saw one of them on their way out of the crash site. They shot one in the head. So we are assuming there are more out here watching us. We will be ready for them tomorrow. Have you heard anything on your end?" she asks.

"No, but if something comes up, I'll let you know. Tomorrow, check in every two hours."

"Okay," she replies.

Brad hangs up and sees Nate walking alongside the fallen angels.

* * * * *

The night has arrived. He doesn't know what time it is, and his hunger has grown strong. With the vision ahead dissipating, it's a suitable time for him to find a place to sleep for the night. He grabs one more drink from the river before he looks for a place to sleep. He takes several small drinks, compared to the bigger drinks he was taking earlier in the day.

Afterward, his bladder alerts him that he needs to relieve himself. He looks behind him to see where he should piss. *I guess I don't need much privacy out here*, he thinks.

Out of habit, he walks behind a tree. After he completes his business, he looks for a flat area where he can lie down and rest. There aren't many options in the immediate area where he is standing, so he walks a little further until he finds a spot that looks flat enough for him to lie down. Desperate for comfort, he looks around for something that he can use to prop his head up and function as a pillow.

He sees nothing he can use, but he does notice that the flat area he will lie on has a raised part to it. He decides to orientate his body so that his head can rest on the raised area, giving his head a little bit of elevation. Fortunately, the ground is not too hard. He lies down, flat on his back, and puts both of his hands behind his head to function as a pillow.

With his eyes already looking up, he peeks through the breaks in the trees. Through the breaks, he can see open sky and bright dots. He doesn't know much about astronomy, but he can appreciate that he is staring at stars. Although he's tired and hungry, he is not sleepy; his thoughts keep him awake. The events of the day weight heavy on his mind.

His thoughts go from stars to angels. *Did they survive? Are they okay? Where are they now?* he thinks to himself.

He feels guilty about it all. A tear runs down his temple to his ear. He is still emotional and still feels like he has let the angels down. "I'm lying in a fucking forest and can't do shit!" he yells up to the sky. *Are they looking for me? Did they find the halo? Does anyone at home even know what has happened? How long is it going to take me to get out of this forest?* he thinks. Question after question after question is all that occupies his mind. He wipes away the trail that the tear has left behind, and he returns his hand back behind his head.

* * * * *

In a different part of the forest, the sun has gone away, and the only things visible are due to the moonshine. Uriah is walking behind Vanessa, and for the last half hour, he has been suggesting that they stop for the night. She can barely see what is in front of her, which makes it a little more difficult in this terrain. She heeds his suggestion this time, and they both stop.

"Where are we supposed to sleep?" she asks.

He walks away from her, further into the forest, looking for space for them to lie down. She sees him go into the forest, so she continues to walk along the river to find a place.

Uriah looks back to see if she is following him; he doesn't see her. "Hey, Vanessa, we shouldn't get too far apart!" he shouts.

"I know. I found a flat spot here!" she shouts back.

"Where are you?" he asks.

"I'm a little further down the river," she says.

He turns around and walks back toward the river then walks to her location. "Oh yes, this should workout just fine," he says.

They drop their gear into a pile.

"We should sleep back-to-back," Vanessa suggests.

"Yeah, that's a clever idea."

Vanessa sits first, then Uriah sits next to her. She reaches for the pouch with the berries in it. She counts them. "Twelve berries left," she informs him.

They look at each other.

"Oh well, better than nothing. It'll have to get us through the night," he says.

"Yeah, hopefully, we find more right away tomorrow," she adds.

She hands him his split of the berries. He takes them and throws them all into his mouth at the same time. He lies down on his back, puts his knees up, and throws his arms out to his sides. Vanessa remains sitting, finishing her berries, eating them one at a time. She puts the last one in her mouth. Sitting next to him; she grabs his arm and throws it across his body.

"That was rude," he says jokingly.

"We are sleeping back-to-back, remember," she reminds him.

She lies down next to him on her side and turns her back to him. She puts her hands together, flat, and puts them under her head. She then brings her knees into the fetal position. Uriah turns his back to her. He tucks one arm under his head to serve as his pillow. Vanessa scoots back up against Uriah's back.

"Oh, you literally meant back-to-back, huh," he says.

"Sorry, makes me feel safer," she says softly.

"I get it. It's cool," he replies.

There is a moment of silence between them. They can hear crickets and the occasional frog around.

"How long do you think it'll take us to get out of the forest?" Vanessa asks.

"I don't know how long. As long as we stay on this river, we're bound to get to a bridge, road, or some sort of path," Uriah replies.

"Right, well, good night, Uriah."

"Good night, Vanessa."

A couple of minutes pass with only the sound of crickets.

"Uriah, you still awake?" Vanessa asks.

"Yeah, but I'm crashing hard," he tells her.

"I just want to thank you for saving me back there," she says.

"No problem, you would have done the same," he replies.

She doesn't know if she would do the same. She wonders if she would have had the strength and bravery to do the same. Historically, she has frozen in moments of confrontation. It has always been one of her weaknesses. She can hear Uriah's heavy breathing, indicating that he is asleep. She smiles about it; she thinks it's cute. She closes her eyes.

Several minutes later, her eyes pop open to a sound. She lies still, trying to make out the sound. She hears it again. It's the sound of twigs or branches cracking or breaking.

Is it walking towards me? she asks herself. She slowly reaches above her head and grabs one of the knives. She brings it next to her chest, slowly to not give their presence away to whoever or whatever is nearby. The sounds are getting closer and closer. She slowly turns to her stomach and slowly gets to her knees; she looks around, but it is pitch-dark in the forest.

She hops onto her feet. She switches hands with the knife and puts it out in front of her. The hand closest to Uriah is now free, so she bends her knees and shake him.

"Uriah, Uriah," she whispers.

He doesn't respond.

"Uriah." She shakes him harder. She turns him onto his back and shakes his jaw "Uriah, wake up."

The sound is getting closer. She can hear several steps, which tells her that there are multiple of them out there. She begins to pinch his nose and slap his face to wake him up. "Uriah, hey. Wake up," she says.

His eyes open. He sees that she is holding a knife.

"So it's like that? I don't want to fight you," he says.

"No, dummy, there is something out there. Get up," she tells him.

He rolls away from her. He reaches for the other knife. He gets to his knees. They can see several pairs of glowing lights coming at them. He stands up all the way and gets into a defensive posture. He quietly counts the pairs of glowing lights.

"I count about five of them," he tells her.

Suddenly, a deer appears on their right. They freeze for a moment. Two more deer make themselves visible.

"It's just a deer," he says.

They relax their postures and lower their knives.

"This must be their watering hole," Vanessa says.

"Yeah, all right, well, I'm going back to sleep," he tells her.

Uriah puts the knife down and lies back down into the same position he was in before. "You gonna be all right?" he asks.

"Yeah, thanks," she replies.

The deer decide to move along and find a different area to get a drink. She sits down next to him, still holding her knife. She watches as the deer walk away. She can't see them but can hear the breaking and cracking she heard when they were approaching. She sets the knife down and takes her position next to Uriah.

"Good night," she tells him. She does not get a response; he has fallen asleep again.

Monday

It's almost 5:00 a.m., and Elise is up preparing for the day's search. She does a quick look to see if anyone else is around. The plan was to meet at 6:00 a.m. She had trouble sleeping the night before. While in bed, her concern for the unaccounted angels grew. She also felt guilty about how late they got to the forest the day before, not giving themselves more time to search.

She walks around, making sure everything they need is in order. About twenty minutes pass when she hears a door close nearby. She turns around to look.

"Sorry to startle you, Elise," Landon says.

"No, you didn't startle me," she tells him.

"What time did you get out here?" he asks.

"About twenty minutes ago."

"All right, well, I'm going to prep these choppers," he says as he jumps inside.

Elise smiles and nods. She starts walking toward him when she hears two angels talking. "Oh, morning, ladies," she says to them.

"Hey, Elise."

She aborts her plan to talk to Landon. *I'll just catch him later*, she thinks to herself. She shakes her hands, and she shivers from the nerves she has just been thinking about talking to him. "That was close," she says. More angels arrive, and soon it's 6:00 a.m. She finds a free moment and realizes that Hayley hasn't arrived.

A little after 6:00 a.m., Hayley shows up. "Hey, girl," she says to Elise.

"Way to be on time," she says sarcastically.

"Well, you know me, I had to stop for me coffee," Hayley says with a scruffy voice. "Well, everyone is here, and everything is set, so let's go review the plan."

All the angels gather. Both knights go over their parts.

"Any questions anyone?" Elise asks.

Lilly raises her hand.

"Yeah, Lilly."

"Do we have any information from home?"

"That's a negative, nothing yet. Anybody else? Okay, let's do this." Elise hops into the chopper "We are good to go."

Landon gives her a thumbs-up then radios to the others, "We are clear for takeoff."

* * * * *

Sara and a large group of devils prepare gear and equipment for their mission into the forest. The devils are spread out around the compound as this mission is a grand undertaking and will require planning for different elements. Sara stands central in an open area issuing commands to devil soldiers as Ty pulls up in his car next to her, window down.

"Hey, brother, what are you doing here? Are you coming with me?" she jokes as she leans into his car.

"Fuck no, but he has some bullshit for me, so I think I would rather go," he tells her.

"It can't be that bad. This mission is going to suck. What's he having you do?" she asks.

"Not sure yet, but it's all working with the triplets. He told me that I need to be babysat. You believe that shit."

"Oh, that should be fun for you," she jokes.

"It's fuckin bullshit, but whatever," he expresses.

"Well, you almost fucked up back at his house, so it could have been worse. I was actually worried a little," she comments.

"That was more about Crystal. She was being a bitch. She was pissing me off," he tells her.

"I know, but you have to keep your cool around her, brother," she reminds him.

"At least you get to go fight. I get shit," he tells her.

"Well again, you let your mouth fuck that up," she replies.

"Anyways, what do you need help with?" he asks.

"Just hang out. I've got plenty of help here," she tells him.

He gets out of his car and walks over to helicopter with her to see the watercraft that's been loaded. I'm getting tired of this shit, aren't you?" he asks.

"What do you mean?" she asks in return.

"This whole thing with the angels—it goes nowhere. We just wait around for orders to do some stupid shit, and it leads to nothing meaningful. It's like we don't have a purpose," he tells her.

"What do you mean we don't have a purpose? We are close to getting the halo. That's what I'm trying to do. This has always been our purpose," she tells him.

"We have been trying to get the halo for thousands of years. Say you happen to find it this time, then what? What are we going to do with it? What is Jason going to do with it?" he asks.

She stops loading the helicopter for a moment. "What are you saying, brother? I've never heard you talk like this before," she tells him.

"I don't know if I even know what I'm saying right now. I've just been feeling a certain way for a while. Don't get me wrong, I still want to rid this earth of angels. I just don't know if Jason is the one to lead us anymore," he tells her.

"Well, if I can get this halo, then we will find out right? Look, why don't I talk them into letting you join me on this one," she tells him.

"Hell no," he says.

"All right, well, get your mind right, because a war is coming, and you will need to be focused," she tells him.

"All right then, if you don't need me, I guess I'll head out," he tells her.

He begins to walk back to his car. He gets halfway.

"Hey!" Sara yells out.

He stops and turns around; she walks to him. "I don't know if I ever asked or if you haven't told me, but why don't you like the triplets anymore? I thought you used to have a thing with them," she asks.

He stands there staring at her. He shakes his head and gets into his car.

* * * * *

In another part of the forest, birds are chirping, and the sun is hitting the forest floor through the trees. Vanessa is woken by the beaming sun on her face. She covers her eyes with her arm. As she fights the sun to stay asleep, she hears voices and laughter. She removes her arm from her face and opens her eyes but turns quickly to avoid the beaming sunrays. The voices are getting closer; the laughter is getting louder. She gets to her knees then to her feet.

She looks down at Uriah, he is still asleep. He is lying with his face away from the sun, and he has an arm over his head, which has shielded the sun from his face.

"Damn it, I should have picked that side." She doesn't want to wake him just yet. She looks around for the voices and laughter; it's getting closer. She sees that the weapons are out in the open, so she grabs a knife and hides the rest. She stays knelt and can see the people coming toward her. She realizes they are hikers. She quickly hides the knife with the rest of the weapons. She hides them in time as six hikers reach them and slow down as they see that Uriah is still asleep.

They cautiously walk around the angels as they greet Vanessa in soft voices and wave. "Hey, all," Vanessa says to them.

"Sorry for being loud," a female camper tells her.

"No problem at all. In fact, I'm glad you were loud," Vanessa responds.

The hikers stop and say nothing as they look at one another.

"Not sure if you can tell, but we are not actually camping out here. We had to sleep out here over night." She clears her throat. "Sorry, my name is Vanessa. The truth is, we are lost," she explains.

The campers look at one another again.

"I know this sounds odd, but it's a long story. We have been out here since yesterday morning, and like I said, we are lost," she reemphasizes.

Uriah wakes up and removes his arm from his head. Vanessa has her back turned to him.

"Do you need some help?" a female hiker asks.

The hikers look down at Uriah, who is trying to look back at the group. "Yes, we do," she says as she looks back at Uriah. "Oh, hey," Vanessa says to Uriah.

"Hey," he replies. He sits up on his butt.

Vanessa turns back toward the hikers. "Yes, we need some help," she tells the hikers.

"How can we help?" asks female hiker.

Uriah gets to his feet and dusts himself off.

"We need to know how to get out of the forest and a phone, if you have one," she tells them.

"We have phones, but they don't work out here. You have to get to a main road to get reception, but we can lead you out of the forest," a male camper tells the angels.

"Yeah, that's a good start. We will take that," Uriah tells them.

"Are you guys heading to or from your camp?" Vanessa asks.

"We are on a hike. We are heading away from camp right now," says a female hiker.

Uriah bends down to grab the supplies, exposing the weapons. The hikers take notice.

"Those are some pretty long knives you got there," says a male hiker.

"Oh yeah, those are the only weapons we have left," Uriah explains.

"Weapons?" asks female hiker.

"Yeah, I know it sounds odd, but we are angels, and this is all we have left from the attack," Uriah explains.

The hikers look both confused and wary.

"Uriah, they have no clue what you're talking about, and you're probably scaring them. Listen, like I said, my name is Vanessa, and that is Uriah. We do not mean to scare you, but we desperately need your help. We live in Portland, and we need to get back there ASAP. Can you help us please?"

The campers look around at one another again.

"Look, we can help you, but things look a little shady, you know. You've got these unusual weapons, in a forest. You're sleeping on the ground, with no camping supplies. Just looks sketchy," a male hiker says.

"I know, it looks odd. I assure you, we mean you no harm," Vanessa tells the hikers.

"We don't hurt humans. It's against our code," Uriah adds.

The hikers look at one another with confusion. Uriah finishes securing the weapons on his person. He tries to hand Vanessa her knife, but she denies it.

"Hold on to it for me," she asks him.

He sticks it into his belt and walks toward the river. "I'm going to get a drink," he tells her.

"What are your names?" Vanessa asks.

"I'm Rosie," "Lee," "I'm Anna," "I'm Selma," "Cody," "And I'm Dexter," they all reply.

"Anna, we had a friend named Anna. She was killed recently," she tells them.

The hikers continue to look confused about what the angels are talking about.

"I know this all looks and sounds weird, but if it would help, we can tell you what happened. If it's too much to ask, I understand. Maybe you could just point us in the direction of a road. Seeing you all out here means we are close," Vanessa says.

"Give us a minute, would you?" Dexter asks.

"Of course, take your time," Vanessa responds.

Uriah returns to Vanessa's side. "What are they doing?" he asks.

"Well, I'm sure this looks weird, and you're not helping with knives and swords sticking out everywhere, so they are deliberating," she tells him.

"What am I supposed to do with them?" he asks.

"Try not to be so weird," she suggests to him.

"Weird? What?" Uriah responds, surprised.

The hikers break their huddle and face the angels.

"So listen, we can lead you back to our camp and then show you the way onto a main road from there. After that, you are on your own," Lee tells the angels.

"Yeah, that works for us, thank you," Vanessa tells them.

"Yeah, thanks, we appreciate it," Uriah adds.

"All right, guys, we will catch up with you later," Rosie tells the group.

She and Dexter have decided to continue their hike. Cody, Anna, Lee, and Selma decide to lead the angels back to camp.

"This way, guys," Selma tells the angels.

"Damn, we were going the wrong way this whole time," Uriah says.

"That is so irritating," Vanessa adds.

* * * * *

Sherri waits at the diner for her friend to arrive. The server comes to the table to check on her. "Can I get you anything while you wait?"

"Yes, I will have a raspberry lemonade and a strawberry lemonade for my friend."

"Okay, coming right up." Sherri checks the menu as she waits.

Becca walks through the door, and Sherri waves at her. Becca reaches the table.

"Hey, girl."

"I ordered you a strawberry lemonade," Sherri tells her.

"Awesome, thanks."

"I'm looking forward to some time off, are you?" Becca asks.

"Sure, but our job isn't hard. I was thinking that we didn't need to take this much time off, but it's done," she says.

"Well, I for one am glad I'm taking this much time. It will be a nice reset," Becca states.

The server returns with the drinks.

"This is the strawberry, and this is the raspberry. Are you ready to order?"

"No, sorry, will need some more time," Becca tells him.

"Cool, be back to check on you."

"He is hot," Becca tells her.

"I didn't notice," Sherri replies.

"Bullshit. You should get his number," Becca suggests.

"Becca, that would be inappropriate. I'm in a relationship."

"Oh, is that what you call that?"

"Knock it off," Sherri commands.

"What to get, what get." Becca looks at the menu.

They both decide on a meal and place their orders with the waiter.

"How is your dad doing with the move?" Becca asks.

"He's good. He would've preferred that I waited to finish school before I moved out. But he is happy for me and being supportive."

"Good."

The server comes around with their food.

"Turkey club and the ham supreme. Is there anything else I can get for you, ladies?"

"Um, yes, how about your phone number for my friend here?"

Sherri freezes with her eyes wide open as the server laughs it off. Sherri looks at Becca then the server, then back to Becca.

"Let me know if there is anything else I can get you," the server tells them.

"Oh my god, why did you do that?"

"He is cute. Hell, if you're not going to take his number, I might take it for myself."

"You're the worst. That was so embarrassing," Sherri says.

"Relax, I'm sure he gets that all the time."

The girls enjoy their meal and prepare to leave. The server returns to leave them their check.

"Thank you for coming in today," he tells them.

"Thank you," Sherri says in return.

"Are you going to leave him your number?" Becca asks.

"I can't do that," she replies.

"Hmm, I see, so you can't do that, or you don't want to do that? There is a difference," Becca explains.

As Sherri gets up from the table, she leans over it and gets into Becca's face, nose to cheek. "*I don't want to,*" Sherri says in a stern tone, emphasizing each word, then leaves the table.

"You're paying!" Sherri yells back at her.

"Whatever. I'll leave mine." Becca leaves the server a note on a napkin with her phone number attached.

They walk out of the diner.

"Why don't you leave your car here, and we'll pick it up after work?" Sherri suggests.

"Sure," Becca replies.

"This way," Sherri points.

They get into the car and pull their seat belts around.

"You need to break up with him, Share Bear," Becca says.

Sherri pauses. "Where did that come from?" she asks.

"Never mind," Becca says.

"Okay," Sherri says as she turns the ignition, staring her down. "Are you okay, Bec?" she asks.

"Yeah, my mind was on something else. That's all. Let's go," she says.

* * * * *

Isaiah is waking up from a long night's sleep. He is taking his time getting up because he is sore from having to sleep on the ground. Fortunately, he was able to sleep heavy, so he slept through the discomfort. Despite the soreness, he has regained some strength to continue. He looks around and hears his stomach rumble.

"I am starving. I need to find something. I might have to start eating bark," he says aloud.

He leans up against a tree and puts his hands on his knees as he continues to look around. He rubs his face and begins to feel around his body. He takes a little more time to gather himself before he moves on. He looks up to check the position of the sun. He may be rested, but being hungry is waring on him. He goes to the river to get water. He stands up and looks down the river, in the direction he will go. He gets one more drink, then he resumes his mission along the river.

An hour passes, and periodically, he's looking up to see if he can see anything promising ahead of him. He stops for drink of water again. He takes a couple of drinks and continues.

About fifteen minutes after his last drink of water, he spots something up ahead. This object looks to be on or over the river. He gets little excited. He turns the walk into a cross country jog. As he gets closer, he can see that it's some type of bridge.

His jog turns into a cross-country run. It takes him less than a minute to reach the bridge. Once there, he sees that there is a gravel road that connects to it on both sides. He walks to the middle of the road and stands a moment, looking around. He stares down one way, then he turns and stares down the other way for another moment.

He can't decide which way to go. He continues to look both ways for a little while longer, trying to make up his mind.

"This must be a logging road, so the likelihood of anyone driving by is minimal, but I'm hopeful," he thinks aloud.

As he debates on which direction to go, he doesn't notice that there is a large amount of blackberry bushes in one direction, lining both sides of the road. He looks back and forth a little longer, then the blackberries catch his attention. He jogs over to the bushes and begins to eat, looking for the biggest ones. He looks down the road to see how far the berries go. He can see that the blackberry bushes line the road quite a way.

"I should go this direction," he says. He continues to feed as he looks around. "Yeah, this is the way, if I want to stay alive," he says.

He continues to eat berries as he is reminded by the beaming sun—that once he leaves the river, he will not have water. "Great, I'm trading food for water," he says.

He gets off the road and goes down to the river. He takes his time at the river to rest and take in as much water as he can. In this heat, he is going to need it. He also has no idea how long it will be before he sees water again. He gets his fill and walks back up to the road. He looks down the road each way one more time, just to make sure he feels like he is picking the right direction.

One direction should take me to civilization. The other direction will take me deeper into the forest, he thinks. He sticks with his original decision and begins to walk. He's rejuvenated because he has found a road. *At least now I have a better chance of getting to a town*, he thinks.

He walks down the middle of the road to make himself visible in the event a vehicle comes around. "Damn, I have no more shade," he says.

Walking on the side of the road will not help any as there is no protection from the sun no matter what part of the road he walks on. He takes his shirt off, stops, and runs back to the river. He soaks it and wraps it around his head. He uses some of it to cover his shoulders. He gets back on the road and continues his journey eating berries along the way.

* * * * *

Vanessa and Uriah arrive at the campsite with the four campers.

"Okay, so this is our camp," Selma tells the angels.

"If you don't mind just hanging out for a moment, we will show you the road," Anna says.

"Yeah, no problem," Vanessa says.

"Have a seat wherever," Selma offers.

There are more campers in the group, but only one is visible, staffing the grill. Lee walks up to him and explains what is happening. The camper is seen slightly moving his head up and down. The angels take a seat and wait patiently as the campers tend to their business. Selma and Anna go into their respective tents. Cody walks up to Lee and the grill master to join the conversation.

Lee walks over to the angels. "Are you hungry? Would you like to eat?" he asks.

"We are in a hurry, but we are also hungry. Yes, we would appreciate some food," says Vanessa then Uriah.

"Cool, we are all about to have lunch, and there is plenty, so hang tight," he tells the angels.

Anna comes out of her tent.

"It's lunchtime!" Cody calls out to the group.

The sound of giggles approaches the camp. The angels look around and see three females walking toward the camp. One of the ladies walks over to the angels.

"Oh, some neighbors. I'm Allie," she introduces herself.

"I'm Uriah."

"I'm Vanessa."

The campers move about to get things set up for lunch.

"Food is ready!" yells out the grill master. Selma emerges from her tent. They all take a place to have their lunch.

"Everyone, this is Vanessa and Uriah. We met them on our hike earlier," Selma explains.

The remaining campers introduce themselves.

"I'm Gina."

"I'm Sandra."

"I'm Alex. We have all types of food here—dogs, burgers, sausages, chicken, and all types of sides. Dig in," he offers.

The angels help themselves.

"Thank you, guys, again for this. We truly appreciate it," Uriah tells them.

"No problem," Cody says.

"Where are you guys camping?" Gina asks.

Vanessa looks over at Uriah with his mouth full. "Well, actually we are not camping, we are lost, or were lost in the forest. Your friends found us. And we are just trying to get back to Portland," Vanessa explains.

Some of the campers look at one another with confusion.

"If you weren't camping, how did you get to the forest in the first place?" Gina asks.

"Gina, quit being so intrusive," Sandra tells her.

"Not trying to be, sorry, just making conversation," Gina explains.

"No, it's fine," Vanessa says. "We gave some nuggets of info to your friends on the way here. The thing is, it's a long story with an even longer background, and well, it's complicated, really."

"I thought you guys were dressed pretty odd for camping," Alex tells them.

"Yeah, you're right. Being in the forest was not our intention. Unforeseen events got us stuck here," Uriah tells the group.

"You see, comments like that make me that much more curious!" Gina exclaims.

"Oh, stop it," Sandra tells her.

"You guys are dressed like you came from a battle," Alex adds.

"Yeah, yeah!" Gina shouts with excitement.

The angels look at each other again, and Uriah shrugs his shoulders, indicating he doesn't mind if they try and explain what has happened to them.

"Okay, I guess we can give you an abbreviated version, but I will caution you first. You may not believe some or all of what I am about to tell you, and we don't expect you to," Vanessa explains.

"Okay, that works for me. I'm ready," Gina says.

"Yeah, me too," Alex adds.

"Hell, I've been curious since we meet you guys," says Lee.

"All right, well, first, we are angels," she says.

"Like from heaven?" Cody asks.

"No, not like that," Uriah replies.

"There is so much more to this, and the more I explain it, the more questions you will have, so again, I'll just give you a condensed version, and we can take questions after," Vanessa tells them.

"It sounds like we are talking to the press," Uriah jokes.

"Again, we are angels. We live in Portland, but there are angels all over the world. There is a larger concentration of angels in Oregon and, especially, in Portland. We were returning to Portland from Bend. We were on a jet that was attacked by a rival group. We were shot out of the air. We had to make a crash landing." Vanessa stops for a moment.

Rosie and Dexter return to the camp.

"Hey, guys," Rosie greets her group.

"Hey, just in time for lunch," Allie tells them.

"And story time," Gina adds.

As Dexter and Rosie settle in, Gina insists, "Please continue."

"We crash-landed, we were ambushed by this rival group, and"—Vanessa pauses as she begins to get emotional—"six in our group were killed. We were the only ones to make it out," Uriah continues the story.

Vanessa wipes away some tears before she continues. The vibe of the campsite changes.

"This happened yesterday morning, and we have not been able to inform our leaders. So this is an emergency for us," Vanessa tells the campers.

The campers are left speechless. They continue to eat but in awkward silence.

"Listen, we really appreciate this food and all your generosity so far, but we really need to get back to Portland ASAP," Uriah tells them.

"Portland is like three hours from here," Dexter says.

"We know it's far, but if you would be so kind as to help us, not only would we be grateful and indebted to you, but you would be generously compensated for your troubles," Vanessa tells them.

"Listen, this is an emergency for us. Time is of the essence, and every hour that goes by puts the world closer and closer to danger," Uriah says.

"Okay, now that is crazy talk, man," Lee says.

"Yeah, we know how it sounds, but it is what it is," Uriah tells them.

There is silence as the campers look at one another uncomfortably. Some make themselves look occupied with their food.

"I'll take you."

All eyes gaze toward Alex.

"Yeah, I'll take you," he repeats.

The angels smile.

"Thanks, Alex," Vanessa says.

Alex looks over at his wife, Allie. "You want to go with me?" he asks.

"Um, I'd rather not," she says in a soft voice.

"I'll go with you," Cody says.

All eyes move to him. He looks at his wife, Anna, and shrugs his shoulders. She, in return, shrugs her shoulders in agreement.

"Right on, Cody," Alex says.

"Yeah, why not? We will be helping save the world, right?" Cody says sarcastically.

"Thanks, Cody," Vanessa says.

The angels don't mind the joke. They have a great understanding for all those who do not believe or understand who they are.

"All right, well, let's finish lunch, then we can head out, yeah?" Alex tells them.

"Thank you all for your hospitality and generosity with the food. We understand that this was not part of your camping plan, and to the wives, girlfriends, thank you as I know that this may cause an inconvenience, but I want to remind you all that you can expect to be generously compensated for your troubles," Vanessa tells the group.

"That really isn't necessary," Sandra says.

"No, we insist. You don't quite understand the amount of assistance you are giving us," Uriah tells her.

"It's settled then. We will head out shortly," Cody tells the group.

* * * * *

The car reaches the gate. Guards approach the car at each side. They lean over enough to see inside. They can see the two angels in the back seat.

"Hey, fellas, can you let us in?" Uriah asks.

"Please," Vanessa adds.

"Go on through," guard number 1 says as guard number 2 steps back to open the gate.

"Fern, you've got two angels and two civilians coming your way," guard number 1 radios.

Leann is standing next to Fernando when he gets the message. "You or your parents expecting company?" he asks.

"No, who is it?"

"Two angels. I wasn't given names."

With a surprised look, she goes to the front door. She opens it and sees the car driving up. Cody and Alex are mesmerized by the property as they attempt to take in the entirety of the estate.

"You can stop here," Uriah tells Alex.

The angels get out of the car.

Leann immediately runs to them upon sight. "Oh my god," she says as she hugs Vanessa.

"Hey, Leann, good to see you," Vanessa responds.

Alex and Cody remain in the car, still wondering what they are currently involved in.

"Is Nate here?" Uriah asks Leann as she walks over to him and gives him a hug.

"Yes, Mom and Dad are both here."

They walk up to the house. Vanessa motions to Cody and Alex to get out of the car. They look at each other, wondering if they should.

Alex rolls down the car window. "You want us to get out?"

"Yeah, I want you to meet Nate and Erin."

The humans look at each other again and agree to get out. Vanessa walks ahead. They get out of the car and hurry to catch up. They reach Vanessa, and they all reach Uriah and Leann inside the house.

"Fern, can you show them to the family room? Let them get comfortable," Leann asks.

"Of course, right this way. Gentlemen, this way please."

The three angels walk to the back of the house. They stop. Vanessa lets out a big sigh.

"Are you okay?" Leann asks.

"Yeah, I just need a second," requests Vanessa. She lets out one more big sigh, then they walk out the back door.

Nate and Erin are tending to their garden. He has always been fond of lilies. They bring him serenity. Erin is fond of orange roses; she thinks they are the most beautiful of the all the roses. They are discussing the plan for the garden for the upcoming season. They are off to the side of the house, so they can't see that Uriah and Vanessa are at the back door. Leann is standing next to them. They all walk toward Nate and Erin. They walk a small distance, enough where Nate and Erin are visible.

Vanessa stops suddenly. Uriah and Leann take a couple more steps before they notice that she has stopped.

They both turn around.

"Vanessa, what are you doing?" Leann asks. Uriah walks back to her. "It's going to be okay," he tells her.

Leann walks a little further toward her parents.

"Mom, Dad," she calls out.

Her mother turns. Nate is in a crouched position and turns around as far as he can. Erin sees Uriah and Vanessa standing off to the side. She puts her hand on Nate's shoulder. He can't quite make out the entire seen, but his wife's hand on his shoulders tells him that it's something significant. He gathers himself enough to get to his feet. He sees his daughter, then his eyes move to Uriah and Vanessa. He begins to walk toward the angels.

He reaches Leann and places his hand on her shoulder as he passes her. Erin stays behind and watches Nate. She wants to give him space to acknowledge the angels and their traumatic experience. She waits a moment then walks to Leann; they embrace. He continues to the other angels; he reaches them and gives each of them a hug. "I am so happy to see you, angels."

They both have a look of defeat as they await what he might say.

"Nate, forgive us. We have lost the halo," Uriah says as Erin and Leann join Nate at his side.

"Never mind that right now," he tells them.

Erin turns to look at her husband. She is surprised to hear him say that but is pleased at the same time. She understands that his number one priority is the halo, but she is happy to know that he is putting the angels first right now.

"How are you? Are you injured?" he asks.

"You must be starving," Erin asks them.

"No, thank you, we are fine, right?" he asks Vanessa.

"Yeah, I'm fine."

"Where are the other angels?" he asks them.

"We were attacked then ambushed by the devils," Uriah tells him.

"It was a complete surprise. We had little time to react," Vanessa adds.

"We were heavily outnumbered." Uriah chokes up a little.

Vanessa takes over. "They are all dead, sir—Rudy, all of them were killed," she expresses.

Uriah gathers himself enough to continue "We fought them off as much as we could, but in the end, there were just too many of them," he says.

"The devils must have known that we were carrying the halo, and they knew the path they would be traveling," Vanessa says as she begins to cry.

Nate puts his hands on her shoulders. "What is it, dear?"

"They are all dead," she weeps.

He brings her in for a second hug. He then places his hand on Uriah's shoulder. There is a moment of silence. He backs away from them both a little. "We must move then," he says with confidence.

"Let's go back inside, angels," Erin suggests.

"Yes, inside is good. You two must tend to any wounds, and rest up," Nate tells the angels. "I will fix you some lunch, my angels. Leann, you will help, yes?"

"Of course, Mother."

"No, that won't be necessary, Erin, thank you. We actually ate a couple of hours ago," Uriah tells her.

"That reminds me, we have some visitors—" Vanessa starts to say.

"They are in the family room," Leann cuts her off.

"It's two men. They were out camping with a group. They stumbled upon us, invited us to their camp, and were kind enough to drive us here during their camping trip," Vanessa explains.

"Yeah, they fed us, and ah, they are good people. They helped us out big-time. If they had not found us, we might still be out in the forest," Uriah adds.

"Well, allow us to go show our gratitude to these men," Nate says as they make their way to the family room.

Alex and Cody sit and talk with Fernando as they wait, wondering what they are waiting for.

Nate walks into the room. "Ah, Fernando has been keeping you company, I see," he says as he walks toward Cody first with his hand extended.

Cody quickly stands up to meet Nate's extended hand. Alex stands up as well, anticipating that he is next.

"I am Nate," he introduces himself.

"I'm Cody," he responds.

"Cody, it's an honor," Nate expresses. He goes over to Alex. "I'm Nate."

"I am Alex. Good to meet you."

"Alex and Cody, I understand that you have provided a great amount of assistance to my angels. For that, I, we are appreciative and indebted to you." Nate motions to Fernando, gestures only understood by the angels.

Fernando leaves the room.

"Oh, it's cool. We are happy to help," Alex says.

"We just saw that some people needed some help, so we helped," Cody adds.

"Well, I know there is much you don't understand, but what you have done is more important than you know. So allow us to show you our appreciation," Nate tells the guests.

As they wait for Fernando to return, he calls for his wife and daughter, "Dear"—he motions his hand to them—"this is my beautiful wife, Erin, and my beautiful daughter, Leann."

They all exchange greetings.

"Thank you so much for helping the angels," Erin tells the men.

"No problem, really," Alex replies.

"Well, that is not true. As I understand it, this is right in the middle of your camping trip, and you left a group of friends back who must be awaiting your return. I would call it an inconvenience," Erin tells them.

The two men smile. Fernando returns with a briefcase. He hands it to Nate.

"Please accept this as a token of our appreciation and gratitude. You have done more for us than you will ever know," Nate expresses to them. He extends the briefcase out, and Alex reaches out for it.

"Um, thank you."

"Yes, thank you," the men say. Alex and Cody stand in awkwardness holding a briefcase with the contents unknown.

"Uh, I can guess what's inside, but can you tell us?" Cody asks.

"Right, of course," Nate says.

Fernando walks up to Alex and grabs the briefcase, turns it toward them, and opens it. Their eyes get big, staring at the briefcase. They look at each other, speechless and frozen. "Please accept this cash in the amount of?" Nate turns to Fernando to get the amount.

"Uh, one hundred thousand, sir," he responds.

"Yes, one hundred thousand."

Still speechless, Alex lets out a cough to clear his throat. "Um, geez, um, we don't deserve this," Alex says.

"Please accept it. We insist," Erin tells the men.

"You can divide that how you see fit. We told you, you would be compensated generously for your troubles, remember?" Uriah reminds them.

Cody clears his throat. "Yeah, but this is way beyond."

"You deserve it, thanks," Leann tells them.

Fernando closes the briefcase and locks it.

"Very well, it's settled. Fernando will see you out," Nate tells them.

Alex reaches the for the briefcase as he looks at Cody, still wide-eyed. They follow Fernando through the house and to the door.

As they reach the door, Vanessa catches up to them and gives them both a hug. "Thank you."

Fernando opens the door. "Have a wonderful day, gentleman." He hands them a business card.

"Yeah, thank you."

"We definitely will," the men say.

The door closes behind them.

"Angels, thank you for your efforts. I would like you to go get some rest, food, and get yourselves cleaned up, then return to give us the full story of the attack," Nate requests.

"Okay, will do," Uriah says.

"Leann, honey, I would like you to accompany them and assist with whatever they need," Nate tells her.

"Yes, Father," she replies.

The three angels turn toward the front door and head out.

"I will have them back as soon as possible," Leann turns and tells her parents.

Nate and Erin are left alone in the family room.

"Honey, what are we going to do?" she asks.

As he stands with one arm across his chest and the other hand at his chin, Nate asks, "How could I let this happen?"

Erin takes a step toward him to console him. "Nathanael, this is not your fault. How were you to know that devils would be attacking?" she tells him.

"I have let the angels down," he says softly.

Erin slaps him slightly on the cheek. "That is absurd. I don't want to hear any of that nonsense anymore. I am clear?" she says in a stern tone.

"Yes, ma'am," he says as he rubs his cheek, surprised that she gently slapped him.

"We are angels. We will get the halo back," Erin continues with optimism.

"I've got to call Bradley, and we have to mobilize," he says aloud.

They walk toward the kitchen as Nate pulls his phone out to call Brad. "Bradley, Vanessa and Uriah are alive. Come over ASAP and bring Christian with you," he says over the phone.

"What? Really? That is great. How?" he asks.

"I will explain everything when you get here. Bradley, time is of the essence!" he exclaims.

"I'll be there ASAP," Brad tells him.

Nate hangs up the phone and walks away, leaving Erin behind.

"Honey, what can I do right now? What do you want me to do for you?" she asks.

He stops and turns around. "Just stay strong and do what you do, my love."

"You got it, my darling," she replies.

He continues to walk away.

"I think I know the answer, but can I make you something to eat or something to drink?" she asks.

"No, my love, but let's prepare to have some guest for dinner, yes," he tells her.

"Of course," she replies.

* * * * *

The men are still in disbelief as they walk to their car. "What the fuck, man?" Alex says.

"What just happened? Cody asks rhetorically.

They get into the car and sit, still trying to make sense of what has just taken place.

"This is crazy, man. Something doesn't feel right, right?" Alex asks.

"I don't know, man. It was definitely weird, but we have one hundred fucking thousand dollars, man," Cody says with excitement.

"What are we going to do with this money?" Alex asks.

"I don't know, dude, but we can't take it back to the camp site," Cody says.

"You're right. We have to leave it here. You live closer. Let's take it there for now, and then we will deal with it after camping," Alex suggests.

"Cool, good, let's go before they change their minds," Cody jokes.

Alex turns the car on and drives through the rounded driveway.

"Hey, man, are we going to give some money to the others?" Cody asks.

"I don't know, you think we should?" Alex replies.

"They didn't come all this way," Cody says.

"Right, this is crazy, dude. I can't believe they gave us this much money," Alex says.

"For a ride they gave us one hundred grand. Easy, like giving someone a gift basket as a thank-you," Cody says.

"Right, who are these people?" Alex asks as he looks in his rear-view mirror. He sees a car speeding up to them.

"Oh shit!" Cody yells out.

"What?" asks Alex.

"We can't take this money to my house. I don't have my keys," Cody says.

"All right, well, I guess we will take it to my house," Alex says. He looks at the rearview mirror again. The car is closer and still speeding. His eyes shift from mirror to road and back. "You know maybe we should give everyone some money." His eyes continue to go from mirror to road.

"Yeah, you're right. Let's do five hundred per couple, then we can split the rest," Cody suggests.

"Sounds good," Alex responds as he continues to look back.

The car has reached them and is now within a car length. He is staying cool about it, trying to figure out what the cars' objective is.

"We should do five hundred each," Alex suggests.

Cody looks over at him. "I just said that, man, and you agreed," Cody says, confused.

Alex is now concerned about the car following them.

"Hey, man, are you cool?" Cody asks.

"Yeah, but this car behind us—"

Cody looks back.

"I've been watching it. It sped up to us, and now it's riding us," Alex describes.

"Yeah, what's up with this dude?" Cody says as he continues to look back.

"I'm going to slow down and let him pass," suggests Alex.

"He looks pissed. What's his problem?" asks Cody.

Alex begins to slow down. The car slows down as well and continues to follow them closely. "He is not passing, man. What is going on?" Cody says.

"This is not cool," says Alex.

"It's not like you can get off to the side either," Cody adds.

"I guess I'm just going to slow down more. I don't know what this guy wants," Alex says.

He reduces his speed from 34 mph to about 20 mph. He checks his mirror as Cody continues to look back. Suddenly the car accelerates around them; they watch as the car goes around and gets in front of them. The car gets about eight car lengths in front of them.

"He's stopping. Why is he stopping?" Cody asks.

The men continue the short distance to reach the mysterious car that is taking up both lanes parked sideways.

"What the hell is this guy doing?" Alex asks.

They stop about two car lengths before the mysterious car and watch. Alex leaves his foot on the brake. The windows to the mysterious car are tinted, so they can't see inside. A guy gets out of the car. Their eyes stay locked on this mysterious man as he takes his time walking to their car.

"Who is this guy?" Alex asks.

"I don't know, man. You think he wants our money?" Cody speculates.

"How would he even know we have it?" Alex asks.

"I don't know. What if he is one of those angels and they want it back?" Cody says.

"I highly doubt that," Alex replies.

The mysterious man reaches the car and approaches the window. He leans over and rests his forearms on the door.

"What do you highly doubt?" Ty asks the men.

They look at each other.

"We were just talking to each other," Alex tells the stranger.

"I see," says the man. He gets down a little lower to see farther into the car and looks around. "Put the car in park," Ty commands.

Alex slowly shifts the car to park as he glances over at Cody.

"What part specifically do you highly doubt?" asks Ty.

"Uh, he was just asking if you were one of those angels, and I told him that I highly doubted it," Alex responds.

"How do you know if I'm not an angel?" Ty asks.

"I don't. I just said that I doubted it. Why would they come after us like this after we leave their house? They were really nice people," Alex says.

"Do you know the angels?" Ty asks.

"No," Cody replies.

"Then why where you at their house?"

The men look at each other again.

"We dropped a couple of them off. That was it. They needed a ride," Cody tells the man.

"Hmm. Why don't you tell me the whole story?" Ty asks.

"What do you mean the whole story?" asks Alex.

"Hold on, man, who are you? Why did you stop us? Why are you questioning us? What do you want?" Cody asks excitedly.

"I want you to tell me the story about you and the angels," Ty asks again.

"We don't even know you," Cody replies.

"Ooahh," Alex gasps as Ty strikes his throat.

"Whoa, what the fuck, man," Cody says, wide-eyed.

Alex grabs his throat with both hands.

"Now tell me," Ty asks again.

"Um, we just met them. They we were camping. I mean we were camping. Um, they were in the forest. We ran into them. They told us they were lost. We invited them to our camp. They asked us for a ride. We brought them to that house, and that's it," Cody explains with urgency.

"How many, what were their names, what other details did they give you?" Ty asks.

Cody stares at Alex as he fights to breathe.

"Focus," Ty says calmly.

"There were two of them, um, Vanessa and Uriah. They told us about some craziness like they were angels and they got attacked and, um, they were lost and they needed a ride," Cody explains.

"That's it?" Ty asks.

"Look, man, we don't even know them. We were just trying to be cool and help them out. That's it. We don't want any trouble," Cody pleads.

"Did they have anything with them?" the man asks.

"Well, I mean, they had some weapons, which was weird. They didn't have much on them. They looked beat up, and they were hungry, but I don't know what else you mean," Cody tells Ty.

"Did they mention anything about a halo or have a circular, skinny shiny ring? It would look like a halo that an angel would wear," Ty describes.

"I don't, I don't think so. They might have mentioned the word *halo* once, but we didn't see one or anything like what you are describing. They did say that there was more to all this and that we would not understand, so they didn't try to explain," Cody says.

"Did they give you anything?" Ty asks.

Cody's eyes roll over to the briefcase. Alex has been able to regain his breathing; he releases one hand from his throat. "They gave us money as a thank-you for the ride," Cody tells him.

"Show me," Ty asks.

Cody sighs and then reaches back for the briefcase. He turns it toward Ty and opens it. He looks up at Ty.

"How much is it?" Ty asks.

"One hundred grand. You can have it, man. We don't want trouble," Cody pleads again.

The man smiles sinisterly. "I don't want your money. I want something else."

The men look at each other again.

"Give me your wallets," Ty demands.

They both slowly reach for their wallets and hand them over. He pulls out their IDs and looks at them. "Alex and Cody, you now work for me."

Behind them a car approaches. Ty looks back at it. It prompts Cody to look back. The car gets close then stops behind their car. The man in the car begins to honk at them. "You will be hearing from me, so stay ready. Consider that money a payment from me for your services," Ty tells them.

The man in the car behind them continues to honk at them.

"Don't talk to the angels about this. I will know if you do, understood?" he tells the men.

They nod to confirm.

The waiting car continues to honk. Ty stands upright and walks back to the honking car. Cody keeps his eyes on Ty as he walks back to the waiting car.

"Dude, look," Cody tells Alex.

They can't hear anything; they see Ty pull out a knife and stab the driver in the neck.

"Holy shit!" Cody yells.

"What the fuck," Alex says with a raspy sore throat.

Ty looks over at them to make sure they are watching. He pulls the knife from the driver's neck and walks back toward their car.

The car moves forward slowly as the driver's foot falls off the break. His hands turn the wheel, causing it to go off the road.

"Don't you guys think about crossing me and leave that alone," Ty says, referring to the man in the car behind them.

They watch in disbelief as they see the mysterious man get into his car.

"Are you cool, man?" Cody asks Alex.

"It's better, but that fucking hurt. I thought I was going to suffocate," Alex says. They see the stranger drive away in his car. Cody looks back at the car behind them.

"That poor dude. Should we wait till he is out of sight and then help?" Cody suggests.

"Hell no. Let's drive ahead, and we can stop somewhere and call it in. I don't want to get chopped in the throat again or, worse, get killed," Alex says.

"Yeah, all right. Then let's get to your house and chill for a bit," Cody suggests.

* * * * *

"Where are my keys?" he asks himself. Brad is gathering some items before he heads out the door. "I'll call Christian from the car," he says aloud. He gets into his car. He does a final check of his belongings. *I know I'm forgetting something*, he thinks. He is a little distracted by his thoughts. He is excited that two angels are alive, but also worried and curious about the whole story. He connects his phone to his car's Bluetooth. "Call Christian," he commands.

Christian sees that it's Brad on his phone and is annoyed that he is getting a call at this moment. He decides to let it go to voice mail, but Brad does not leave a message and, instead, redials. Christian checks his phone again. He rolls his eyes a little. He decides to answer this time.

"Hey, Brad," he answers, a little annoyed.

"Nate is asking for you to come in. Emergency status," he tells Christian.

"Seriously, man, I'm kind of busy right now," Christian expresses with more annoyance.

"Yes, Nate requested you specifically, ASAP," Brad tells him.

"What time does he want to see me?" he asks.

"Us and now. I'm on my way now," Brad tells him.

Christian goes quiet.

"Christian, you need to be on your way now. That is an order," Brad commands.

"Damn it, Brad, this isn't a good time… All right, I'm on my way," Christian reluctantly agrees to go in.

He sets his phone on the table. He looks across the way to his lady companion. "I'm sorry, but I have to go."

She expresses disappointment, "I'm not going to let you leave until you promise to make it up to me."

He smiles then gets out of his chair and walks over to her. He leans down and whispers something into her ear that makes her smile big.

"You better," she giggles.

He kisses her on the cheek and leaves money on the table.

*   *   *   *   *

Brad arrives at Nate's house; he walks up to the house and lets himself in. "Hey, Fern."

"Erin is in the kitchen, and Nate is in the study," he tells Brad.

"Thanks," Brad replies.

He decides to go say hi to Erin first.

"Hello, Bradley," she says.

"Hi, Erin," he replies.

They exchange kisses on the cheeks.

"How is the old man doing?" he asks her.

"Things are not good, Bradley, but I won't delay you any longer. He's waiting for you in the study, I believe," she tells him.

"Good to see you, Erin," he says.

"Hopefully, seeing you will bring him some relief," she tells him.

"I'll see what I can do," he responds.

He heads toward the study. He finds Nate standing with his eyes closed. "Nate," Brad calls out.

Nate doesn't respond as he is in deep thought. Nate opens his eyes. He remains in deep thought.

Erin walks to the study and stands next to Brad. She sees Nate in deep thought. "Nathanial… Nathanial, honey," Erin calls out.

Nate comes out of his daydream. He sees Brad and Erin at the doorway. Brad walks forward as Erin walks back to the kitchen. "Yes, come in, come in. Thanks for getting here with urgency," Nate tells him.

"Of course, I got here as fast as I could. So what's going on?" Brad asks.

"Well, as I told you, Vanessa and Uriah are alive. They stopped by earlier. I sent them home to rest and clean up. Did you call Christian?"

"Yes, he's on his way."

"Good, good. They will be returning to tell us what happened. In the meanwhile, I want to discuss what we are going to do next, when Christian arrives. Make yourself comfortable," Nate suggests.

Erin enters the room with drinks. "Ah, thank you, dear, but I'm going to have some of the hard stuff," Nate tells his wife.

"Thank you, Erin, but I'll be joining Nate with the hard stuff," Brad says.

"Well, you can use these as mixers," Erin offers.

Several minutes go by when Fernando and Christian enter the room.

"Ah, Christian, you made it. Thank you, Fern," Nate says.

"Late of course," Brad follows.

"Would you like a drink, son?" Nate offers.

"Hell yeah, since I was having one already when I was interrupted," he says as he looks at Brad.

"Blame the guy pouring you a drink," Brad responds.

"Christian, let's catch up first. I have great news. Uriah and Vanessa are alive!"

"Cool, I'm happy for them," he says without emotion.

Nate and Brad stare at him for a moment. "What? Why are you guys staring at me like that?"

"Why would you respond like that?" Brad asks.

"How should I respond. Am I missing something?" Christian asks.

"Do you know? You don't know, do you?" Brad asks.

"About what guys?"

"The jet, the attack on the jet."

"What? No, what are you talking about?" Christian asks with a confused look.

Brad and Nate look at each other for a moment.

"The jet from Bend was attacked yesterday morning by the devils," Brad tells him.

"Until today, we hadn't heard from the jet and didn't know what had happened until Vanessa and Uriah showed up here, about an hour ago," Nate says.

"What?" Christian says confused and a bit lost with the story. "Uriah and Vanessa are returning in a while to give us a full account of the event. We all have many questions, but I think it's best to hold those for them. Right now, I want to discuss what we are going to do about this. We have confirmed that the devils are responsible for the attack. Hayley and your sister confirmed this yesterday. They are still out there, searching for the missing angels and the halo. We know that three angels were killed, so far. Three are unaccounted for."

"Who? Who was killed?" Christian asks.

Brad and Nate look at each other again.

"Dom, Anna, and Angela," Brad tells him.

"Damn, motherfuckers! Yeah, so what are we going to do?" Christian asks.

"We are going to pay Jason a visit," Nate says as he hands Christian his drink.

"Fuck yeah!" exclaims Christian.

Brad looks confused and surprised. "That was unexpected," Brad says.

"He has gone too far this time," Nate responds.

Leann, Uriah, and Vanessa arrive at Nate's home. They get out of the car and make their way up the stairs.

Fernando opens the door for them. "Good to see you again, angels."

"Good to see you to, Fern," the angels say.

Uriah offers a smile as Vanessa pats him on the shoulder.

"They are waiting for you in the study," Fern informs them.

They make their way to the study.

"Ah, angels, welcome," Nate shouts.

It grabs everyone's attention.

Christian turns around then stands up. He walks over to them. "I just found out, guys. Sorry for what happened," he offers.

The angels acknowledge his sympathy.

"Hey, Christian," Leann says.

"Hey, Leann," he says as he walks over for a hug.

"All right, everyone, make yourselves comfortable. You will all be staying for dinner. Grab something to drink, and we will get started in a bit," Nate tells the group. Erin enters the room to greet everyone as well.

"What can I get for anyone? Please don't be shy," she offers.

Each angel takes a turn giving their request. The angels find a comfortable place to sit. They all engage in small talk as they wait for their drinks and snacks.

* * * * *

Uriah and Vanessa sit quietly as they consume their drinks.

"Can I get anything for anyone else?" Erin asks.

No one responds.

"Very well then, everyone will be staying for dinner," she tells the group.

"Yes, Nate has informed us," Brad tells her.

"Ah, thank you, dear," she says to her husband. Erin exits the study.

There is a tense disposition and an atmosphere to match.

"How are you guys feeling?" Nate asks them.

"Not good, Nate," Vanessa responds.

"We are as good as can be, considering the circumstances," Uriah adds.

"Of course, that is understandable," Nate says.

"Take some deep breaths, and begin when you're ready. Take your time," Brad tells them.

Uriah and Vanessa look at each other.

"Okay then, when you're ready, angels," Nate tells them.

On their way to the meeting, they had decided that Uriah would start, then Vanessa would add as necessary.

"Well, as you all know, we were on our way home," Uriah starts.

"Oh, oh oh oh oh oh oh oh oh oh oh oh oh, caught in a bad romance. Oh, oh oh oh oh oh oh oh oh oh oh oh oh, caught in a bad romance, ra ra ah ah ah ah, ra ra ah ah ah ah," Uriah sings as he pulls his laptop out of his backpack. The song catches the attention of the other angels.

"I want your ugly. I want your disease. I want your everything as long as it's free. I want your love love, love, love, I want your love," Uriah continues to sing as Isaiah walks by him.

"I love that song, man," Isaiah comments.

"I find it surprising that you would like a song like that," Angela tells Uriah.

"Why is that, Angela, 'cuz I'm a dude?" he asks.

"No, that is not the case. I'm just surprised that you like this song. That's all," she explains.

"Yup, I do love this song, who doesn't?" he asks.

"So do I!" shouts Isaiah from the back of the jet.

"There you go, now there are two of us you can be surprised about," he tells Angela.

They laugh along with Anna, who is listening in on the conversation.

Domingus looks over at Vanessa. "Take a break. I can take it from here."

"Sure, Captain," she jokingly replies.

Vanessa gets out of the cocaptain's chair and moves to the back of the jet. "Hey, y'all, we are five minutes from home," she tells the other angels.

There is a pause. She is silent because she is joking with them and waiting for one of them to realize it and call her out.

"Hmm!" Uriah exclaims as he is unsure if he should believe her.

"Seriously, is that true?" Angela asks.

"No, not true, we have been in the jet for about twenty minutes. There is no way," Anna says.

"Ah, you got me," Vanessa giggles.

She sees Isaiah at the back of the jet. She walks to him. "Got it figured out yet?" she asks.

He has been staring at the halo for several minutes without moving. "No, not really trying to. I don't really know anything about it. It just amazes me how this is the source of everything we are," he tells her.

"Yeah, it's pretty crazy, but I guess you have to be one of the elders to really understand it," she tells him.

"I hear you. It's just crazy to think about," he adds. "Well, let me know if you figure it out," she says as she walks away.

She makes her way back to her seat and passes the other angels on the way. She gets into her seat and reaches for her buckle; she looks over at Domingus who is rubbing his forehead. "Are you okay? she asks.

"I'm fine," he tells her.

"Doesn't look like it."

"Just some small headaches, had them for a while now."

She inquires a little more out of concern. "How long has this been happening?"

"It's been about four or five days now, since before Bend," he tells her.

"Hmmm, how bad are they?" she asks.

"It's nothing to crazy or concerning, just annoying," he says.

"Are you dehydrated?"

He thinks about it for a second.

"That could be it," he says.

"Let me get you some water."

She unbuckles again. She walks to the back for some water. This time she sees Uriah staring out the window.

"I love the view from up here," he says loud enough so that the others can hear.

"So do I, but I can't wait to get back," Angela replies to the group.

"Really, why?" asks Rudy.

"What? You have a special someone waiting at home for you?" Isaiah pokes fun.

Angela smiles then giggles. Anna giggles along with her. There is a brief silence as Anna stares at Angela. Uriah then turns to stare at Angela as well.

"Are you going to tell them? Go ahead, I think you should," Anna tells Angela.

Angela stares back at Anna with a pair of wide eyes as she tilts her head at her.

"Tell us what?" asks Vanessa as she walks by again.

Angela smiles at Vanessa. She thinks for a second.

"Well?" Isaiah asks with suspense.

"Okay, fine."

The angels make themselves a little more comfortable. Vanessa remains standing at her chair, forgetting to hand Domingus the water she got for him.

"Okay, well, I met someone, and he—"

Boom! The jet gets rocked by an explosion. The back of the jet lifts, sending the front pointing toward the ground. It quickly levels out horizontally and begins to spin. Isaiah gets blown back against the jet wall toward the middle. Vanessa falls away from her seat and hits the floor. JR, not seated and standing closest to the blast, gets sucked right through the hole, his body and head hit the jet on his way out.

"JR!" Anna yells out.

As the jet continues to spin, the angels fight to get into a seat and strapped in.

"Everyone, hold on!" Rudy yells out to the angels.

Isaiah grabs ahold of some straps that are flinging around. Vanessa gets to her knees and crawls her way back into her seat.

"We are going down, guys! Everyone needs to get buckled in!" Domingus yells from the front of the plane.

Debris blows all around the jet. The suction from the opening begins to rattle the crate, holding the halo. Domingus struggles to maintain control of the jet as it continues to spin toward the ground.

"We have to stop the spinning," Domingus tells Vanessa.

"I will activate the stabilizers," she tells him.

"After that, activate the boosters," he replies.

"Got it, twenty-four thousand feet," Vanessa tells Domingus.

"Come on, baby, stay with me," Domingus sweet-talks the jet.

"Stabilizers on!" Vanessa yells out.

Domingus corrects the jet, stops it from spinning. The jet is now falling toward the ground with the left side leading the way.

"22-5, getting boosters on now," she tells Domingus.

"Okay, guys, we can't keep the plane in the air for long. Hang on!" Domingus yells back at the angels.

Between the alerts coming from the jet and the sound of the suction, the angels can barely make out what is being said at the front.

"Boosters on, twenty-one thousand feet!" Vanessa yells out.

As they hang on, Angela looks up; out of her peripherals, she sees the crate with the halo in it, rattling on the ground. She also sees Isaiah nearby hanging on. He is watching the crate as well. The crate is slowly rattling toward the hole, centimeters at a time.

"Isaiah, the halo!" Angela yells out.

It gets the attention of the other angels.

"We are falling too fast," Domingus tells Vanessa.

"Yeah, booster indicate they are on, but it looks like the they are damaged—nineteen thousand feet," she tells him.

Isaiah continues to work toward the crate.

"You have to get it now!" Rudy yells out.

Isaiah pulls himself within arm's length of the crate. He reaches for it, then the jet rattles. The rattle is so strong that it makes the crate bounce against the top of the jet, busting open. The halo in a clear cube encasing flies out of the jet. The angels are left wide-eyed as they hopelessly see the halo leave the jet. Isaiah pulls himself to his feet. He looks back at Rudy briefly then looks at the hole. He looks at Rudy one more time and then gives him a small nod and a smile. He grabs one of the parachutes that hangs right behind him. *I don't have time to put it on*, he thinks to himself, so he clutches it against his chest.

"What are you doing?" Uriah yells out.

Isaiah releases his hold from the straps and runs toward the hole, diving out of the jet. The remaining angels look at each other and look at Rudy for a reaction. He says nothing.

I hope he catches up to the halo, he thinks to himself.

"15-5, boosters are not responding," Vanessa tells Domingus.

Both Domingus and Vanessa are unaware of what is taking place at the back of the jet. Vanessa vigorously continues to work on the boosters, "13-7!" she yells out.

As the jet drops lower in elevation, it is getting less chaotic inside the jet. Uriah quickly undoes his belt.

"Uriah, what are you doing?" Rudy asks.

Uriah gets up from his seat. He moves toward the parachutes. Rudy quickly unbuckles his belt.

"Uriah, don't!" Anna yells out.

Rudy rushes to him and grabs him by the arm and shoulder. "You can't do this," he tells Uriah.

"I have to. He needs help. We need to get the halo back," he responds.

"We have to trust him. I have faith that he will find the halo and JR," Rudy says.

Uriah tries to lightly get free from Rudy to get a parachute.

"Eleven thousand feet," Vanessa tells Domingus.

"Okay, let's just keep her steady," he responds.

"Listen, we need you here. You know who did this, and they will be waiting for us when we hit the ground. We need you," Rudy expresses to him.

Uriah stops for a moment.

"We need you, Uriah," Angela tells him.

Uriah looks at Rudy and closes his eyes in acknowledgment. Rudy releases his grip and pats him on his chest.

"Okay, good, let's strap in. We have to brace for this crash landing," he tells Uriah.

"9,100 feet!" she yells out.

"Okay, check the integrity of the reverse thrusters," he instructs her.

"Checking thrusters now," she replies.

Rudy and Uriah make their way back to their sets and buckle in. "Thrusters are operational, Dom. 7-9," she says as she looks back at the other angels. She looks at the dashboard again. "We are at seven thousand feet to impact."

"Vanessa, at five thousand feet, activate the reverse thrusters. We have to slow our velocity," he instructs.

"Got it, 6,100 feet," she reports.

"When I say 'Go,' I will shut down the engines, and then you will hit the thrusters, got it?"

"Got it," she says.

Domingus looks back. "Guys, hold on. You're going to feel a full stop in midair. It's going to rock you," he explains.

She begins a countdown, "Fifty-six...fifty-five...fifty-four...fifty-three...fifty-two...fifty-one...five thousand!" she calls out.

Domingus shuts down the engines. "Go!" he yells out.

Vanessa activates the reverse thrusters. The jet begins to slow down, then it comes to a complete stop in midair. All angels feel the jerk of the full stop.

"Okay, shut down thrusters," Domingus instructs Vanessa.

"Thrusters off," she says.

He turns the engines back on, allowing the jet to again continue its acceleration. "All right, we are going to do this one more time," he tells Vanessa.

"4,100 feet," Vanessa reports.

"All right we are going to do this again at one thousand feet, got it?"

"Got it," she replies.

"Go ahead and drop the landing gear," Domingus instructs.

Vanessa looks over at him, confused.

"Why do we need landing gear? We are going to crash."

Domingus looks over at her. "You're right, sorry, habit." He chuckles.

"3,200 feet, Dom," Vanessa reports.

"Guys, we are going to hit hard, but I don't think we will explode on impact," he tells the group.

That draws a stare from Vanessa. "What do you mean? Why would you say that?" she asks.

"Oh, that is comforting!" Anna shouts.

"Sorry, poor choice of words. Never mind, just hang on," Domingus tells them.

"2,300 feet," Vanessa reports.

"Guys, get ready. A second jolt is coming in about ten seconds," Domingus tells the group. "Eighteen…seventeen…sixteen…fifteen…fourteen." Domingus shuts the engine down again. "Eleven—one thousand feet. Now!" Domingus yells.

Vanessa turns on the thrusters again. The jet comes to stop in the air again. "Engine back on. Okay, guys, brace for impact in about fifteen seconds," Domingus tells the angels.

Vanessa stays fixed on the altimeter and begins her final countdown. "900, 850, 800, 750."

"Come on, baby, I got you," Domingus continues the sweet talk.

"700, 650, 600, 550, 500, 550, 400, 350, 300."

The jet reaches the tree line and contacts some of the taller trees.

"250, 200, 150, 100," Vanessa ends her countdown.

The jet makes its way through the trees, breaking limbs and branches on its way down. Domingus fights to keep the nose up. The jet hits a thick part of a tree, tearing its wing off.

"Damn, that sucks. I had control of this thing," Domingus tells Vanessa.

It slides along the ground hitting several trees like a pinball. The contact with the trees causes the jet to slow down. It comes to a stop. A cloud of dust, branches, leaves, and forest debris flies all around. Everything is still for a moment as everyone on board is a little rattled. There is dust and smoke inside the jet. Electrical wires spark as well. The angels look around at one another.

"Hey, are you good?" Domingus whispers to Vanessa.

She gently nods her head.

"Is everyone okay?" Rudy asks the angels.

"We're good up here," says Vanessa as she stares across at Domingus.

"Good, good," Rudy says.

"I'm okay," Anna responds.

"I'm okay too," says Angela as she looks over at Uriah.

She sees that his eyes are closed and he is nonresponsive. "Uriah!" she yells out.

The other angels look over at him.

"Guys, Uriah is not responding," she says. She tries to unbuckle herself but can't. "I'm stuck. My belt won't unbuckle," she tells the angels.

"Shit, I'm stuck also," Anna tells the group.

"Anna, hang on, I'm going to undo myself, then I'll help you," Rudy tells the ladies.

He unbuckles his belt and goes over to assist Anna. He struggles initially but gets her freed.

"Thanks," she tells him.

Anna goes to Uriah, and Rudy goes to help Angela. Vanessa and Domingus take their time getting out of their seats.

Anna tries to wake Uriah. "Uriah, Uriah," she calls out. She shakes him but does not get a response. She calls out his name again, "Uriah." She shakes him some more, and he finally regains consciousness.

He looks around, not completely aware that they have made a crash landing.

"Uriah, you're fine. You're good," Anna tells him.

"Can you move?" Anna asks Uriah.

"Yeah, I'm good to go," he responds with a rasp in his voice.

"Can I help? Is everyone good?" Vanessa offers.

"What just happened to us?" Anna asks openly.

"This is the work of the devils," Rudy tells the group.

"Ahhh, fuck them," Uriah says angrily as he gets out of his seat.

"Okay, listen up, everyone. We have to assume that this isn't everything. I can assure you that they are on their way right now. We need to get ready. Gather every weapon. Bring it all here so we can take inventory and divvy it up," Rudy tells everyone.

Domingus unbuckles his belt and begins to check the radio.

"Dom is working on the coms," Vanessa tells Rudy. "That's good, but help is not going to get here in time. He has until they get here, then he joins us," he instructs her.

"Got it," she replies.

She goes to assist Domingus with the radios.

Rudy walks toward the opening, at the rear. He looks around, into the forest, wondering how close the devils are. *I should probably get back in. If they can see me, they will take me out*, he thinks to himself.

Domingus and Vanessa join the others.

"No, go on the comms," he tells the group.

"That is fine. What do we have for weapons?" Rudy asks.

As they begin to divide up the weapons they have available, a sound on the outside catches their attention.

"You hear that?" Anna asks.

They all pause for a second. "That sounds like helicopters," Vanessa says.

"And they are not here to pick us up," Domingus adds. "Angels, we have to hurry. Our best shot is to get into the forest. It will be much harder for them to find us out there. Let's get our gear and go," he instructs them.

They all rush to grab all weapons and relevant gear they may need. Vanessa rushes to the front to grab a set of knives she keeps up there. After grabbing them, something outside the window grabs her attention. First, she sees a leg to her right, behind a tree. A couple of seconds later, she sees a body move from one tree to another. She slowly backs up while she keeps her eyes on them. "Guys, we're too late. The devils are right outside the jet. I just saw them," she tells the team.

Rudy looks to the front of the jet.

"Shit, we are too late. They must have been right behind us the entire way," Uriah says.

Rudy backs up. "Okay, angels, it's time. Take cover. Don't be visible. Get ready to fight. Okay, here is the plan," he tells the angels.

Angela and Anna walk to the opening. Now knowing that the devils have them surrounded, Angela and Anna are curious if they can see them. They reach the opening—Anna on the left, Angela on the right. They each look in opposite directions.

"Do you see anything?" Anna asks Angela.

"No, do you?" she asks in return.

"No, I don't either," Anna responds.

Domingus looks over at the opening as sees the ladies standing there. "Ladies, you've got to get away from there," he tells them.

Rudy looks back. "Come on, ladies, that is dangerous," he tells them."

* * * * *

Vanessa and Uriah pause from the story. They both look at each other.

With the memories of the attack still very fresh in his mind, Uriah looks shaken. He stares ahead in a daydream.

"Do you need a break?" Brad asks.

"This must be so difficult for you angels," Leann says.

Uriah and Vanessa are no strangers to confrontation with the devils, but this attack was different for them. The fashion in which they were attacked was rare for them, and they lost close friends in the process. This is the first time they lost angels to whom they were close.

"We don't need a break," Vanessa says.

They just take a moment to gather themselves.

"Sorry, my angels, this is difficult for me to hear. I must excuse myself right now and go check on dinner. Excuse me, my darlings," Erin tells the table. She gets out of her chair and leaves the room.

"Go ahead when you are ready," Brad tells the angels.

Uriah decides to continue the story, but not before he lets out a big sigh. He looks over at Vanessa. "You good?"

"Yeah, let's do this," she tells him.

* * * * *

Anna and Angela begin to back away from the hole, maintaining sight to the outside. As they back in, they move closer together. Suddenly, Anna falls into Angela.

Surprised, Angela struggles to catch her. "Anna," she says.

The other angels look over at the ladies.

"I'm hit," Anna says with an airy voice.

Angela struggles to hold her up as the other angels come to assist Angela.

"Anna," Angela calls out again.

"What happened?" Rudy asks.

"I don't know. She just fell into me," Angela responds.

"You three, set up some cover. Angela and I will tend to Anna," Rudy says to the other angels.

Domingus and Uriah approach the opening with weapons drawn to provide protection. They are careful to not expose themselves considering what just happened to Anna. Vanessa goes to the cover the front of the jet.

"Oh my god!" Angela says.

Rudy doesn't comment on it but stares in surprise at the hole in Anna's side. The hole is about two inches in diameter.

"What is it?" Anna asks with her soft voice.

"Shhhh, don't talk. You are going to be fine," Angela tells her.

"We have to make her comfortable," Rudy says.

"Anna, breathe, just keep breathing," Angela tells her.

Anna's eyes close.

"Shit, there is so much blood," Angela says hysterically.

"Angie, you need to stay calm." Rudy looks around for anything he can use as dressing. Rudy stops looking for a moment and looks at Angela, with tears running down her checks. He finds some blankets. He throws one at Angela. "Cover her up with that." He uses the other blankets to address the wound.

"Guys," Anna says softly.

"Don't speak, Anna. You have to save your energy," Angela tells her.

Anna musters up a little more energy to get their attention. "Guys," she says louder.

The angels look at her from where they stand.

"You're all sweet. It's okay," Anna tells them.

"Shhh, we're going to get you out of here," Angela tells her.

"I love you all. I'm not going to make it. You have to save yourselves," she tells them.

"We're not leaving you behind," Uriah tells Anna.

"You have to. I don't want to slow you down," Anna tells the group.

"This is not up for debate, Anna. We are all getting out of here together," Rudy replies.

"I love you all," Anna says softly.

Uriah, Domingus, and Vanessa remain standing guard. Domingus, kneeling, looks back at Anna as he wipes a tear away. He resets his defensive position. He sees movement across the way behind a tree. He waits to confirm what he thinks he saw. He sees it again, so he locks onto a devil. He waits until he has a clear shot. He focuses his bow, takes aim, and releases the arrow. The devil falls to the ground with the arrow sticking out of his forehead.

Ty looks over at Sara. "Well, we know they have one bow. I wonder what else they have," Ty says over the comms.

Domingus reloads his bow. "I just killed one," he tells the group.

"Nice work, that's one less," Rudy says.

"I love you," Anna says as she opens her eyes slightly.

Angela continues to cry. "I love you too, honey," she says back with a sniffle.

"Guys, we are losing her," Angela cries out.

Rudy grabs both her hands as he begins to cry. "I am so sorry, Anna," he says.

Angela's crying intensifies. Vanessa looks back and begins to cry as well as she momentarily loses focus of her watch. Uriah drops his head.

Domingus gets angry and stares out at the forest. "Fuck you!"

"Angels...hey, angels. Let's make this easy, huh!" Ty yells from outside.

"Just got another one," Domingus tells the team.

Ty and Sara stare at each other again.

"Angels, come on, make this easy on yourselves. We have the jet surrounded. You ain't going anywhere," Ty tells them.

The angels don't respond.

"Anna, come on, Anna. We are losing her! Guys, we are losing her," Angela says emotionally.

Rudy looks at Angela and shakes his head.

"You know why we're here. Throw it out, and we'll be on our way," Ty says.

Anna's eyes close completely. "Anna, honey, open your eyes," Angela says as her voice cracks. She caresses Anna's face.

"Hey, Rudy, why won't you talk to me? You busy or something? You have killed two of my devils. You are ahead, 2-1. I'm assuming it's 2-1. Is it too early? Is it still 2-0? Either way, it can remain at 2-0, and we can all go home," Ty tells the angels.

The angels have tuned out all communication from Ty as they remain focused on their angel sister.

"She's gone, she's—" Angela says in a screechy voice.

"Let's move her over here," Rudy suggests.

Angela doesn't move. "Angela, we have to move her now!" he yells.

She still doesn't respond. Rudy gets up and pulls Anna away from Angela and relocates her.

"You're going to a better place, angel," Rudy says to Anna as he sets her down. He turns to Angela. "Angela, we need you right now. I wish we had the time to honor and mourn Anna, but we don't. We need to get ready to fight, or other angels will die. Do you understand me?" he asks her.

He gets up to look outside.

"Rudy, hey, Rudy. Come on, man. I am trying to work with you here. You're making me look bad," Ty says.

"You had your turn. It's not working," Sara tells Ty.

She has grown impatient. She looks over at a devil and gives him a signal. Three devils move into position and shoot into the jet. One shoots a flash-bang, and the other two shoot smoke bombs.

"Incoming!" Uriah yells to the others.

The angels take cover by crouching, closing their eyes and plugging their ears. Rudy jumps on Angela to provide protection. Smoke begins to fill the jet but dissipates quickly because of the openings at each end. The flash-bang follows a couple of seconds later. BANG! The piercing sound moves throughout the jet, accompanied by a bright, blinding light.

The angels stay low to the ground to avoid the smoke. Angela is not able to cover her ears in time, so she is now disorientated. The smoke causes some of the angels to cough.

"Is everyone all right?" Rudy asks.

Each angel responds that they are okay. Rudy gets to his feet. "You three, as soon as you see them loading up, take them out," he tells Vanessa, Domingus, and Uriah. He then looks down at Angela. "Angela!"

She is moaning, waiting for her hearing to return.

"Angela!" he calls again.

She slowly reaches over to try and reach Anna.

"Angela!" he says again. "I need you to get up right now."

"She's gone," Angela says as she continues to sniffle.

"If you want her life to have any meaning, then we need you to focus now," he says in an elevated tone.

She continues to stare, as if she doesn't understand what he is saying. He walks over to her and gets down on one knee to her level.

"Are you with me? We need you to focus. Do you understand, angel?" Rudy asks her.

In a soft voice, Angela slowly responds, "Yes, I hear you."

"Good, we have to prepare to fight. Let's do this for Anna," he tells her.

She gets to her feet. Sara signals three of the devils to go into the jet. Three devils come out from behind the trees and approach the jet with their crossbows drawn.

"We got devils approaching, three that I can see," Domingus tells the angels as he draws his bow.

Uriah draws his as well, but he isn't fully recovered from the flash-bang.

"Are they coming straight at us?" Rudy asks.

"Yes," Domingus responds.

"Okay, take them out," he instructs.

Uriah and Domingus let their arrows fly, striking two of the devils. One in the throat and the other in the heart. The third devil stops momentarily, looks down at the fallen devils, and looks back up again just in time to catch an arrow in his eye. It is a quick reload by Uriah.

"That was a stupid move," Ty tells Sara.

"Shut up. You weren't doing anything, so I will," she responds.

"At least be more tactful. Don't send them right into their face. Flank them," he tells her.

Ty signals to a bigger group of devils to flank the jet as he walks away.

"Where are you going?" she asks him.

"I'm going to lead an assault from the front," he tells her.

"Listen, angels, I don't think they're all going to be that easy, but if you have it, take the shot. I want to try and conserve our ammo. Here is what we're going to do. If they are going to come from that hole, let's invite them in and fuck them up in here," Rudy explains.

Devils approach the jet. There are four on one side and five on the other.

"We have more approaching," Domingus tells the group.

"Okay, angels, devils are stupid right? Let's play with them. Everyone, hide. Let them come in, and we'll ambush them. Uriah, you jump up above. Hang out there." He points above.

"Vanessa, you go and hide behind the seat. Angela, you get inside the paneling. Dom, you and I will lay down and play dead. Uriah, wait for my thumbs-up, then come down on them. We'll join the party," Rudy explains.

The angels move into position. Domingus and Rudy select their places to play dead. The devils move toward the opening, along the sides of the jet. Both sides reach the opening and wait. The lead devil on each side exchange signals about how to enter. They enter slowly, weapons drawn. The first two enter completely then pause. They then move along the walls until there is enough room for the next two to enter. They continue this pattern until the last devil enters. The angels wait. Sara and Ty wait. The devils are cautious and confused. They are expecting angels to be alive and offer resistance. They break formation to look for the halo.

"Where are they?" a devil asks.

"This don't look right," another responds.

"Does anyone see the halo?" a different devil asks.

The devil closest to the front stares out the front window and can see other devils. He continues his way to the cockpit, still cautious. He gets closer and closer to Vanessa's position. He reaches the back of the seat, still unable to see her. He takes one more step closer and sees Vanessa, leaning on the control panel giving the appearance that she is dead. The devil looks away briefly to look for the halo. Vanessa opens her eyes as the devil looks at her again. His reaction is too late as Vanessa drives her dagger through his throat. The noise draws the attention of the other devils, but all they can see is his back. Vanessa pulls the dagger out, allowing the devil to fall to his knees. The other devils are stunned for a moment when they see Vanessa. Two devils nearest to Vanessa charge at her. Uriah jumps down onto the two devils standing closest to the opening, driving a knife down each of their necks.

One knife goes through the spine, and other misses the spine and goes through the trapezius muscle. All three fall to the ground.

Domingus slices the Achilles tendon of one of the devils charging at Vanessa. That devil falls to the floor. Rudy stabs the other devil charging at Vanessa, through the calf muscle. That devil falls to one knee. Domingus climbs on top of the devil and slices throat. Vanessa comes out from behind the seat and drives her dagger through the throat of the devil on one knee.

Two devils closest to Uriah look back at the commotion; they begin to spit fire balls at Uriah. He grabs the dead devil and uses him as a shield against the spitfire. Angela steps out from her hiding spot and engages one of the five remaining devils. She swings down at a devil, but he blocks her sword with his. The devil spits a fire ball at her, hitting her in the shoulder. She releases one of her sword hands and grabs her shoulder. The devil grabs her by the throat and slams her against the wall. He brings his tail out and wraps her sword wrist to keep her from using it. She grabs his wrist attempting to remove it from her throat. Rudy, Domingus, and Vanessa are all engaged with other devils as Uriah continues to shield himself from the fire balls.

The devil with the trapezius wound wraps his tail around Uriah's throat as they lie on the floor. Uriah quickly grabs at the tail and tries to remove it. Seeing that Uriah has a tail around his throat, the devil shooting spit at him turns and goes to assist the other devils. Pressed against the wall, Angela continues to try and free herself from the choke hold, but she isn't strong enough.

The devil draws his sword back, above his head. Rudy sees the trouble Angela's in and does a tuck roll to get away from the devil he is fighting; he comes out of the roll to a foot and knee and throws his sword right through the side of the neck of the devil about to kill Angela.

The devil is stunned, drops his sword, and falls to his knees, alleviating the pressure on Angela's neck. Angela lowers to her feet as the devil falls. She grabs at her throat. The devil Rudy is fighting now turns his attention to Domingus.

"Thanks, Rudy!" he shouts sarcastically.

Vanessa and her devil continue to battle; she must continuously make quick moves to make up for the devil's strength. Rudy sees Uriah struggling. He gets up from his knee, runs to pull his sword out of the neck of the devil he has struck, and runs to help Uriah.

Angela gathers herself and runs over to assist Vanessa. With the devils back to her, she drives her sword through his back. It stops just short of Vanessa's stomach.

Vanessa freezes; her eyes grow wide. "Wow, close, don't you think?" she asks sarcastically.

Angela looks around the devil's body to see how close. "Oh yeah, sorry. I wanted to make sure I got him," she tells her.

Angela and Vanessa move to assist Domingus with the two devils he is fighting. They each take a side and stab the closest one to them. One in the back the other in the rib cage.

Angela's devil drops to the ground. Vanessa's devil looks back at her. Domingus drives his knife through the neck of Vanessa's devil. Angela slices the throat of the devil she has attacked.

The remaining devil fights Rudy as he maintains a grip on Uriah's throat. Uriah continues to struggle to loosen the devil's tail from this throat. His eyes begin to close as he loses oxygen. Unable to be mobile because of having Uriah by the throat, the devil is restricted and allows Rudy to dispose of him quicker than normal. Just for good measure, Vanessa runs over and cuts the tail off at the base, freeing Uriah.

"Uriah," Vanessa calls.

Uriah coughs as he regains his breathing.

"Are we good?" Rudy asks the angels.

They all look around at one another.

"Yeah, we're good," Domingus says.

Rudy looks down at Uriah as he lies on the floor with the devil's tail still wrapped around his neck.

"Here, let me help you with that." Vanessa unwraps the tail.

"Are you good?" Rudy asks him.

"Oh yeah, I'm good. I'm always good," he responds with a light cough.

The angels gather themselves. "I really hate that they have tails. I hate their tails. Why didn't we get tails?" Uriah says, siting holding the tail.

"Yeah, and the fire spit, that shit burns. Why did they get all the cool shit?" Angela adds as she tends to her burn.

"We have extra weapons now. Everyone, load up," Rudy instructs.

Domingus grabs the devil's tail and throws it out the opening. It lands next to Sara. She has a face of displeasure.

Ty can see the angels moving around inside the jet. "I don't know how many you sent in there, but they are all dead," he radios her.

"Yeah, I know that," she says with annoyance.

"I wonder why they haven't stormed us with everything they have?" Vanessa asks.

"Don't worry, there are more of them out there. I'm sure that is next," Angela responds.

"Well, we fucked their first wave up, so yeah, I'm sure they will bring the heat next," Domingus says.

Sara signals for five more devils to approach the jet. She signals them to reach the opening and wait.

"All right, at some point we're going to get overwhelmed. We've got to start thinking about getting out of here," Rudy tells the team.

"What are you thinking?" Uriah asks.

"I've got to draw them away from here. If I do that, then you all have a chance to get out of here," he says.

"How do you plan on doing that?" Angela asks.

"They think we still have the halo, so I'll just make it look like I have the halo on me," he explains.

"Sara, next time you send a wave, we will attack from the front," he tells her.

"I'm setting up for the next hit," she tells him.

"Good, we are ready," he responds.

"Hey, we've got more movement out here!" Uriah yells back.

"Yeah, same thing up here," Vanessa adds.

Rudy turns around and walks toward the opening to check things out.

"Okay, here is what we are going to do," Rudy says as he begins to grab supplies.

"I'm going to lure them away, or as many as I can," Rudy explains.

"Shouldn't we stick together, Rudy?" Vanessa questions.

"Listen, guys, we don't know how many of them there are out there. They will just continue sending wave after wave, eventually wearing use down. They want the halo. They think we have it, so I am going to make them think that I have it and lead them away from here. They might leave some, but I'm confident you can manage them," Rudy explains.

The angels stay quiet for a moment.

"I don't like this, Rudy!" Angela exclaims.

"This is the best option, angels," Rudy responds as he prepares a bag.

Sara sends more devils into position. Ty also moves his devils into position at the front of the jet.

"All right, I'm ready to go, but before I go, here are my last orders. We are going to take these dead bodies and pile them up at the opening. That will give you some cover and more space in here. Continue to invite them in. They are less effective in a small space against us. One of you get back up there and pick them off. Let's get these bodies over there. Ladies, cover us," Rudy asks.

The angels finish placing the dead devils and get into position.

"Those guys are fuckin heavy," Domingus says.

"We're all going to make it out of this, angels. We just have to get into the forest. We will lose them in there. I'm going to try and find a river. When you guys get into the forest, find a river. It should be the same one, and we can find each other that way," Rudy tells them.

He walks over to give Angela a hug, then Uriah, Domingus, and Vanessa. With bag in hand, Rudy walks to the front. "I'll see you all soon," he says as he looks back with a smirk on his face.

He jumps out, and right away is engaged by devils. He makes light work of them. Ty sees the action and is a little surprised to see Rudy outside of the jet. "Hold on, Sara," he tells his sister.

"What? What's going on?" she asks.

"Rudy just jumped out of the jet. He is trying to escape. I'm going after him!" he yells.

Rudy begins to run through the forest as he continues to evade the devils around him. He draws the attention of many devils. Ty begins to chase him as well as he signals to other devils to join the chase. Domingus looks out the window and sees Rudy running away.

"He made it. They are chasing him. He is drawing them away!" he yells back to the other angels.

"He is carrying a bag. Looks like he has the halo," Ty radios to Sara.

"You better catch him," she says. She motions to the devils to move around the jet and cover the front.

"Guys, this might work, if we leave out the front. Their reaction time is slow," Rudy yells back.

"He was able to get a lot of them to chase him," Domingus tells the group.

"Dom, they're coming now," Uriah yells back.

The devils begin to move in at the rear. Vanessa jumps up to the top while Uriah and Angela stand ready with bow and arrows.

* * * * *

Uriah and Vanessa again pause from the story. Nate tells the group to take a break.

"Let's say twenty minutes. Get a drink, restroom," he tells them.

They all disperse to various parts of the house.

"Christian, walk with me," Brad requests.

They go into the living room.

"What's up?" Christian asks.

"You know I can't help but wonder how this happened. Things lined up to perfect for the devils," Brad expresses.

"Yeah, I know what you mean. They were at the right place at the right time to take that shot," Christian says.

"You can't just happen to be along the exact flight path of the jet without being detected and then strike it," Brad adds.

"Yeah, there had to be some type of tracking system on that jet, but the jet is designed to detect any type of tracker. So this one went undetected. They weren't alerted, and so unless there was a defect in the jets defensive systems, there was no tracker," Christian says.

"That is the part that is concerning to me. If there was no tracker on the jet, the devils had another way of knowing this information," Brad expresses.

"That's what I'm saying," Christian says.

Neither of them says it aloud, but they are thinking same thing, that one of the angels must have feed information to the devils to allow them to conduct the attack.

"What do you want to do?" Christian asks.

"Not quite sure yet. I am having a tough time believing that any angel would do this," Brad says.

"Yeah, well, I don't want to believe it either, but if it's true, it raises so many more questions," Christian says.

"Let's finish this, no conclusions just yet. Right now, this is all on Jason," Brad tells Christian.

They walk outside to join the other angels getting fresh air.

"Don't mention any of this to Nate just yet. I don't want to give him one more thing to worry about. Especially something like this," he tells Christian.

"Got it."

"Although he's probably already thinking it," Brad says.

* * * * *

"What is taking them so long?" Vanessa says.

"Give us the first two, then take them out," Uriah tells Vanessa.

Rudy continues to run through the forest, but he can hear the devils behind him. He is dodging a consistent number of bolts from the devils. At the jet, the first two devils take positions on their knee using the devil wall the angels built as cover to provide cover for the other devils who will enter. They toss a canister inside.

"Flash-bang!" Uriah yells.

Boom! The canister explodes, causing another piercing sound. Uriah and Angela hit the ground. From the floor, Uriah loads his bow and shoots one of the devils in the face. Now only one is providing cover and takes a shot at Angela. He misses. Vanessa can't see them yet, so she waits. Two devils enter. Angela takes aim with her one arrow and catches a devil in the shoulder.

"Shit. My vision is messed up," she says.

They draw their metal, inviting the devils to enter further. Two more devils enter, then two more. They finally move into Vanessa's view, so she begins to fire down at them as more enter slowly. Vanessa continues her assault from above, but now the devils are slowing because of the down bodies and they are now aware that she is picking them off from above. Uriah and Vanessa engage the devil who are still alive, after a shot from Vanessa.

Domingus turns and sees the number of angels that have entered. "Fuck this, I'm wasting my time up here," he goes to assist them.

The devils press forward and attempt to overwhelm the angels. Vanessa's attention shifts to the front. She sees devils attempting to enter through the front windows. She looks down at her arrows.

"Guys, they're coming in the front." She looks down to see that she only has six arrows left. She waits until the devils are halfway through the window, so they block it when she hits them. Rudy can hear water nearby; he pauses a moment. He decides to change his direction and head toward the river. As he does, a bolt catches him on the shoulder. It drops him to the ground. He gets to his knees and quickly removes the blot. He gets to his feet and continues to run toward the sound of water. Having shot her last arrow and plugging up the front windows for now, she jumps down to assist the others.

Angela gets her wrist wrapped up by the tail of a devil. She tosses her sword to her free hand. She blocks an oncoming ax, but only enough that it still slices down her arm. Uriah sees that she is struggling, so he works his way to her. The devil spits fire at Angela's sword hand. She drops her sword. The devil follows up with a punch to her chest that takes her off her feet but is held up by the devil's tail at the wrist.

Her legs go weak, and she falls to the ground. The devil drives his sword down and catches Angela in the arm, through the bicep. The sword has her pinned her to the jet. Domingus sees that Angela is struggling as well. He fights his way toward her. Two more devils enter the jet, along with Sara. She stops at the entrance. She surveys the action, looking for the halo. Uriah reaches Angela and chops the tail that had her bound. Domingus reaches her as well and together with Uriah dispose of the devil attacking Angela. Domingus pulls the sword out of Angela's arm and gets her in a seating position.

"Are you good?" he asks.

"Yeah, I think so," she responds.

"We are almost done, and we are going to get out of here," he tells her as he smiles.

"I don't see the halo," Sara thinks.

"Ty, that knight has to have it on him," she radios. She isn't concerned about the angels in the jet as they aren't a barrier to her obtaining the halo.

"Yeah, well we are close behind him," he responds.

"Don't lose him. I'm coming out there," she tells her brother. Before she walks out, she looks over at Angela, and pulls out a dagger. Vanessa sees this "Domingus." Sara lets the dagger fly, Domingus looks her way to the opening and sees the dagger coming toward Angela. He turns to shields her from it. It sticks him in the upper back near the shoulder. He falls forward, on to Angela. She attempts to catch him with her one good arm.

"Dom, oh no," she says.

Sara leaves the jet.

"You all, with me. The rest of you, finish them off," she instructs.

Vanessa raises a sword and throws it at Sara but catches a devil instead. "Come back here, you demon bitch!" she shouts.

Devils have cleared the front windows of the dead bodies that were obstructing it. Two devils set their crossbows at the front windows and take aim at Domingus and Angela.

"Guys, arrows at the front!" Uriah yells.

Angela doesn't have much time to react as she is holding Domingus. One of the bolts catches her injured arm, just inches away from an existing wound. The other misses.

"Aw, damn it. This arm keeps getting hit!" she shouts.

Uriah raises his sword and throw it. He hits one of the two devils at the window. He looks back to check on Vanessa. He looks over and sees an ax on the ground. He picks it up and throws it at the second devil at the front; he misses. "Fuck." He sees a second ax and grabs it. He throws it, but not before the devil gets a second shot off, the bolt catches Angela in the lower back. Domingus lays her down. Isaiah returns to help Vanessa with the remaining devils inside. Rudy reaches the river.

Cross the river or keep running? he questions himself. He looks back and sees they have closed on him. He decides to run along the river. As he does, another bolt catches him in the hip. He falls to the ground. He reaches to pull out the bolt. He gets up and limps to a nearby tree to hide and catch his breath. The angels have finished off the devils inside. They huddle up to check on each other and think about next move. Devils that remain outside the jet. They are hesitant to go in now that Sara has left. A couple of them attempt to recoordinate their efforts. This allows the angels time they need to plan.

"We have to get out of here," Uriah tells the angels.

"We go out the front, just like Rudy," Vanessa says.

"Everyone can run, right?" Uriah asks.

"Good, weapon up and let's get out of here."

Ty and the devils reach the river; they saw Rudy get hit and saw that he took a right at the river. "Everyone, spread out," he instructs the devils.

Rudy can hear them getting close to his position. Two of them reach the tree that Rudy is using for cover. They each take a side. First devil sees him and then takes a knife to the throat. Second devil attacks, but Rudy makes quick work of him as well. More devils approach as Rudy hobbles along the river. He doesn't get far before he is struck in the back with another bolt. He falls to the ground. He grabs the bag and takes it off his person. Ty gets to Rudy.

"Hand over the halo," Ty commands.

"Come and get it yourself," Rudy responds as he gets to his feet.

Ty chuckles as Rudy continues to bleed from his wound.

"I don't have time for your games," Ty tells him.

"Like I said, come and get it yourself," Rudy repeats.

"That would not be fair to you," he says to Rudy as he signals at two devils to attack. "I don't underst—" Ty begins to say as Rudy tosses the bag over his shoulder into the river.

The two devils approaching stop and look at Ty for direction. Ty stands, staring at the river. "You two, in the river. You two, chase it downstream," he commands.

"Now why would you do that?" he asks as he scratches his head. "You're a fool. Guess now I'll have the halo, and I will kill you for fun," Ty says.

Rudy laughs aloud. "Okay, what's so funny?" he asks.

"You actually think that I would hand over the halo and believe that you wouldn't kill me after handing it over?" he asks as he continues to laugh.

"Your best chance is for you to come at me," he tells Ty.

"Go!" Ty tells the two devils to continue.

Rudy battles the two devils but isn't as effective as he normally would be. He manages to kill one of the two but then is stopped by Ty, who grows impatient. He sustains a cut on his forearm and another on his back. He is growing weaker and weaker as the wounds from the bolts are taking their toll.

"Back away," Ty orders the remaining devil.

"Told you, it's got to be you," Rudy tells ty.

Ty advances on Rudy. Rudy puts up a valiant defense but succumbs to the superior fighting skills of Ty. Ty finishes Rudy with a stab to the chest. Rudy falls to his knees before falling onto his face. Ty turns his attention to the halo. He sends the rest of the devils downriver to assist in the recovery.

On their feet and equipped with weapons, the angels move to the front. Uriah and Vanessa each have a bow and several reclaimed arrows.

"Okay, her and I are going to step out and provide some cover. I'll go first. You cover me. Then you, then you two," Uriah tells the group. He looks at Vanessa. "You ready?" he asks.

"Let's do this," she replies.

Between them they have seventeen arrows. Vanessa loads her bow to provide Uriah's cover. Uriah steps out and sets himself up. He scans the area in front of him but doesn't see much. Most of the devils have moved to the other side. Only few remain on the front side.

"Now," Uriah whispers to Vanessa.

She sets up.

"Now," he calls out the other two.

Angela steps out guided by Domingus. She gets behind Uriah.

"Over here. They're coming out the front," a devil radios to another devil at the back.

The devils run to the front; some devils stay at the back. Devils come out from behind the trees to begin taking shots at the angels. Domingus steps out and leans against the jet. He reaches for Angela's hand. As she moves closer to him, she is struck in the chest by a bolt. She falls back against the jet. "Angela, shit," Domingus says. With tears in her eyes, she looks at him, "I'm sorry, I'm so sorry, you guys."

"We have to move!" Vanessa shouts.

"SShhh, save your energy. We are going to get you out of here," Domingus tells Angela.

"Let's go!" Uriah shouts.

"I'm going to carry her. You two will lead," Domingus tells the others.

He struggles to get her to her feet as her body is weak and loose. He gets down on one knee and lets her body fall over his shoulder. He gets to his feet.

"Let's go!" Domingus shouts.

Uriah and Vanessa grab their remaining arrows and begin to lead. As they move into the woods, Domingus is hit in the calf with a bolt. He falls to the ground, dropping Angela. She lands face up. Uriah and Vanesa stop and look back.

Vanessa hands Uriah her two remaining arrows. "Make them count," she says as she goes to Domingus and Angela.

"Dom, can you move?" she asks.

"Yeah," he replies.

They look over at Angela as she struggles with her last breaths. She can hardly keep her eyes open.

"Stay with us honey," he tells her. Uriah is out of arrows and joins the group.

"You have to leave us. Go! GET OUT OF HERE! I'll hold them off," Domingus commands them.

"You're out of your mind. We all go," Uriah responds.

"We will only slow you down. Just leave us and save yourselves. Go catch Rudy," he tells them.

Vanessa and Uriah look at each other. Simultaneously, two bolts hit a tree nearby, and the other catches Domingus in the neck.

Domingus grabs at the bolt. "Go," he says softly as blood pours out of his mouth.

He falls on top of Angela. He looks at them again.

"Go." Vanessa looks down at Angela.

"She is gone," she says.

"Shit, we're coming back for you," Uriah tells the fallen angels.

Uriah and Vanessa take off through the brush and further into the forest. The two devils in the river haven't been able to catch up to the bag. The two devils leading the way along the banks have caught up to the halo and are now ahead of it. They figure they are far enough ahead to jump in and intercept it. They are successful and manage to bring it to shore. They walk it back to Ty as he is walking toward them. Ty opens the bag and doesn't see the halo. There are a couple of random items in the bag, but no halo.

"What the fuck is this? The halo isn't in here!" he shouts. "That angel tricked us. Fuck!" he shouts. "It's probably at the jet," he says angrily. He throws the bag to the ground.

"It could be in the river?" a devil says. "The bag was open," he adds.

Ty thinks for a moment. "You're right. All of you get in the river and find it."

The devils stand around looking at one another.

"For how long?" a different devil asks.

"Until you find the halo, or you drown!" Ty tells him.

The devils remove some of their gear and enter the river.

"You're a fucking idiot," one devil says to the other.

"Why?" the devil asks.

"You should have kept your mouth shut about the bag being open," he says.

"Sara!" he calls.

"What?" she responds as she approaches him.

He turns around. He stares at her as she walks right up to him.

"What is it?" she asks.

"The halo isn't here."

"What do you mean it's not here?"

"It's not here in the bag. This is the bag Rudy was carrying," he says.

"Well, it wasn't in the jet, so where is it?" she asks.

They think about it for a moment.

"Why are all those devils in the river?" she asks.

"The bag was open. It might have fallen out of the bag."

"Right, well that is possible," she says.

"We have to search again," she says.

"What do you mean again? Search what?" he asks.

"We have to search the jet, the river, the forest—everywhere," she says.

"No way," Ty responds.

"If Rudy didn't have it in this bag, he left it in the forest, or he took it out and threw it in the river. Or the other angels hid it somewhere else before we got there. Or it was not in the jet when it crashed. Now that I think about it, there are two angels missing from this group," she expresses.

"What?" Ty asks, a little confused.

"Think about it: We have one angel here. There were five at the jet. That's six. There were eight angels that left Bend," she says.

"So where are the other two?" Ty asks.

"I don't know, but that's where the halo might be, and we can't go back empty handed this time," she tells her brother.

"So what the hell do we do now?" he asks.

"You will coordinate searching downriver and the forest from here to the jet. I am going to go back to the jet and sweep it. If it is not there, I will come back to help you. If we can't find it," she pauses for a second. Ty and all the devils around stare at her.

"What? What's going to happen if we don't find it?" Ty asks.

"I don't know, let's just start with this, and then we will see," she says.

* * * * *

The angels take another break.

"Let's make this one a quick one, yes?" Nate tells the group.

All the angels go outside except for Christian who uses the restroom. As soon as he finishes, he walks to the back to see the others.

"I'm ready to go!" he yells at them. Nate and Uriah decide to go back inside. Vanessa, Leann, and Brad remain in the yard talking.

Before they make their way inside to join the others, Erin walks to the backdoor.

"I hope you all have a big appetite this evening," Erin waves Leann over. Leann is confused for a moment.

"Excuse me, guys," she says as she makes her way over to her mother.

Erin guides her into the kitchen. "Dear, will you help me with dinner?" she asks as she puts her arm around her daughter.

"Mother, I can't. I have to get back to the meeting," Leann responds.

"Maybe you should help me instead. I could use the help," she adds.

"Mother, you never ask me to help you," she says with a suspicious tone.

"Well, maybe we start tonight, huh. What do you say?" Erin tries to tempt her daughter with some playful gestures.

"I kind of feel like you're trying to keep me from the meeting, Mother. Why don't you want me in there?" Leann asks.

"Well, of course, I don't want you in there. I don't think you should be involved," Erin says.

"Father doesn't have a problem with it. In fact, he wants me in there."

"Honey, when does your father ever tell you no?" Erin asks.

Leann smiles big and kisses her mother on the cheek. "I love you," she says as she leaves the kitchen.

She goes to the back door to see if the others are still outside. Vanessa sees that Leann is at the door; they make eye contact and smile at each other. Brad turns around to see what Vanessa is smiling at.

"Are we resuming?" Brad asks Leann.

"I'm not sure. I'll go ask," Leann says.

Brad and Vanessa continue to talk while Leann checks with the others. Leann returns.

"They would like to get started again." She turns around and returns to the study. Brad and Vanessa walk in together as they keep talking. Vanessa takes her seat next to Uriah again. She looks at him as she reaches for his hand and squeezes it. He smiles at her. Just before they resume the story, a phone rings. Everyone looks around. It's Brad's cell phone.

"Sorry, everyone. Give me a minute. It's Elise."

Brad gets up and leaves the room.

"Hey, Brad."

"Hey, Elise."

"Brad, hold on, I'm putting you on speaker. I'm here with Hayley."

"Listen, girls, I'm in a meeting, but I have some good news."

There is a slight pause.

"Yeah, so do we. That's why we are calling," Elise says. "Well, you go first," Elise says.

"Vanessa and Uriah are alive. In fact, they are here with us now at Nate's house."

"What?"

"No way. That is so good to hear," Elise and Hayley express.

"Why didn't you tell us earlier?" Hayley asks.

"My apologies, girls."

"So we found Rudy's body. It was along the river. We have him loaded, and he should be heading your way soon," Hayley tells him.

"That is good news. Thank you, girls, for your work."

"So that means we are only missing Isaiah and JR," Elise says.

"That helps us out with the search," Hayley adds.

"Right, well, listen, we are learning so much right now. I will call you later this evening to give you more details that I hope will help you. Hold on to Rudy until you get my call. I'll tell you when to send him," Brad tells the girls.

"Sounds good. Looking forward to your call," Hayley tells him.

They hang up. Brad walks into the den to find the group waiting. "Sorry, everyone. That was Hayley and Elise. Continue when you're ready," Brad tells them.

* * * * *

Uriah and Vanessa continue running through the forest. Uriah stops; he turns to check how far back the devils are. They are barely visible but still a threat. Vanessa doesn't notice that Uriah has stopped until she realizes she doesn't hear him behind her. She stops, turns around, and can still see him, but she is several yards ahead of him. She runs back to him, wondering why he has stopped.

"Uriah, what are you doing?" she asks.

"We can't keep running. We need to fight these guys," he tells her.

She looks back; she can see the devils getting closer. "I really don't want to, but you're right. We can't keep running."

The devils get closer.

"Okay, let's do this," she tells him.

"Here, let's get over here," he suggests.

They set up for an ambush by hiding behind some trees. They get in place and wait until all three devils get closer. They both move around their tree as the devils pass them. Vanessa jumps out.

"Hey, animals!" Vanessa yells at them.

All three devils stop and turn around. They can only see Vanessa between two trees. They charge at her. The trailing devil reaches her first; they engage in combat. The other two devils go after Vanessa as well, but as soon as they pass Uriah, he steps out behind them and throws a knife at the back of one of the devils, dropping them to their knees. The other devil looks over at his partner on his knees then looks back to see where the knife came from. The wounded devil stays on his knees and tries to get the dagger out of his back. The other devil charges at Uriah recklessly, making it easy for Uriah to dispose of him. He looks up at Vanessa and sees that she has just tripped over a tree root. He runs to her aid, and as he passes the devil on his knees, he pulls the knife out of the back of that devil and throws it at the back of the devil fighting Vanessa. It stuns the devil, allowing Vanessa to escape from the devil's grasp. He jumps on that devils' back and slices his throat.

"Are you good down there?" Uriah asks.

"Yeah, I'm fine," she replies as he extends his hand out to help her up.

She gets to her feet and picks up her sword. She looks behind Uriah and sees a devil charging at his back. She lets the devil get close enough to Uriah before she drives her sword in between Uriah's torso and arm, right into the devil's stomach. The devil stops. Uriah looks down at the sword, with his palms out. He realizes what's happening, grabs his dagger, and turns to slice the devil's throat. The devil drops to the ground.

"Okay, well done," Uriah says. He looks back from where they came.

"I think that's it. I don't see any more," he tells her.

"Thank goodness. I was tired of running," she replies.

They both relax and gather themselves briefly.

"Good call on stopping and fighting," Vanessa tells him. She smiles at him. "Let's get going. I'm sure they sent more after us," she says.

"Maybe we can catch up to Rudy," Uriah says.

"Hopefully," she replies.

* * * * *

"How did you guys make it back to town?" Brad asks the angels.

"We continued to work our way through the forest. Eventually found a river. We used that to guide us. That's where we found Rudy's body. While we were with him, we saw devils in the area, so we went the other way along the river. We stopped for the night because it got dark. We couldn't see anymore," Vanessa explains.

"We kept going until we found a place to lay down. We slept for who knows how long," Uriah adds.

"We eventually came across some campers. You, of course, met two of them earlier," Vanessa says.

"So that's what happened," Uriah concludes.

Vanessa puts her head back and sighs.

"I want to thank you angels for your time and courage," Nate expresses.

"Thank you. What you have been through has been very traumatic, so rest up and clear your minds," Brad tells them.

"I want to help. I'm ready to get back out there," Uriah tells Brad.

Vanessa is not ready to get back to work, so she remains silent. But she is curious to know how they will respond to Uriah.

"We appreciate your dedication, but you need to rest and gather yourself," Brad tells him.

Uriah gets up from the table. "We need all hands out there looking for the halo and the other angels," Uriah tells the room.

"I'm sorry, I can't let you come in yet," Brad tells Uriah.

Uriah continues to advocate for himself some more then is cut-off by Brad as he smiles.

"The answer is no. You need to rest," Nate chimes in and backs up Brad as he gets up from the table.

"He is right, Uriah. You guys have been through enough already."

"We'll take care of this, man. You will be back in the game soon," Christian tells him.

Uriah nods and softly smiles. Nate turns to Brad.

"Give those girls a call. Make sure they have all the details we can offer them," Nate instructs Brad.

Brad pulls his phone out and walks out of the study. As he walks out, he passes Erin, who is walking in.

"Is this a break?" she asks.

"No, we are done," Brad replies.

"Great," she continues on to the study.

"Why don't you all make your way to the dining room. Dinner will be served in ten minutes," Erin tells the group.

"What's for dinner?" Christian asks.

"We are having ricotta shells," Erin replies.

"Hmm, that might be worth staying for," Christian says.

"You are such a brat, and you don't have a choice," Erin jokingly tells him.

* * * * *

"Hey, Brad, what do you have for us?" she asks.

"Are you in a position to write this down?" Brad asks.

"I've got Hayley here to write for me, and I'll put you on speaker. Give us a sec," she asks.

"All right, go, Brad."

"JR was sucked out of the jet shortly after the explosion."

"What? Geez, that's horrible," Elise expresses.

"Yeah, very unfortunate. So he should be furthest away, but if you can pinpoint the location in the air where the jet was hit, then JR was sucked out about five seconds after that. So that should narrow his area. Isaiah, on the other hand, jumped out of the jet."

"What?" Elise asks.

"Yes, he went after the halo and, presumably, JR. He managed to get a parachute before he exited the jet, so he might be alive. Look for a parachute about a minute after the hit," Brad explains.

"Got it," Hayley tells Brad.

"Where you able to get the black box?" Brad asks.

"Yes, Becky is still working on it. We were able to get some info on it, but there is more I'm sure," Elise tells Brad.

"Yes, there is. Take care of that box. We need to look through it thoroughly," he tells them.

"Got it," Hayley says.

"Good job, angels," Brad tells them.

* * * * *

Sherri walks to the counter with a clipboard in hand. Her shift at the vet clinic is ending, and she can't wait to go home. As she walks away from the counter, a boy holding a kitten and his father walk through the door. The boy's father walks up to the counter.

"I know it's late, and it looks like you're about to close, but can you help us out?"

She looks at the father and then the little boy.

"Hey, Doctor, can you fix Sampson please?" asks the little boy.

She lowers herself down to the boy's level.

"So this is Sampson, huh. What is wrong with Sampson?" she asks the boy.

"Well, he is sick," the boy says.

She smiles at him as she plays with Sampson through the carrier.

"Okay, well, we are going to fix Sampson and make him feel better, okay?" she tries to comfort the boy.

"Thanks, Doctor," the boy replies.

"And what is your name?" she asks the boy.

"My name is Arny."

"Okay, Arny, I'm going to talk to your dad for a second, okay?"

"Okay," Arny responds.

Sherri stands up.

"The cat has been vomiting for two days now. At first, I thought it was a hair ball, but then it kept happening. Then it carried over to today," the father explains.

"Okay, so the doctor has gone home for the night, so I can check Sampson in tonight without being seen, or you can bring him back tomorrow morning," she tells the father.

"Oh, I thought you were the vet," the father says, surprised.

"No, not yet, I'm working on it," she explains.

"Got it. All right, well, it's probably easier if we just leave him tonight," the father says. The father goes over to his son and explains the plan to him.

The boy agrees to the plan. They both return to the counter. The father grabs the carrier from the boy and sets it on the counter. Sherri comforts the cat some more.

"Thank you, Doctor," the boy says to Sherri.

Sherri hands the father some paperwork on a clipboard. "We just need some contact info for now," she tells the father. "You will be getting a call tomorrow late morning after the doctor has done an initial exam," she explains.

"Thank you, Sherri," he says as he grabs his son by the shoulders and turns him around to exit the building.

She locks the doors behind them and then walks the cat to the back. She gets through the door and is intercepted by Becca. She doesn't notice the cat carrier in Sherri's hand at first as she is on her phone.

"Let's get out of here," she tells Sherri without looking at her. She looks up because she didn't get a response.

She now sees the cat. "What is that?" she asks rhetorically.

"Don't worry, I'm going to crate him. We will check him out tomorrow," she tells Becca.

"That better be the case!" Becca exclaims.

"A little boy and his dad brought it in," she tells Becca as her phone rings. She hands the cat off to Becca.

"Can you please?" she asks.

Becca takes the cat and sets it inside a kennel. "You know there are some margaritas waiting for us," she reminds Sherri.

"Don't worry, Beck, there will be plenty of drinks waiting for us," she reassures her friend. Sherri walks into the staff lounge to answer the phone.

"Hey, babe." She pauses. "Yeah, I'm just getting off, and then I'll be out with Becca," she pauses again.

"Yeah, remember I told you?" she says to her boyfriend. "All right, I love you," she says to an abrupt click on the other end. She grasps her phone with both hands and looks down and to the side.

Becca pops her head in. "Hey it's time to go."

"Yeah, um, I just need to get my stuff," she responds with her back turned. Becca closes the door. She knows who was on the phone.

"Time to cheer my friend up, again," she says aloud.

* * * * *

The angels have decided to wrap up their search for the day. Visibility is still good, but it's getting late, and they are hungry. They have been searching for the entire day.

"I'm exhausted," Lilly tells Ariah.

"Yeah, me too, but for me, it's more emotional, I think," she responds.

"I think you're right, same for me."

They continue to talk as they walk to meet up with others. In a different part of the forest, Bella, Katy, and Ernesto are walking to meet up with other angels.

"Do either of you know which way to the jet?" Katy asks.

Ernesto laughs a little. "Are you serious? Look around you," he says.

"Don't be a dick," Bella defends Katy.

"Seriously, though, like we have radios, but I can't tell where the jet is from here," Katy says.

The other two angels stay silent as they look at her.

"Ernesto, you should shout, yell out, so others can hear us," Bella suggests.

"Yeah, yeah, that is a great idea," Katy says.

"Why me?" he asks.

"You have bigger lungs. You are louder," Bells tells him.

"Well, I guess that is true," he responds. He looks around to see if he can see any angels in the immediate area.

Seeing none, he begins to yell out, "Angels, angels!" He pauses. "Angels, hey, angels!" he continues.

"Hold on, shit. we shouldn't have don't that," Katy says.

"Oh fuck, devils," Bella adds.

"Fuck, um, yeah, that was not good," Ernesto says.

"Let's stay alert. Radio others to check in.

Somewhere else in the forest, Kelsey is alone trying to get to the jet. She hears the faint shout from Ernesto. She doesn't know it's him but assumes it's an angel calling.

"Did any angels shout?" she asks.

"Yeah, that was me," Ernesto responds.

"Okay, why did you do that? We have radios," she tells him.

"Yeah, I fucked up. Are you heading back to the jet?" he asks.

"Yeah, I'm on this path of debris, so I'm right on track. I'll see you there," she tells him.

* * * * *

Isaiah is now facing his second night in the forest. He's exhausted from walking all day. He's low on energy and hasn't had water since the morning. The berries he came across only lasted him a short while. The initial bunch he found when he first got on the road ended soon after. There were spots that provided tiny amounts along the way, but those were few and far in between. He doesn't know exactly, but he is guessing that it's been at least five hours since his last berry. He decides to get off the road and look for food, water, and a place to lie down for the night. Visibility is lessening, so he is looking for food first. As he does, he is listening for water.

"There has to be another river around here," he says.

He doesn't hear any water, and he is too exhausted to keep looking. He can't remember a time that he was in this amount of pain because of hunger. He finds a tree to sit up against. He stares out ahead, slowly scanning the area around him. With an empty stomach and the onset of dehydration he wonders if he will make it through the night. He knows he won't die, but the helpless feeling he has is causing his mind to wander to dark places. As he is in that dark head space, his thoughts take him to the attack. For him, though there is little imagery to think about other than what he saw before he jumped out of the jet. Fortunately for him, he has no idea of what took place with the devils. He can only imagine. He closes his eyes.

"No need to find a resting place on the floor."

Tuesday

Franco pulls up to Jason's home. He sees Jason, Crystal, and some devils loading up two vehicles parked out front. He gets out of the car and walks up to Crystal.

"I figured you were going with him?" he asks her.

"No, not this time. I've already been to Costa Rica, and on trips like this, I find myself sightseeing alone. So I'll just wait until he returns, and I'll make him take me somewhere else, where we can spend some time together," she answers.

"Makes sense," he replies.

"Why aren't you going?" she asks in return.

"Don't know, didn't get invited," he responds.

Delaney walks out of the house and walks by Franco and Crystal.

"Hey, Franco," she says.

"Hey, Delaney," he greets her in return. He continues to stare at her as she walks to the vehicle and loads a briefcase and a bag. Crystal notices that Franco is fixated on Delaney.

"Are you sure you don't want to go on this trip?" she asks.

"No, I wasn't invited."

There is a small pause.

"Why do you ask again?" he asks.

"Oh, I don't know, so maybe you can be closer to a certain someone," she suggests as he continues to stare at her.

It takes him a moment to realize that she is referring to Delaney. He snaps out of it and turns to look at her.

"Come on, I've seen the way you look at her. It's clear you have feelings for her. You don't hide it well," she tells him.

Jason walks up to them both. "Franco, lets walk," Jason requests, saving him from the awkward position he was just in with Crystal.

"If you don't tell her, then I will," Crystal tells him with a muffled voice just before he begins to walk down the stairs.

He stares her down as he walks down the steps to meet Jason, wondering if she would go through with it. He reaches Jason and they being to walk and talk, away from the house.

"Any updates on the halo?" Jason asks.

"Nothing yet. The angels have been out there searching. We are tracking them. The halo is still lost, as far as we know," he reports.

"Good, good," Jason responds.

"Listen, I know that you might think me leaving right now is bad timing, but I assure you that there is a good reason for it," he says.

"Are you going to tell me?" Franco asks.

"No, not yet. So while I am away, you're in charge. Just don't try and give Crystal orders. I can't even do that," he tells Franco.

"Anything with the halo, I trust you will make the right call, so make it. Everyone reports to you," Jason explains.

"Got it," Franco replies.

It is typical for Jason to leave Franco in charge during his absences, but Jason wanted to make sure Franco understood what that meant during this time with halo in play.

"Do you want any extra precautionary measures for your home?" Franco asks.

"That won't be necessary, unless Crystal requests it, then go ahead," he tells him.

They stop for a moment.

"The only thing you have to focus on while I'm away is getting us the halo. So do whatever you have to do to make that happen," he tells Franco.

The sound of a yell catches their attention; they both turn to the house. They see Delaney waving, signaling that they're ready to go. Jason nods. They turn back toward the house as they finish their conversation.

* * * * *

Leann is sleeping face down. She pops her head up off her pillow and looks around as if she's lost. She reaches for the clock to check the time. She sees that it's a little after 6:00 a.m. She lays her head back down. She's upset that she is awake this early and wondering why or what woke her up. She remains lying awake for a couple of minutes before she decides to get out of bed. She walks downstairs and into the kitchen. She stops and stares ahead, with a surprised look.

"I couldn't sleep. I made coffee. I hope that is okay," says Vanessa.

"Oh yeah, of course. It's nice to have it made already," she responds.

Vanessa smiles.

"How long have you been up?" Leann asks.

"I don't know, to be honest. I was up most of the night. I know I slept some, but not very much," Vanessa tells her.

"Yeah, I get it," Leann says as she joins her at the table.

They continue to talk for a bit until Leann notices that Vanessa is not paying attention.

"Hey, are you okay?" she asks.

"Yeah, sorry, just thinking. I feel like I should call Elise and Hayley," Vanessa responds.

"What would you tell them?" asks Leann.

"Not quite sure, but I feel like I should do more to help," she states.

"Yeah, I get it. I think that I would feel the same way too," Leann says.

Fearing that this might take Vanessa to a dark place so early in the morning, Leann attempts to change the subject without coming off insensitive.

"I'm going to cook you a phat breakfast. With a *ph*, anything you want," she tells Vanessa.

Vanessa smiles and nods at her.

"Okay, what do you want to eat?" Leann asks.

She thinks about what she's in the mood for. Leann stares at Vanessa as she waits for the decision.

"Crepes," Vanessa says with a smile.

"Crepes," Leann repeats, surprised.

"Yeah, fruit crepes," Vanessa specifies.

Leann's eyes get big as she smiles. "Crepes." She doesn't know how to make crepes. When she offered to make breakfast, she was thinking bacon and eggs, toast, or maybe some pancakes. She takes a sip of her coffee, wondering how she is going to pull this off.

"I'm going to invite Danny over," she tells Vanessa. Before she calls him, she begins to blast his phone with text after text, telling him to wake up. She is desperate to get his attention.

"You should jump in the shower, and I'll get going on these fruit crepes," Leann suggests to Vanessa. Vanessa takes her up on the idea.

"Go on up, and take your time. I'll bring you up another cup of coffee. I'll need just a little extra time for these crepes," Leann tells her.

"Thank you, why the special treatment?" she asks.

"You have been though a lot," she tells her as her phone chimes. She looks, and it's Danny. She walks out of the kitchen and gets on the phone. Danny answers on the other end. He is confused, worried, and still sleepy.

"Listen, I need you to get over here asap with some fruit crepes!" she exclaims.

"What?" He pauses.

"You need to hurry. I need crepes here stat!" she tells him.

"What is going on man? It is so early," he says while still waking up.

"Listen, I'm going to call ahead and place the order. Just swing by and pick it up. It will be in your name," she informs him.

"I don't want to do this right now. It's so early," he expresses.

"Okay, thanks, see you soon. Hurry up. I need those crepes her now," she tells him as she hangs up.

Danny lies in bed, still confused. As he lies, his phone continues to go off. It's Leann, continuing her barrage of texts. He tosses his phone to the foot of his bed and lays his head down.

Leann sits with her phone in hand waiting for Danny's updates. He has been sending progress texts. Leann has made every effort to keep Vanessa upstairs, including running another cup of coffee to her, like she said she would. There is a knock at the door. She rushes to get it; it's Danny.

"You are crazy," Danny says as he enters.

"Took you long enough," she responds.

"What, I'm not even awake yet. What is this for?" he asks.

"I'll explain later. Help me make this look like I made it all," she tells him.

"What are you doing?" he asks again.

"Fine. Vanessa is upstairs. I wanted to do something nice by cooking her breakfast. She chose crepes, but I don't know how to make crepes, so..."

There is a pause.

"Oh, I get it," he says.

"Well, my work here is done. Can't wait to eat," he adds.

She looks at him. "You have to help me," she tells him.

"No, I think I'll just wait till you're done cooking," he tells her with satisfaction.

"Don't do this. Please!" she pleads.

"I don't know, you did just rudely wake me up," he tells her.

"Please."

"You're not going to fool her, you know," he says as he moves to help her set up.

As they finish the setup, Vanessa walks down the stairs. She sees Danny.

"Hey, Danny, you got here pretty quick," she tells him.

"Yeah, I had a rude awakening, then I was on a mission," he responds.

This prompts Leann to look up at him.

Vanessa walks toward the kitchen. "Cool, well, thanks for picking up breakfast for us," she tells him as she smiles at Leann.

Leann drops her shoulders and head.

"Dang it," she says.

"It's fine really. I know you don't know how to make crepes. I love them, but I just wanted to see what you were going to do. I was expecting to go out to breakfast, but this works. I actually like this better," Vanessa says.

"Oh well, I tried. Let's eat," says Leann.

Danny walks over to sit with the girls at the island.

"I wanted to invite Uriah over, but I'm guessing he's still sleeping, so didn't want to disturb him," Leann tells them.

"Yeah, I'm sure he is. Let's let him sleep. We could invite him to lunch," Vanessa suggests.

"Good idea," Leann replies.

"You going to stick around until then Dan?" Vanessa asks.

He thinks for a moment. "I think that depends on where we eat," he says.

* * * * *

Isaiah didn't move from his sleeping position. He is still sitting upright against a tree. The sunlight is breaking through the trees, shining bright on his face. He slowly begins to wake up. He moves his head around to avoid the sunlight but can't, so he raises his hand to block the light. He leans over and lays on the ground, using his hand as a pillow, to get out of the sunlight. He opens his eyes slowly. He lays on the ground just long enough to hear the rumble in his stomach. He pops up and begins to look around.

I've got to piss, he thinks. He gets to his feet and unzips his pants. He looks around as he pisses. He looks down at his piss and sees that it's dark yellow.

"Damn, that ain't right. I need to find some water," he says. He finishes and walks back to the road he was on. It doesn't take him long to get to it, and when he does, he stops to wonder if he chose the right direction. The sun above is reminding him that it's going to be another scorcher.

"Fuck, am I wasting my time going this direction? And getting fried in the process," he says aloud. *Why change now? Might as well keep on the same direction*, he thinks to himself.

He gets onto the road and resumes his walk to find food, water, or better yet, civilization.

*　*　*　*　*

It's still morning, but residents are taking advantage of the early-morning summer sunshine. Brandon has assigned the mowing duty to Jayce, with Franky standing guard. As Jayce mows, his father does lawn maintenance in a different part of the yard. Upstairs, Sherri dances as she folds her laundry to ready for packing. She loves to dance. She's thinking about the upcoming move to her new place with her friends. She's feeling excitement and a little nervousness if she's being honest with herself. She dances her way out of her room and over to a window where she can see her father and brother sharing the yard work.

I am really happy with my life, she thinks to herself.

She dances back into her room, to the basket of clothes on her bed. Jayce continues to mow as he listens to music and his father edges the grass. Jayce turns the mower away from the fence to head back in the other direction. Right before he completes the turnaround, the mower goes over a golf ball lying in the grass, sending it flying across the yard, hitting his father on the back of his head. It knocks him unconscious. At first, Jayce is oblivious to what has happened to his father. He eventually looks up and sees his father lying on the ground. With no regard for the mower, he jumps off and runs to his father's side, leaving the mower unattended.

"Dad…Dad, Dad!" Jayce cries out as he pushes on his shoulder. "Dad!" he calls out again. He looks around then back at the house. He pushes on the shoulder a couple more times. He looks up again.

"Sherri, Sherri!" he calls out for his sister. He gets no response. He wants to cry but is so preoccupied with trying to get his father to wake up that he doesn't. He finally decides to run inside to grab Sherri. As she continues to dance, she doesn't see Jayce come into her room.

"Sherri, Sherri, come outside. Hurry. Dad is not moving!" he cries out.

"Jayce, stop," she tells him.

"No, no, Dad is not moving," he says again.

Sherri is skeptical about Jayce's excitement; after all, he has developed a reputation for being a bit of a jokester. So she assumes he is at it again.

"Please, come on, please." He grabs her by the wrist and pulls her downstairs.

"Come on, come on," he continues to plead with her.

They run down the stairs.

"If you are playing a joke on me, you're going to regret it," she warns him.

The door is already open when Jayce entered. She walks out back with a confused look. She sees her father lying on the lawn and Franky standing over him licking this face. She runs down the stairs and runs over to him.

"Dad, Dad!" she calls out.

Franky moves away, to make space for Sherri. She checks his pulse and checks to see if he is breathing.

"Okay, he is breathing, and he has a pulse." She thinks for a second; she isn't sure if she should do CPR.

"What happened?" she asks Jayce.

"I don't know. I was mowing, and then I saw him laying down," he responds as he stands over her shoulder.

"Okay, run inside and grab some water," she instructs.

Jayce rushes into the house and gets to the sink. Meanwhile, she decides to do chest compressions. Jayce returns with a small cup of water.

Sherri looks at him. "Really, Jayce," she says annoyingly.

"I was in a hurry," he replies.

"Of course, you were, little brother," she says.

He brought out less than a cup's worth of water. Worst, most of it fell out as he was running it to her. She grabs the cup of water from him and tosses the water at her father's face. No response.

"Go in and get more. This time get more than the first time, a bigger cup," she instructs him.

Jayce runs inside again. This time he grabs the same amount as the first time then returns.

She pauses the chest compressions. "Come on, Jayce, you're killing me!" she yells out.

"What, I can't carry more," he tells her.

"Whatever," she says with even more annoyance as she nods and rolls her eyes.

"There was more, but it was spilling as I was running," he tries to explain.

"Give me that," she grabs the cup. She tosses it at her father's face, again no response. She gives him a couple mini slaps to the cheek, no response.

"Step back," she instructs Jayce.

"I hope this works." She cocks back her arm and lets it fly.

Slap! Brandon comes to. He takes a couple of seconds to realize where he is.

"Man, what happened?" Brandon asks.

"I don't know, but Jayce ran upstairs and told me that you're not moving. When I came out here, you were out," she says.

"My head is killing me," Brandon says as he rubs his head.

"Let's get you inside," Sherri tells him.

"I don't know what happened. Last thing I remember is mowing the lawn."

"Something must have knocked you unconscious," Sherri suggests.

"You were edging, and I was mowing, Dad," Jayce adds.

"Come on up, we have to get you inside, mister."

As she helps him to his feet, the golf ball becomes visible.

"There's a golf ball," Jayce points out.

"That seems like the likely culprit," Sherri comments. She puts her arm around his waist and puts his arm around her shoulders.

"Jayce, go shut off the mower," she directs him.

"I guess I'll finish later, huh," Brandon says.

"You need to not worry about that right now. We need to get you inside and lying down," she replies.

They make their way into the house as Jayce goes to deal with the mower. Franky follows Sherri and Brandon first but then turns his attention to Jayce and follows him to the mower.

They get inside, and Sherri lays him down on the couch. She goes to grab him a pillow and an ice pack for his head.

She returns with the items. *He might need some aspirin*, she thinks.

Jayce walks into the house. "Franky, you're staying outside for now," he tells the dog.

She sees Jayce walk into the house. "Jayce, go grab the aspirin," she commands him. She continues to talk with her father as she tries her best to make him as comfortable as possible. Jayce returns with the aspirin.

"Can I help?" he asks.

"No, I got it in here. I need you to go finish the yard, thank you," she tells him.

He pouts a little as he walks right back out the door to his sister's command.

"I'll be out there shortly to help you finish, bud," Brandon tells his son.

"No, you won't," Sherri tells her father.

* * * * *

They finish with breakfast. There is a knock at the door. Danny is closest, so he gets up to answer it. It's Kyleigh.

"Hey, Danny, haven't seen you in a while," she says as she gives him a big hug.

"Good to see you too."

Leann and Vanessa can hear a female voice but can't make out who it is.

"Were you expecting anyone?" Vanessa asks.

"Nope," Leann says.

They hear the door close, and soon after Kyleigh comes into view.

"Hey, sis," Kyleigh says.

Vanessa is a little surprised but happy to see her big sister. They hug each other.

"Why didn't you call me right away? I should have been your first call," Kyleigh tells her.

"I know, but things happened fast. I just needed some time to process, and I didn't want to interrupt your vacation," she tells her.

"That is absurd. You should have at least called me."

"I was going to today."

"Well, I'm just glad you're okay. I was worried when I heard."

"Yeah, I don't have a phone right now, and I've just been hanging here with Leann."

"Oh, hey, girl," Kyleigh acknowledges Leann.

"How did you find out?" Vanessa asks.

"Leann called me. There wasn't a lot she could tell me, but I got a general idea. I thought I would hear it from you if you were up to it at some point."

"Yeah, I could do that," she tells her sister.

"You said you weren't expecting anyone," Vanessa questions Leann.

"I wasn't. I spoke with her yesterday but didn't know she was showing up this morning," Leann responds.

"Why don't you guys go to the living room to talk. I'm going to pick up," Leann tells the ladies.

Vanessa and Kyleigh move to the couch. Danny decides to help Leann. Vanessa begins to give Kyleigh an abbreviated version of the attack. Danny is close enough to hear, but he wants to hear it clearer.

"Hey, I'd like to help, but I'd rather be over there," he tells Leann.

"Sure, whatever."

The cleanup doesn't take long, and soon Leann joins the others in the living room. They all sit around visiting for a while when the doorbell rings. Leann gets up to answer it. It's Uriah at the door.

"Hey, glad you made it."

"Thanks for inviting me," he says as he gives her a hug.

"We have a nice little group going here," she tells him.

"Oh yeah, who else is here?" he asks.

"Well, Vanessa stayed the night. Kyleigh and Danny are also here," she tells him as they walk into the living room.

"Uriah!" Kyleigh shouts as she jumps off the couch to hug him. Danny stands up to greet him as well.

"Hey, Uriah, how did you sleep?" Vanessa asks him.

He nods. "Surprisingly well. I was exhausted. You?"

"I didn't sleep as good as you, but I got some."

"Can I get anyone something to drink?" Leann asks.

She provides drinks for those that request something. She makes a delivery then returns to the kitchen for other items. Uriah sits on a stool.

"My sister was telling us about the attack. I'm sorry you had to go through that," Kyleigh tells them.

"I should be out there right now. I should be out there helping them," Uriah says. Kyleigh stands across Uriah at the island.

"Listen you two, very carefully, there is a tremendous amount of guilt you are feeling right now because you survived and other angels didn't. You two have been through something that most of us angels have not experienced, so it's hard for us to understand how you feel, but you can't beat yourselves up over this. You need to be strong and focus up because this thing is not over. It's just getting started. Right now, the halo is lost, and there is a fight coming and you two need to be ready. Right now, you're doing what you need by getting back to one hundred percent, you understand?"

"Yes," Vanessa tells her big sister.

"I guess I would feel better if we were actually doing something and not just sitting around. Brad won't let us do anything," Uriah tells Kyleigh.

"And that's the right move. Remember, you got to take care of yourself first. This is all still fresh. Hell, you just got attacked forty-eight hours ago. Brad and Nate just want you to rest up and recover. You will be back in the game soon enough, trust me," Kyleigh says to reassure him.

Danny puts his hand on Uriah's back. "When you get back in the game, I'll be right there with you."

* * * * *

Christian arrives at Nate's house. He dismounts from his motorcycle and sees angels moving around, prepping to move out. He walks up to Brad and asks him why there are other angels here.

"They are coming along," Brad tells him.

"Why? You think we need help?" Christian asks.

"Not I. Nate wants this. It's not for fear. It's for security. We are going to need them. We don't know what to expect," Brad tells Christian.

"Come on, Brad, you know that between you, Nate, and me, we can take their entire army." Brad laughs a little.

"Tell me, Christian, do have eyes on the back of your head?"

"Well, no, why does that matter?" Christian asks.

"Think about it. Anyways, don't ever underestimate the devils. They have been around as long as we have, and they need to be respected."

Christian pauses a moment. "You respect them?" he asks with a baffled look.

"I respect the fact that they are dangerous and they are out to destroy the angels. Respecting them doesn't mean liking them," Brad adds.

"I guess you're right, but we got this," Christian says.

"Yes, I think we will be fine, and the reason they are here is because Nate wants them here," Brad tells him.

Nate walks out of the house.

"Glad you can join us," Nate says as he stares at Christian.

"Sorry for being late," he tells Nate.

"It's all right, as always," Nate says sarcastically. "Just wish it wasn't a habit," he adds.

"It's not a habit," Christian replies.

"Oh, you're right. It's a problem," Brad interjects.

"In fact, I can't remember a time when you were on time," Brad adds. Christian gives him a look of doubt.

"Very well then, how close are we to leaving?" Nate asks.

"We are ready when you are," Brad tells him.

"Great, let's move out then."

They move to the vehicles.

"Not so fast, mister," they hear behind them.

All the angels outside look back. They freeze like they just got in trouble. It's Erin, standing at the doorway. Everyone stays still for a moment. She walks up to Nate, Brad, and Christian.

"You all better be careful out there," she tells them.

They nod at her.

"I am counting on you two to bring this one back to me unharmed," she tells Brad and Christian.

"We will," Christian responds.

"Erin, you underestimate your husband. He will be the one bringing us back in one piece," Brad says next.

Erin shakes her head and smiles as she straightens Nate's clothing and then gives him a kiss.

"Everything will be fine, my love. I love you," he tells her.

She rubs his face. "Be careful, boys."

The men turn around and get into the car.

* * * * *

Sherri is lying out in her backyard while reading. She prefers to lie out during the early part of the day during the summer to avoid the scorching sun in the afternoon. Although she looks relaxed, she is lying concerned for her father. She is annoyed at her father's bullheadedness, which prevents him from seeing a doctor. She wanted to make sure he didn't have a concussion or something worse. He insisted on just resting and sleeping it off. She's in deep thought when she hears the voice of her boyfriend Matt.

"Hey, babe," he says.

"Hey, baby," she replies.

He sits beside her. She looks at him with a concerned expression. He looks then turns away from her.

"I'm bored. Let's do something." He fails to notice the look of concern that sits on her face. She looks down and away then turns to look at him a second time, giving him a stronger expression of concern.

"What? I want to do something," he says.

Sherri continues to stare.

"Are you even going to ask me what's wrong? At the very least, how am I doing?" she asks.

A confused look comes over Matt.

"With who?" he asks.

"With me, you jerk. And it is, with *whom*, not *who*," she corrects him.

"What?" he says softly. He is a bit thrown by her emotions and confused by the grammatical correction.

"What's the matter? How are you doing?" he asks out of obligation.

Sherri fills him in on what happened to her father.

"Damn, that sucks, babe. Let's go do something. It will make you feel better," he says.

Sherri's shoulders drop. The look of concern turns to a look of disappointment. There is a brief pause.

"Is that all you have to say?" She is quickly reminded of how insensitive he is.

"I can't believe you," she says.

"What? I said that sucks."

She sits up and turns away from him. He quickly resorts to an apology.

"You don't even care. If it's not about you, then you don't care about it. You didn't even ask if he was okay," she says.

"I figured he is okay because you're not sad," he tells her.

"Not sad? I'm sad and worried. It's still considerate to ask if someone is okay, especially if it's your girlfriend's father," she tells him.

There is another small pause between them.

"Is he okay?" he asks with a look of uncertainty, not knowing how the question will be received.

"Whatever," she replies.

She closes her eyes and shakes her head. She lies flat on her stomach to continue her reading. Matt decides to try another tactic to get back on her good side. Unfortunately, for him, it's an old tactic that has long lost its effectiveness. Nevertheless, he gives it a go. He begins by lying down next to her and begins to kiss her shoulder. She quickly pulls away, but he follows.

"Stop! That's all you ever want," she says with annoyance.

"Come on!" he replies with frustration.

"Why can't you just lay here with me and talk? You definitely know how to ruin moments," she tells him.

"Come on, Sherri, why do we always have to go through this? I love you. We love each other, right?"

"Well then—"

"I'm out of here," he cuts her off.

She is surprised but then remembers that this is normal behavior for him.

"We are supposed to spend time together tonight," she reminds him.

"You need some time alone tonight. You're emotional," he tells her.

"Wow, you are so considerate," she tells him.

He gets up to leave.

"Yeah, there you go. That's what I'm used to—"

"I'll see you later," he interrupts her again.

"Right," she says. She is once again left with an all-too-familiar feeling that she is all alone in this relationship.

* * * * *

Nate, Brad, and Christian arrive at Jason's home. They reach the gate and are meet by two devils. The devils are surprised to see angels at the gate. They look at each other and begin to draw their weapons cautiously. They are aware that these are three of the best angels, so they move slowly.

"No need for that," Nate tells the guards.

"I am here to see Jason."

The guards look at each other again.

"He isn't here," devil number 2 says.

"He isn't? Hmm, how convenient," Nate says.

"Well then, I'll speak with his wife. Inform her that I am here."

Devil number 2 radios to the house. Devil number 2 gets off the radio and steps toward the car.

"She doesn't want to see you."

"Is that right? Well, tell her that I am coming through this gate. It's just a matter of how. I'm sure you have a preference?"

The devil steps back again to the radio again. He steps forward again.

"Okay."

He nods to guard number 1 to open the gate. Crystal walks through the house, irritated about the company.

"Keira, call Franco and tell him to get over here right now."

Nate and his angels reach the house. They park the cars and wait a moment. They see one guard standing at the front door. They get out of the vehicles and wait again. After looking around a little, Nate begins to walk up to the house. The knights follow. Crystal and Keira come outside before the angels make it to the stairs.

"What do you want, Nate?" she asks.

Nate gets straight to the point. "I am here to see Jason."

The guard and Christian lock eyes in a stare down.

"He isn't here," Crystal responds.

"Do you know how long he will be or where I can find him?" Nate asks.

"He is out of town. You look like you came here to start a fight, Nate," Crystal says.

Nate smiles. "I didn't start this fight, but I do want to talk about it."

Christian and the guard continue their stare down.

"He came to talk. I came to fight," Christian tells the guard.

Crystal looks over at Christian then back at Nate.

"Are you sure about that?" she asks Nate.

"Lady, it wouldn't be much of a fight," says Christian.

"Let's find out," Keira tells Christian.

Nate looks over at Christian.

"That is not why we are here. Not another word about combat," he tells Christian. "Like I said, we are not here to fight," he reassures Crystal.

"Well then, what do you need, Nate?" Crystals asks.

"We should talk inside," he suggests.

"You're wasting your time," she says as she turns and enters the house.

Keira follows.

"Brad, you stay out here." Then he tells Christian, "You can come with me, if you behave."

Nate and Christian follow Crystal and Keira into the living room.

"So when will Jason return?" he asks again.

"Like I said, I'm not sure. He's gone for several days," she replies.

"Out of town, huh. Where did he go?"

Crystal walks over to the bar and pours herself I drink.

"I'm not going to tell you that."

There is a brief silence as Nate looks around the room.

"Can you call him and ask him what day and time he will be home?"

"I'm not going to do that either. What makes you think I'm just going to tell you what you want. We are not friends. I don't like you. I don't owe you anything," she tells him.

"You're right, but right now, I'm grieving, and I'm not in the best state of mind. My patience is short, and so I don't want my time wasted," he says.

"You're wasting your own time, Nate, by coming here," Keira says.

Nate looks at Keira. "You seem strong, young one, but you have much to learn," he tells her.

"I know enough, and you don't scare me," she tells him.

"Young lady, I would hope that I don't scare anyone. What good would that serve?" he responds.

* * * * *

Isaiah has been walking on this road for several hours now. He is still unsure where this road will take him. The sun is high, and there are clear skies. Nothing but direct sunrays beam down on him. When he first got on the road, there was an abundance of black berries on both sides of the road; this kept him from starvation. Further down the road, the berries became less and less available. The berries are now few are far between. He sees what looks like more berries up ahead. He doesn't run; he doesn't have the energy to. Berries are confirmed, so he eats.

He thinks about packing for the stretches without, but he has no way to carry them other than his hands and pockets. Neither of which is ideal. The tradeoff of berries for water is now taking its toll on him. He is growing increasingly dehydrated under this beaming sun. He fills his hands with berries and begins his walk. He walks for about twenty more minutes until he looks ahead and sees an object with dust circling it. He stops; he takes another small step and freezes. He can't decide if he should stop or keep walking, but there is something on the road.

"Is that a truck?" he asks himself. He stops walking. He waits for the semitruck to get closer before he tries to get its attention. The semi is going about thirty-five miles per hour, but it looks to be slowing down. Isaiah walks to the middle of the road and waves his arms in the air, tossing the few berries he has in his hand. The truck driver has no choice but to see Isaiah in the middle of the road and slow down. He looks up at the sky with a smile.

Finally, some relief, I can finally go home, he thinks to himself.

The truck comes to a stop. He looks up at the driver. The driver looks perplexed as he sets his forearms on the steering wheel. They stare at each other for a moment. The driver opens his door as Isaiah falls to his hands and knees. The driver steps out, leaving one hand on his door.

"Are you okay, son?" the trucker asks.

"I am hungry, thirsty, and tired, but I am okay right now," he tells the trucker.

"What are you doing out here, in the middle of the road?" the driver asks.

"It's a long story. Do you have a phone?" Isaiah asks.

"I left my phone at home with my wife, but I've got a radio in my rig," the trucker tells him.

Isaiah gets to his feet and drags himself to the trucker.

"Where are we?" he asks the trucker.

"In the forest, middle of nowhere," the trucker replies.

"Of course, we are. Uh, where are you headed?" Isaiah asks.

"I'm headed back into town, got to take this timber in," the trucker responds.

"Well, can I bother you for a ride please?" he asks.

"No bother at all, hop in." He points to the truck with his thumb.

Isaiah walks to the passenger's side of the truck and climbs in.

"There's my CB radio, if you need to use it," the trucker offers.

"Thanks, but that won't work. I'll just wait for a phone," Isaiah expresses.

The driver pulls out some water and hands it to him. He then reaches for his lunch box and opens it.

"Here you go, son, eat this. It's cold, but I'm sure you will find it mighty delicious right now," the trucker says.

A big smile comes over Isaiah. "Thank you, sir," he says gratefully.

The driver adjusts himself and then his hat. "You don't look so good, son," the trucker comments.

Isaiah is in mid-drink.

"What are you doing out here all alone in this condition?" the trucker asks.

Isaiah lets out a big sigh after a big drink of water. "It's a long story and pretty complicated, but I'll tell you after I eat this food," he says.

"Of course, take your time," the trucker says.

"That reminds me, you mentioned that you are going into town. That would mean that I was going the wrong way, is that right?" Isaiah asks.

"That is correct. Don't know what business you had going further into the forest," he tells him.

Isaiah closes his eyes in disbelief and lays his head back. "I can't believe I chose the wrong direction," he says aloud.

The trucker adjusts his hat again and reaches for his seat belt. He puts the truck in drive, and they head toward town.

"You got a name, son?" the trucker asks.

The driver doesn't get a response.

"Don't feel like talking much, huh?" the trucker asks.

Again, no response. He turns to find that Isaiah has fallen asleep, leaning against the door, food on his lap. The driver nods a little and adjusts his hat again.

"I'll bet he was out here doing the partying and got lost from his camp. Younger people," the trucker says aloud as he shakes his head.

* * * * *

"So, Crystal, why has your husband decided to break the peace we had in place?" he asks.

"I don't know, Nate. Why don't you ask him yourself?" she tells him.

"Well, that's why I'm here, right?"

"Six of our angels are dead because of him, you witch!" Christian yells out.

Everyone in the room looks over at Christian. There is a brief silence.

"Hmm, only six," Crystal comments.

"Does that amuse you?" Nate asks her.

"I don't understand why we don't just take these ones out right now. That would definitely get Jason back here ASAP," Christian adds.

Crystal's eyes widen as she grips her drink a little tighter.

"That is not our way. You know that, son. Why don't you wait outside with Bradley?" Nate tells him.

He looks at Nate then looks at Crystal with a dagger of a stare then spits at the floor in her direction. He turns and walks, bumping shoulders with a devil standing at the doorway.

"As you can see, this has been hard on all of us," Nate tells Crystal.

"I really don't know what you want. I'm not going to apologize. I'm not going to answer for my husband, and I don't feel bad about what has happened to your angels. That shouldn't surprise you," she tells him.

"I'm not surprised, Crystal, but I would suggest that be the extent of your thoughts about my angels. We are done for now, but just know that your husband has made a big mistake, and none of you should feel immune to the repercussions to come."

She stares at him and then looks down and away.

"I have to burry six of my angels now."

"All those angels deserve to die, and so do you!" shouts the devil at the doorway.

Crystal and Keira quickly look over at the devil then at Nate. Nate looks at Crystal, and before the devils next blink, Nate reaches for the dagger in his belt, turns, and throws it at the devil, sticking him right in the throat. Crystal lets out a yelp as she backs up to the wall, covering her mouth. Kiera reaches for her weapon.

"Unless you want to meet your devil friend in hell, you will reconsider," Nate tells Keira.

The devil looks forward, grabs his throat, and falls to his knees. He struggles to breathe, looks up at Nate, then falls to the floor.

"Told you, we are very sensitive right now," he tells Crystal as he exits the room. He gets outside.

"Let's go."

As they begin to go down the stairs, they see some cars pull up. They continue toward their vehicles. The cars come to a stop. Franco, with several devils, get out.

"Now we'll see some action," Christian says.

"There will be no action. Especially since Jason is not here," Brad responds.

"You have some big balls showing your ugly faces around here," Julian tells the angels.

The four accompanying angels stand alert.

"So this is what he sends instead of coming himself," Brad says to Franco.

Crystal comes out of the house. "They just killed my guard!" she yells.

Only Christian looks back at her. The devils release a unified growl. The devils draw their weapons, and Keira begins to make her way down the stairs to join the other devils. All the angels draw their weapons except for Nate. Instead, he walks up to Franco.

"There will be no fight here unless you want to die today. We were just leaving, so save yourselves for another day," Nate says, staring at Franco.

"You can't come here and kill one of us and walk away," Franco replies.

"You just killed six of my angels and walked away. Consider yourself extremely fortunate that there will be no fight right now."

"Kill them now!" Crystal commands the devils.

They begin to circle the angels.

"If they attack, you will also die, witch. We are leaving daemon," Nate says while maintaining eye contact with Franco.

Crystal continues to shout out commands to attack, but the devils wait for the command from Franco. They are in conflict but must wait to hear it from him.

"You do have the numbers for a fight right now. Think about it," Nate advises him.

"You underestimate us, and you shouldn't have come here if you weren't expecting a fight," Franco tells Nate.

The devils move closer and closer to the angels.

Crystal looks at Kiera. "Go kill them."

Kiera slowly approaches the angels. Christian looks up at her and smiles.

"I think that if you wanted to fight, you would have given the command already," Nate tells Franco.

"Kill them all, Franco!" Crystal yells out.

Christian positions himself to meet Keira first.

Just before Kiera reaches Christian, Franco instructs, "Lower your weapons."

"What are you doing?" Crystal asks with disbelief.

Kiera pauses.

"What are you doing?" she repeats.

"Smart. Let's go, angels," Nate says while maintaining eye contact. Nate turns around and walks to the car. The rest of the angels cautiously back up and get into their cars. Crystal continues to yell and berate Franco for not following her directives.

"You are a coward, and the rest of you should expect some punishment when I tell my husband!" Crystal yells at the group.

Franco watches them drive away and then walks up to Crystal. "Don't worry, I'll tell him myself. I only showed up here to make sure you weren't harmed, no other reason."

"He killed my guard. That is reason enough."

"Those were three of the best angels. This was not the time or place, Crystal. Were you so brazen before I got here?"

She stares at him for a second and turns around. "Clean up the mess inside," she says as she turns around and goes into the house.

Franco looks at a couple of devils and signals to them to go inside to clean up.

* * * * *

Isaiah is sleeping as the truck pulls into town. The trucker stops in an open parking lot.

"Son, hey, son."

No movement form Isaiah. The trucker tries again. This time, he nudges his shoulder. Isaiah wakes up. He pops up, eyes wide open, and he freezes for a moment. He begins to look around, trying to figure out where he. He sits up in his seat.

"We are in a town called Sisters," the trucker tells him.

"Oh, okay, um, did I sleep the whole way here?"

"Oh yeah, I must have been pretty boring conversation," the trucker says jokingly.

"No, no, that's not it. I was just really tired."

"What are you fixin' to do now?" the trucker asks.

"Find a phone." He opens the door and climbs out of the truck.

"Hold on there, son." The trucker pulls out his wallet and pulls a ten-dollar bill out of it.

"You're going to need to eat," he tells Isaiah.

Isaiah laughs a little.

"What's so funny?"

"Just forgot that I was hungry. Thank you."

"Listen, I've got some quick business to take care of, then I'm going to head on home. If you have trouble finding a phone, then you can come on back with me and use my home phone. I'll be about an hour, then back here at my rig."

"Sounds good, thanks." Isaiah begins to shut the door but stops and opens it up again. "Hey mister, what's your name?" he asks.

"The name's Malakai."

"Malakai," Isaiah repeats.

"That's right."

"My name is Isaiah, thanks again."

"You betcha, son," replies Malakai.

Isaiah closes the door and walks toward food as the Malakai looks on.

* * * * *

Isaiah walks into a multifunctional retail building. It's the type that has a restaurant or two and a convenience store, typical of a rest stop. This one happens to have a Taco Bell and a Burger King in it.

I can't wait to have a whopper, he thinks to himself. He walks up to the counter to place his order.

"Do you guys have a phone I could use?" he asks the worker. The worker is a little caught off guard.

"I'm from Portland, and I am kind of stranded here."

"I'm sorry, our phone is not for public use," she replies.

Isaiah drops his head.

"But you can barrow mine," she says as she hands him his change.

He looks up as he extents his hand.

"Wait here," she tells him. She returns to the register.

"Here you go."

"Oh, thank you so much," he tells her. He steps away from the counter but stays in sight for the girl to see him. He doesn't want her to think he is going to run off with it. He dials his sister's number. It's the only number he has memorized. The phone rings on the other end. After the fourth ring, the call is answered.

"Hello," Isaiah hears on the other end.

"Hey, sis," Isaiah says.

There is a silence.

"Noemy, it's me," he tells her.

He waits for a response. Noemy is frozen on the other end as tears begin to roll down her face. She has her mouth covered but then uncovers to exhale. He can tell that she is crying. His eyes begin to well up.

"Z," she asks.

"Yes, yes, it's me."

She cries a little louder. "How?"

They both sniffle and attempt to gather themselves.

"I thought—*we* all thought you were dead. I was told you fell out of the jet," she tells him.

"I didn't fall. I jumped out!" he exclaims.

"You little shit, why did you do that?"

"I went after the halo, and I had a parachute," he explains.

"Arrrg, I heard different, okay." She catches her breath.

"Well, I'm alive, sister."

"Oh my god, I'm so happy you're alive. I thought I lost you," she says.

"Well, I'm tired and hungry, but I'm alive," he says.

The young lady at the counter calls out his number. He's preoccupied with his sister that he doesn't realize that it's his number getting called.

"Listen, I'm at a Burger King using a girl's phone right now."

She interrupts him.

"Stay right there, I'm on my way!" she shouts.

"No, no, listen. I'm riding with this trucker. He is willing to take me back to his place. That is my best move. When I get there, I will call you again from his house, got it?"

"How long until I hear from you again?"

"I don't know, maybe about two hours from now."

"Okay, I'll be waiting," she tells him.

His number gets called again. This time he hears it but still doesn't go up for it.

"Just tell everyone that I'm fine and I'll see them soon," he tells her. He walks toward the counter. He sees the girl at the counter point to his food.

"Okay, sis, I've got to go. I have to eat and return this phone. I'll be calling you soon, okay?"

"Okay, I love you so much," she says.

He giggles. "I love you too." He hangs up the phone and hands it to the girl at the counter.

"Thank you so much for letting me use your phone," he tells her.

"No problem. Are you okay?" she asks.

"Yeah, I'm good now. I'm better," he tells her.

"Tears of joy, I hope." She points to his eyes.

"Yes, good tears. Thank you again," he says as he grabs his food. He walks back to the truck and finds that Malakai hasn't returned. He checks the door and finds it unlocked. He jumps in and settles himself and begins to eat.

* * * * *

Noemy can't stop pacing. In all her happiness and excitement, she has forgotten to inform the angels that her brother is alive.

"Oh shit, I have to tell the others." She runs around her apartment looking for her keys and purse. She finds them and walks to the door. Before she closes the door. "I feel like I'm forgetting something." She thinks for a couple of moments. "Oh yeah, my sunglasses. It's bright outside."

She closes the door behind her. She walks to the building elevator and waits. She gets in and gets to the parking garage. She walks out of her building to her car. She settles in. The pedals feel odd to her. She looks down at her feet and sees that she isn't wearing shoes.

"Balls!" she shouts out. She contemplates going back inside. "Oh well." She turns the car on and drives out. On her way, she runs a red light and cuts off some pedestrians at a crosswalk. Distracted, she finally makes it to Nate's house. She gets out of her car and runs up to the house. Fernando greets her at the door.

"Hey, Fern, I need to see Nate."

"Nate isn't here at the moment, but Erin is."

"I'll see her then," she says.

Fern goes to summon Erin.

He returns. "Erin is in the backyard. You may go."

Erin sees her coming out. "Well, hello child," she tells Noemy.

"Hey, Erin."

"How are you holding up, honey?" Erin asks, knowing she is in mourning over the loss of her brother.

"I am doing great. That is why I'm here," she tells Erin.

Erin looks confused then looks down at her feet. "What do you mean, child? Is everything okay?" she asks.

"Isaiah is alive! Isaiah is alive, Erin!" she shouts out.

Erin is quiet and doesn't know how to react.

"Why would you say something like this, Noemy?"

"I know it sounds crazy, but he called me, called my phone. He is in a small town right now getting a ride with a trucker of some kind," she explains.

"Come, let's have a seat," Erin suggests as she guides her to a bench.

"You don't believe me, do you?" Noemy asks.

"I just don't understand where all this is coming from. You arrive saying your brother's alive. You look a mess, and you're not wearing any shoes," Erin explains.

"Yeah, I know. I forgot them. Look, my brother called me. I spoke to him. I heard his voice. I need to tell Nate and Brad and everyone," she tells Erin.

"How about you slow down, dear?" Erin suggests.

Noemy pulls her phone out and shows Crystal the number Isaiah called from.

"You see this number? We can call it. He won't be there, but it's some girl who is working at a Burger King. Go ahead, call it," Noemy suggests.

"Okay, let's call it," Erin obliges.

Noemy presses Call on her phone. It rings until it goes to voice mail. She hangs up and doesn't leave a message.

"Ugg," Noemy lets out.

"Where is Nate, please? Never mind, I'll just call him," she says as she walks away from Erin back into the house.

"Noemy, wait!" Erin shouts, trying to get her to stop.

She passes Fern. "Z is alive, and she doesn't believe me," she tells him.

* * * * *

Isaiah and Malakai are on their way to Redmond. They have been making small talk, but Malakai's curiosity is too strong. He really wants to know what Isaiah was doing out there alone on that logging road. He looks over at Isaiah and decides to ask him.

"Let me ask you something, son. Why were you out there today where I found ya? You say you're from Portland. Were you camping? How'd ya get lost? I don't understand why you were out there the way I found ya?" he says.

Isaiah stays silent for a moment. Angels aren't shy about revealing who they are, but Isaiah has some reservations about this time.

"So what happened, son?"

"You know, Malakai, I appreciate everything you have done for me so far, and especially inviting me to your home, just to use a phone and making sure I eat," Isaiah says.

"So you don't want to tell me, huh," Malakai responds.

"I don't know that you would understand, but more importantly, for your own safety, it's probably best you don't know," Isaiah tells him.

"Son, at my age, I understand most things. As far as my safety goes, at my age, there isn't much, I fear. Don't you think I'd be better prepared to defend myself if I knew what I was up against?" he tells Malakai.

Isaiah laughs a little. "You make some great points." He thinks a little more and decides he will tell Malakai.

"You are familiar with angels and devils, right?"

"Of course, I am, son, we are in God's country," Malakai responds with authority.

"Right." He clears his throat.

"Well, I am an angel, but not the ones you are familiar with," Isaiah says.

Malakai looks over at him with curiosity.

"There are many of us around the world, but there is a large population in Oregon. Like I mentioned, I live in Portland. We look, talk, and live the same way as humans. We just have some enhanced capabilities," he tells Malakai.

"Like special powers, you're like those X-Men or them Avengers?"

"Kind of, but not exactly. You see, we do have heightened senses and extraordinary capabilities, but we don't live in heaven, we don't have wings, and we aren't always dressed in white clothes, and we don't wear halos," Isaiah explains.

Malakai continues to look at Isaiah as if he is on some sort of hallucinogen. "Are you on the drugs son?"

Isaiah laughs. "Yeah, I get it. There are a lot of folks out there who find what I just told you hard to believe. There are many who are aware of us and have witnessed what we can do. I didn't really expect you to understand or believe me."

"Well, it is a crazy story, and you have been without food and water for a couple days, so your mind might be playing some tricks on ya. I think once you've had a proper meal and get hydrated, you will return to normal," Malakai tells him. Isaiah laughs harder this time.

"You mention that you fight the devil?"

"Oh yes, devils. There are thousands, also around the world. Not just one," Isaiah adds.

"Well of course, the angels and devils are enemies, but there is only one devil," Malakai says.

"Well, they have a leader, but he's not the devil. He is actually a daemon."

"You are quite the storyteller, son. Do me a favor, huh, let's keep this story between you and me. Don't need the misses hearing how there are thousands of devils. In her world, there is only one devil, and that is more than enough."

Isaiah laughs again. "Yes, sir, will do."

* * * * *

Noemy is almost to Brad's house. She is upset that Erin dismissed her so blatantly. She is hoping to get a better reaction from Brad. She knows that he will believe her. Since hearing of her brother's apparent death, she remained reclusive until she heard from him. So she doesn't know about the efforts in the forest. She is unaware that Vanessa and Uriah are alive, and she doesn't know that some of the angels' bodies have been recovered. She doesn't realize that Nate and Brad have been busy with this matter while she has been tucked away. She has tried both of their phones, but they are not answering. She gently runs to the front door without her shoes. She knocks and rings the doorbell. She is constantly checking her phone waiting for her brother to call her again. She tries the doorbell a couple more times as she peeks into a window. She begins to get emotional as she feels like she might be letting her brother down. She gathers herself and takes some time to breath.

I'll just wait until Isaiah calls me again with his location. It's not like they could do anything right now if I told them anyways, she thinks to herself. She wipes away some tears and slowly walks back to her car. She looks at her phone and decides to dial the number back. Again, no answer.

"Geez, why isn't anyone answering their phone," she says aloud.

* * * *

Brodie and Becca arrive at Sherri's house. They knock on the door. Jayce answers.

"Hey, Jayce," Becca says.

"Sherri in her room?" Becca asks.

"Yeah, she is."

They walk upstairs to her bedroom.

"Hi," they greet Brandon on their way. They reach her room and knock as they walk in. Sherri is lying on her bed, belly down with the side of her face buried, hugging the pillow. Unlike her boyfriend, her friends quickly notice that she is not in the best of spirits.

"What's wrong, Share Bear?" Becca asks. Deep down inside, she knows what the source of the problem is, but she still asks.

"Oh, oh, oh, I know, I can answer that," Brodie says sarcastically.

"Don't do it," Sherri says, half muffled.

There is a brief pause as Brodie and Becca look at each other.

"Well then, tell us why you put up with him?" Brodie asks.

"Don't do this to me right now, please?" she pleads with them. She gets to her knees and hugs a pillow to her chest.

Becca backs off a little. "What happened this time?"

"What's the point?" Sherri states.

"He is a piece of shit," Brodie says.

Both girls turn to him, each with a different expression. Sherri gives him a look of displeasure. Becca's expression is one with a smirk as she is much more in favor of the comment. Sherri then turns to Becca; Becca quickly changes her expression to one of support for her friend.

"He's a nice guy, and we have had some really good times," Sherri conveys to her friends.

"Honey, I find that hard to believe. We have been here the whole time, and I can't say that I agree with you," Becca responds.

Brodie backs up Becca's statement, "We haven't been fooled. Matt hasn't changed since the first day you met him."

Becca chuckles mildly because of the glaring look that Brodie is getting from Sherri. Brodie attempts to recover. "We love you."

"And it's because we love you, we know you well enough to know that you haven't been the same since you got together. It's time for you to leave him," Becca tells her.

There is a short pause in the room.

Sherri looks out the window. "I'm not going to leave him."

The more her friends talk about her relationship, the more she breaks down, knowing that they make strong points.

"We love you. We are here for you," Becca reminds her again.

Brodie looks at his watch. "We should get going if we want to catch the movie," he tells the girls.

"I'm going to pass on the movie, guys," Sherri tells them.

"WHAT?" Brodie yells out.

"No! You see, this is what he does to you," Becca says.

"I just need a little more time, and I will be fine," she tells her friends.

Brodie shakes his head as he has thousands of times before about her relationship with Matt. Brodie and Becca stare at each other.

"Well, let's go, Brod," Becca says with a disappointed tone. With their heads down, they walk toward the door. Becca opens it.

Brodie turns around. "Do you even plan on making it to the signing tomorrow?"

"Yes, of course, I am. Please don't be mad at me," she replies.

"We are not mad, just disappointed."

With the disappointment on their faces, they walk out the door. Sherri's left sitting on her bed to think. She scoots to the window to watch her friends leave. She is feeling very guilty about how her friends feel, but she knows they only have her best interests at heart. A smile comes to her face. She quickly gets up and darts out the door. She races downstairs and out the front door.

"Bye," she says on her way out.

"Hey, guys, wait up!" she yells out.

Brodie and Becca turn around. Brodie smiles, and Becca jumps and cheers with glee. The girls hug.

"I'm sorry, I love you guys. You're right: I am not going to let him ruin my time," she tells them.

"We are happy you changed your mind," Brodie says.

"Let's go," Becca says.

They get into the car and drive away to catch their movie.

* * * * *

"My baby brother, I'm surprised to see you here. You have been quite busy back in Oregon," Jamie says.

"Only recently," he responds as he leans in for a hug.

"And who is this young pretty new thing?" she asks as she looks over at Delaney.

"My name is Delaney, ma'am. Nice to finally meet you. I have heard so much about you," Delaney responds.

"Ma'am! Oh, make me feel old," Jamie says as she walks away.

"I am so sorry, that is not what I meant," Delaney explains.

"You are old, and she is my assistant," Jason says as he takes a seat.

"Is that all she is to you?" Jamie asks suggestively.

Delaney looks over at Jason as Jamie looks at Delaney.

"No need to answer. She just told me," Jamie says as she takes a seat.

Delaney quickly looks over at Jamie with a surprised look.

"Have a seat, dear. You're not being punished. Can I get you a drink?" she offers her guests.

"I'll have some tequila on the rocks," Jason requests.

"And for you, dear?"

"I'll have some red wine, if you have it," Delaney asks.

"Of course, I do. Does it look like I can't afford it?" she sarcastically asks Delaney.

"No, of course—"

"Leave her alone," Jason chimes in to save Delaney.

The assistant nearby walks away to retrieve the drinks.

"How are my girls doing?" Jamie asks.

"They are good," he responds.

"Good, those little brats. They rarely ever call me," Jamie complains.

"Maybe they still feel like you abandoned them."

"Oh please, they are grown young women, and they have each other. They don't feel abandoned. When I was living there, they were never home. That's in part the reason I left," she says as she looks over at Delaney.

Her assistant returns with the drinks. He sets the tray down.

"And how is your wife?" Jamie asks.

"She is great," he responds.

The assistant hands Jamie her drink first, then Jason's, and then Delaney's.

"Thank you," Delaney tells the assistant.

"Well, I can tell that you're not interested in small talk, so why are you hear?" Jamie asks.

"Good, I'm glad you read that. As you know I've launched my plan to get the halo. We are closer than we have ever been. I attacked their jet carrying the halo, but the halo fell into the forest, where it remains. The angels are looking for it, and we are watching them, in addition to looking for it. If we find it, then a phase two won't be necessary, but I don't want to wait around for that. So I want to launch phase two of my plan," he tells her.

"Phase two, you say. Wow, there are phases," Jamie says with sarcasm.

"What is phase two?" she asks.

"Kill the angels," he says as he takes a drink.

"That sounds so generic. We always want to kill the angels. We have been doing it for thousands of years. You came down here to tell me that?" she asks.

"No, I wanted to get away for a bit, but also, to do this, I'm going to need your entire legion," he requests.

"All of it? This sounds big-time, little brother."

"Well, I'm not fucking around anymore. The time is now," Jason says as he takes another drink.

"Well, this just sounds like you're going to war again. That's nothing new. I hope you have a plan, because just killing them isn't one," she tells him.

"Of course, I have a plan. So your legion?" he reminds her.

Jamie thinks about it for a moment. "Well, it would be nice to visit Oregon right now. Sure, you can use them," she tells her brother.

"Excellent," he replies.

"It will be nice to see my brats, even if they don't care to see me," Jamie says.

* * * * *

The truck pulls up to Malakai's home. Malakai's wife, Shawna, is outside watering plants. She puts the hose down and walks over to greet her husband. She doesn't see Isaiah yet as she is on the driver's side. Malakai gets out of the truck.

"Hi, dear."

"Hello, my darling, how was your day?" she asks him.

"It was good, but interesting," he piques her interest.

As she waits for him to explain the interesting part of his day, the passenger door closes.

"Is someone with you?"

Malakai sees her confusion.

"We've got a guest, dear," he says as Isaiah walks around the front of the truck.

"Hi," Isaiah says.

"Dear, this is Isaiah. Isaiah this is my wife, Shawna."

"Hello there, I'm Shawna, Mal's wife," she says.

"Only she calls me Mal," he tells Isaiah.

"Hi, ma'am," Isaiah says.

Malakai closes his door. They walk to the house as Malakai tells Shawna about his day. She figures that Isaiah has something to do with making his day interesting. They walk up the stairs and into the house.

"Are you hungry, Isaiah?" Shawna asks.

"Not yet, um, I actually came here just to use your phone," he tells her.

Malakai is reminded about the cell phone.

"Oh, that's right, let me go grab the phone for ya."

"Have a seat, dear. You look like you can use a break, some food, and a bath," she tells him.

"Thank you, but I don't want to be a burden. If I could just call my sister, I'll have a ride here in a couple of hours."

"Well, you'll definitely be here for supper then," she says.

"How did you meet Mal?"

"I was camping, went on a hike, and got lost. Ended up on this road, and that's when Malakai found me." He tells her.

"Were you with your sister?" she asks.

"Yeah, that's who I need to call," he reiterates.

Malakai returns with the phone. "Here you go, son."

"Thanks."

"Honey, would you like something to drink?" Shawna offers Mal.

"Is there a room I can make this call in?" Isaiah asks.

"Yeah, right down that hall to the right," Malakai directs.

Isaiah heads down to make the call. He dials the number, and it rings.

Waiting with her phone in hand, Noemy answers right away. "What took you so long? I have been waiting, running around trying to find people, trying to call everyone, and no one's picking up. Some people think I'm crazy making up the fact that you're alive. Can't stop thinking about you. Haven't eaten. I'm going crazy. Why aren't you talking? Say something."

He laughs. "Are you sure it's my turn?" he tells her.

"Yeah, sorry, I'm just stressing."

"Okay, lets back up a little. Who have to told?"

"I went to see Nate. He wasn't home, so I told Erin. She thinks I'm crazy. I went to Brad's house. He wasn't home. I've called both. Neither has answered."

"Okay, that's fine. I'm sure they will call you back," he tells her.

"Where are you? What are you doing?"

"I'm at Malakai's home. That's the trucker I've been riding with, and his wife, Shawna."

"Where?" she asks.

"Redmond," he tells her.

"Oh well, that's not far from Bend, right? We can have Emily send someone for you," she suggests.

"No, let's not do that."

"Well then, I'll just come get you then," she tells him.

"No, no, no, you can't drive out here. That's a three-hour drive, and it will be dark soon. We wouldn't get back home till after midnight."

"Well then, what are you going to do?"

"I don't know that I can leave this area yet. I want to talk to Brad or Nate while I'm here. I'll call you later tonight, and hopefully, you will have gotten ahold of them."

"You can't stay out there," she tells him.

"Noemy, it'll be fine. I'll call you later tonight. I love you."

"Z, you need to come home!"

"I need to find the halo. I can't leave yet."

"Fine," she says reluctantly.

"Don't stress, and don't lose sleep. I'm doing fine here. I love you," he says.

"I love you too."

He hangs up the phone.

* * * * *

Jason and Delaney arrive at their hotel and head straight to the bar.

"Grab us some comfortable seating. I have to use the lady's room," she tells Jason.

He walks around the bar. He comes across a table with a couch on one side and two chairs on the other side. He sits and pulls his phone out. "Uh, wife, wife, wife, wife, Franco, wife, wife...okay, I should probably call Franco first," he says.

Franco sits on his back porch enjoying some company. His phone rings; he puts it on speaker.

"Can you tell me why my wife keeps calling me?" he asks.

"Have you spoken to her?" Franco asks in return.

"No, but she has been calling me nonstop pretty much, and that means she's upset. So do you know what she's upset about?"

"Yeah, Nate showed up at your house today. I got there as he was leaving. He killed a guard. She wanted me to fight, but I didn't. So she wants us all punished," Franco explains.

"I see. Did you and Nate talk?"

"Not really, just a standoff."

"Well, I'll call her next. How is the other thing going?" Jason asks.

"You mean the halo? The angels are still searching. We have eyes on them. Sara is watching their every move," Franco reports.

"Good, good, well, call me if anything changes," Jason tells him.

"Will do. Say, boss, you ready to tell me what your plan is?"

"Not quite," Jason says.

"We just attacked the angels and there is a war brewing. It just seems like this is something I should know," Franco explains.

"True, true, in time. Just be ready for phase two," Jason tells him.

"Phase two?" Franco asks with curiosity.

"Yeah, I'll explain it when I return," he tells his captain.

"All right, well I'll be waiting, and so will Nate," Franco says, causing Jason to laugh aloud.

"That is funny," Jason says as he hangs up.

Franco sits, wondering how Jason can seemingly be calm and not worried about the recent events.

Jason dials his wife next. "Hey, honey."

"It's about fuckin' time!" she yells into the phone.

Jason backs his ear away. "Babe, stop," he tells her. "What is going on?" he asks her, already knowing.

"I could have been killed today, and you are nowhere to be found," she tells him.

The server comes around to take his order. He puts the phone down and covers the speaker with his hand.

"I'll have a tequila, on the rocks," he tells her.

The server walks away, and he resumes his conversation. He makes attempts to comfort her, but Crystal won't stop talking. Delaney finds Jason and sits. She can tell that it's Crystal on the phone. She lies back and begins to check out her nails. Jason is finally able to get a word in.

"Babe, I spoke with Franco already, and everything is fine," he tells her.

"First of all, why has it taken you so long to return my calls, and why would you call Franco before calling me? Is he more important? If I'm calling you over and over, don't you think there might be an emergency? Did Delany tell you I was calling?" she asks him.

"Babe, Franco caught me during a break," he attempts to explain.

Delaney smiles and laughs a little because she knows that he is lying to her. The server arrives with Jason's drink and sets it down. Delaney quickly sees that Jason did not order for her. She gives him a look of displeasure. The server asks Delaney what she would like to drink.

"I'll have an Amaretto sour," she orders.

"Coming right up," says the server.

Jason tries to wrap up the conversation, but Crystal continues to talk.

"Babe, listen, I'm going to call you in a little bit, and we can finish this conversation, okay?" he tells his wife.

"You have something more important to do right now?" she asks.

"I am a little exhausted, and I'd like to relax, have a drink, maybe shower then settle in. I can call you then," he suggests.

"Fine, whatever," she replies with annoyance.

"Let me call you later on, and we can finish up, okay?" he tells her. As he hangs up, Delaney's drink arrives.

"That sounded brutal," she tells him.

"Yeah, Nate went by the house. She still freaking out. He killed a devil," he tells her.

"You don't look too upset about that," she says.

"Considering what we just did to them, I am surprised that that is all he has done. I'm surprised he didn't hurt Crystal," he tells her.

She looks at him with inquisitiveness.

"So you were hoping for that?" she asks.

"No, of course not. Here's the thing, when you get to know someone as long as I've known Nate, you learn certain things about them—tendencies, habits, weakness, etc., etc. One thing I have learned about Nate is that he has a tremendous amount of honor, and that honor demands that he doesn't hurt the innocent," he explains.

Delaney nods.

"Oh, that is why you are comfortable being out of town right now," she says.

"Precisely," Jason responds.

"This is all part of a grander plan my demon," he tells her.

"So what comes next in the grand plan of yours, boss?" she asks.

"When we return home, I'll have to see where things are with the halo, but I am sure you will love what I've got it store, and don't worry, you will have a key role in it as well," he explains.

She raises her eyebrows as she is surprised.

"I will?" she asks.

"Yes, you will. We all will," he tells her.

"What are we doing for dinner?" Delaney asks.

"Not sure, let's have some drinks first. We can eat here. We're here already," he tells her.

"Sure, we can eat here, makes sense," she agrees.

They have a couple of drinks each as they continue their conversation.

"I want to go up to my room before dinner," she tells him.

They walk to the elevator. Delaney presses the button as she is standing slightly in front of Jason. Far enough in front that he can stare at her ass. He isn't trying to be discrete about it, and she welcomes it. The elevator door opens, and they walk in. She stands next to the numbers and presses the floor. He again stands behind her and continues to stare at her ass. They have a little small talk on their way up to the top floor. The doors open and they begin to walk out.

"What are you in the mood for, for dinner tonight," he asks her.

"Oh, something savory," she says as she looks back at him with a smirk.

"Hmm, okay, and we can have some dessert after," he suggests.

"Or before," she says as she reaches the door to his room.

"I think I would like some pasta tonight," she says.

"Excellent choice," he tells her.

"And what for dessert?" he asks.

She leans into him to whisper in his ear. "I am in the mood for some devil's cake," she says with a sexy voice.

"Let me freshen up. Call in our dinner, but not too soon. I have to get a little more comfortable," she tells him.

She turns and walks to her door that is right across the way.

"I trust that all of your personal business will be concluded by the time I come over," she suggests to him.

Jason waits to watch her go into her room. He thinks about how much he enjoys that view. Delaney opens her door, takes a step in, and looks back. She holds the look until she closes the door. He's left staring at a closed door when his phone rings again; it's his wife. He answers it before he opens his door.

"Hey, babe, what's up?" he says as he enters his room.

* * * * *

Malakai and Shawna are outside on their back deck talking when Isaiah joins them.

"How you feelin', son?" Malakai asks.

"I feel like I just stripped off like eight layers of dirt, sweat, and skin, so I feel better," he tells them.

"Well, you look better," Malakai tell him.

"Those clothes fit ya right, so that's good," Shawna adds.

"Yeah, not exactly my style, but they fit, and I'm grateful to you for offering them."

"Isaiah."

"Call me Z. That's what my friends and family call me back home," he explains.

"Very well then, Z, there is some raspberry pie there for ya on the table," Shawna tells him.

"Oh, wow, so that's what I was smelling. I love raspberry pie. I'll go grab some right now."

"He's a nice young man. He reminds me of Jake," Shawna tells Malakai.

"Yeah, I know what you mean. I was getting that when I first picked him up," Malakai says.

Isaiah walks back outside with his pie.

"Talking about me, huh. I leave for less than one minute, and you're talking about me," Isaiah jokes.

The couple laughs.

"We have been talking about you this whole time," Shawna tells him.

"What kinds of things?" he asks.

"Well, here is the thing, Z, I don't think you were camping out there. I don't know what you were doing, but you weren't camping," she tells him.

He looks down at his pie, then at Malakai, who has a smirk on his face.

"You tell her, old man?" Isaiah asks Malakai.

"I didn't say nothin'," Malakai says as he crosses his arms.

"He didn't have to. Something wasn't right about you," she says. He takes a bite of the pie and wipes his face.

"Well, I don't mind telling you, but I got the sense that I'd be wasting my time on account of your beliefs. So I thought I would spare you the insult and time."

"How considerate of you," she says.

"But...but I'll tell you," he offers.

"Sure, let's give it a shot," she tells him.

* * * * *

Brad sits down to a drink. He takes some time to relax. He takes a sip and checks his phone. He has been ignoring it most of the day, using it only to make calls really. He sees that he has some missed calls from Noemy and Nate, among others.

"Hmm, that's a lot of missed calls," he says to himself.

Lupe walks to his side, puts her hands on his shoulders, and begins to rub them.

"How are you doing, honey?"

"I'm kind of exhausted," he tells her.

"Is Lisa out?"

"Yeah, she went down fast."

"Ahh, I wish I would have been here to kiss her good night," he says.

She continues to rub his shoulders.

"Come to bed, you need to rest," she suggests.

"I will, after this drink." She kisses him on the cheek. He dials Noemy's number, considering she had the most missed calls.

"Finally," she says as she lies in bed thinking about her brother.

"Hey, I saw that I missed your call, a couple of times, actually."

"Yeah, you did."

"Sorry, it's been another busy, emotional day."

"Yeah, tell me about it. I've got some great news that I hope will make your day better."

"Good, I could use it. What is it?"

"Z is alive."

There is a brief pause.

"Your brother, Z?" he clarifies.

"Yes, yes, my brother."

"How do you know this?"

"So earlier today, I get a call from a random number. It's him. We talk, he tells me that he is in a random town, getting food with a trucker. He told me that he would call be back later. It took awhile, but he did. This time he asks me if I had spoken to you or Nate. I told him that I couldn't get a hold of either of you. I told him to have Emily pick him up because he is in that area. He didn't want to do that. I told him that I would go pick him up. He said no. He said that he was just going to stay at the trucker's house, and he would call me in the morning again. That was about two hours ago, I think," she explains.

"So he's alive. Oh, man, that is great. We weren't sure, but this is great news. Um, you're sure it was him?"

"Bradley, that's my brother. Of course, I'm sure. Geez, you sound like Erin," she says with annoyance.

"What does that mean?" he asks.

"Like I said, I was trying to get ahold of you and Nate, I even went to both of your homes. Erin was home. I told her, but she thought I was crazy. She was patronizing me."

"This is crazy. He made it. This is great!" he exclaims.

"Oh yeah, he is in Redmond. That's where the trucker lives."

"Redmond, okay, we have people in Sisters right now, not too far from there. That's a quick pickup. Elise and Hayley are out there right now."

"Damn, I wish I would've known that. I would've called them directly," Noemy says.

"How did you not know that?" he asks, surprised.

"Brad, I thought my brother was dead. I've been disconnected," she tells him.

"Yeah, of course, you're right."

"So he said that he is going to call me again tomorrow morning with directions."

"Okay, good. Listen, let's meet up tomorrow morning. I want to coordinate this with the team down there," he explains.

"Okay," she replies.

"I'll come over early tomorrow morning," he tells her.

"Okay, see you then."

* * * * *

There is a knock at the door. Jason opens it to find Delaney standing there wearing an overcoat. She walks in and brushes his shoulder as she walks by. He smiles a little. He takes a drink as he closes the door. She walks into the restroom. He walks to the window as he takes another drink. Delaney opens the bathroom door and stands at the doorway, arm up, supporting her body wearing a lacy, barely-there bra-and-thong combination.

She comes out and walks right up to him, just enough for him to sense her presence. She runs one finger down his shoulder, down his back. He turns halfway, grabs her wrist, and swings her around and up against the window. He takes one more drink and tosses his glass to the side. Her chest rises rapidly.

He leans back a little to take it all in. He runs his hands down each side of her body. He begins to kiss her chest and work his way up to her neck. She presses her hands against the window. He brings his hands up to her tits and around her chest. She brings her hands to his shoulders and begins to run her nails down his triceps.

He moves his right hand down into the front of her thong. He begins to rub her clit. She grabs him by his neck and pulls him in as she looks up to the ceiling, biting her lower lip. She grabs his hands and moves them away, allowing her to kneel in front of him. She looks up at him as she undoes his belt and pants.

His pants drop, but his drawers remain. She fondles his cock with her face, clockwise, up, and down. She pulls his drawers down using her teeth. She sticks out her tongue and licks his cock several times and then sticks it in her mouth, still no hands.

Jason lets out a beastly growl, letting her know that he is thoroughly enjoying her talents. This continuous for a bit until he grabs her by the shoulders, raises her up, turns her around, and presses her against the window. Her chest continues to rise rapidly, accompanied by heavy breathing.

He pulls down her thong, kisses her ass, slaps it, then bites it. He spreads her legs and gets down on his knees. He sticks out his tongue and takes his time licking from front to back, ever so slowly. Delaney lets out a growl of her own, expressing her pleasure.

He stands up.

"Just one lick, you're such a tease," she tells him.

"That's the whole point. I want you to want more," he replies.

She arches her back, sticking her ass out. He steps into position and drives his cock into her glistening wet pussy, slow at first. Her hands press against the window; she begins to scratch at it.

"Fuck me harder!" she shouts.

He picks up the pace and adds more power to his thrusts. He moans and groans.

"Harder, fuck me harder!" she continues to yell. Her hands slide down the window. She begins to slam the window. She pulls herself away, turns around, and pushes him to the bed. She grabs his cock and begins to suck it vigorously. She mounts him and sticks his cock inside of her. She aggressively begins to thrust her hips in the cowgirl position.

Jason closes his eyes and growls again. He can't help it. He can't stop it; his climax is nearing. The way she is working her body is driving him crazy.

"Fuck, you're going to make me cum hard," he tells her.

"Just go, I'll meet you there," she replies. She continues to work her hips aggressively.

"Come on, baby," she tells him.

"Shit, here I cum!" he shouts.

"Yes, yes!" she screams then lets out a loud screech as she arches her back and throws her head back.

They growl together as he grabs her tits. She lies over him, both breathing heavy. She continues to move her hips ever so slightly as they both compose their breathing.

Wednesday

Undisturbed, the halo lies on the ground near a river. The crate acrylic case it was in broke open during its fall from the sky. Now it lies bare and exposed to the sun and anyone who walks along the river. It is giving off a glorious shine because of the sun so much so that it would be virtually impossible for anyone in its vicinity to avoid it.

After three days of lying unnoticed, the shine catches the attention of a bull elk. The elk walks over to investigate. It stares at it for a moment then looks around. It stares at it again, but this time, it lowers its head to smell it. It's not often wildlife get something so shinny in the forest. But the halo happens to be in a familiar area for the elk. This spot happens to be his watering hole, or one of them.

He decides to skip the halo for now and grab a drink. As he drinks, he cautiously scans the river and the area around him. He stands tall looking around. He is enjoying the day and the view. He takes his time grabbing more drinks, occasionally looking back at the glorious shine.

Once he's had his fill, he turns into the forest. He goes a few yards into the forest when his curiosity gets the best of him. He turns to see the shine again. He walks back to the halo. He sniffs it again. He decides to tap it with his hoof, moving it a couple of inches toward to river. He is still curious. He gives it a couple more taps, moving it closer and closer to the river. He is intrigued by it, so he continues to tap. He continues to tap until the halo finally falls into the river.

The elk looks on in disappointment as he has just lost his new toy. He doesn't spend much time sulking as he turns around right away and walks into the forest.

* * * * *

Brad gets into his car. He takes a moment to reflect on the amount of time he has spent in his car the last three days. He turns his car on and begins to pull away. He gets on the street. "Call Nate," he commands his Bluetooth. It rings a couple of times.

"Hello," Erin answers.

"Erin, good morning, it's Brad."

"Well, Bradley, good morning to you as well," she responds.

"Is the old man awake?" he asks.

"Yes, he is. Let me grab him for you."

Nate comes to the phone. "Good morning, Bradley."

"Good morning, sir. Listen, I'll make this quick. I've got some great news."

"What is it?" Nate asks.

"Isaiah is alive!" he shouts mildly.

"Really?" Nate asks with doubt.

"Yes, Noemy got a call from him yesterday. He's going to call her again this morning with an address. He's in Redmond. I'm on my way to Noemy's now to be there for the call. Once I learn of his location, I'll send some angels to go pick him up."

"This is incredible. He survived. Wow, okay, great. Please keep me updated."

"Will do." Brad hangs up.

Nate stands alone in deep thought, rubbing his chin.

Erin walks up to him. "What is it, dear?"

He looks at her with a puzzled look.

"Well, what is it?" she asks again.

"Isaiah is alive," he says with a soft voice.

"Isaiah, you say?"

"Yes, that was Bradley."

"Yes, I know, dear. I answered the phone."

"Of course, Noemy called him telling him that Z called her from Redmond yesterday," he tells her.

"Oh, that is wonderful news. Oh, dear, I owe Noemy and you an apology."

"What do you mean?" he asks.

"Noemy came by yesterday looking for you. I forgot to mention this to you, I'm sorry. She was a little hysterical about Z being alive. I didn't believe her. Something didn't sound right. She was telling the truth. I feel horrible."

"Oh, it's fine honey. There is much going on right now. The good news is that he is alive. Let's prepare for his return, yes."

* * * * *

Malakai walks into the kitchen where Shawna has prepared coffee and muffins.

"Hey, dear," she hands him a cup of coffee.

"Thank you, honey," he says as he takes a drink.

"I checked on your friend. He's still sleeping," she tells him.

"Not surprised. It'd been awhile since he got some decent sleep on a real bed," he says.

"So what is the plan for when he wakes?" she asks.

"Not sure, he said he wanted to call his family, or some friends. Though he was going to do that last night, but he just fell right asleep," he tells her.

They continue to talk for a while longer and finish their breakfast. Malakai leaves the kitchen and goes back to their bedroom to prepare for work. Shawna stays in the kitchen preparing his lunch. They meet at the front door, and she hands him his lunchbox.

"Have a wonderful day, my love," she tells him.

"You too, my dear," he replies.

She holds his hand and walks him out the door.

"Are you sure you don't want to wake him? I can take him with me," he asks.

"No, no, we'll be just fine. Let him sleep. I'll call you when he wakes," she tells him.

He walks off to his truck. She stays out front to see him off like she does every morning without fail. A couple more hours pass before Isaiah wakes up. He lies in the bed for a while; he is in no hurry as he is enjoying the feeling of being rested. He eventually gets out of bed and walks to the bathroom. Shawna can hear that he is up. She walks toward his direction and meets him outside the bathroom.

"How did you sleep, dear?" she asks.

"Good, really good. I really need that," he tells her.

"Good to hear. Would you like some coffee and breakfast?" she offers.

"Yeah, definitely, please," he says.

They walk to the kitchen.

"Is Mali still asleep?" Isaiah asks.

"Oh no, dear, he is at work," she chuckles a little.

"Oh, right, of course, yeah. My sense of time is a little off right now," he tells her.

She serves him coffee with muffins and eggs.

"Thank you so much for this," he expresses.

"No problem, eat up. Let me know if you would like anything else?" she tells him.

He finishes his breakfast as they continue to talk.

"What is your plan, dear?" she asks.

"Well, if I can borrow a phone, then I can call my sister and arrange for a pickup," he tells her.

She gets out of her seat and goes for her phone. As she returns, she texts Malakai, like she told him she would. She finishes the text and hands the phone to Isaiah.

"Thank you," he says as he grabs it.

"I'm going to call my sister, and oh, can I get this address please?" he asks.

"Oh, that is wonderful. She will be happy to hear from you," she says as she gets up from the table to grab a pencil and some paper.

"Yeah, well, it is the only number I have memorized, so…" He pauses to dial. The phone rings on the other end.

"You asshole, I have been waiting all night, last night, this morning. Why didn't you call me when you said you would? Where are you? Are you okay? I've got Brad here with me, and you're in trouble."

He takes the phone from his ear to his hand.

"Sorry," he tells her.

Shawna smiles as she finishes writing the address. She can hear every word from across the table. She raises her eyebrows and stand up.

"I'll give you some privacy," she says as she walks out of the room.

* * * * *

The big day has arrived for Sherri and her friends to sign the lease to their new apartment. Their plan is to wake up early, grab some morning beverages, and be at the complex for an 8:00 a.m. appointment. The drive the to the new apartment is about a half hour away from where Sherri currently lives, but they are picking Brodie up on the way. Becca stayed with Sherri the night to ensure shed be on time. Brodie is ready when they arrive at his place.

"Let's get some breakfast," he suggests.

"That is not part of the plan, sorry. Breakfast after," Sherri tells him.

"Here, we got you a drink though," Becca hands him his morning beverage.

"Could just hit a drive through, really fast, on the way," he suggests.

"We are right on schedule, breakfast after," Sherri reminds him.

"Besides, there are no drive-throughs on the freeway," Becca adds.

"We won't lose—"

"No!" they both yell, cutting him off.

"You guys ain't right," he tells them with displeasure.

"You should have eaten at home," Becca tells him.

They arrive at the apartment complex and park the car. All three get out of the car with smiles on their faces, except for Brodie, who is hungry. There is a sense of growth and freedom for Sherri. This isn't a new feeling for Brodie and Becca, though, as they were previously sharing an apartment together before this one. The girls have also brought along their dogs to introduce them to their new home. They both call their dogs out of the car. Kiara and Franky jump out of the car. They move around with excitement, but not for the same reason as their owners. They all walk into the leasing office and are greeted by the leasing agent. They exchange pleasantries.

"Please have a seat," the agent offers.

The girls tell each of their dogs to sit. They make small talk as the agent prepares the paperwork.

"I have two dogs myself," the agent tells them.

They close the dog conversation and then begin the paperwork.

"So I just need to go over some information with you. Then get some signatures from the three of you, and I can officially hand you the keys," the agent tells them.

They spend about twenty minutes going over the paperwork, then they each take a turn signing the lease. The agent hands them all keys to their new apartment.

Sherri has an exceptionally large smile on her face as they walk toward their new apartment. They make their way up to the seventh floor. They have nothing with them currently because their intent was to sign and then move later that day. They reach the apartment door. Sherri unlocks it and walks in first. They walk in slowly as the dog's race by them into the house. They start slow, but they quickly pick up the pace and begin to run around the apartment in celebration. Sherri decides to go outside onto the balcony to get a view of the river that sits right outside their apartment building. She sees that just a small walk gets her to the riverbank.

Only trees and a jogging/biking path stand between them and the river. One at a time, her friends join her outside. First Brodie then Becca. The dogs join them outside as well. They all take in the sights for a moment and then gather for a group hug.

Becca breaks the hug. "I have something for us," she says. She runs inside and gets to her bag. She pulls out a bottle of tequila.

"Come inside!" she yells at them.

Sherri sees the bottle and grins. "Oh my god, it's still morning," Sherri says.

"And this is a celebration, bitches!" replies Becca.

"You know I'm down, and it looks like you don't have a choice," says Brodie as he looks at Sherri.

"What did I get myself into?" Sherri yells out.

"The best time of your life!" Becca yells back. They all laugh.

Brodie proposes a toast. "To friendships, freedom, fun, and to us!"

"Yeah!" the girls shout excitedly.

They each take their shot and then slam their glass on the table with painful expressions on their faces.

"Another," Becca suggests.

"No WAY!" yells Sherri. She quickly moves away from the others.

"Where are you going?" asks Brodie.

"We should go check out the rooms. I'm going to go claim mine," she tells them as she runs upstairs.

Brodie and Becca look at each other and chase after her to claim their rooms as well.

* * * * *

The sun is shining through the drapes, hitting Jason in the face. He turns his head to avoid the light. He reaches across the bed to feel for Delaney. He feels nothing, so he moves his arms across the other side of the bed. He opens one eye and sees that she isn't lying there. He opens the other to confirm. He lifts his head slightly and looks around. He sees her curled up against the window ledge, drinking her coffee, overlooking the city.

"Hey, sexiness, what are you doing over there?" he asks her.

She looks over at him and smiles. "It looks beautiful out there, the ocean," she tells him.

Jason scoots up into the sitting position on the bed. "Why don't you come back over here?" he asks her.

"I got you a coffee also," she responds.

Not the response for which he was hoping. "Did you sleep well?" he asks.

"Yes, I did," she says.

He gets out of bed naked and walks over to his coffee. He picks it up to gauge the temperature and goes for a drink. He walks over to her and puts his hand on her shoulder. She looks up at him and smiles again.

He runs his hand through her hair. "You know I love you, right?" he tells her.

"Yes, I do." She looks back out the window.

"What's wrong, D?"

There is a pause between them.

She takes a sip of her coffee. "Well, nothing we haven't talked about before. It's just that I'm tired of hiding and lying whenever she is around. I think it hits me harder in times like this when we are alone and don't have to hide. I get a sense of what it would be like if we were free. That's all. It is what it is," she explains.

He nods. "I don't want to lie to—"

She cuts him. "You don't have to, I get it. I've always gotten it. That doesn't mean that certain emotions won't come up from time to time. I'll be fine," she tells him.

He walks away and goes to the bathroom. "Do you want to get breakfast in or go out for it?" he shouts from the bathroom.

"Let's go out. It's bright and sunny out," she responds.

He walks back to her and grabs her by the chin. "Look, I know that this arrangement is difficult, but I am doing the best that I can. And in the spirit of that effort, I do have a surprise for you."

She smiles.

"You should expect on it Thursday or Friday. I think you will really enjoy it," he tells her.

"I'm looking forward to it," she says as he gestures her for a kiss.

* * * * *

"So some of us were talking about going to bar for a bit," Hayley tells Elise.

Elise looks at her with a puzzled expression. "That's not a bad idea," she says.

"Awesome, let's do it."

"But we got some shit to do first," Elise reminds Hayley.

"What, really, like what?" Hayley asks.

"Listen, why don't you guys go ahead, I'll finish up, then I'll meet you'll there."

"Works for me." Hayley turns around and heads to her room.

"Where is Becky," she says softly. She pulls her phone out to dial her, no answer. She goes back to her room.

Hayley and a group of angels meet in the lobby.

"Is this everyone?" Jed asks.

"There are others, but they will meet us there," Lisa tells Jed.

"How far is this place?" Serena asks.

"The front desk said we can walk," Jed says.

"That doesn't answer my question. I don't want to walk far, or at all, actually," Serena says.

"It's really nice out," Kelly tells her.

"Okay, well I'm gonna walk. If anyone wants to drive, do it. But no driving back," Hayley says.

"Ugh, I'll just walk also," Serena says.

They walk out of the hotel lobby.

"Wait up, wait!" the group hears behind them.

They stop and turn around.

"Becky, nice," Aiden says.

"No, I'm not going yet. I was looking for Elise. Thought she was with you guys," she explains.

"No, she is meeting up later," Hayley tells her.

"Okay, I'll find her. I'll call her," she tells the group.

The group continues to the bar.

Elise's phone rings It's Brad. "Hey, Brad."

"No, what's up?"

"What, no way, wow."

"Redmond, okay, we are on way." She hangs up and runs across the hall to Hayley's room. She knocks but gets no answer.

"Shit, she must have left already," she says aloud. She goes down the hall knocking on doors to see if anyone is around. She finally gets one.

A door opens. "Ernesto! Oh, good. We got to go," she tells him.

"Okay, where to?"

"Redmond. Z is alive. We have to go pick him up," she says.

"What the shit!" Ernesto yells.

"Hurry, get ready, you're driving," she tells him.

"Cool, give me two minutes," he requests.

"I'm gonna find another angel. Meet me down in the lobby," she tells him. She moves on to knock on more doors. Finding no one else on that floor, she goes down one more floor. Another door opens.

"Bella, great."

"Hey, Elise."

"Listen we got to go. Z is alive. We have to go pick him up in Redmond ASAP.

"Holy shit, he made it. That is awesome," she says.

"Look, meet me down in the lobby in five minutes. Ernesto should be down there already. I'll see you down there," she tells Bella.

She runs back upstairs to her room to grab some items. Ernesto gets out of the elevator and goes into the lobby. He finds Becky on her phone.

"Hey, Beck. Have you heard?" he asks.

"Heard what?"

"Z is alive!"

"Oh, wow, no way," she says.

"Yeah, Elise just told me. We are heading out to go pick him up right now. I'm waiting for her. She was looking for someone else, maybe you?"

"Um, I could, but I'm working on something else right now," she tells him. The elevator bell chimes. It's Elise. She walks up Ernesto and Becky.

"Hey, Becky, Z—"

"I know, Ernesto just told me. If you could, though, Paloma is on her way with more angels. Help them get settled in, and let Hayley know about Z. I'll call her, but just in case," she instructs Becky.

"Will do," she replies.

"Ernesto, you want to grab the car. I'll wait for Bella."

"On it."

* * * * *

Elise and the angels arrive at Malakai's house. Isaiah comes out to greet them. Bella jumps out of the car and runs to Isaiah; she throws herself into his arms. Elise is the next one out of the car. She walks up to Isaiah but must wait because Bella is still hugging him. She decides not to wait any longer and hugs them both. As the driver, Ernesto takes a little longer to get off the car. He doesn't run; he takes it easy and lets the girls have their moment.

Shawna comes outside and stands on the front porch watching their reunion. She smiles, happy for Isaiah. She is curious at why the angels keep repeating that they can't believe that Isaiah is still alive. Ernesto reaches Isaiah, and they hug.

Shawna hears Ernesto say the same thing, "Glad you're alive, man."

As they continue to embrace, Isaiah looks up at Shawna. "Guys, this is Shawna. This is her home."

They all introduce themselves.

"Her husband is Malakai. He is the man who picked me up, out there in the forest."

The angels thank Shawna profusely for saving and helping their friend.

"Well, we should get going then," Elise tells Isaiah.

Isaiah looks up at Shawna. "Yeah, almost. Shawna has prepared lunch for us. I told her that you would be staying for lunch, so…"

"Ah, I see," Elise says. She pauses a moment.

"Well, I suppose it's the least we can do to thank you for helping our friend, right?" she says.

Ernesto and Bella seem to be more than okay with the invite.

"Oh, wonderful," says Shawna as she claps her hands.

"Cool then," Isaiah adds.

"Come on in please," Shawna says as she opens the screen door. They all walk into the house.

"You know that us being here puts her in danger, right?" Elise tells Isaiah in a soft voice.

"I know, but they, she insisted, and I promised them. They are curious about us. Even though she's the one feeding us, we are showing our gratitude by staying to eat," he explains.

"I get it, but we shouldn't stay to long. We eat, and we are out," she tells him.

"Got it," he replies.

Shawna passes them on her way to the kitchen. "Please make yourselves at home," Shawna tells the angels.

Elise looks at Ernesto. "Do a perimeter check."

"On it," Ernesto replies.

"Have you told her anything about us?" Bella asks.

"Some, they had questions, but I kept it vague. I wouldn't be surprised if she asks more questions from you all. She is deeply religious, though."

"Oh, fun," Elise replies. Elise steps into another room for a moment to call Brad.

Shawna comes back into the living room, lunch is almost ready, would anyone like something to drink?" she asks before she realizes that there are two angels missing.

"Where are your friends?" she asks.

"Elise is on the phone in another room and Ernesto is outside," he tells her.

"Is he coming back?" she asks.

"Yes, yes, he just had to get something out of the car," he tells her.

"Okay, what can I get you to drink dear?" she asks Bella.

"Oh, some sort of juice would be fine."

"I've got orange juice," Shawna tells her.

"That will work."

"Shawna, we can all have orange juice," Isaiah tells her.

Elise walks back into the room.

"Okay, updated Brad, so we are good there."

Shawna returns to the living room. "Okay, lunch is ready. Come on now."

The three angels follow Shawna to the kitchen.

"Your other friend back from the car yet?" Shawna asks.

"No, not yet. He will be in soon," Isaiah tells her.

* * * * *

Two devils pull out binoculars to get a closer view. A third calls Sara to report. Sara sits around a table with devils discussing a portion of their plan when her phone rings.

"Yeah," she answers.

"We are in a town called Redmond. We followed some angels out here—Elise and a couple of others. It looks like they are here to pick up Isaiah," the devil reports.

"Isaiah, huh, so he survived as well, interesting. Stay with them and report as soon as they make their next move. He may have the halo," she instructs them.

The devils sit around discussing how Isaiah got there, and if he was there, when they attacked the jet.

"Was he hiding somewhere in or around the jet?" devil number 2 asks.

"He didn't survive the attack because he wasn't there. We did a sweep of the area," says devil number 1.

"If he was there, it's not like an angel to just hide, while other angels are getting slaughtered," says devil number 4.

"Listen, the attack happened over the forest. He is in Redmond now, getting picked up. Why come all the way out here?" asks devil number 5.

He must have jumped out of the jet after it got hit," devil number 3 suggests.

They think about it for a second.

"If he did jump, why would he and why only him?" devil number 6 asks.

"Look at him. He is dirty and looks beat up. He would've had to have landed in the forest, found his way out."

"Hold on, there's an old lady coming out of the house also. It must be her house. Do any of you recognize her?" devil number 5 asks.

They each take a turn looking. None of them recognize the old lady.

"Is she an angel?" asks devil number 3.

"Some of them live out in this area also," says devil number 2.

"I got it. He obviously had a parachute, but I'm thinking he jumped after the halo. I'll bet the halo fell out of the jet and he went after it," devil number 6 theorizes.

"That makes sense," says devil number 4.

"We thought the halo was in the jet, then we thought Rudy took it from the jet. Neither of those was right," says devil number 2.

"He must have caught up to the halo. What if he has the halo on him right now?" asks devil number 6.

"Yeah, you might be right," devil number 1 tells him.

"Don't you guys think they would have sent more angels to pick him up if he had the halo?" asks devil number 5.

They think about it for a moment. Devil number 5 has doubts about Isaiah having the halo on him.

"Look, they know we are watching them," he tells the group.

"You don't think he has the halo, do you?" devil number 3 asks devil number 5.

"No, I don't."

"What do the rest of you think?" asks devil number 3.

"They did send Elise to pick him up," devil number 2 points out.

One by one they give their answer.

Devil number 3 takes a count, "One, two, three, four, and I'm five," he says.

"All right, Luis [devil number 5], looks like it's 5-1."

"Are you guys thinking about going in there?" Luis asks the group.

They look around at one another.

"That's a bad move. We don't know for sure," Luis reminds them.

"This is a good time to strike. If they have it, Jason would reward us big-time," devil number 1 tells the group.

"You guys even going to check with Sara?" Luis asks.

"Naw, she even said that he might have it. I say we just do it," says devil number 1.

"Let's do it," confirms devil number 6.

* * * * *

Vanessa lifts her head up from the couch. She has dozed off for a while, as she is still emotionally exhausted. She lies her head back down and draws the attention of Leann, who is in the kitchen getting the others some drinks. Vanessa lifts her head again and sees Kyleigh and Uriah playing a game of cards.

"Hey, sleepyhead," Leann calls Vanessa from across the room.

Uriah and Kyleigh look back.

"How long was I out?" Vanessa asks.

"I'd say about two hours," Uriah tells her.

"You feeling better?" Kyleigh asks her.

"Yeah, a little better," Vanessa tells the group.

"You want to join us?" Uriah asks her.

"No, thanks, I'm going to use the restroom," Vanessa says.

As she walks toward the restroom, a phone rings.

Leann recognizes that it's hers, so she grabs it. "Hey, Dad."

There is a pause.

"Uh, yes. Vanessa's in the restroom, but they are both here."

Vanessa hears her name and returns to check on why.

"What's up?" Vanessa asks.

"It's my dad. He's asking for you and Uriah," she tells them.

"Dad, I'm putting the phone on speaker."

Vanessa comes to the table.

"Hello, angels," Nate greets them.

"Dad, you should know that Danny and Kyleigh are here also," she informs him.

"Ah, hey, angels. I have some great news."

They all freeze for a moment.

"What is it, Dad?" Leann asks excitedly.

"Uriah, Vanessa, you will be most excited to know that Isaiah is alive."

Uriah stands up. Vanessa looks at Uriah. Kyleigh stares at her sister. They are all quiet.

"Did you guys hear me?" Nate asks.

"Yes, we heard you," Leann tells her father. She claps her hands and jumps then turns to hug Danny.

"What, oh my god," Kyleigh says continuously.

Uriah and Vanessa embrace each other as Vanessa bursts into tears. Kyleigh gets out of her seat to join the hug. Leann and Danny break from their hug to join the others.

"Ah, man, this is awesome," Uriah says.

"Angels, listen, I don't have many details, but I can tell you that he will be connecting with Elise at some point, if he hasn't already. Soon after that, he will be coming home."

"This is so exciting," Kyleigh says.

"Hang tight, angels. I'll let you know when he is back in town."

Nate hangs up the phone, and the five angels continue to hug.

"Isn't this great news, sis?" Kyleigh asks.

Vanessa gathers her thoughts. "Yes, of course. I'm so happy. I still need to pee. I'll be right back," she tells them.

The four others remain to celebrate. They decide that they should prepare to see Isaiah.

"Listen, I'm going to head back to my place. I'll be by to pick you all up," Kyleigh tells them.

"I'm going to head out also," Danny says.

"Hold on, guys, why don't we just wait until my dad calls? We don't know how long it's going to be," Leann tells them.

* * * * *

Becky walks outside to see the jet arriving. Brad has sent additional angels to help with the efforts in the forest. The jet lands in an open space of the hotel. Becky walks over to the jet as its cabin door opens. She greets the angels as they deplane. Paloma steps out. She pauses a moment when she sees Becky. She makes her way to the ground.

"How is it going?" Paloma asks.

"Well, we have most of the hotel booked, I think. As for the search, well, that's why you're here right?" she jokingly laughs.

Paloma stares at her with confusion as they continue to walk. "Why is that funny?" Paloma asks.

"Well, I was just pointing out the obvious to you. Thought that was funny."

"Right," Paloma says.

"Anyways, I do have some good news. Z is alive."

Paloma stops. "Our Z?" she asks.

"Yeah, Isaiah," Becky confirms.

There is a short pause.

"Well, tell me more!" Paloma shouts.

"Right, well, we just found out about an hour ago, I think. He's in Redmond. Elise and a couple of other angels went to pick him up. That's all we know right now."

"Oh, wow, this is great news. I assume everyone at home knows?"

"Yes, that's how we found out. Z called Noemy, and she started calling everyone else."

They reach the hotel lobby.

"Oh, that is wonderful. So then all that is left is the halo and JR, is that right?"

"Yes, that is correct," Becky says.

"Okay, let's get settled in, and we can talk about next steps," Paloma says as she walks up to the counter. She gets herself checked in and comes back to Becky.

"So who is running point right now?" Paloma asks.

"Um, not sure. Hayley is around, but she and a couple of others are at a bar having some fun, so it looks like it's you," Becky replies.

"What, that can't be. I just got here, and I have no idea where here is," she says with frustration as she shakes her head. How far is Redmond from here?" she asks Becky.

"I don't know. I don't know this area either," Becky says.

Paloma turns to the counter. "Excuse me, how far is Redmond from here?" she asks the front desk.

"It's about a half hour, ma'am, a little less," he tells her.

"Thank you," she responds as she looks back at Becky. "Okay, you said they left about an hour ago. We've been here for about fifteen, so they should be arriving soon, right?"

Becky shrugs her shoulders. Paloma lets out a big sigh.

"I need to get settled in. I need to figure out what's going on. If Hayley is in charge, that is concerning. I think we will need to wait for Elise to return. I'll come check in with you in a bit. Until then, give her a call and find out when they will be back," Paloma commands.

"Will do," Becky responds.

* * * * *

The angels are midway through their lunch. The topic of conversation has been the existence of angels and devils.

"Like I told you yesterday, there is so much more to us, to this, and why I am currently sitting in your house right now," Isaiah tells Shawna.

"Shawna, you have to understand that our presence in your home puts you in danger," Elise tells her.

"You bein' followed?" Shawna asks.

"It's possible. We know that the devils are in the area also," Elise tells her. Elise turns to Isaiah. "We spotted some in the forest while we were recovering the others."

"The others," Isaiah asks with a concerned face.

Bella and Ernesto drop their heads.

"Yeah, uh, some of the angels were killed, Z," Elise tells him.

"How? The crash?" he asks.

"No, actually, they all survived the crash. The devils got to the jet. They were trapped, it appears. They tried to fight their way out. Only Vanessa and Uriah survived," she tells him as she holds his hand.

Isaiah drops his head onto their clinched hands and begins to cry.

"I will pray for your friends," Shawna tells Isaiah.

"I should have been there. I could have helped," Isaiah says with his head buried.

"You did what you had to do, Z," Bella tells him as she gets emotional.

"Yeah, bro, you shouldn't feel guilty. We all would have done the same thing. You did what you had to do to get that halo, man," Ernesto tells him.

Elise looks around at the table.

"I forgot that you have no clue what happened out there. We should finish here and get going," Elise tells the group.

They finish with lunch as Shawna gets up from the table and begins to clear it. The angels stand up as well.

"You boys have a seat. Ladies, you can come with me," Shawna says.

The boys look at each other, shrug their shoulders, and sit again.

"Old-fashioned, are we?" Bella whispers to Elise.

"Yeah, looks like it," she responds.

"I wonder what else she is going to have us do while the boys just sit there," Bella jokes as she glares at the boys.

* * * * *

The devils have the house surrounded. They didn't have much time to think it through, so their main strategy is to surprise the angels and enter from both ends of the house. The angels are inside cleaning up after lunch. Isaiah and Ernesto have moved to the living room and Elise and Bella are helping Shawna in the kitchen. Bella is staring out the window as she washes and rinses the dishes. She sees something go across the window. She gets on her toes to get closer to the window. She sees the back of a devil making his way to the back of the house. She puts a cup down and grabs a hand towel.

"Elise, devils outside." Elise looks up at her, then she looks at Shawna.

"Stay with her," she tells Shawna as she leaves the kitchen.

"What's going on?" Shawna asks Bella.

"Devils followed us here. Stay with me," Bella tells her.

"Guys, we have devils outside," Elise says as she looks out a window.

The guys get to their feet.

"Shit, they followed us here," Ernesto says.

Three devils position themselves at the back door. Three more at the front door.

"Shawna, are these the only two doors to the house?"

"Yes, the front and the back."

"Okay, we know there is one, but no doubt there are more, and of course, we left our weapons in the car. Shawna, get yourself upstairs please, and lock your door. Take my phone, call, and text Hayley. Give her your address and tell her what's going on. Bella, you position yourself at the stairs and protect her. You two, take the back. I'll cover the front."

Shawna speed walks up the stairs. Bella gets into position, and the guys walk to the back door in the kitchen.

"There are knives and shit we can use in here," Isaiah says.

They look around and grab knives. Outside, devil number 2 checks the door.

"It's unlocked," he tells the other two. Ernesto sees the doorknob move.

"Let's get set," he tells Isaiah.

Up front the three devils line up at the door. Devil number 3 is closest. He checks to hear for something inside. Both groups coordinate their entry. Ernesto walks up to Isaiah.

"Hey, I'm gonna go out the window of a bedroom, catch them from behind."

"Good move," Isaiah says.

Ernesto leaves the kitchen. The front door opens slowly. Elise is standing right behind it. It opens about halfway when Elise kicks it, hitting devil number 3 in the face. Does little to the devil but surprise him. Devils number 4 and number 6 shoot their crossbows into the house. Elise takes cover. They reload as number 3 gathers himself. The door remains open so they can see inside. Elise comes out and runs at devil number 3 and jumps with a knee to his chest. It knocks number 3 into the devils behind him then to the ground.

Devils number 4 and number 6 remain on their feet. She turns to number 3 on the ground and kicks him in the face. She is now close enough that the other two devils don't have comfortable shooting space. At the back, Isaiah doesn't know how many devils to expect, but he knows that Ernesto will approach from the rear.

I've got to take them right away, he thinks.

The devils bust through the door, crossbows drawn. Isaiah sees one pass then lunges out at the next one leading with the knives to his neck. The devil grabs at him with his opposite arm as they fall to the ground. Number 1 turns to see then continues further into the house. With the action in front him, Luis stops and takes aim.

He shoots at Isaiah, but Isaiah shields himself with the dead devil. Ernesto gets to the door, drawing Luis's attention. Luis tries to reload but doesn't have enough time before Ernesto engages him.

Number 1 continues through the house. Bella peeks into the hallway and sees number 1 approaching. She pulls back and waits for him to reach her. Right as he does, she lunges off the third step leading with an elbow to the head. It throws him against the wall and causes him to drop his crossbow. He defends himself from the barrage of elbows to his head until he gets an opening to counter with a punch to Bella's chest.

She falls back onto the stairs, holding her chest, gasping for air. He hovers over and begins to choke her. Bella grabs at the devil's wrist with both hands attempting to detach them. Isaiah gets up from the floor and sees Ernesto fighting with Luis and struggling.

"No, go help the girls!" Ernesto yells to Isaiah.

He hesitates, conflicted about leaving him. He pulls the knives out of the devil's neck, puts them in his back pockets, and grabs the crossbow. He trots through the kitchen and sees a devil hovering over Bella. He raises the crossbow and shoots at number 1 piercing him through the side. The devil releases his grip of Bella and falls off. Isaiah extends his hand to Bella to help her up.

"Elise," Bella calls out with a hoarse throat.

"I'll go. You stay here," Isaiah tells Bella.

At the front, devils number 4 and number 6 have managed to fight Elise back into the house. Number 3 gets off the ground grabs his crossbow and tries to shoot at Elise. He doesn't get a clear shot. "You two take care of her, I'll go look for the halo," he tells them.

Isaiah gets to the front where he sees Elise. He takes aim.

"A devil got past me, in the house somewhere. Find him!" Elise shouts.

Before he goes to find the loose devil, he takes a shot at number 6 but only catches his forearm.

"Shit."

"Go!" Elise yells.

Upstairs, Shawna tries to call Hayley but keeps getting her voice mail. She comes down the stairs to see Bella and sees a devil lying at the bottom of the stairs.

"Oh my, what is that?" She turns to Bella.

"Shouldn't we just call the police?"

"No, that would just put them in danger."

Shawna grips the phone. "Well, this Hayley girl isn't answering."

"Just keep trying."

"Oh shit," she sees number 1 get up, with a bolt stick out of his side.

"Please get back upstairs and lock your door," Bella instructs.

Number 1 grabs at Bella, and she attempts to kick him off. They are powerful, so when he grabs an ankle, he pulls her onto her back, down the stairs. He drags her onto the floor and mounts her. He begins to punch her repeatedly. Number 3 comes into view and figures number 1 is about to kill Becca, so he goes upstairs.

Elise has managed to dislodge the flail from number 6 and use it against him. He now lies over the couch dead. With a weapon and the odds even, she takes little time to dispose of number 4. Isaiah gets back to the stairs and sees that Bella is mounted again. With two knives in hand, he charges at number 1 and lunges at him, striking him on both sides of his upper chest, then landing on him. The devil looks up, and Isaiah knees him in the face. He pulls both knife out and stabs number 1 on each side of the neck. Bella is slow to get up.

She uses the wall as a crutch. "Shawna!" she shouts as she stumbles to the stairs.

Isaiah gets up and goes to the kitchen to find Ernesto sitting at the table hunched over.

"Ernesto," he shuffles to him. Ernesto lifts his head and leans back. He is holding one wound with another exposed. Upstairs the devil has broken into Shawna's bedroom. Bella reaches the second floor. Elise runs to the kitchen; she sees Isaiah and Ernesto.

"Upstairs, Shawna and Bella!" Isaiah shouts.

Elise turns and sprints to the stairs.

"Go, go help her. Can't let Shawna get hurt, go," Ernesto shouts.

"What about you?" Isaiah asks.

"Go! I'll be fine," he says as he lays his head against the table.

Shawna has been hiding under her bed, and although number 3 knows she is in the house, his interest is in finding the halo. Shawna is covering her mouth as she breathes heavily. Number 3 gets to his knees and looks under the bed, pointing the crossbow at her.

"Ahhh!" Shawna lets out a loud scream.

Bella gets to her room and sees that the devil is about to grab her. She runs at the devil. He rolls onto his back and aims his crossbow, shooting Bella in the arm. She falls to the ground. Number 3 gets to his feet and walks to Bella. Elise reaches the room and sees Bella on the ground and number 3 standing over her. Number 3 pulls out his flail and begins to swing it.

Elise engages the devil. They battle as Isaiah gets to the room.

"Bella." He goes to her side.

"Help her. I'm fine Bella tells him. She begins to scoot over to Shawna. Isaiah gets up, runs, and slides at number 3, slicing both of his calves with both knives. The devil lets out a loud growl. Isaiah gets to his feet. Carelessly the devil faces Elise and continues to swing his flail at her. She kicks him back into Isaiah as he drives both knives into his back. Number 3 reaches back for the knives as he walks in front of the window. Elise runs and drop kicks him through the window, sending him to the ground causing the knife to continue through his body. The angels look out the window.

"Come on out," Bells invites Shawna.

"Are you okay?" she asks.

Shawna is visibly shaken by what she has just witnessed.

"Here, come over here and sit," Bella offers.

"I'm going to make sure that's all of them," Elise says.

"I'll go check on Ernie," Isaiah says.

Bella keeps Shawna upstairs until she gets an "all clear" from Elise. Isaiah walks into the kitchen and finds Ernesto hunched over again.

"Oh man, Ernie." Ernesto leans back in the chair.

"Hey," he says softly.

"You've lost a lot of blood," he tells him.

"We're all clear!" Elise yells throughout the house.

Bella and Shawna make their way back downstairs to the kitchen.

* * * * *

Sherri and her friends arrive at the new apartment building with all their belongings in two moving trucks. They have also enlisted the help of some of their friends. Brodie gets out to coordinate the positioning of the trucks for unloading. While they wait, Sherri and Becca take a group of friends up to the new apartment for a quick peak. Brodie gets the trucks positioned and begins to unload. He and others run items up the apartment.

"You guys are welcome to help unload now," Brodie tells the folks in the apartment.

"Yeah, yeah, we got you," Becca replies.

"Hey, let's get this mattress," Sherri suggests to Becca.

"Uh, no," Becca reacts.

"Why not? We can use this wheel thing," Sherri suggests.

"Or we can have the guys get it. They can carry all the heavy shit. That's why we brought them," suggests Becca.

"Come on, we can do this," Sherri replies with encouragement.

They set the mattress on the mini trolleys and guide the mattress toward the elevator. They stop to adjust it.

"It was awfully thoughtful of your boyfriend to lend you a hand moving today," Becca says.

"Please don't start," Sherri begs Becca.

"I'm just saying, he is super sweet for helping out today. That's a compliment," Becca adds.

"You mean sarcasm. Learn the difference," Sherri tells her.

Brodie was in earshot of the conversation. "I'm not surprised," he says as he walks by them.

"You both need to stop right now," she commands. Brodie stops and turns around with a smile.

"Break is over, it's not like either of you brought boyfriends to help," he says.

"He is busy, okay?" Sherri says in Matt's defense.

"We actually prefer that he wasn't around. We all have much more fun without him around," Becca says. Sherri stands with a sad expression on her face.

"Honey, we are just giving you crap," Becca says.

"I know, but this is supposed to be a joyful day for me, for us. I don't need these reminders," Sherri tells Becca.

"You're right. I'm sorry. I'm done. Let's get this inside." Sherri had asked Matt to help her move several weeks ago. He told her that he would. Deep down, there was a part of her that expected this from him. She just didn't care for the reminder on a day that is supposed to be exciting for her. He told her two days before the move that he had a basketball game. Although she knows it's true, she also knows that the game is only about an hour long and he can very easily come right over to help after. She knows that he would much rather hang out with his friends than to help her move.

* * * * *

Isaiah and Shawna join the other angels downstairs. They go to the kitchen where Bella and Elise are tending to Ernesto's wounds.

"We've to get him some medical attention," Elise tells the others.

"I have some medical supplies. Let me grab them," Shawna offers.

"We have to move him," Elise tells the group.

"I'm gonna be fine. I just need to clean up, but I'm gonna be fine," Ernesto responds.

"Well, we still have to go," Elise tells the group.

Shawna returns with the medical supplies. Elise and Bella grab the medical supplies and address the wounds. Isaiah grabs Shawna by the arm and walks her away from the others.

"Shawna, you have to come with us. It's too dangerous for you here."

"Oh, I ain't going anywhere, Isaiah. This is my home. No devils, or whoever these guys are, are gonna scare me from my home. I'm staying put," Shawna responds.

"Shawna, please, there are many more, and they may come back here."

"I'm not going anywhere, Isaiah. Besides, Mali will be home soon. Can't leave him either."

"He can come with us also, please, Shawna," Isaiah pleads.

"It's sweet of you to be concerned, but this is our home. Daemons or devils can't scare us away," she tells him as she rubs his cheek.

"Please, Shawna," he pleads some more.

"I'm gonna go clean up," Shawna leaves the kitchen. Isaiah turns toward the other angels. "Fuck, I shouldn't have come here," he says.

"You can't be surprised, Z," Bella says.

"I can't leave her here or him," Isaiah says.

"Listen, Z, I'll have some angels come out here, watch over them," Elise offers.

Isaiah nod.

"But I got to get you and Ernie home. Bella, call Hayley. Get a group out here."

"I'll try. Shawna couldn't get ahold of her at all during our fight."

"Get ahold of someone, and arrange for a group to get out here. Z, let's get Ernie in the car," Elise instructs.

Isaiah goes over to help with Ernesto. He and Elise put his arms around their necks and grab his hands to support.

"I'm gonna wait here until the other angels get here," Isaiah tells Elise.

"You can't stay here. You've already been through enough. We have to get you home," Elise responds.

"I can't leave them here alone, Elise. I'll meet up with you when the other angels get here," he tells her.

"We can have Bella stay with them."

"No, Elise, it should be me. It has to be me. I'm the reason they are in this mess," he says as they set Ernesto up against the car.

* * * * *

Becky and Paloma arrive at the bar where Hayley and the other angels are. They walk in cautiously, wondering if they have the right place. Lisa spots them and yells their names. It gets the attention of the other angels and all the patrons in the bar. They walk in to see Serina rocking some "Cruel Summer" by Bananarama. They reach the table and Hayley, and the others greet the ladies.

"You all made it," Kelly says to them.

Paloma doesn't look happy, and she isn't trying to hide it.

"Angels," she greets them with a disturbed tone.

"Grab a seat, P. Have a drink," Hayley offers.

Paloma wastes no time in addressing what she thinks is reckless behavior considering the circumstances.

"I'll have a seat," Becky says as she reaches for the pitcher of beer.

"Why are you guys here when there is work to do?" she tells Hayley.

Aiden repositions himself and grabs his beer to get a better view. He anticipates this exchange will be entertaining.

"What is wrong with what we are doing, Paloma?" Hayley asks.

"Oh, I don't know, where do I start? We have an angel missing in the forest. There are devils in the area, and oh, yes, we have a missing halo. Did I miss anything?" she asks.

Hayley laughs a little and takes a drink of her beer. "Everything is fine."

"Your guard is down, and you have yourself and these angels in a vulnerable position if devils attack," she tells Hayley. Hayley takes another drink. "Elise and I have everything under control," she tells Paloma.

"I see, this must be part of the plan, and where is Elise right now?" Paloma asks.

"Um, back at the hotel with the other angels," she says with confidence.

"Um, no, she's not," Becky chimes in.

"What do you mean she is not?" asks Hayley.

"They have been gone for a while now. She left in a hurry and took Ernesto and Bella with her. She said she was going to Redmond to pick up Z. Oh yeah, Z is alive, y'all," she tells group.

Hayley stands up and pulls her phone out as the other angels react to the news.

"Shit." She realizes it's dead.

"Does anyone have a charger?" she asks the group.

No one has one on them.

"Did Elise call anyone else?" As they check, she walks to the bar and asks the bartender if she has a charger.

"Yeah, I do, just a minute," the bartender says as she goes to the back to retrieve it.

The bartender returns with it and hands it to Hayley. Hayley looks for an outlet.

"All right, everyone, the party is over, wrap it up."

"Come on, Paloma, relax, have a drink," Lisa tells Paloma.

"This isn't what we came here for," she tells Lisa.

Serina finishes her song. She expected some cheers from her table but didn't get any. She looks on and can tell that there is some tension at her table. She hands the mic over to the DJ and walks off the stage to the table.

"Hey, ladies," she says to Paloma and Becky.

"You know, right now you are not our lead," Lisa tells Paloma.

"If I'm here, I am," she responds.

"Come on, Paloma, you know how it works. You brought a team. They report to you. Right now we report to Hayley," Jed reminds her.

"What is going on here?" Serina asks. She looks around. Everyone stays silent. Hayley gets enough power to turn her phone on. She can see that she has some missed calls from Elise and Brad and a text from Elise. She dials her back.

Elise answers, "Dude, where have you been?" Elise asks.

"My phone was dead. I'm charging it now," Hayley explains.

"Listen, you are not going to believe this shit," Elise says.

"What?" asks Hayley.

"Z is alive."

"Yeah, I just found out from Becky."

"And we had some shit to deal with also. We are close to heading back. Are you still at the bar?" she asks.

"Hell yeah, we are. You gonna join us?" she asks.

"Can't, we have some shit to take care of. Ernie's hurt pretty bad, and others are banged up."

Hayley looks over at the table.

"What are you guys talking about?" Serina asks.

"Oh yeah, Z is alive. Elise went to pick him up," Becky catches her up.

"Holy shit. That is great," she expresses.

Hayley finishes her conversation with Elise. She walks over to the table.

"Listen, guys, I have to go, but you guys can stay if you want," she tells the angels. Paloma walks up to Hayley.

"So you're going to leave your team here?" she asks.

"It's up to them," she responds.

"Very nice, we are almost at war and your team is just going to sit around and be drunk and vulnerable," she tells Hayley. Paloma shakes her head as she goes to the exit. Hayley is left silent, questioning her leadership style.

"Don't worry about her, Hayley. We love you," Lisa tells her. She smiles at the table.

* * * * *

Elise, Bella, and Ernesto have returned to Sisters. Isaiah stayed back with Shawna like he insisted. Malakai arrives home. He walks into the house unsuspecting of any abnormal events in his home. He stops at his front door to make sense of the damage to his front door and surrounding area. He walks in and sees additional destruction right away.

My wife is his first thought. He closes the door slowly. Isaiah walks into the living room.

"Hey, Mali." Malakai is stunned.

"Where is my wife?" he asks.

"Shawna!" Isaiah shouts.

"Yeah," she yells back.

"Mali is home."

She makes her way downstairs. "Oh dear, I am so happy to see you," she says as she gives him a hug.

"Are you okay?" he asks with concern.

"Oh yes, I'm fine, dear," she tells him.

"Well then, what the hell happened here?" he asks.

"Maybe you should have a seat," Isaiah suggests.

Malakai looks at his wife, and she nods at him to indicate that he should sit.

"Malakai, first off, I am really terribly sorry that this happened. This is the last thing I wanted for you, your wife, and your home. If you remember, I mentioned a couple of times that telling you who I am, or what I am, could put you in danger, especially coming to your home. Well, today I was able to get ahold of my sister and arrange for a ride back to meet my group. Three other angels came out to pick me up. Shawna was gracious enough to treat my friends to lunch. Shortly after lunch, as far as we know at least five devils came into your house and tried to kill us."

Malakai's eyebrows drop with disbelief.

"My friends and I were able to fight them off—kill them, actually. Some came in through the front, and some came in through the back. Unfortunately, your kitchen looks like this. And there is some damage upstairs."

"Our window is busted out, dear," Shawna adds.

"What the hell!" Malakai shouts.

"Look, it's dangerous for us, or even you guys, to be here right now. The devils could come back. They aren't nice to any humans that associate with us. I asked Shawna to return with us, but she wouldn't."

"I'm not leaving home," Shawna says.

Malakai shakes his head in agreement.

"I wanted to stay behind just in case," Isaiah says.

"Wow, that's quite the event." He gets up to walk around.

"I want to make sure you two are safe. Please consider coming with me," Isaiah asks.

"My wife is right: this is our home, and no devils or nothing is gonna scare us off."

"Geez, you two sound like twins," Isaiah says.

"We are staying put," Malakai adds.

"Well, after talking with Shawna and expecting you to feel the same, I need to make sure you guys aren't harmed any further. So I've got a team coming out here to watch over you. They are going to help get your home repaired as well. All expenses are on me. They will stick around for a while just to ensure you're safe."

"We don't need all that, son," Malakai expresses.

"Listen, I don't know what would have happened out there when you found me. I was tired, dehydrated, hungry. I owe you. You brought me here, fed me, put me up. I owe you. I'm not going to let anything happen you because you two decided to open your hearts and home to me. Once the house is repaired, if the angels make you uncomfortable, then we can reposition them, but they will be watching your house," Isaiah tells them.

"You're a good kid, Z." Malakai laughs in disbelief.

"Well, it would be nice to get some help with the house. I can't do it, and Mali can only do so much these days," Shawna adds.

"In addition to that, expect a check in the mail from me, or maybe I'll come back down soon to check on you and hand it to you."

"A check for what?" Shawna asks.

"Angels are incredibly grateful to those that go out of their way to help us. We are very generous with our form of appreciation. So you will be receiving a sizable amount in the form of a check, maybe cash, not sure which. I'll have to see how Nate does it," Isaiah explains.

"Who is Nate?" Malakai asks.

"He is the leader of the angels. Super sweet guy," Isaiah says.

"Well, I'm gonna settle in and check out the rest of the house," Malakai says.

"Be extra careful, dear," Shawna cautions.

"Just a reminder that, uh, there are five dead devils here. They are piled in the backyard," Isaiah reminds him.

"Right, devils, you say. Can't wait to see that," Malakai says.

"Yeah, remember, our enemies. I told you about them. Maybe now you will believe what I was telling you about the angels and the devils."

* * * * *

Luis finishes getting himself cleaned up from the fight. He goes around looking for some food while he waits for Sara to return. He finds some fruit lying around. Eventually, Sara arrives. He sees her pull up. He goes to the door then stops.

Eh, I'll just let her come in here, he thinks.

Sara gets out of her car and walks in a different direction.

"Ah, shit," he says. He goes to the door. "Sara!" he calls out. She turns to look. She gestures to give her a minute. He leaves the door open. A couple of minutes pass, and she walks in.

"So what do you got?" she asks.

"Nothing good, I'm the only one that made it back," he tells her.

"What? How? Why?" she asks.

"The others got it in their heads that they had the halo in that house. I was the only one who objected. They took a vote, decided to attack. I objected again, but they were all in. They wanted to be the heroes, surprise you, and impress Jason. I went along, bailed after I killed an angel, but, uh," he explains.

"I gave no order," she states.

"I know, I reminded them. They had already decided it. It was Gino who got everyone else riled up. I suggested we call you first, but they didn't want to, and they were moving fast," he continues.

"Goddamn it," she says as she paces around.

"Well, it actually doesn't hurt us or change anything. They got what they deserve for not obeying," she tells him.

"What now?" he asks.

"I'm gonna call Franco soon and get us out of here. This mission is shit. It's going to take forever to find the halo. We are wasting our time here. I think the halo is in the river. That's where we need to focus, but that has to be someone else. I have to get out of here," she tells him.

"What about me?" he asks.

"I'll take you back with me. Franco keeps talking about this plan that Jason has, but no one knows what the hell it is. What I do know is that we need to do something different. Jason isn't even in the country. None of this makes sense. I'm starting to understand why Ty feels the way he does," she says.

"What does that mean?" Luis asks.

"He has been upset lately with the way Jason has operated. He is losing confidence in him. He thinks that he's gone soft on the angels. Someone like Ty is a killing machine. He needs to be out there killing angels. Part of his frustration is that he doesn't even care about the halo. He just wants to kill angels in any manner. Anyways, he's on Jason's shit list right now, and Crystal's got this bull's-eye on him."

Luis stares at her. "I know there are others that share his sentiment," he tells her.

"Yeah, I know, and that is a little disturbing," she responds.

* * * * *

Malakai is in the living room picking up destroyed home furnishings. He is moving slowly as he tries to visualize what took place in his home. He hears a car pull up to the house. He goes to the window. He sees three vehicles park out front. He remembers Isaiah telling him to expect friends, but he didn't make clear how many. Malakai wonders if it might be the devils again, especially in three vehicles with blacked-out windows.

"Hey, Z!" he yells back.

Isaiah comes to the front of the house. "Yeah, what's up?" he asks.

"I hope those are your friends out there," he says with some concern.

Isaiah walks to the window. "Yeah, good they are here," he confirms. He opens the door and walks outside.

Shawna walks into the living room to check on Malakai.

"His friends are here," he tells his wife.

"All right, well, maybe now is a good time for me to start dinner then," she responds.

They look at each other and walk outside. Isaiah walks up with his friends.

"Everyone, this is Malakai and his wife, Shawna. I got them into this mess, and now we have to make things right. This is Kelsey, Rafael, Danny, and Janie," Isaiah tells the couple.

"You can call me Raf."

"Pleasure to meet y'all," Malakai says.

"Likewise," Kelsey replies.

"Why three vehicles for four of you?" Malakai asks.

"Oh, never mind him," Shawna slaps Malakai on the arm.

"Just askin'."

"Well, fair question. Um, the car is for Z, and the other two will stay with us. We understand that there is some work to be done. So we wanted to make sure we had the space to do it," Janie explains.

"So what's the plan here?" Rafael asks.

"All right, well, you're going to repair any damage that was caused. Mainly in here and the kitchen, but there was some action in the hallway, stairs, and upstairs. Basically, whatever they tell you needs fixing. Mali, Shawna now is a good opportunity to add some projects you've wanted but haven't been able to. Well, take care of that as well."

Shawna stares at Malakai as he raises his eyebrows.

"Second, there are five bodies in the back. Please dispose of them."

"What you gonna do with them?" Malakai asks.

"We have a thing," Danny says.

Malakai and Shawna look confused.

"Third, protect them and this house. Not sure if devils will return, but stay ready," Isaiah says.

"You're in good hands. We will take care of you and your home," Kelsey tells the couple.

"Is there anything else, Z?" Janie asks.

"No, just, um, these people are very important to me. Please take care of them," he asks.

"Got it, bro," Danny confirms.

"Okay, well, these are for you." She tosses the car keys at him. "And so is this." She tosses a cell phone at him.

"The address to the hotel is in there, map it. It has Elise, Hayley, and my number in it."

"All right, I should get going then," Isaiah tells the group.

"Malakai, Shawna, do you mind if we take a look around so we can get started?" Rafael asks.

"Go right ahead," Shawna tells them.

The four angels walk out of the living room to various parts of the house.

"I'm gonna come back and see you soon. I have to go home first, so maybe in about a week or so. Thanks, you two both, so much. You don't understand what you have done for me." He goes in for some hugs.

"Well, son, it's been interesting around here, to say the least. I wish you the best out there. Look forward to seeing ya again," Malakai says.

"Please take care of yourself, Isaiah," Shawna tells him.

* * * * *

Sherri and Becca are unpacking their apartment while Brodie is out with friends. Becca is unpacking in the living room listening to music. There is a knock at the door, but she doesn't hear it. It's the barking of the dogs that prompts her to check the door.

"Okay, okay, I hear it," Becca tells the dogs. She looks through the peephole and sees that it's Matt.

"Fuck," she says softly. She slowly backs away from the door. He knocks again. Dogs continue to bark. She tells the dogs to hush as she continues to back away, hoping that Matt will think no one is home and he will go away. He knocks again, this time he rings the doorbell. Kiara continues to bark at the door while Franky just stares at it. Sherri couldn't hear the knocks but can barely hear the doorbell over both of their music. She comes out of her room.

"Becca you going to get that?" she gets no response. The knocks continue as she walks down the stairs.

"Hmm, I thought she was down here," she says to the dogs. She makes her way to the door to open it.

Kiara and Franky are there to greet the visitor as well. As soon as they see that it's Matt, they begin to bark.

"Quiet you two." She greets him with a kiss as he walks in. Becca walks out as if she had not heard the door.

"Hey, did I..." She stops.

"Oh, you," she says, with a look of displeasure. She walks over to the box she was working on when she heard the knock.

"Never mind her," Sherri tells Matt.

"I never do," he replies.

"Right, never like you never showed up to help your girlfriend move."

"Drop it, Bec," Sherri says loudly as they walk upstairs.

They reach her door.

"Sorry, babe, sorry about that. I'll make it up to you," he says.

"It's done," she tells him.

"I know that an apology is not enough, so I'll make it up to you." He begins to caress her back and arms trying to send her a signal that he wants to have sex.

She's not interested, so she shrugs her shoulders.

"You don't need to do anything. I am fine. I just want to finish unpacking." He persists with the kissing of her neck and shoulders.

"We can make bedtime right now. Let's break in this bedroom," he suggests.

She breaks away from his kisses and walks toward the closet.

"What's wrong with you?" Matt asks.

Downstairs Brodie walks into the apartment.

"Hey, Bec."

"FYI, asshole is here." He shakes his head.

"How was hanging out?" she asks.

"Good, good, good...good."

"Okay, that's a lot of goods."

"Yeah, good, good," he reiterates.

"Okay, what did you do?" she asks.

"So we are throwing a party this weekend," he tells her.

"Wait, what, here?" she asks with confusion.

"Cool, so you're on board," he says as he walks away.

"Brodie, the place isn't even put together yet. We need more time."

"Don't worry, we will be fine," he reassures her.

"Even worse, Sherri is going to freak out. She needs more time to process these things," she reminds him.

"I know, you will make her be okay with it," he tells her.

"Oh, I am?" she asks.

He makes his way to his bedroom. "We will talk details later," he tells her.

* * * * *

"FUCK, MAN!" Brodie and Becca freeze and look upstairs. Matt comes storming out of the room and down the stairs. They act like they don't know what's going on. Brodie makes eye contact with Matt.

"What the fuck are you staring at?" Matt says to Brodie as he walks through the living room.

"The biggest loser I've ever known," he says in return.

Matthew rushes Brodie. "You want to go, bitch?"

"I'm not gonna fight you," Brodie tells him.

"Yeah, that's right, bitch."

"But I'm also not gonna take your shit," Brodie replies. They stare at each other for several more seconds, then Matthew walks out of the apartment.

"Your cool, right?" Becca asks Brodie as she runs up to Sherri's room. She arrives to a closed door.

"Hey, honey, are you okay?" Becca asks.

"Yes, come in," she tells Becca.

She opens the door and finds Sherri clutching a pillow.

"He's pissed because I didn't want to have sex with him."

"Way to stay, strong girl," Becca says.

"Yeah, I guess," she replies with a sad tone.

Thursday

The halo is on its journey, after a literal kick-start from an elk. The river has a slow flow to it, as it is the summertime, and the depth is low. Still, the halo flows calmly downriver in a west-southwest direction. Its speed depends on what part of the river it's in. Occasionally, it will move to the middle of the river giving it a boost, but most of the time, it remains on the edges where it is slower. This river is in the main forested area, so it hasn't been seen by a single human. Only wildlife, fish mainly. Periodically, a fish will get curious and come swim near and around it. Sometimes, a fish will peck at it. The halo has been on its journey for about twenty-four hours now, and unless it gets removed from the river, it will soon come into the McKenzie River. The McKenzie is the biggest river in the area and is a tributary to the larger Willamette River. On the McKenzie the halo will experience a more eventful river journey.

* * * * *

The angels continue their search of the forest. The search is slow and thorough. There are scores of angels out searching, but they have much ground to cover, and it's difficult to establish starting and stopping points from one day to the next. It's also difficult to remember which paths they have taken and which areas they have covered. Katy stops her movement; something has caught her attention. She looks around to see if any other angels are visible. She sees none. She refocuses on what caught her attention initially. She slowly makes her way in that direction. As she creeps, she can see that a person has stood up. She stops to make sure. She gets behind a tree. She can tell that this person is intently looking over something.

Are they staring at the halo? she thinks. She crosses over to a nearby tree. She peeks around the tree, but the person is gone. She comes out from behind the tree entirely and begins to walk to the spot she last saw this person. As she gets closer, she draws her bow. She pulls an arrow out and puts it across her bow. She reaches the spot and notices a body lying facedown. She does a three-sixty scan to check for anyone else around. She puts her bow and arrow into one hand and kneels to the body. She can't see the face right away, so she repositions herself.

"Holy shit, JR," she says softly. She hears a noise behind her. She turns to look. She sees a devil with his crossbow aimed at her. He shakes his head at her. It's too risky to draw her bow.

"What do you want?" she asks. He doesn't answer.

"This is an angel, and he belongs to us," she tells him. He stays quiet and stares at her for a moment, but to Katy, it seems like an eternity. Katy's heart is racing, and so is the devil's. He lowers his crossbow slowly as their eyes stay locked on each other. He begins to back away slowly. An arrow whisks by him, right in front of his chin. Katy sees it and looks to her right. The devil ducks and looks to his left in the same direction.

Katy sees Ariah running toward them, drawing a second arrow. She releases it, and it misses the devil again. The devil takes cover behind a nearby tree, but still within sight of Katy. He stares at her more intently. The devil turns and runs away, looking back one more time.

"Katy…Katy," she can hear as she lets out a big breath. She takes a moment to gather herself as she reflects on what just happened.

Ariah reaches her. "Are you okay?" she asks.

"Yeah, I'm fine. Thanks for that."

"Yeah, no problem. What happened?" Ariah asks as she sees the body on the ground.

"Um, not sure," Katy begins to explain.

"Is that JR?" Ariah asks.

"Yes, it is."

"Oh, wow, that's great. Good job."

"Yeah, well, I didn't find him. The devil did. I saw the devil and approached him. Anyways, we found him. I'll call it in," Katy tells Ariah. Her attention returns to JR.

"Angels, I found JR. I'm turning on my transponder," she radios. Ariah moves into position to help with JR's body.

Brandon sits patiently in the doctor's office, waiting to get called. Brandon is a bit stubborn when it comes to his health and so Sherri took over her mother's duties of making sure he follows through with check-ups and his overall health. Brandon didn't tell Sherri about this visit. He didn't want to burden her with it, especially since she is moving into her new place this week. She would be proud to know that he made this appointment by himself.

"Mr. Everdeen," the nurse calls out.

"Yeah, right here." He walks back to the exam room. He does the prescreen work with the nurse and waits. Several minutes later, the doctor walks in.

"Mr. Everdeen."

"Hey, Doc."

"I understand you came alone?" he asks surprised.

"Yeah, my little girl moved out this week, and, ah, I didn't want to bother her."

"Got it, well, I'm glad you came in. First, I want to tell you that we didn't find any head trauma from the golf-ball impact. No concussion or fractures to worry about. Just some area soreness," the doctor reports.

"Great, that was easy. That'll make Sherri happy," Brandon says.

"Mr. Everdeen, there is something else."

"Your lab work came back, and I'm sorry to inform you that you have cancer."

Brandon freezes for a moment.

"Mr. Everdeen, you with me?" the doctor asks.

A minute passes before Brandon returns to the conversation. He takes a deep breath.

"Cancer, huh," he says.

"Yes, specifically colon cancer. Now there is some good news," the doctor tells him.

"There's good news about cancer?" Brandon asks.

"Well, depends on how you look at it, but in the medical field, this would be good news."

"Well, what is it?"

"Your cancer is at stage zero."

"What does that mean?" Brandon asks.

"So in cancers, such as this one, there are five stages of cancer. Some have four, but colon cancer has five. You're at zero, which means it's super early, and we caught it in time. Zero means that the cancer cells are present, but they are localized and haven't spread. So that is really good news," the doctor explains.

"So what do we do now?" Brandon asks.

"Well, because you are in stage zero, a simple surgical procedure to remove it can be done."

"So you're going to cut me up?"

"No, not exactly." The doctor goes on to explain the procedure in detail.

"All right then, I've got to think about it. Is that it?" Brandon asks.

"Mr. Everdeen, this is your best option, and it's a safe procedure. Please don't take too long to think about it. I would like to get you scheduled ASAP," the doctor tells him.

* * * * *

Three other angels have joined Katy and Ariah on the ground to help with JR's body. A chopper hovers above to airlift JR's body to Portland. Below, angels load the body onto the carrier and watch it get rise.

"Listen, nice job finding him," Jed says.

"Yeah, all that's left now is the halo," Ariah tells the group.

"It took us what? Three, four days to find JR. Imagine how long it's going to take to find the halo," Jed says.

"Right, well, at least we found him," Ariah says.

"Have you told Elise or Hayley yet?" Jed asks.

"No, I haven't," Katy replies.

"I can do it. I'll do it," he says as he walks away with two other angels, leaving Ariah and Katy alone.

Ariah turns to face Katy. "What happened earlier?" she asks.

"What do you mean?" Katy asks.

Ariah smiles. "You know what I mean. You're still thinking about it," she tells her.

"I'm not sure what you mean?" Katy says again.

"When I saw you and that devil, he had you direct, and he didn't take a shot. I shot at him twice, and he still didn't take a shot. I've never seen that before. And you, you didn't even take a shot at him as he was running away. So that's what I mean. What happened?"

They walk to join the others.

"I really don't know, I guess. I know that I froze. I mean he had me, so I didn't have a choice. He just kept staring at me. It's like he knew me or something," she says.

"Did you know him?" Ariah asks.

"No, that's the first time I've seen that devil," she tells Ariah.

"It almost looked like he was taken with you, and you with him, if I'm being honest. That's the only reason I can think of for not killing you," Ariah tells her.

Katy stays quiet. She isn't quite ready to tell Ariah that there was some sort of connection between her and the devil. She is still trying to figure that out for herself. She agrees that that the devil could have and should have killed her.

"You know, there are stories of angels and devils hooking up before. I've never known of one specifically, but I have heard of them," she tells Katy.

Katy stops. "This isn't that," Katy responds with a disturbed tone.

"Relax. I'm not implying anything. I just know what I saw," Ariah says.

"Well, I'm just glad he didn't pull the trigger," Katy says.

* * * * *

Jason sits in his jet with his eyes closed. Delaney boards the jet.

"We are ready to go," she tells him.

"Great," he says, eyes still closed. A devil lifts the stairs and closes the door.

"What did you get us to eat?" Jason asks. The devil and Delaney look at each other. Neither of them answers.

"Are you there?" Jason asks.

"Yeah, but I didn't get anything. We didn't talk about it. I assumed you would eat on the jet," she tells him. The jet begins to move and get in position for takeoff.

"Hmm, a, does anyone see Emilio on the jet?" Jason asks.

Delaney and the devil look at each other again. The pilot speaks over the intercom.

"Prepare for takeoff."

"Tell them to hold up," Delaney instructs the devil.

"What do you want to eat?" she asks Jason.

"I don't know, I can do either some pad Thai or some teriyaki chicken."

A puzzled look comes over her. "Jason, you understand that we are in Argentina. Those options aren't readily available," she tells him.

"Well, find them," Jason instructs.

Delaney gets up from her seat and walks over to the devil. She gives him instructions to pick whichever option is closest to them. She returns to her seat.

"Did you want to be in Costa Rica by a certain time, because finding either one of these foods is gonna take awhile."

"We are in no hurry," he says, still with his eyes closed.

She gets on her phone to help locates some potential areas for the food. The devil gets off the jet, and the copilot goes out to close the door behind him.

"I don't want to be disturbed until the food gets here!" Jason shouts to the copilot.

"Of course, master," he replies as he closes the door to the cockpit.

Delaney continues to look on her phone when she feels Jason's hand grab her forearm. She looks up. She instantly realizes what he just did.

"Come sit on me," he tells her.

She smiles and puts her phone down. "So you set this little thing up so we could be alone, huh. Are you even hungry?" she asks.

"Of course, I am." She sits on his lap. He opens his eyes. "I have two different appetites right now, and I want to satisfy one of them before the other," he tells her.

"I see, well, I can definitely help you with that then." She stands up and stands in between his legs. She sets her hands on his thighs and spreads his legs. She gets down on her knees and runs her hands up to his belt.

* * * * *

Elise runs over to Hayley's room. Hayley opens the door.

"Hey, have you heard?" Elise asks.

"No, what's up?" Hayley asks.

"They found JR!"

"Oh, no shit," Hayley responds.

"Yeah, he is in a chopper on his way to Portland."

"Oh, that is great news. Come in," Hayley offers.

"So I think it's time to leave this operation to Paloma," Elise says.

"Right, okay, hold on. I need to pee. I guess you can keep talking."

"We go meet with Paloma, then we can call Brad after," Elise proposes.

"Wait, no, by the time we do that, JR will be home. We should call Brad first and just tell him that we are passing this thing off," Hayley suggests.

"Oh yeah, okay, that does make sense. I'll call Brad, you get ahold of Paloma," Elise suggests.

"Um, no, let's switch," Hayley strongly suggests.

"Oh, okay, weirdo. Sure," Elise says.

Hayley finishes in the restroom. Elise makes her call first; it's a quick one, and then she uses the restroom. Hayley gets on her call after, but hers takes longer. Elise finishes in the restroom and gets on the TV. They both expect Hayley's call to take longer, so Elise will just relax. Hayley relays all the info to Brad. She finishes her call with Brad.

"Geez, sometimes it's hard to get off the phone with him," Hayley says about Brad.

"Okay, we are going to go up to Paloma's room and talk there. But first, what's going on with switching people we call? That was weird. So what's up?" Elise asks.

Hayley lets out a big sigh. "Um, nothing, really, but just something that happened yesterday, at the bar. She's just pissed at me and thought I was being reckless and irresponsible," Hayley explains.

"She told you that?" Elise asks.

"Yeah, she didn't like the idea of us at the bar. She said I was leaving my team vulnerable," Hayley adds.

"Well, you know how she is, and you know how you are, so I think you were both right," Elise offers.

"What, that's, what?" Hayley asks with confusion.

"Let's go," Elise says.

"You do all the talking, okay? She's still pissed at me probably," Hayley says.

"Sure, Hayley, sure," Elise replies.

They leave Hayley's room and go up a couple of floors. They knock on her door.

"Hey, ladies?" Paloma says.

"You got a minute?" Elise asks.

Paloma looks at Hayley. "Sure. Come on in," she offers.

They all take a seat.

"Glad to see that you are still with us," Paloma tells Hayley.

Hayley looks up at her. "What, of course I am. Why wouldn't I be? Whatever," Hayley replies.

"Paloma, we have some good news first. About a half hour ago, they found JR's body," Elise tells her.

"Oh, good, finally," she replies.

"Right, right."

"So all the angels are accounted for then," Paloma states.

"Yeah, so now it's just the halo, and Hayley and I are going home today, and we have to get Z home. We will also leave you with folks from our teams. Use them however you see fit. With the angels accounted for, that will leave you with the halo to focus on. So the show is all yours," Elise tells her.

"Good, that all sounds good to me," Paloma tells them.

"Any questions for us?" Elise asks.

"What day did you guys start on the river?" Elise looks at Hayley.

"Um, I think it was right away, but I can say we weren't very thorough."

"Hmm, okay, well, I think I'm going to switch out that team in the river and start over. I'm going to line boats up and drag a net," Paloma explains.

Elise and Hayley have surprised expressions on their faces.

"That is fucking genius," Hayley says.

"Yeah, no doubt," Elise adds.

Hayley stands up. "Listen, Paloma, sorry about yesterday. You were right. No hard feelings?" she offers.

"Of course not. I would hope you would do the same for me," she tells her.

"All right, well, we already called Brad and told him about JR and this meeting with you, so you can follow up with him whenever," Elise tells her.

"What time are you guys leaving today?" Paloma asks.

"Oh, I don't know, early afternoon maybe."

* * * * *

As part of the preparations for tonight's dinner, Brodie and Becca stop at the market. They have what they need but are missing a couple of items, including alcohol.

"Where are you going?" Brodie asks.

She stares at him with a ridiculing look. "To get the wine, duh."

"You know we will get there eventually, right?" he tells her.

She continues her way. Becca gets to the wine section of the aisle and looks around for a specific brand. She gets on her phone and dials Sherri's number. It rings a couple time and then goes to voice mail. "Hey, call me. I'm at the store trying to get you some wine."

She looks around a little more and finds the wine she was looking for. Brodie is in the middle of an aisle getting spices. He is looking over two different ones, one in each hand. He hears the giggle of a female at the end of aisle, at the back of the store. He looks over to see. The female stops in his view and looks back as if she is waiting for someone. She turns forward again as a male joins her.

Brodie's mouth opens as he is stunned to see that it is Matt at the store with another woman. He stays still for a moment as he thinks about what to do. He doesn't want to be seen by Matt, but he also knows that if Becca see him, she will not stay quiet about it. She will confront him on the spot. It's a scene he desperately wants to avoid. He decides to go behind Matt and his significant other.

He figures he is less likely to be seen if he stays behind them. He hopes to find Becca fast so that he can get them out of the store fast. He continues to follow as they reach one end of the store. He looks around for Becca and doesn't see her. He quickly turns around looking down every aisle on his way to the other side of the store.

He gets halfway when he sees Becca come out of an aisle at the front end of the store toward Matt. He quickly runs up the aisle to try and catch her. He knows they are headed right for each other. He gets to the end of the aisle at the front of the store and sees her back.

"BECCA!" he shouts.

She turns around. He waves her back. She turns and walks toward him. As she gets near, he begins to back into the aisle. He had to call her name aloud, so several people heard it, including Matt. Concerned that it might be the person he knows, Matt leaves the side of his significant other and cautiously peeks around the corner at the front of the store. He doesn't see the Becca he knows, but hearing that name has him paranoid, so he returns to his significant other.

"Hey, I'm not feeling well, can we get out of here?"

"Ah, sure, I think we have everything we need, anyway," she tells Matt.

They move quickly to the checkout.

"Why are you being so weird?" Becca asks.

"I'm not, but we need to go this way really quick," he tells her as they continue down the aisle to the back of the store. They stop.

"Okay, what is going on?" she asks as she grabs the cart. She waits for his response as she puts her items in the cart.

"We have to stay low for a bit," he tells her.

"There's a girl I'm trying to avoid. She did me really dirty," he tells her.

"Aw, that sucks, Brodie. I'm sorry, honey," she comforts him.

"It's cool, I would just like to avoid her, especially since she is there with another dude," he tells her. He positions himself to see the exit.

"Can I check out some fruit?" she asks.

"Ah, sure, but we have to be ready to move out of the area."

"Can I see her? I want to see what she looks like."

"No, not yet," he tells her.

"Fine," she replies as she pouts her way to the fruits. He finally sees Matt leave the store.

"Okay, the coast is clear. We can move on."

"I think I'm going to make a fruit salad for tonight, what do you think?" Becca asks.

"Can't go wrong with that. I love fruit salad," he replies. He is both happy and sad about what he just discovered. Sad that his best friend is getting cheated on, because she will be crushed, but happy that now they have something on him, and they can get him out of her life.

"Now, the hard part," he says.

"What, what do you mean the hard part?" Becca asks.

"Oh, nothing, I didn't mean to say that," he responds.

They walk to the checkout as he wonders how, when, and where they will tell Sherri. First, he will tell Becca so they can do it together.

*   *   *   *   *

Ty stops in front of the café where Franco is waiting for him; he looks inside to see if he is inside. He doesn't see him, but it's the place he told him to meet. He looks back and sees that there is an open spot behind him on the same side of the street. He puts his car in reverse, and without any consideration for traffic, he backs up.

A couple of cars are approaching and see what he is doing, so they slow down. The nearest car is late to see Ty's car and must suddenly stop short. They meet at the open parking space. The driver of the other car honks his horn at Ty as they are at an impasse. Ty looks at the driver in his rearview mirror. He can see the driver throwing his hands up and around. Ty revs his engine, but the driver is adamant about getting through. Ty puts his car in park, gets out, and walks toward the driver. The driver begins to cower a little as he rolls up his window.

I should have just gone around, the driver thinks to himself. Ty gets to the car door.

CLINK! The sound of glass breaking fills the air. The driver covers his face as Ty stands outside his car with his fists clenched.

"Okay, I'm sorry, I'll back up," the driver says.

The other drivers behind him back up as much as they can. The driver gets enough space to pull out of the lane and get into the opposite lane, creating more room. Ty gets into his car and backs into the space. He enters the café and scans for Franco.

He doesn't see him right away, not until he hears, "Quite a show you put on out there." He looks over and sees Franco sitting at the front near the window.

"If fucking humans knew their place, there wouldn't have to be shows like that," he responds. His words catch the attention of other patrons, who don't appreciate the comment. Ty isn't concerned about any type of retaliation. It was evident Ty meant for all to hear it.

"So why are we here man?" Ty asks.

"Relax, I just want to talk about what's been going on with you lately," Franco tells him.

"What do you mean?"

"You know what I mean. You haven't been yourself lately. You seem off. That attitude you had back at Jason's," he specifies.

Ty stays quiet a moment.

"You know, that was more about Crystal. She is starting to get on my nerves," he explains.

"Okay, I get that, but what about the rest of it?" he asks.

"What do you mean the rest?"

"You haven't been right, even before you left for Bend. There's been something up with you. So what is it?" he tells Ty.

"I guess I just don't like the direction we are heading in. I have been thinking lately that Jason isn't the one who should be leading us anymore, especially with Crystal by his side. I think she has made him soft," he tells Franco.

"Jason is the strongest among us. He is our leader. I trust him to lead us," he tells Ty.

"I know you do. I mean, we used to fuck the angels up, any chance we got, and before this last attack, we hadn't done shit for a really long time. We haven't been the same, and I don't like it," he explains to Franco.

"Okay, I hear you, and I agree with you to a large degree, but you must remember that Jason is our leader, and I suggest you trust him," he reminds Ty.

"That reminds me, why didn't you call me the other day when Nate showed up at Jason's?" Ty asks.

"That conflict was resolved with little loss. That's a good thing. If you were there, it would've had a vastly different, not-so-peaceful outcome," Franco explains.

"That's a bunch of crap," Ty expresses.

"You are too unpredictable right now, which is why we are here talking," Franco tells him.

"The reason I haven't gone over the edge is because of you and my sister. Otherwise, Jason would have another battle to fight," he says.

"I appreciate you trusting me and hang in there. Things will get better. I know they will," Franco reassures Ty.

"Listen, there is something else, about the attack," Ty says.

"What is it?" asks Franco.

"We didn't tell you guys everything back at Jason's."

"What do you mean, what are you saying?" he asks with a look of confusion.

"Two angels got away," Ty tells him.

"What the fuck. You're kidding me." Franco scowls.

"I didn't like the way things were going down back there, and so I didn't mention it," he says.

"Did Sara know?" he asks.

"Yeah, but she was just covering for me," he says.

"Shit, Ty, this is not good, do you understand that?"

"Look, man, I'm telling you because I trust you, and you know how I feel about Jason right now," he tells Franco.

"Fuck, man, this is not good, Ty," Franco says as he wipes his face from forehead to chin. "I'm going to have to tell Jason, you know that right?" he tells Ty.

"Yeah, I figured, but here's the deal. I went by Nate's place to check things out. I intercepted two humans leaving his house. I stopped them and questioned them. They confirmed that the two angels that escaped were Uriah and Vanessa. They didn't have the halo with them, so it's still out in the forest. Those two human cockroaches work for me now."

"All right, well, I'll work out a story about those angels. In the meanwhile, stay strong. Clean your shit up. You know it's going to get super crazy when Jason gets back. He is working on another plan that I sure will restore your faith in him. I don't have any details yet, but I know he has something big planned," he tells Ty.

"It better be big," Ty says.

"Did you go by and talk with the triplets?" Franco asks.

"I'll do it on my way home," he responds.

* * * * *

The jet lands at the hanger. Most of the flight was silent for the angels. Elise gets off the plane first and sees the car waiting for them nearby.

"I have a little surprise for you," Elise tells Isaiah who is right behind her. He looks up and see Noemy running toward him. They can hear her screaming the whole way to them. Noemy slams into her brother.

"I'm so glad you are here. I was so worried," she tells him.

"I'm glad to see you too sister. I love you so much," he replies. Elise and Hayley move ahead to the car and give them some time to rejoice.

"Noemy, can you pop the trunk!" Hayley yells back.

"Keys are in the car," she yells return.

"I'll get them," Elise tells Hayley.

Isaiah and Noemy walk back to the car. They all settle in.

"Where to?" Noemy asks.

"I'm going home," Hayley tells her.

"Yeah, I think we are all just heading to our own place right now," Elise follows up.

"It will be nice to just relax in my own place tonight," Isaiah says. The car begins to move.

"Ha, that's funny, you actually think you're going to get to relax today?" Noemy tells him.

"Why couldn't I?" he asks.

"Nate's putting a little get together for you tonight. If you want to relax, you need to hide," Noemy tells him.

"Don't worry, Z, as a favor to you, I didn't tell Brad what time we left, sisters, and I arranged this pickup, so you have some time, but it's only a matter of time before they find one of us home," she tells Isaiah.

"There's a party tonight?" Hayley mumbles with her head leaning against the window.

"I thought you would be excited about it, Hay Hay," Elise says.

"Not right now, I'm not," she mumbles.

"Bro, I'll take you back to your place, and we can hang there for a while. When you're ready, we can let Nate know your home. Is anyone hungry?" Noemy asks.

"Nate is going to have to reschedule this thing 'cuz I'm not doing a party tonight," Isaiah says.

"Does anyone want me to stop anywhere, before I drop them at home?" Noemy asks.

Elise and Hayley decline the offer.

"Definitely for me. Let's stop at Burger King. I am craving a whopper," Isaiah says.

"Whoppers, coming right up."

* * * * *

Sherri sees a new text on her phone. She waits till she is stopped before she checks who it's from. She's on her way from the store. She has one more stop before she gets home. The low mileage beep goes off indicating she has fifty miles left until her tank is empty. She pulls into an ARCO for gas. While waiting for her tank to fill, she checks the message. It's a text from Matthew. It's a message telling her that he loves her. She smiles. She doesn't get these often, so it makes her really happy to receive them.

She responds by telling him that she loves him too. He sends another message asking her how her day was. She tells him that's it's just okay. He asks her what she has done so far that day. She tells him that she went to the gym, the store, ran some errands, and now she is getting gas. He is rarely this inquisitive, but she is enjoying the extra attention from him. He asks what store. She tells him that she went to Wal-Mart. He asks if that was the only store. She tells him yes. Although she loves the attention, she is now starting to wonder why he is asking these questions. Little does she know that his behavior stems from fear and not genuine feelings. She hears the gas nozzle click, indicating the tank is full.

"You want a receipt?" asks the gas attendant as he returns the nozzle.

"No, thanks." She turns the car on and pulls away from pump.

He sends another message, so she stops briefly to check it. She is adamant about not texting while driving. The message is asking her if she is mad at him. She tells him that she didn't like what happened on Monday but that she is getting over it. He apologizes and tells her that he would like to make it up to her by taking her out to dinner that evening. She tells him that she has dinner plans at home with her roommates. He tells her that he understands and asks for a rain check. She tells him of course. He tells her to have fun.

She doesn't respond; instead, she sits confused about how nice he is being. He isn't this understanding and has never told her to have fun with her friends. She is now suspicious that he is up to something. Another text comes through telling her that he loves her. She tells him the same in return. She waits in her car a little longer. She is confused about his attentive and positive behavior. She shrugs her shoulders, smiles, and drives out of the gas station. She figures that it must be guilt from the other day.

* * * * *

Jason and his devils pull up to a gate. The devil guards quickly see that it's Jason and allow him through.

"I should warn you, if you thought Jamie was rough, well, she's nothing compared to this one. Jocelyn is known as the mean one of the group. She is fierce and strong. Don't let her size fool you, and don't take any of what she says personally, at least at this meeting," he warns Delaney.

"Great, thanks for the heads-up."

They reach the front of the house. Jocelyn comes out to see them. Delaney gets out first and looks at Jocelyn.

Wow, she is really small, she thinks to herself.

Jason gets out next.

"Glad you came to visit, finally," Jocelyn says to Jason.

"I told you I would someday," he replies.

"Hi, I'm Delaney."

"I think I've heard of you. Are you my brother's current assistant?" she asks.

"Uh, yes, I am," Delaney says with some uncertainty.

"So you're fucking him then?"

Delaney's eyes widen. Jason shakes his head as he enters the house.

"I'll just give myself a tour as you two catch up," he says.

"Why would you be interested in that?" Delaney asks.

"So that's a yes," Jocelyn says.

Delaney remains quiet.

"You can wait out here," Jocelyn tells Delaney.

She turns around to go inside and find her brother. Delaney remains outside, confused.

I thought I would like this sister more than the other one, she thinks.

"Where is my brother? Find him," Jocelyn tells her butler. She continues to her kitchen. Moments later, Jason comes into the kitchen.

"Jamie told me you were coming."

"Where's Delaney?" he asks.

"I told her to wait outside."

Jason has a disgusted look on his face.

"Why did you do that?" He looks around. "Get her in here," he tells her.

She summons her butler and has him go grab her.

"So I know you aren't here to visit me. I'll make this quick for you. Tell me your plan in detail, and I'll consider letting you use my forces," she explains.

Delaney walks into the kitchen.

"I happen to like Crystal, and I don't like women that can't honor a marriage," Jocelyn tells Delaney.

"Leave her alone. She isn't doing anything wrong. It's me you should be upset with."

"Oh, I am, so much so that right now I don't want to lend you my army. But like I said, I'll hear your plan then determine if it's worth the time. So what's this plan of yours?" Jocelyn asks.

"Right, well, I made a move on the angels this past Sunday, phase one. We shot down a jet carrying the halo, but the halo is lost in a forest. Phase three is dependent on having the halo. Phase two is to kill the angels, large-scale simultaneous assault on Nate's group specifically. With them out of the way, phase three will be much easier. You know what takes place in phase three."

Jocelyn walks to a window with her hands behind her.

"Jamie gave you her army. I'm glad you are finally doing something about the halo. We have been waiting for a long time. Your plan isn't detailed. It sounds messy. I can't give you what you need right now. I could have told you this over the phone. You're welcome to hang around, or stay if you want, but I can't help you. I think you have enough with your army and Jamie's help."

"I didn't expect this. Why wouldn't you want to crush the angels for the last time?" he asks.

"I do, but I just don't know that you have a plan to do this."

"I do have a plan," he expresses.

"Well, you're being lazy describing it. But look, at the end of the day, you have the power to just take my legion, so you let me know what you're going to do," she tells him.

"I figured there would be more buy-in if you agreed, but maybe not. I know I can take them, but like I said, it's good to know I have not only the loyalty, but the trust. I'll let you think about it. Call me," he tells her.

A young female dressed in bikini climbs the stairs to reach the top of the slide to the pool. She is cheered on by two other young ladies' poolside with drinks in their hands. She reaches the top and sits on her butt. She raises her arms into the sky as she begins her slide. She lets out a loud cheery scream as she slides down into the pool.

She splashes in as the other two girls by the pool cheer on. Nearby Franco is engaged in conversation with two other females a safe distance from the splash zone. There is no occasion for having a pool party for Franco; this is part of his lifestyle. He enjoys keeping the company of females, five for this occasion. When he is not involved with devil affairs, he is often engaged in some type of social gathering, with a heavy female presence. He is lying on a cabana-style bed with the two females involved in the conversation.

"I'm going to get some ice," says a female by the pool. She walks into the house and to the kitchen. When she reaches the kitchen, she hears a phone ring once. She doesn't pay attention to it. She grabs her ice and checks in on her social media for a moment. As she walks out of the kitchen, the phone on the counter begins to ring again. She looks back at it; she knows it's Franco's phone. She is curious about it, so she answers it.

"Hello," she says.

"Franco?" Sara asks.

"Um, no, I'm Whiney, Franco is outside," Whiney says.

"Put Franco on, you skank," Sara says.

Whiney scoffs. "Fuck you," she says and hangs up the phone. With phone in hand, Whiney walks out to Franco. The phone rings again.

"Here you go, Franco," Whiney tosses the phone onto his stomach. The phone continues to ring. Franco grabs it and looks at the caller ID.

"Ah, yeah, I should take this," he says aloud. He gestures to the two ladies lying with him to give him some space. He answers the phone.

"Why are you letting your skanks answer your phone?" Sara asks.

Franco looks confused and stares at Whiney.

"I'll address that later," he tells her.

"Isaiah is alive," she reports.

"He was on that jet, wasn't he?"

"Yes, he was," she replies.

"A group of devils followed some angels out to Redmond. That's where Isaiah ended up somehow. They thought he had the halo and attacked. Only Luis returned. He said they didn't have it," Sara tells him.

"So what now?" he asks.

"More angels have arrived in the area. That tells me they need more support in the forest to find the halo. All the angels are accounted for now except for our friend. I say we focus on the river, let the angels work the forest and we can sweep the river," she suggests.

"Okay, set up the river and return to Portland. I'll send Julian out there to lead the river sweep," he instructs.

"Cool, I'll see you later then," she says.

He holds the phone out. "Whiney, did you answer my phone?"

All the women look at Whiney.

"Yes," Whiney says.

"Let me make myself clear. No one answers my phone, is that understood?" he says.

They all respond in agreement.

"Now, Whiney, come over here so you can be punished," he says with a smile.

* * * * *

Sherri pulls into the driveway of the house she used to live in. She sits in her car for a moment. She sees Jayce look out the window. He runs outside and runs to the car. She gets out of the car before he reaches it. He gives her a big hug.

"Hey, buddy, good to see you," she tells him. Brandon walks out front with a smile. Sherri and Jayce walk up to the house as they talk. She gives her father a hug.

"Hey, honey, how are you?" Brandon says.

"I'm good, Dad, what about you?"

"Can't complain, honey. Come inside. What's the occasion, honey?"

"Just running some errands. Thought I'd stop by and see how my boys are doing."

"Me and Jayce here, have been holding down the fort, you know. We've been talking about what we want to do with the place," he tells her.

"Now that's it's just the guys!" Jayce shouts out.

They all chuckle a little.

"Dad says that we are going to make a game room," Jayce informs Sherri.

"Wow, not even gone a week and already turning my room into a game room," she says.

"No, you will always have a room here, honey," Brandon assures her.

There is a short silence.

"It's my room, isn't it?"

"It's your room," Brandon responds.

"Yeah, I figured," she says.

"It's the only one that makes sense. Dad still needs his office," Jayce tells her.

"Yeah, I get it. I think it's a fantastic idea, guys. Looking forward to coming over here and playing against you," she tells them.

"How is the move going, honey?"

"Not quite there, but most of the big stuff is set. Just some smaller boxes, but it's great. I feel grown up."

"That's great, honey. How are your friends?"

"They are good. We are all excited to be doing this. And, oh, Brodie has been talking about getting a dog."

"What kind?" Jayce asks.

"Not sure yet."

"Good, good. How is Matt? Haven't seen him around in a while," Brandon asks.

Sherri looks down at the ground and puckers her lips. The expression on her face is enough to tell him that something isn't right in that department.

"How about we save that one for later?" he suggests to her.

"Thanks. How is your head?"

"I am solid, honey." She looks over at Jayce.

"Is that true, is he better?" she asks him.

"Yeah, I think so, he went to the doctors," Jayce tells her.

"Oh good, I'm glad to hear that. What did the doctor say?"

"Son, give us a minute. Go watch some TV."

"I didn't want to tell you yet because I didn't want you to overreact. But you're not my little girl anymore. You're a young woman and I should treat you as such. First, my head is fine. Doc said no serious issues or concerns."

"Oh, that is great news," she responds.

"This is no big deal, but a..." He drops his head and looks around.

"Dad, what is it?" she asks impatiently.

"I've got stage zero colon cancer."

Sherri covers her mouth and begins to sob.

"Honey, I'll be fine. It's stage zero, and the doctor said that it's super early and it's local and so they just have to go in and take it out," he tells her.

"I'm moving back in," she says.

"No way!" Jayce screams from the other room.

"Shut it, Jayce!" she yells back.

Brandon laughs a little.

"Honey, you're not moving back in. I'm fine. I'll be fine. You need to go live your life now. I'll have this procedure, and I'll be good," he tells her.

He walks into the kitchen, and she follows.

"I'm making Jayce's favorite for dinner, country fried steak, mashed potatoes, and corn on the cob," he tells her.

"Well, you're going to have to include me for dinner tonight," she insists.

"Weren't you telling me that you have some sort of special dinner with your friends tonight?" he asks.

"Yes, but we can to that some other time."

"Sherri, honey, you need to not worry. The doctor said that they aren't even concerned right now."

She walks to him and gives him a hug and buries her face in his chest.

"Sherri, everything is going to be fine, I promise you." He kisses her head and pets her hair. He pulls her head away from his chest and kisses her forehead.

"You have done your job here. You have done an amazing job helping me with your brother, and you have been the best daughter a father could ask for. Now it's time to go explore the world, build a career, and live your life. Your brother and I are going to be fine," he tells her.

She looks at him and closes her eyes in acknowledgment. Jayce pokes his head around the corner.

"She's not moving in again, right?" he asks while concealing his body.

Sherri turns and grabs the first thing she sees and throws it at him.

"Shut it, you brat," she says as the roll of paper towels hits the corner where his head was.

"Fine, well, just so you know, I want to know about all your appointments, your reports, and expect to see me here more often," she tells him. She goes into his chest for another hug.

* * * * *

Ty arrives at the building where the triplets live; he parks across the street. He takes a drink from his flask. He waits in his car dreading the idea of having to go into their apartment. He takes out a cigarette and lights it. He's in no hurry to be around the triplets. He lays his head back and exhales. He spends about five minutes savoring his cigarette and relaxing. He sees a boy on his bike riding his way. He takes one last puff of the cigarette and flicks it at the boy as he passes his car.

"Hey, you asshole!" the boy yells back as he continues to ride.

Ty laughs as he gets out of his car. He walks around his car and cross the street without looking each way. He reaches the building; the main door is locked. He doesn't want to wait around so he kicks the door open, instead of asking to get buzzed in. He walks in and goes to the elevator. The door opens and he gets in. He presses the Eleven button and heads up to the eleventh floor. He steps out of the elevator then pauses a second, looking down the hallway at both ends. He reaches their door and knocks. Laura answers the door. She quickly greets him with a smile.

"Oh wow, what a sweet surprise." He walks right by her without acknowledging her compliment.

"Hey, sisters, look who's here!" she yells out to her sisters.

Lucy walks down the rounded staircase. "To what do we owe this visit?" she asks.

"Don't get so excited. Jason sent me. I'm not here by choice," he tells them.

Leti walks out of her room to the living room.

"Shit's going down with the angels, so Jason wants you to go by his place sometime next week.

"Hmm, he could have just called," Lucy says.

"Yeah, I know. That's what I told him."

"Well, it's been a while. We're glad you're here. How about a drink?" Laura offers.

"No, I won't be here long."

"There is always time for a drink," Leti replies.

"You're right, just not here," he responds.

"So what is the job?" asks Leti.

"I don't know. He didn't tell me."

"So you came all the way over here to tell us that we have an assignment, but don't know what it is?" Lucy asks.

"Yeah, Jason is punishing me, I'm sure. It's something we will be working on together, I guess," he tells the ladies.

"Ew, that sounds fun. You shouldn't view this as a punishment, Tyler," Leti says.

"Just see Jason next week. He is out of town right now," he tells them.

"I hope it's as fun as your assignment, attacking the angels and taking the halo," Laura says.

"We didn't get the halo. It was lost during the attack. It's somewhere in the forest," he explains.

"You guys lost the halo?" Lucy asks.

"He should have sent us instead," Leti adds.

Ty stares at them for a moment. "Just go to Jason's," he says as he makes his way to the door.

"You should hang out and have a drink so we can catch up," Laura suggests.

"I already said no," he responds with an elevated tone.

"Somebody's in a poopy mood," Lucy says.

"Why are you such a dick to us, Ty?" Laura yells out. "You never had a problem when you were fucking us before," Leti tells him.

He turns around before he reaches the door.

"Oh, I know what it is," Laura says.

Leti and Lucy look at her.

"What is it?" Leti asks.

"You're still pissed about that little butthole thing we did to you, aren't you?"

He turns around and continues to the door.

"Oh, my hell, that's it, isn't it?"

Ty remains silent as he opens the door, walks out of the apartment, and heads to the elevator.

Lucy closes the door.

*   *   *   *   *

Hayley paces from her living room to the kitchen, phone in hand. She can't get him off her mind. She wants to talk to him. She has had this feeling since she got back to town. She's very hesitant and scared of his reaction to her. She paces a while longer, taking breaks on the couch in between the pacing. She darts out to her balcony, takes a deep breath, and begins to dial. The phone rings on the other end.

"Yeah," Christian answers.

"Hey, it's me," says Hayley.

"Yeah, I know. What do you want?" he asks her.

"Nothing," she stutters a little.

"So nothing? You have nothing to say?" he asks.

"Well, I was hoping we could talk," she says.

"About what?"

"I just have some things to say, I guess," she tells him.

"Go ahead and say it."

"It's kind of hard to explain over the phone, can we get together?" she asks.

A strong emotion comes over him at the idea of being close to her again; it's upsetting him.

"Why are you doing this? If you want to say something, then say it," he tells her.

"Can we get together please? I can come over if that makes things easier," she offers.

"What's the point of this?" he asks as he grows more upset with the conversation.

"Please, I really need to talk to you."

"If it's about us getting back together, then sure. Otherwise, not happening. She remains silent.

"Well, is it?"

"Why do you have to complicate things? I just want to see you and talk," she says.

"I'm not doing this anymore. You can't do this anymore," he tells her as he hangs up the phone.

She keeps the phone at her ear for a moment, sad that he doesn't want to see her. She lowers the phone and cups it with both hands staring at it. She wants to call him again, but she knows that it will only upset him even more. She walks over to her couch and curls up.

* * * * *

Becca is setting the table while Brodie puts the final additions on dinner. Sherri is currently out and has been for most of the day. They are celebrating their first dinner together in their new place. Becca smiles.

"Doesn't this feel good?" she asks Brodie.

"Yeah, but this isn't new for us. You and I have been out of our house for a while now," he reminds her.

"Don't downplay it, bro. You know what I mean," she tells him. "We have been looking forward to this for some time now," she adds.

"Yeah, I know. I will tell you what I am not looking forward to is having that jackass around more," he says, referring to Matthew.

"You and me both," she says.

Brodie wants to tell Becca about what he saw at the store. He is trying to gauge her mood, because he knows that she could very well storm out the door and go looking for Matthew in that moment.

"I have something to tell you. But before I do, you must promise to stay in the house, and we will deal with it another time. You have to agree that this is about someone else and not you, and we will have to be careful about what I'm going to tell you," he tells her.

"What, so serious. What is it?" she asks with intent.

He has Becca's attention.

"Stay in the house, never heard that one before," she tells him.

"Do you promise? You need to promise," he stresses.

"Yeah, I promise," she says without thought.

He waits and stares at her.

"All right, I promise, I'll stay in the house and not overreact," she commits.

"All right, I'll tell you then," he says.

"You know when we were at the store today. I told you that I was hiding from a girl. I was lying about that. The reason I lied is because I saw something else," he says. Before he can go any further, the front door opens, and Sherri walks in.

"Hey, guys, I'm home," she announces.

"Oh, just in time, Brodie was about to tell me something serious," says Becca.

Brodie looks at Becca wide-eyed.

"Oh, is it private, or is it about me?" Sherri asks jokingly.

Brodie decides to play along. "Yeah, it's about you, so you should go to your room, and I'll tell you when you can return," he jokes back.

Becca looks back at Brodie.

"Is it really that private?" she puts Brodie on the spot.

He bunches his lips as he looks at both girls. "Uh, well, I was about to tell Becca that, ah, we were at the store today and I told her that I was hiding from a girl that did me dirty, but I was about to come clean and tell her that, that wasn't the exact truth," he tries to explain.

Both girls wait in silence; they can tell something is off.

"Okay, we're waiting, weirdo," Becca says to him.

"Yeah, right, well the truth is…I…think I love her," he tells them.

Both girls look at each other with confusion and doubt.

"That was it?" Becca asks with ridicule.

There is a silence. Sherri walks to the counter.

"I picked up three wines for us to celebrate this occasion," she says.

She proceeds to describe each wine while Becca goes to the fridge and pulls out the two bottles she purchased. They completely disregard Brodie or the big news he had for Becca. He begins to nod with pride as he grins. He was able to elude having to tell them the truth at that moment. Sherri turns around as she continues to describe the wines and sees Becca holding two bottles.

"Oh, well, I guess we have more than enough," Sherri says.

"It's cool, we can never have too much wine, right?" Becca tells her.

They continue to put the final additions on dinner and decide which wine to open first.

"I'm going to run up and shower. I should be back down in time to eat," Sherri tells them.

"Cool, dinner should be ready by then," Brodie says.

Sherri runs out of the kitchen and upstairs to her room.

"You're in love, huh," Becca asks, surprisingly.

Brodie thought that he was in the clear, but now he must try and explain his way out of this story. Sherri returns a short while later and joins her friends at the table. Dinner plated and wineglasses filled, Becca calls for a toast. They all raise their glasses.

"To best friends forever, and a fun-filled time living together," Becca says.

They all cheers and enjoy their night of celebration.

* * * * *

Hayley arrives at Christian's building. She waits in her car; she really wants to go in but is stalling because she understands the repercussions of going in. She can't help herself; she gets out of the car. She walks up to the building but must wait around until a tenant arrives to open it. It's the type of building that only tenants can access. The wait is a little long, but it gives her a little more time to think about what she was wants to do. Eventually, a couple shows up to enter the residence, and she walks in behind them.

"I'm going to check the mail," the female says to the male.

The male walks to the elevator and waits. Hayley casually waits by the elevator as well. They make brief eye contact. Hayley smiles. She has no choice but to wait for them to access the elevator. The man's wife rejoins him. The man accesses the elevator, and it opens.

"Thank you, my boyfriend didn't answer the ringer. He is probably in the shower," she explains.

"Yeah, I've seen you here before," the lady tells Hayley.

"Forty-second floor, please," Hayley requests. There is no further discussion on the way up. The elevator stops for the couple first.

"Have a good night," the lady says.

"You as well," Hayley replies.

She reaches Christian's floor. On her way to his door, she stops a couple of times to check herself. She is typically not the nervous type, but this will be the first time they will be alone since they ended the relationship—*she* ended the relationship. They have had a couple of conversations over the phone and some encounters, but usually with others nearby.

She gets to the end of the hall where his apartment is. She lifts her arm to knock. She comes within an inch of the door and pauses. She drops her arm and turns around to walk away. She gets about twenty feet away while fighting with herself then stops. She talks herself into going back. She turns around and walks back toward the door. She gets to it and raises her arm again, ready to knock. She pauses again.

What are you so afraid of? she asks herself. She closes her eyes and knocks. She can hear him walking to the door. As soon as there is enough room for her to get through the door, she lifts her head and lunges at him. Her lips meet his, and she flings her arms around his neck.

He is surprised initially then reacts by putting his hands on her waist. He tries to push her away. She fights to hold the kiss. He puts more force into pushing her away, but she also counters with a stronger hold with her arms. He tries to pull his lips away from hers, but she is dug in deep. He grabs her arms from around his neck and begins to get separation. One final push away, and their lips unlock. He steps back.

"What the hell are you doing, Hayley?"

"I miss you, and I just want to touch you."

Christian is confused; he is having trouble understanding why she is doing this.

"You said you had something to tell me, over the phone," he says.

"I kind of lied. I just wanted to see you."

He looks up and closes his eyes. "Man, what are you doing? Why are you doing this?"

"I really miss you. I want to stay with you tonight, please," she asks.

"You're crazy. You didn't want this anymore, remember? You didn't want us anymore. Remember that," he says with an elevated tone.

She walks around him, inviting herself inside. "Tell me you don't want this. Tell me to leave," she says to him. She begins to get a little sassy with him.

"You ain't right. You can't keep fucking with my head," he tells her as he stares out into the hallway. He closes the door slowly.

"Turn around. Look at me," she requests.

He does it slowly as she walks up to him. Before she gets to him, he moves away from her. She stops and looks at him then walks to him again. This time he stays in place. She begins to caress his face, hair, and chest. His breaths get heavier while he stares down at her.

"I know you want this. Why are you fighting it?" she tells him.

"Because you broke my heart, remember?"

"SShhh," she puts her fingers over his mouth.

"Don't fight it. Just let it happen and enjoy it. I know you want it too," she says with a soft, whispery voice as she runs her hands around his body.

"Have you been drinking?" he asks her.

"Just a couple, but that is not what's driving me," she tells him.

"Then what is?" he asks.

"You, my heart, our love," she responds.

He bursts into laughter. He gathers himself for a moment. "You killed all that, remember? You ended it."

"SShhh," she puts her finger over his lips again.

She takes him by the hand and leads him to his couch. There is silence between them on the way there. They reach the couch, and she stands him in front of him then pushes him down. She mounts him and begins to kiss his neck. He is enjoying the feeling but knows that this will hurt later. Still, he lets it go. Her power of persuasion has gotten the best of him again. The weakness has taken over, and now his hands begin to reciprocate hers. He is getting lost in the moment and the kissing becomes intense, filling with passion.

Hayley can't help but be excited in knowing that she still has control over the man that she still loves. It's a victory for her, but just for the moment. While straddling him she begins to thrust against his waist. She knows this is something that he can't resist. His hands begin to move about her body. Hers move around his face and head. He takes command of her body and picks her up to lay her on her back.

He hovers over her to kiss some more. She pulls his shirt off; he undoes a belt she is wearing. She pushes him off; he falls back onto the couch. She gets up in front of him and turns her back. She bends over and looks back at him. She lifts herself and begins to take her skirt off, ever so slowly while her hips move side to side.

The skirt comes off completely leaving only a lacy thong. He has lost control, and now she is in complete command. He scoots up to grab her hips and kiss her ass. He pulls down the thong as he runs his nose around her ass. The thong comes off. She rises up and walks over the kitchen counter. She leans over it as she swirls her head around slowly, occasionally looking back at him. He gets up and walks to her. She feels him behind her and reaches back to pull his shorts and drawers down. She turns and lifts herself onto the counter. She lies back as he lowers his mouth to her pussy. She feels her own body as the sensation increases. The pleasure intensifies as her body begins to joggle at the cunnilingus she is receiving. She lifts her head to see for herself as she puts her hand on top of his head.

"I want you inside of me now!" she tells him.

He rises, and she leans to him to kiss. He slides her off the counter, grabbing her by her ass.

She whips her legs around his waist and arms around his neck. He carries her over back to the couch and lays her down, he arms and legs open, inviting him in. He hovers over her to kiss her as he teases her pussy with his cock. Suddenly she breaks from the kiss; she lets out a loud moan as he slides inside of her. He begins to thrust at various paces as she moves her body to indicate her satisfaction.

It is obvious to both that the sexual chemistry is alive as they both know and understand what the other desires. He turns her over into doggystyle. He slides inside of her again, and she reacts as if it's the first penetration. The sensation increases for him in this position, and so does his thrusting.

She looks back at him both out of pleasure but also out of caution. She puts her hand at his stomach to let him know that he has the potential to overextend his abilities. She doesn't stop him as there is a deep hunger for the way he moves. She decides it's her turn to take command.

She pulls away from him and shoves him back. She mounts him; he puts his hands on her hips. She begins to grind vigorously as she knows that this position drives him wild. It's his favorite position. He thoroughly enjoys the way she moves her hips. They move about the room, taking turns fucking each other.

They move from the floor to the kitchen table, to the kitchen counter. The fucking takes them to the bathroom, then to the bedroom. They stay up late fucking through the night as they did time and time before. Christian has lost his power of resistance to Hayley for the night, but this is something that he is not concerned about now. It won't be until the morning when it's time to face the truth again.

Friday

The halo reached the McKenzie River during its second day. It is early Friday morning, and the halo has been floating for about forty-eight hours now. Unless taken out of the river, the next checkpoint for the halo will be the much larger Willamette River. But it's in no rush. It's enjoyed its time on the McKenzie. So far of the ninety-plus miles that is the length of the McKenzie, it has traveled about seventy-five miles. It will be meeting the Willamette in the next couple of hours. During its time on the McKenzie, it passed three dams. At one of those dams, it had to wait about nine hours until water was released. Because this river is larger, it has a higher rate of velocity which has allowed it to travel at a faster rate, the hold up at the dam notwithstanding. The halo has been more exposed on this river than the arterial river that feed into it. More people use this river recreationally, especially during the summer. The halo has crossed the paths of a couple hundred unsuspecting boaters, fisherman, floaters, and swimmers. Still only the fish is the only life that is willing to acknowledge the halos existence.

* * * * *

Christian and Hayley lie asleep in his bed. Hayley's eyes open as the sun shines through the window into the bedroom, but it was the knock on the door that woke her up. She hears a couple more knocks accompanied by the voice of Christian's mother, Emily. She lies there until the knocking stops. She doesn't want to get up and answer the door because she doesn't want the awkward interaction between her and Christian's mother. She watches Christian hoping that the knocking and calling of his name doesn't wake him up also. She continues to lie there until the visitors leave. She is wrapped by Christians arms, one under her neck, the other over her chest.

She takes in the familiar feeling his arms provide. Those feelings begin to make her little emotional, so she decides to try and slip out. Christian is a heavy sleeper, and she is counting on that for her escape. She slowly takes his top arm off.

She gently rolls off his bottom arm and gets off the bed, on to her knees. She gets to her feet and looks around for her clothing. She grabs what is near her, then moves around to get the rest of it that is spread around. She starts to dress herself slowly, away from the bed, so she doesn't wake Christian. She gets her bra and panties on when she hears him.

"Leaving so soon?"

"Yeah, uh, I've got to get going now," she responds. "Sorry I woke you," she adds.

"You didn't wake me. It was my mother, but I didn't want to answer her."

"Yeah, me either."

"So that's it, huh?"

"Look, Christian, this is all part of the process," she tells him as she continues to look for her clothing.

"What process?" he asks.

"What we did is nothing unusual. When two people break up, there is a phase. This is it," she tells him.

"I'm not going to keep letting you do this to me," he responds.

"It's all still fresh, I know, but this hurts for me as well. I get lonely, and I just want to be with you," she explains.

"I'm not going to feel sorry for you. You did this to us," he tells her. He gets out of bed, and he walks to the bathroom.

"I'm sorry, but I let my emotions get the best of me, but we had an exciting time last night, didn't we?" she asks.

"It's not how I want it, and you know that," he says.

"Well, I'm sorry," she answers.

"No, I'm the one who is sorry. I shouldn't have let this happen. I knew better," he tells her. He finishes in the bathroom and walks back out to find his draws.

"Christian, stop. I love you. I just need to figure some things out," she expresses to him.

"Well then, you can't do this to me. I'm not your toy. This doesn't help you figure it out," he tells her.

"I'm doing this because I love you," she reiterates.

"That is hilarious," he laughs aloud. He pauses a moment. "Well, I can't handle it, so don't do it anymore. Don't call me again for this," he tells her.

"What are you saying, Christian?" she asks him.

"I'm saying that the next time I hear from you, it better be to tell me that you want to get back together. There is no other reason for us to talk otherwise," he says.

"Do you mean it? Do you really feel that way?" she asks.

"Yeah, I do. I don't want to feel like this again," he tells her.

"Fine," she says with attitude. She is fully clothed, but she cannot find one of her shoes and a belt she was wearing.

"Where is my shoe?" she asks while holding the other in her hand. "And my belt, I can't find my belt," she says as she looks around helplessly.

"Can you help me, Christian?" she pleads to him.

He doesn't answer her and instead walks into the kitchen for some water. Hayley finds her belt and puts it on as she stares at Christians back.

"Where is my shoe?" she asks herself again.

Christian continues to ignore her and focus on his water. He turns around to see her searching. She stands still in front of the couch, looking down at it. She begins to cry as Christian continues to ignore her. She turns around and sits on the couch and buries her face in her hands. A minute passes.

"Did you check under the couch?" she hears from the kitchen.

She takes her face out of her hands and wipes away her tears. She gets down on her knees and looks under the couch. She sees her shoe and grabs it. She gets to her feet, and while holding her shoes in one hand, she wipes her face with the other. She straightens herself out. "I'm going now," she tells him. She walks to the front door. There is a part of her that wants to stay, and a part of her wants him to follow her, but he does not. She turns back and sees him standing in the same spot.

"Well, I guess I'll see you around," she tells him.

"You won't," he responds.

She walks out and closes the door behind her. She stops and turns around to face the door. She raises her fist to knock. She wants to go back in, but she decides against it. She turns around again and leans back against the door. She looks up and begins to tear up. She is struggling with the breakup and wonders if it was the right decision.

* * * * *

"What does this do to your plan?" Delaney asks regarding the denial from his sister.

"I'm not concerned. I know she will come around. Second it doesn't change the plan, just less devils, but still have thousands to work with."

"So what is your grand plan? Can you tell me now?" she asks.

"I know it sounds generic, but we are going to take out the angels. We will target the knights and their leadership. The attacks will all happen simultaneously so they don't have time to react. It will all be timed and coordinated. We will then move on to the rest of the angels, but by then they will have lost their best warriors. This will be different in that we have always face them head-on, in large battles. Never really worked out for us. This time they will be unsuspecting," Jason explains.

"I see. I like it…I do. It sounds fun."

"That is one way to look at it. I think it will be fun as well," he agrees.

"What time do you want to leave today?" Delaney asks Jason.

"Oh, I don't know. I don't think we have to go home yet," Jason responds.

"Okay, well, what else is there to do? I thought the only business was to visit your sisters?" she asks.

"How does Cancun sound? I don't see the need to get home right now, do you? We should finish out the week in Cancun, don't you think?" he asks.

"Well, I would not be opposed to that. No work, right?" she checks.

"No work," he confirms.

"What about home, your wife? Isn't she expecting you home today?" Delaney asks. She gets up to grab another drink.

"I'll take care of my wife. I told her that I would be gone for an entire week. We left Tuesday, well, go home Tuesday. Let's go to Cancun."

She sits down again. She gives him a look of suspicion. "If I didn't know any better, I would say that you had this planned," she questions.

"Truth be told, I did. I wanted to spend some extra time with you," he confesses.

"Well what time do you want to leave then?" she asks.

"Whenever, the rest of this trip is about you, you're in charge, so you make the call."

"Wow, I'm in charge." She smiles.

Jason's phone rings. "Franco, tell me something good. I should be home by Tuesday… Yeah. We can meet then or Wednesday to talk about our next course of action. It will be huge. I think you will love it," he tells Franco. Jason gets out of his seat to get another drink.

"Yes, see you then," he hangs up the phone.

"Franco and the rest of the devils will be happy about this plan," Delaney tells him.

"Yes, and I was saying, this trip is about you. Surprise! This is what I was talking about. Once we get there, we will do everything you want to do. And I've got some other little surprises in store for you as well."

"Wow, this is so sweet. Thank you. I love it. This will be great," she tells him.

* * * * *

Sherri walks through the door and sees Brodie sitting on the couch. She lets Franky off his leash and pulls her headphones out. She goes to the kitchen to refill her water bottle. She returns to the living room and sits near Brodie.

"How was the walk?" he asks.

"It was good. It's always good," she responds.

"Is Beck around?" she asks.

"Yeah, I think she's upstairs," he tells her.

"Are you busy right now, or can you talk?" she asks.

"I'm just looking at some stuff on the internet. I can talk. What's up?" he asks.

"Let me grab Becks then, see if she is free right now. Hold on."

"All right." She walks up stairs to her room first. She removes her shoes and exchanges a top she is wearing. She walks over to Becca's door and knocks.

"Come in," Becca says.

"Hey, you got a sec?" Sherri asks.

"Yeah, what's up?" Becca asks.

"I have something I want to tell you guys, can you come downstairs?" Sherri asks.

Becca gets out of her seat. "Are you sick? Are you okay?"

"I'm fine, just something I want you guys to know."

They get downstairs and join Brodie.

"What is it, Sher Bear?" Becca asks impatiently.

"My dad is sick. He has cancer."

"Holy shit!"

"Oh my god!" the friends react.

"It's colon cancer," she tells them.

"I'm so sorry, Sherri," Brodie says as Becca walks over to sit by her. She puts her arms around her and squeezes tight.

"I found yesterday, but the good news is that it's early and my dad says that the doctors aren't concerned," she says as she begins to weep.

"Well, that is good news," Brodie agrees.

"My dad isn't even worried about it, and he tells me not to worry, but I can't help it," she tells them.

"Why isn't he worried?" Brodie asks.

"Um, I guess they can just go in and take it out because it's small and early. He called it stage zero out of four or five stages. He isn't even worried about the procedure. I just wanted to tell you because I might be spending more time over there for a while. Especially after the surgery."

"That makes sense," Brodie says.

"Well, if you need anything from us, just let us know," Becca adds.

"Thanks, guys," Sherri says as Brodie moves in to join the hug.

* * * * *

Emily arrives at Elise's home. She reaches the front door of her apartment. A couple of her assistances accompany her. She stands by as her assistant rings the doorbell. Elise comes to the door still half asleep; she looks through the peep hole before opening it. She sees that it is her mother and leans her forehead against the door.

"Open up dear, I know you're at the door," Emily says from the other side.

Elise lifts her head from the door and puts on a happy face to open the door. Emily stares at her daughter and can tell that she just woke up.

"Mother, why are you here so early?" she asks.

"Early! You think it's early?" Emily answers with a surprised look.

"Yeah, it's…" She turns to check the time on her clock. Slowly she responds, "It's five till ten, not even ten…oh, maybe it's eleven."

There is a short pause. Elise looks on, expecting a follow-up comment from her mother.

"All right then, come on in, Mother," Elise says.

"Thank you, darling," Emily responds. Emily and her assistants walk into the apartment.

"I stopped by your brother's place before this, but there was no answer. Do you know where he might be?" Emily asks.

"Most of the time, no one knows where he is, Mother," she replies. Elise shuts the door and turns to see her mother with open arms. Elise moves in for a hug. Emily squeezes and kisses her daughter.

"Oh, how I miss my little baby," Emily says.

"Very good to see you, Mother," Elise says.

"Yes, indeed. So the service is at 1:00 p.m. Will you be ready in time?" Emily asks.

"Yeah, I'll be ready... I think I'll just keep my preparations to a minimum," she answers.

"Very well then, would you like to ride with us?" Emily asks.

"So that would mean you would hang out here until then?" Elise asks in return.

"Of course, why not. I'm here already. I was actually thinking I would take my little girl out to lunch before the service," Emily says.

"Right, well, I guess I'll just go get into the shower then," Elise tells her guests. She turns to walk to the bathroom.

"How soon do you think you will be ready dear?" Emily asks.

"I will be as quick as possible, Mother," she responds.

"Would you like any assistance getting ready?" Marvin asks Elise.

Elise stops and looks back only half ways at the assistant. Emily and Georgia stand with big smiles on their faces.

"Thanks, Marvin, but I think I got this. I've done it a couple times before," Elise tells him.

"Of course, well, let me know if I can help in any way," Marvin offers. Elise smiles at him and continues to her shower.

* * * * *

"Three countries in one week, but this time we get to relax," Delaney says as she stares out the window overlooking the beach.

"We are going to have all types of fun, baby. But first I have to make a call," he tells her.

"You said no more work, remember?" she reminds him.

"I wouldn't call this work. I have to call Crystal back," he tells her.

"Of course. Well, I'll be down on the beach, 'cuz who knows how long you're going to be," she tells him.

He slaps her ass as she walks by him to leave the room. He gets up to pour a drink. He takes a sip as he undoes a button. He pushes the Speaker button on the phone, then presses Call, and sets it down.

"Hello," she says.

"My love, how are you doing?" he asks.

"Not good, Jason!" she says with an angry tone.

He takes a sip as he cowers a little.

"I'm still pissed about Nate. I want you home now," she commands.

"Right, well we just landed in Costa Rica…"

"Jason, what the fuck. Why?" she asks.

"Well, I thought I would spend some extra time with each of my sisters. Spend three or so days with each of them," he explains.

"No, you don't like your sisters that much, Jason!" she exclaims.

"This is some serious business we are discussing, and I wanted to spend a little nonbusiness-related time with them to ease the fact that I am asking them for their legions," he tells her.

"That's a bunch of bullshit, Jason. You don't need their permission. What are you really doing?"

"I just told you, in Costa Rica. I'm not going to see Joselyn until tomorrow. I asked you to come with me," he says as he takes a drink.

"I don't know what you are doing, why it has to take so long. I'm just pissed. I have to go," she hangs up.

He takes another drink as he raises his eyebrows. He stares out the window to the beach. "This is going to be fun," he says as he smiles.

* * * * *

The angels have gathered for a midday service. Angels both local and from out of town are in attendance. Also in attendance are human associates and colleagues to pay their respects. All five fallen angels are being remembered at the service. Each is spoken of and highlighted individually by different angels in attendance. It's a sweltering day, and for some in attendance, sweat is mixed in with the tears they shed. The service lasts for about an hour. At the conclusion of the service, most folks leave, but some stay to visit. Brad and Nate walk to their cars with Erin and Leann following, side by side.

"What a beautiful service that was," Erin comments.

"Yes, it was, Mother," Leann responds.

"Hey, Leann," she hears from a distance. She looks up at Brad and her father, but they are facing away from her.

Erin turns around to see Noemy approaching them from the rear.

"Behind you, honey," she tells Leann. Noemy reaches them.

"I'm going to grab a coffer. You want to join?" Noemy asks Leann.

"Yeah sure. I'll meet you there. I drove here," she responds.

"Cool, see you there."

"Noemy, dear," Erin says.

"Yes, Erin. Hi."

"Listen, dear, I just want to apologize about the other day, when you came over. I didn't mean to make you crazy or make you think you were crazy. I just didn't understand what was going on," Erin explains.

"It's okay, Erin. It's been crazy the last couple of days. I'm only glad my brother is alive."

"As am I," Erin replies.

"Okay, I'll see you there," Noemy tells Leann.

Erin and Leann continue their walk to the car to join Nate and Brad who are still conversing.

"It's concerning, but I'll find out how this happened," they hear Brad tell Nate.

"Let's also meet Monday with some of the knights to see how we can increase or improve our efforts," Nate tells him.

Leann helps her mother into the car after their embrace. She walks to her father and gives him a kiss on the cheek, and touches Brads forearm on her way out.

"Very well, Bradley, thank you for everything you have done. I can't express how appreciative I am."

"Don't mention it, sir," Brad opens his door.

"Bye, Erin."

"Bye, Bradley." He closes the door and walks over to his car where his wife and daughter await.

* * * * *

Luis pulls up to Robert's home. Robert's wife answers the door. "Hey, is Rob here?"

"Yes, come in. Let me grab him for you." Robert comes to the door.

"Luis, come in, man," Robert says.

"Thanks, you got some place we can talk?" Luis asks.

"Yeah, let's go in the back. You sound serious," Robert jokes.

"It is, actually," he says as he chuckles.

"Oh shit, okay, you've got my attention," Robert tells him.

They reach the patio outback and sit.

"Oh, shit, man, a beer?" Robert offers.

"Yeah, definitely," Luis responds.

Robert runs inside to grab the beers. Luis adjusts himself in the chair as he is a little nervous about this conversation he is about to have. Robert returns and hands Luis a beer.

"Thanks. All right, I got to put this out there first. I have never thought about this. And really, I'm only doing this because I share the same thoughts as you all, I might be stuck in the middle of it, so this is risky for me. The way I see it, though, is that I'm just sharing information," Luis prefaces.

"Damn, man, this is serious," Robert says.

"I told you, I'm serious it is," Luis tells him.

"All right, well, shoot," Robert says.

"So I'm hearing that Ty is not happy with Jason," Luis starts.

"Really?" Robert has a surprised look.

"Yeah, from a pretty reliable source too," he adds.

"Sara?" Robert guesses.

"Yeah," Luis confirms.

"So I'm hearing that Ty is on Jason's shit list and Ty is questioning everything about Jason—his leadership, intentions, decisions, everything. To the point where he is thinking about challenging him," Luis explains.

"Shut the fuck up!" Robert exclaims.

"I'm serious, this is all from Sara. Let's put it this way, she is concerned. That's my girl, so she can't know this is coming from me, but Franco has had to keep him calm."

"Okay, this sounds legit. I like it. I just want to make sure, though, why are you telling me?" Robert asks.

"Because it's no secret how your father feels about Jason, and by extension, you and your brother. With Ty on board, that would really tip the scales, don't you think?" Luis asks.

Robert thinks about it. "I mean, yeah, I think you're right. I think that would cause a rift." Robert laughs.

"Damn, devils are so shady." Luis smiles.

"All right, well, I agree. Did you think this out any further?" Robert asks.

"Well, the next step is to talk to Ty. I was thinking that I could do that, and you talk to your brother. I don't think we bring your dad into this yet. We have to make sure Ty is in," Luis explains.

"Yeah, good call, I agree. Well let's move fast. I'll get with my brother right now. You talk to Ty. Let's connect in about an hour and see where we are," Robert proposes.

"Sounds good," Luis confirms.

* * * * *

Brad arrives at Uriah's apartment. He knocks on the door.

"Hey, Brad, come on in."

"Hey, Uriah, good to see you." Brad makes his way to the couch.

"How are you doing?" he asks Uriah.

"Better, but it's still fresh. Knowing that Z made it helps."

"Yeah, definitely. Have you seen him yet?" Brad asks.

"No, I haven't."

"You?"

"No, I'm sure he's been resting."

"Yeah, makes sense," Uriah agrees.

"Listen, we need to figure out how this happened. For as long as I've been alive, I've never known an angel to betray their own, but right now that is the leading theory."

"You think one of us, did it?"

"I hope you understand."

"I do actually. It makes sense. As Vanessa I were running from the jet, we would stop to rest. I remember having the same thoughts. I want to know what happened as well," Uriah says.

"Good. Let's just start with the ride there. Talk to me about it. What seemed different? Think about each angel individually. Take your time. Was there anything unusual about them, compared to your other experiences with them?" Brad asks. Uriah takes a moment to think about it. He thinks about the other angels, one at a time.

"On the way there, everything was normal. Everyone acted normal," he tells Brad.

"Okay, what about your time in Bend? Anything out of the ordinary there?" Uriah thinks again.

"I didn't think anything different there either."

"Okay, so what about the fly home?" Uriah thinks about each angel again.

"It was such a short amount of time. Dom and Vanessa were up front. You know the only thing I thought was different was JR. He was quiet. I don't remember him talking on the way home, at all, actually."

"Was he quiet in Bend?" Brad asks.

"I don't think so, not when I was around him."

"So JR was quiet. That's it, huh," Brad recaps.

"Yeah, you know coming back was such a short period of time, and it all happened so fast. Everything seemed normal," he tells Brad.

"Yeah, I get it. Let's talk about the attack. I noticed that when you and Vanessa were recounting the attack, it was you who described how Ty was communicating with Rudy. And it seemed like Ty knew Rudy was in the jet already. Think about that communication again? Can you talk more about any communication between any devil and angel?"

"Ty did all the talking. I don't know if any other daemons were there. Ty called Rudy out right away. How would he have known that Rudy was on that jet? He also mentioned at one point that we were down to seven angels after Anna died," he explains.

"They knew Rudy was on board. They knew there were eight angels on board. They must have not realized yet that JR and Z were not on the jet when they got there," Brad points out.

"That's specific detail about us that someone would have had to have told them. There is no way they would have known that detail otherwise," Uriah says.

"My thoughts exactly."

"Do you plan on talking to anyone from Bend?" Uriah asks.

"Yeah, I do. Anything else about that communication with Ty?"

"No, there wasn't much said. Rudy never responded. It was Ty, and that was short," Uriah says.

"Okay, listen, Uriah, you should know that I'll be pulling phone records for this group," Brad informs him.

"Makes sense. I hope you get something from it," Uriah tells him.

"All right, well, if anything else comes up, just let me know. It's gonna take me awhile to figure this out, assuming I will, so call me," he tells Uriah.

"I will. So I'm glad you're here. I wanted to talk about getting back out there."

* * * * *

It has been a busy week for Sherri. With the move and the emotional stresses of her father and her relationship, she needs an outlet. She decides to hit the gym and release some stress. There is a twenty-four-hour fitness in the neighborhood, so she runs there as part of her workout. Generally, she focuses more on cardio, but today, she wants to release some real tension, so she is going to add some weightlifting.

After a lengthy period of stretching and warming up, she sets her sights on the bench press. She starts off with a manageable weight. After a couple of sets, she is feeling really good, so she decides to add more weight an amount she hasn't tried before. She stands back and stares at the bench. She is staring seventy-five pounds square in the face. She takes a deep breath then claps her hands. She lies down on the bench and aligns her body. She reaches up for the bar and spaces her hands. She pulls her upper back up, arching it, and lets out a big breath as she lies back down. She closes her eyes. She opens her eyes and lifts the bar off the rack. She moves the bar above her chest. She begins to lower it.

Lowering it is the easy part, she thinks to herself. It's slow at first, then her elbows begin to bend faster than she anticipated.

"Shit, no, no, no, no," she says as she struggles to talk. A fellow gym goer is close by watching. As soon as the bar reaches her chest, he swoops right in to help her. He grabs ahold of the bar.

"Keep pushing, I got you." He assists her to the rack.

Her arms drop to the floor. She closes her eyes. She opens them again. She looks up at him smiling down on her. She is speechless. She gets off the bench, to her feet.

"Are you good?" he asks.

You are a beautiful man, she thinks to herself.

"Um, I am so embarrassed," she tells him.

"Don't worry about it. We'll just tell people that you were doing a negative," he suggests.

"Negative, that sounds bad, what is that?" she asks.

He explains a negative to her.

"I guess we can call it that," she says to him. It didn't make her feel any better.

"Thank you for helping and for trying to make me feel better about it," she tells him.

"No problem," he says. He tells her to have a good day and returns to where he was working.

She begins to unload the bar. She is a little disappointed at her attempt. She moves on from the bench press and goes from one machine to the next. Physically, she is feeling really good, but mentally, she is not. Earlier that day in her room, she had a feeling for the first time. After her last interaction with Matthew, in her bedroom, she began to doubt the strength of her relationship.

Until then, she had always felt optimistic and thought that Matthew had her best intention at heart. Now, she doesn't believe that to be true. It is overly concerning to her because she has always felt like her relationship was rock-solid. She's close to finishing. She is happy with her overall production at the gym. She has one more set left, so she sits, resting until it's time. She is staring straight ahead in deep thought.

"You gonna need a spot on this one," the gym goer says.

No response.

"Hey, hi," he adds as he waves his hand in front of her face. She snaps out of her gaze.

"Oh, hi," she says, surprised.

"Sorry didn't mean to startle you," he says.

"Ah, you didn't, I was just in a zone for a strong finish," she tells him.

"Yeah, I can see that," he tells her.

"Well, I'm heading out, but just wanted to check on you and make sure you didn't need a spot," he tells her. She giggles.

"Thanks, but no." She freezes her face.

Stop it, you shouldn't be flirting, she thinks to herself.

"Cool, well, my name is Ruben."

"I'm Sherri, nice to meet you," she replies.

"Good to meet you as well."

There is a moment of silence.

"So would you like to have a drink sometime," he asks.

"Yes!" she shouts mildly.

"No," she says right after.

"No, um, no, ah, I can't, um, no, um, sorry, you're nice, no," she says. She gets out of the seat and faces him. She starts backing away as she apologizes.

"I'm so sorry. I can't. I'm in a relationship. You're really nice, gorgeous, and thank you for helping me, but no," she tries to explain. She continues to apologize as she backpedals. She trips over a piece of equipment and falls on her butt. Ruben moves in to help her.

"No, I got it, thank you. Have a lovely day," she tells him as she gets herself up. She faces him again and bows, then turns around and walks away.

"Why, did I bow. I'm such a weirdo," she says aloud.

* * * * *

"What did you think of the service, dear?" Erin asks Isaiah.

"It was nice. It was nice. I'm glad we were able to include JR," he replies.

"Yes, I'm so glad he was found. I can't imagine how hard it is to look for anything out there in a forest," Erin adds.

"It's been so long since we've had to bury an angel," Isaiah says.

"Indeed, it has," Nate agrees.

"Well, it's so good to see you, Z. I'll let you two talk," Erin says as she goes to a different part of the yard.

"I'm so glad you are alive, Z. I wanted to meet with you to check in. See if there is anything I could do for you," Nate offers.

"There is, in fact, but first, I want to apologize. When I jumped out of that jet, I went after the halo. Then I saw the devils in the air, and I panicked. I shifted my focus to the angels. Lost sight of the halo. I'm sorry. I know that the halo is the most important thing," Isaiah explains. Nate smiles.

"You know, Z, I'm going to tell you something that might be a surprise to you. The halo is the most important thing to us. It is the source of our being. It's our life source. But something that is more important, even more than the halo in many ways, is the life of an angel. You see, protecting the halo is something we do because we must. In the grand scale, it impacts everyone equally. But protecting the life of an angel, well, we don't do that because we must—we do it because we want to. Life has more meaning to us than a halo. We do it because without the angels, the halo would fall into the wrong hands. So you don't need to apologize. You decided with your heart, and it was the right decision. We'll find the halo. I'm confident in that," Nate explains.

"Yeah, I have to say that my guilt lies more with the angels than it does with the halo right now," Isaiah adds.

"That's perfectly normal. Don't feel bad or guilty about that. The last couple generations of angels, like yours, have shifted priorities. Where life has become more important than the existence of the halo. I blame myself for that and a couple of generations before me. For thousands of years, the halo was the only thing that mattered and was worth dying for. Now you feel that it is more important that you give your life for another angel instead of the halo. To be honest, I'm a little envious about that," Nate says.

"Well, I know that I would sacrifice myself for the halo," Isaiah tells him.

"I know you would. You did by jumping out of that jet," Nate points out.

"Yeah, well, you know, still feels like I failed everyone."

"That you did not," Nate reassures him.

"So there is something else. While I was out there, I was found by a man named Malakai. He is a trucker. He found me, fed me, took me into his home. I met his wife, Shawna. They went out of their way to help me. I owe them big-time. Unfortunately, they got caught up in this mess because of me. The devils followed Elise to their home when she went to pick me up. Of course, you know that there was a fight. Parts of their home were damaged. When I left, I assigned four angels to help them repair their home and watch over them. I'd like to give them some additional money and keep them under our protection until I feel that it's safe for them," Isaiah asks.

"Done. Anything else?" Nate asks.

"No, thank you."

"When were you hoping to deliver this money?" Nate asks.

"Not sure, I was thinking about going down there soon to check on them."

"Tell you what, you can come with us if you'd like. I asked Brad to set up a visit for next week. I would like to visit the angels down there. You can join us then if you'd like?"

"Yeah, I might do that, thanks."

"And if you don't mind, I'd like to join you, to meet your friends," Nate asks.

"Sure."

"Well, the money is here for when you are ready, and just get with Brad about the protection detail for your friends," Nate tells him.

"Thanks, that's all I've got for now," Isaiah says.

"Okay, well, I wanted to tell you that we are having a celebration of life tonight, but I also want to celebrate you, Vanessa, and Uriah, so be here at eight," Nate insists.

"Yeah, cool, that sounds fun."

* * * * *

Becca is in her room on her computer doing schoolwork. Brodie knocks at the door as he opens it.

"Hey, Becks."

"Yeah, come in."

"I need to talk to you before Sherri gets home." She turns quickly to face him. She enjoys anything that is gossip, drama filled or secretive in nature.

"What is it? Is it about Sherri?" she asks.

"Yes, so, I was trying to tell you yesterday before dinner, but then Sherri got home. I still need you to hold to your promises from yesterday," he tells her.

"Okay, sure fine," she says.

"So remember the other day at the store, I told you some shit about a girl. Forget all that. I saw something else. This is big-time. So I was in the aisle. I look to the end of aisle, and I see a girl. I was checking her out. As she walked by, I saw Matt walk behind her, with her."

"That motherfucker. I always knew he was scum," she says as she gets out of her seat.

"I went down the aisle and basically chased them. I followed them for a minute, and it was clear they were together," her explains.

"Ew, that pisses me off. I want to rip his head off!" she yells.

"So then of course I found you and took you to the other end of the store until I saw them leave."

"Goddammit, poor Sher Bear," she says as she paces around.

"How do you want to do this?" Brodie asks.

"Fuck, she is already stressing about her dad. If we tell her before the party, that will kill it for her and us, but more her," she says.

"I think we just wait till Sunday, then tell her early," he proposes.

"Ew, the thought of him at the party now just pisses me off even more. I feel like I would have been better off not knowing till after the party, but I'm glad you told me," she expresses.

"All right, we'll do it Sunday. You should be the one to tell her since you saw him. You're sure it was him, right?" she asks.

"Yeah, I know what he looks like, man," he responds, a little insulted.

"Ew, I want to be there when she dumps his ass. I hope I'm there," she says as she continues to pace in her room.

"You won't be, but you can be here for after, 'cuz she will need you," Brodie tells her.

She continues to pace. "Now I can't focus. I don't know that I can continue with school. Ew, I need to get this anger out. I should pay him a visit," she says.

"Absolutely not, we just agreed on a plan," he reminds her.

"But I want to punch him in the face!" she yells out.

* * * * *

Luis pulls up to Ty's building. He presses the intercom that connects to Ty's apartment.

"Yeah," Ty says over the intercom.

"Hey, Ty, it's, uh, Luis. Can we talk?" he asks.

"About what?" Ty replies.

"I'd rather tell you in private. It's pretty serious," Luis tells him.

"I'm busy right now man. Call me later," Ty tells him.

"Ty, it shouldn't take much time. It's about you and others, but mainly about you," Luis elaborates.

"Why don't you just tell me man. I've got company," Ty explains.

"Look, we don't have a lot of time. It has to do with Jason also," Luis says.

The door buzzes open. Luis enters the building and goes up to the apartment. When he gets there, the door is already open, so he lets himself in. As he enters, he sees a lady standing nearby with a robe on. He walks over to Ty.

"So what's going on, man?" Ty asks.

"Look, first, Sara doesn't know I'm here. Her and I have talked, but she doesn't know I'm doing this, so just so you know, I'm taking a risk here," Luis explains.

Ty motions to Luis to move it along.

"Right, all right, look, Sara was telling me how your relationship with Jason has become a little fractured. I just met with your cousin Rob, told him about you and Jason. You know how your uncle and cousins feel about Jason, and I just wanted to remind you about them, I guess. If you are feeling the way your sister describes, then I think it would be a good opportunity to talk with them and go from there," Luis explains.

"What exactly has my sister told you?" he asks.

"Uh, that you're on Jason shit list pretty much. You've been questioning his leadership. So much so that it feels like you might turn against him," he tells him.

The lady walks over to sit next to Ty as she snacks on an orange.

"She told you all that, huh," Ty confirms.

"Yeah."

"So what do you want, what are you trying to do here?" Ty asks.

Luis doesn't respond right away. He is distracted by the lady's exposed boob.

"Hey, you with me?" Ty asks.

The lady realizes that her boob is out; she smiles as she covers up.

"Yeah, well, all I'm doing right now is bringing some folks together to talk. I agree with you all, but I'm loyal to Sara, so. I'm just saying. Don't you think it's worth talking to your cousins? See what they have to say. You know how they feel already. Having someone like you on their page, well, that's worth a chat, I think," Luis explains.

Ty thinks about it for a moment. He gets off the sofa and walks around.

"So they want to meet? They want to talk?"

"I only spoke with Rob. He was going to talk to Curt, and I with you, then hopefully, meet up."

"When?" Ty asks.

"ASAP," Luis responds.

"What's the rush?" Ty asks.

"I think it's more about not letting this fester. They are pretty excited to hear that you are in this space right now," Luis explains.

"Is Franco involved?"

"No, right now it's just me, you, Rob, and Curt," Luis tells him.

"All right, let's do it. Set it up," Ty instructs.

Luis gets on his phone to send a text to Robert.

"Hey, baby, I have to head out for a bit. Just hang out. I won't be gone long," he tells her.

"I wait in your bed," she responds in a thick German accent, drawing Luis's attention.

* * * * *

Brad arrives at the park. Vanessa asked him to meet her at a park instead of her home. He looks around for her and doesn't see her.

"Boo!" Vanessa screams out.

Brad isn't startled.

"Oh, you're no fun," she tells him.

"Sorry to disappoint you, but I'm glad to see you in better spirits."

"I've had some great support around me, so that's helped. Thanks for meeting me here. I just wanted to get out of the house, such a lovely day," she says.

"No problem, this was a good call. It is beautiful out here. Let's find a spot, yes."

They find a park bench on the other side of the park.

"So what's going on? What did you want to meet about?" she asks.

"I'm trying to figure out why and how this attack happened."

"Right, right. You think an angel was involved?"

"I would hate to think that, but to pull something like this off, the devils would need some help from the inside.

"So I want you to take me through your experience. Now you and Uriah gave us a detailed description of what happened, but I would like you to dig a little deeper if you can.

"In the forest, Uriah kept bringing this idea up also. I didn't say much because it's hard to imagine an angel would set us up like that. But not Uriah. He was convinced the whole time that something wasn't right. The devils had help."

"Let's start with the flight there. Did anything or anyone seem different to you?" he asks.

"Um, it's hard to say for me. I was up front with Dom the whole time pretty much. I got up occasionally, but you know it's hard for us to hear anything up there with headsets on," she explains.

"True, I forgot about that. Guess you would have missed out on all the interactions. Well, let's talk about the time in Bend. Same questions." She takes in a big breath.

"Anna and I spent a lot of time together. Didn't see Rudy, Uriah, JR, or Isaiah much, so can't say for them."

"So the guys, you didn't see them much?"

"Yeah, I guess not. Didn't think about it like that, so I guess I spent most of my time with the ladies."

"No problem. Focus us them, anything off about the ladies?"

"No, they all seemed normal to me," she says.

"Okay, the ride home, I know you didn't get to interact with them much, but when you did, did anything stand out?"

"Right, well, nothing that I would consider out of the ordinary, but I will mention, and not because I think this suspicious, but I did observe Isaiah fixated on the halo. We chatted about it briefly, but he was just very curious about it," she explains.

"Yeah, that's not out of the ordinary. I've observed other angels do the same. I'd like you to think about the attack. Did any of the devils and angels talk? They were yelling at us. It was fuzzy for me because I was so preoccupied with Anna. Also, I was covering the front of the jet. All the yelling was coming from the back. I thought I heard one of them say it was Ty who was yelling. But I was in a zone. I had devils in front of me, waiting to attack. So I don't remember what was said, sorry," Vanessa expresses.

"No problem. I'll be working on this for a while, I'm sure, so if something comes up, please let me know. There is one more thing you should know Vanessa. I'll be pulling phone records for you and the other angels. I'll probably go beyond that group, but definitely the Bend crew. Thought you should know," Brad informs her.

"Oh, no problem. Let me know if there is anything else I can do or provide," Vanessa offers.

"Thanks. Well, I'll get going now. Good idea meeting out here. You heading over to Nate's?"

"Yeah, I've got a couple things to do, but I'll be there."

"Good, I'll see you there," he tells her.

* * * * *

It's a little past eight, and there are quite a few people already at the celebration. Both angels and humans are present. Uriah, Vanessa, and Isaiah have already arrived. Nate asked them to be present by 8:00 p.m. This is the first time they have seen each other since the attack. They keep to themselves for a while as Vanessa and Uriah tell Isaiah of the attack. Periodically, both angel and human associates approach them to chat them up about the attack, or to just express their happiness about them being alive.

Hayley walks into the house. She does a quick scan for Elise and Christian. She doesn't know if he will be there, but chances are that he will be. She doesn't see either of them, so she goes for a drink.

"Hayley, my dear," Emily says as she flanks her.

"Emily! Hi."

"Oh, young lady, it's been so long."

"It has, it has."

"You don't come to Bend anymore. Why not?" Emily asks.

"You know, Emily, it's just been super busy lately, and, um." She pauses. She isn't prepared with a response. She is feeling uncomfortable because she knows questions about Christin are coming.

"Well, I just miss seeing you. You and Christian need to visit me soon," she says as Hayley looks around desperately for Elise to show up.

"Actually, I'm in town for a couple of more days, why don't I take you two out?" Emily offers.

"You know, Emily, that sounds great. We need to talk before that. Will you excuse me for a moment? I really have to use the restroom," Hayley tells her.

"Of course, dear," she says as Hayley rushes away from her.

It's close to nine, and more people have showed up. Hayley keeps checking her phone for a response from a text she sent Elise. Kyleigh goes the bar for a drink and stands next to Erin.

"Hi, lady," she says to Erin.

"Hey, honey, how are you?"

"I am great. Just trying to be there for my sister, you know."

"Yes of course. You are a great big sister. What are you drinking?" Erin asks Kyleigh. "Oh, it's wine for me tonight," she responds.

"Same for me. Two reds please," Erin orders.

Elise finally shows up. She casually walks in and begins talking to some folks. She navigates her way through the crowd looking for someone she wouldn't mind talking to. She spots Landon.

"Oh, I'm not ready for that yet, where is the bar? I'm sure I will find Hayley there."

"Oh, not surprised, I was right, hey," she says aloud, trying to get Hayley's attention.

"Oh my god!" Hayley shouts as she grabs Elise by the wrist and pulls her to the restroom.

"Where have you been?"

"What's wrong?" Elise asks.

"Your brother hasn't told your mother that we are broken up. That's what's wrong."

"Are you asking me or telling me?" Elise asks.

"Both, either. I don't know, but your mother is wanting to take us to lunch. So it sounds like she doesn't know," Hayley says.

"Well, he is kind of private, even with his family, you know that. I wouldn't be surprised if he hasn't," Elise tells her.

"Oh, geez, I should go. I shouldn't be here," Hayley expresses with a mild level of anxiety.

"Why not? I just got here. Look, it's not a big deal. Who care if she does or doesn't know? Hell, I'll tell her," Elise offers.

"No, no. I'm just freaking out. Your brother is going to be here, I'm sure, and I don't want to see him," Hayley says.

"Why not?" Hayley doesn't respond.

"What did you do?" Elise asks.

"I went over to his place last night," Hayley whispers.

"What the—you shit. Goddamn it. Why? Are you serious right now? What the hell, Hayley," Elise expresses.

There is a knock at the door.

"Go away," they both yell.

"Oh, you fucked up," Elise says.

"I know, I know," Hayley pouts.

"I have to piss," Elise walks to the toilet.

"I don't know if I can be here. Your brother, your mom. There is no way we can hide this tonight," Hayley expresses.

"Look, it's not a big deal, who cares if my mother doesn't know. It doesn't matter. What? Are you gonna get grounded? I'll talk to Christian. Just do what you do best," Elise tells her.

"What's that?"

"Drink."

Hayley rolls her eyes as Elise flushes. She goes over to wash her hands.

"Okay, let's get out there. Don't stress," Elise tells her friend. They open the door.

"Wow, there are so many people here. I was not expecting this," Elise comments.

"Me either. There are a lot of people here. I thought it was a small gathering," Hayley adds.

"We might not have to go out tonight," Elise tells Hayley.

"Oh yeah, we still have to," Hayley replies.

"Let's just see how the night goes, huh," Elise suggests.

* * * * *

"Cousin!" Curt yells out when seeing Ty.

"Hey, Curt."

"I don't know what you guys are drinking these days, so we didn't order for you," Robert says as he waves the bartender over.

"So after Luis came to me, I spoke with Curt, so he is caught up. I gotta say, I'm pretty surprised that you are feeling this way," Robert adds.

The bartender gets to the table.

"What are y'all having?" Robert asks.

"I'll have a pale ale," Luis requests.

"I'll take a Hamm's tall boy," Ty requests.

"Got it," the bartender says.

"And a round of boilermakers!" Curt shouts out.

"So, Luis, you got us here. You know, after you and I spoke, I got to wondering about you. You know, why are you doing this? What's your angle here?" Robert asks.

"Yeah, what do you have to gain?" Curt follows up.

The three men stare at Luis.

"Well, like I told you two, I feel the same way you do, but I'm not going to do anything about it. I'm not a daemon. I don't have that kind of pull. But I do think there is an opportunity here, so my role in this is to bring the heavy hitters together. I'll support whatever, but I can't lead it. I want to remind you that Sara doesn't even know I'm doing this. You know how loyal she is to Jason. I don't imagine it has changed, but you might know different," Luis says as he looks at Ty.

"So I have no more to gain than any of you. Your family has felt this way for a long time, and I was just telling them, that if you feel the same as them now, well, that changed the landscape. Everyone knows what you can do, Ty. If something were to change with Jason, the chances would be greater if you were a part of it, instead of against it," Luis explains.

The bartender shows up with the drinks.

"So you're proposing a coup," Ty asks.

"Just the idea right now. I wouldn't go against Jason alone. All I'm saying is, if there is something here, then I'm in," Luis tells them.

"Ty, you know where we stand. What are you thinking? I want to hear it from you," Robert asks.

"Not sure. It's true. I do think that Jason has gone soft. I guess I haven't reached that point of turning on him. There is a lot I have to think about. My sister, my mom, Franco. It's not that easy for me," Ty conveys.

"But you agree that Jason has to go?" Curt asks.

"Yeah, I think so. But I'm not gonna commit to anything," Ty makes clear.

"Well, that is a start. That's good news. That will make Pops happy," he tells Robert.

"Let's do these boilermakers," Robert suggests.

"Have you talked to your dad about this? Ty asks with suspicion.

"Not really, we just quickly mentioned that we were meeting with you to talk," Robert tells him.

"That's all this is right now right, just conversation," Curt says.

"Do you guys have a plan?" Ty asks.

"No, I mean we have wanted Jason out for a long time now but, obviously, never done anything about it. But having you, Luis, is a game changer," Robert says.

"And think about it—if you two are feeling this way recently, then how many others are feeling this way also, but are too afraid to say anything. I'll bet there are more than we think," Curt says.

"How would your mother feel about moving against Jason?"

"I know that she has expressed some anger towards him, but not sure how far that goes," he explains.

"Well, it's no secret how our pops feels," Curt says.

"I think that is the next move, talking with our parents," Robert suggests.

"Mine would have to be over the phone," Ty says.

"We can meet with our parents ASAP," Curt points out.

Ty takes a drink and looks around the bar.

"I need another beer," he says.

They wave the bartender over.

"Luis, you said you have a plan?" Curt asks.

"Nope, hell no, I didn't say that. I said I have some ideas, not a plan. More like thoughts," he clarifies.

"Well, what are you thinking?" Curt asks.

"I mean some of it has been brought up already. Number one, finding others who share this sentiment. Two, who takes over as the new leader. That person should create a plan, be prepared to take over. Three, this might be too soon, but I know that Jason isn't returning until Tuesday. Not a lot of time, but a window of opportunity to strike with an element of surprise," Luis explains.

They think for a moment.

"Something this big requires more time, Tuesday ain't enough," Robert says.

"Why don't we just talk to my pops first and your mom," Curt suggests.

"How do you think your mom will receive this idea?" Curt asks.

"I don't know. I don't know that I want to talk to her about it yet," he says.

The next wave of drinks arrives.

"Well, let's just start with my pops. There's no harm in that, right?" Curt asks.

"Sure, I'll hear what he has to say. I just want to remind you that I'm not committing to anything right now," Ty reminds them.

"For sure, for sure," Robert says.

"Let's meet here tomorrow night," Curt suggests.

* * * * *

It's a quarter past 10:00 p.m. as the celebration is in full swing. There is plenty of food and drink as is the norm for angel parties. By now, all the ceremonial acknowledgments, speeches, and toasts have been made, and so all that is left is for some relaxation and fun. More angels have arrived at the party, including Christian. The first person he looks for is Isaiah.

"Damn, there are a lot of people here," he mutters.

He makes his way through the crowd. He greets some people and waves at others, but he would rather continue moving.

"Shit, your brother is here. I'm gonna go hide," Hayley says.

Elise looks around frantically until she spots him. She cuts through the crowd and reaches him. She punches him in the shoulder.

"What the hell," he says aloud.

She grabs him by the ear.

"Dude, I'm not five!" he yells out as she pulls him to the bar. "What are you doing? What was that for?" he asks.

"Hayley is here."

"Yeah, I figured."

"Why would you sleep with her?" she turns to the bartender. "A rum and coke please." She faces him again.

"Why?"

"Whatever, she came to my place. I don't want to talk about it," he says with annoyance.

"Fine, we'll come back to that. Why haven't you told Mom that you split up?"

He stares at her with a look of slight. He turns to the bartender. "Coors Light. I don't know, haven't gotten around to it."

"Yeah, I get it, two months isn't enough time to tell your mother something like that. Well, Mom is offering to take you guys to lunch. Would you like that?"

"Who cares. I'll just tell her here when I see her," he tells her.

"No, you won't!" she says.

"What is all this? Why are you bombarding me with this? You know what, hey, Landon."

Elise freezes.

Christian grabs him from behind Elise and puts his arm around him.

"How you been, man?"

"Good, you?"

"Better now that you're here. Listen, has Elise told you that she has had a massive crush on you for a very long time?"

Landon stares all around, avoiding all eye contact with Elise. Elise is still frozen, but with eyes wide open. Christian grabs his beer.

"I'll leave you two to talk," Christian tells them.

* * * * *

Uriah sees Patricia near the door, putting her coat on. He walks over to her as she reaches for the door.

"Patricia, hey, you are leaving?"

"Hey, Uriah, yeah, I'm tired. I just want to get home to the kids," she tells him.

"I hear you. I'm sure this is emotional and overwhelming. Listen, I just want to say that I'm sorry. If there is anything I can do, please call me," Uriah offers.

Patricia's eyes well up. She smiles at him.

"I just want to tell you that I know I'm alive because of him. He sacrificed himself for the rest of us."

She rubs his shoulder. "Rudy always talked about you the most. He loved you so much," she tells him.

Uriah's eyes begin to well up. He goes in for a hug. "Please call me for anything," he reminds her.

"Thank you, Uriah. Be safe tonight."

* * * * *

"So are you enjoying the party?" Landon asks.

"Um, I." She clears her throat. "Sorry, yes, I am. Aside from some minor drama, yes. Are you?" she asks in return.

"Yeah, this is a big one, but yeah. So, what's your brother talking about? That was random, and if I'm being honest, awkward."

"Right! I think he is really drunk. I'm concerned." She struggles to get any more words out. "Will you excuse me? You know that minor drama I mentioned, well, I kind of have to deal with that right now." She whisks right by him as he is left speechless.

* * * * *

"You know, I love these types of parties, but I'm just a little surprised that your parents are down like this," Kyleigh tells Leann.

"I know what you mean. I'm a little surprised also. Mom has done a lot of work on loosening Dad up."

"Girls," Emily approaches them.

"Hey, Emily."

"Hey, Auntie."

"You girls are beautiful," she tells them with a slight slur in her speech.

"Thank you."

"Can I tell you girls something?"

They look at each other.

"Love your parents. Mine don't even like me. The girlfriends and boyfriends don't even like me. Hayley has been avoiding me all night. My son has turned his girlfriend against me," she slurs as she hiccups.

Leann and Kyleigh look on with confusion.

"You do know about Christian and Hayley, right?" Kyleigh asks.

"Well, of course, I do, she is going to be my daughter-in-law someday. Soon, I hope. I think, they are both staying away from me."

Kyleigh and Leann look at each other with surprised looks, realizing that Emily is unaware that Christian and Hayley are broken up.

"Auntie, are you drunk?"

"No and yes, and some."

"Okay, I think that's a yes. Where is um…did your assistant come with you, Auntie?" Leann turns to Kyleigh. "Do you remember his name?"

Kyleigh shakes her head.

"Do you want to go home, Auntie?" Leann asks.

"Heavens no, I want to talk to my children," she says.

"Okay, um, why don't you just have a seat right here, and we will go get them for you," Kyleigh tells her.

They assist her to a seat.

"Oh my god, she doesn't know," Kyleigh tells Leann.

"Oh, Christian's right there," Leann points out.

"I say we stay out of this one," Kyleigh suggests.

"Yup, let's go this way," Leann says.

The party continues late into the night. Drama is avoided, and so is any interaction between Christian and Hayley. Inhibitions lower the later it gets, and emotions elevate. There is a mixture of grief and celebration, throughout the night, but overall, the mood stays positive as the grief is focused on remembrance of the joy and happiness the fallen angels brought the world.

Saturday

The halo is now on the Willamette River. It is now on a north-bound direction toward Portland and the even much larger Columbia River. If it manages to stay undetected on this river and reaches the Columbia, it will then flow in a west-northwest direction and eventually dump into the Pacific Ocean. At this rate, that is highly likely. The halo has missed several opportunities to be seen by thousands of people, the first being the city of Eugene, as it bypassed the city entirely. The confluence for the McKenzie and the Willamette sits on the north end of the city limits. The Willamette passes through several midsize and smaller towns, but the river sits on the edge of them instead of splitting them. Still, the possibility of getting seen is greater, and because it's summer, people are out on the river still.

Currently, the halo is about to enter the Salem City limits. This will be the first city that the Willamette splits, so there will be resident on both sides. Salem has a midsize population of about 180,000 people, and it boasts a city park that lies along the Willamette. This is a popular spot for residents. Its chance of getting found is much greater here. Still, the halo floats calmly through the city and past the park without a single person realizing it's around.

* * * * *

Bread pops out of the toaster. Brodie walks over to grab it.

"Ah, hot!" he shouts. He grabs the toast and sets it on the plate. He goes to the fridge to grab butter.

"Morning, Brod."

"Hey, Sher."

"What are you having?" Sherri asks.

"Um, some eggs and toast and a yogurt," he responds. "What about you?" he asks in return.

"I am going to have some oatmeal and my usual coffee."

They move around each other to prepare their breakfast. Brodie finishes preparing, so he sits at the table.

"Are you excited about the party?" she asks him.

"Hell yeah. It's going to kick ass," he says.

She laughs.

"I'm pretty excited also."

"Look, I just want to remind you to invite every girl you know," Brodie tells her.

Sherri laughs louder this time.

"So this party should be full of females then?" she asks sarcastically.

"Damn straight," he responds.

Sherri continues to laugh as she finishes preparing her oatmeal.

"I'm surprised Becks isn't up yet," Brodie says.

"You know her, she is always the last one up," Sherri says as she sits at the table.

"Talking shit so early in the morning," Becca says as she walks into the kitchen.

"The truth is not a lie," Brodie tells her.

Becca goes for some coffee. Sherri sits quiet at the table as Brodie and Becca continue with small talk.

"Sherri...Sherri," Brodie calls out as she's in a daydream.

"Huh, sorry, yes," Sherri responds.

"What do you mean yes? We didn't ask you a question," Brodie tells her.

"Oh, well then...I don't know," she tells him.

"Are you okay?" Becca asks.

"Yeah, I was just thinking."

"Oh yeah, what about?" Becca asks.

"Nothing important," Sherri says.

"No, no, no, you got something, so spill it," Becca demands.

Sherri sits there thinking as Brodie stares at her. Becca takes a sip of her coffee, then reaches for cereal.

"I met a guy," Sherri says.

Becca drops the cereal box and rushes to an empty seat at the table. Brodie looks frozen as he stares at her wide-eyed.

"You met a guy?" Becca asks.

"Relax, not what you think."

"We will be the judge of that," Brodie says.

"Tell us!" Becca yells.

"I said relax. Yesterday, I was at the gym, and I needed some help, and a nice guy helped me. That's all," Sherri tells them.

Becca glares at her. "There is no way you're daydreaming about a guy who just helped you. There's more, I know it," Becca tells her.

"Yeah, there is definitely more," Brodie agrees.

"Okay, well, I might have flirted, I think, and he did ask me out."

"Oh, I'm really hoping you said yes," Becca says.

"I most certainly did not. I am involved. It wasn't a big deal, guys. He helped me. I thanked him. He asked me out and I said no."

"Did you think he was hot?"

"That is not important."

"So that's a yes," Brodie says.

"I did think he was attractive, but that doesn't mean anything."

"What's his name?"

"I don't remember, and I have somewhere to be." She gets up from the table. Becca and Brodie look at each other with excitement. Sherri leaves the kitchen. Becca leans over to Brodie.

"We have to find this guy. I'm not letting this go." She gets out of her seat and runs to her room.

* * * * *

The angels continue the frustrating search for the halo. When Elise and Hayley turned the lead over to Paloma, she made it a point to refocus their efforts to the river nearby. The plan doesn't lessen the number of angels searching in the forest; it just adds a more thorough search of the river. They started a sweep of the river yesterday morning and were able to get through the creek that runs into the McKenzie. Once on the McKenzie, the angels had to and will have to continue adjusting their plan. The McKenzie is wider, and its width constantly changes naturally, so they must adjust the number of boats to use with their dragnets.

They are currently east of Eugene, where the McKenzie will end and join the Willamette. So far on this portion of the McKenzie, the other barriers they have had to overcome are lakes and reservoirs. This river flows into each of those bodies of water a couple times requiring the angels to again adjust their sweep to open water spaces. They have also encountered several dams along the way, causing them to exit the river then set up on the other side. Perhaps the biggest challenge the angels face on this river is when the river splits. This happens often along the McKenzie. Even worse, the river will split a second time or split into a dead end, from the original split.

Either way, the angels must adjust to cover all lanes of the river. All together, these barriers have created a time-consuming process, but still progress is felt compared to the efforts on land. Paloma has had to rethink the way they search the forest so that they aren't retracing their steps. It's been seven days since the halo fell into the forest, and in that time, the angels have been able to cover several square miles of forest ground. Paloma herself has been a part of the forest search.

"Paloma, come in," Lilly radios.

"Yeah, go ahead."

"I've completed this section of forest. What's next?" she asks.

"Stand by," Paloma tells her. Paloma pulls out her map and crosses off the section just completed by Lilly. "Lilly, move on to section two-sixty-seven. That should get you to lunchtime," Paloma tells her.

"Roger that," Lilly replies.

Paloma has only been on this mission for about three days now, but she is now starting to grow discouraged with the search. She continues to think of ways to make the search more efficient—all the while trying to make sure she doesn't lose the motivation of the two-hundred-plus angels searching the forest.

She gets on her radio. "Hey, angels, I just want to remind you to stay strong, be thorough, and take breaks as needed. Lunchtime is coming up, so recoup then as well. Remember that there are devils around, so do not let your guards down. Continue to check in with your partners every fifteen minutes. Thank you, angels. You are appreciated," she relays.

* * * * *

Both girls are in the living room. Brodie comes out of his room to stretch.

"You both sent all your invites out, right?

"Yes, we have," both ladies respond.

"Good, good, good. Have you told Jackass about the party?" he asks Sherri.

Becca looks over at her.

"He is my boyfriend. Of course I did. I can't not invite him," she tells them.

"You can not invite him, in fact."

"Guys, please don't start," Becca says as she frowns a little.

"I'm still stressing out about my dad. I just want us to have fun at this party."

Becca and Brodie stay silent because of the guilt about her father.

"Jackass and fun don't go together, honey," Becca says out of the side of her mouth.

"Guess we will have to wait and see," she tells the roommates.

Brodie and Becca stare at each other, each wondering if now is a good time to tell her about Matt's alternate life. They both decided that he would be the one to bring it up. He shakes his head.

"Well, if he does show up, he better not bring his barbarian friends," Brodie tells her.

"He won't bring his friends," she snaps at Brodie.

The friends look at each other because they think it's cute when she raises her voice for any reason. There is a short pause as she remembers that she hasn't told Matt about his friends not being invited. Before they can question her about it, she decides to tell them some news, "Hey, I have to tell you guys something."

Both friends look on with curiosity.

"But…before I do, I have to go upstairs really quick. She quickly runs upstairs to her room to call Matthew and let him know not to bring his friends. As the phone rings, she can already hear the rant that she is going to get from him. Matt is such a 'bro' kind of guy. Him and his friends do everything together, and he takes it very personal when it comes to them. The phone continues to ring, and he finally answers.

"Hey, baby, what's up?" he says.

"Hey, babe, not much, just reminding you that the party is tonight."

"Yeah, man, I'm ready. We'll be there a little late, but we will be there," he tells her with confidence.

"Oh good, I'm excited to see you, but listen… You have to come alone. You can't bring your friends," she tells him.

"What the fuck!" he screams into the phone.

"I just think it's best if they don't come," she says.

"Fuck that. It's your friends that said that," he says.

"It was my decision and mine alone," she tells him to avoid further hatred between the two sides.

"I want you to focus on me, is that so bad?" she asks.

"They're a couple of sorry bitches," he says about her friends.

"Stop it. Those are my best friends," she answers in return.

"This is a disrespect to my friends," he tells her.

"I'm not disrespecting your friends, Matthew."

"This is some bullshit, and fuck your friends," he says as he hangs up on her.

She lets out a huge sigh. She wonders how much longer she can withstand this tension between her best friends and her boyfriend. She goes to her bed to lie down. She needs peace for the moment.

* * * * *

Brad drives up to Isaiah's apartment. He knocks on his door. It takes Isaiah longer than normal to answer the door. Brad knocks a couple more times. Isaiah finally answers.

"Sorry, Brad, you caught me right in the middle of a deuce," Isaiah explains.

"Thanks for sharing, Z."

"Yeah, no problem. Come on in."

"How did you enjoy the party last night?" Brad asks.

"It was good. I was glad to see everyone, especially Vanessa and Uriah." It was nice of Nate to bring everyone together. What about you, how did you enjoy it?" Isaiah asks.

"It was nice. I do those things more often than the rest of you, so it's a little different for me. But this one was better, having more angels present made it much more pleasing," Brad tells him.

"I hear that. So what did you want to meet about?"

"We need to figure why this happened. So I just want to go over that day. I appreciate what you did that day, but I hope you understand that you, along with Vanessa and Uriah, are under investigation, if you will. I believe the devils had some help on the inside. It's really hard to believe, but I don't see any other way," he explains.

"Oh, hmm," Isaiah mumbles.

"Let's start with the ride there. Was there anything different about it? Anyone acting differently?"

"Um, not really. I don't remember anything standing out," Isaiah says.

"Okay, what about the time in Bend?"

"I didn't see everyone as much. The girls stuck together. Some of us guys hung out but again, nothing out of the ordinary."

"Okay, what about the ride home?"

"Well, it was short. I remember Uriah singing. Some small talk. We weren't up there long, a half hour maybe," Isaiah explains.

"Think about each angel separately, and tell me if anything was different about them?" Brad asks.

"Dom and Vanessa were up front. Vanessa came back once I think. Uriah was cool. Angela and Anna were talking about guys. Rudy was doing his thing. JR was hanging out. I don't know."

"Would you say that they each acted normal?" Brad asks.

"Yeah, JR kept to himself, but he was by me most of the time. I didn't talk to him. He didn't talk to anyone."

"You weren't there for the attack so can't tell me about that."

"I wish I was. I think things might have been different," Isaiah says.

"I'll be reaching out a couple times as things come up. This process might take awhile, so please be patient," Brad asks.

"Got it. It's hard to imagine any angel doing this. What would cause them to betray us?"

"I hope to find that out soon, but for now, the focus is finding the halo. One more thing. You should know that I'll be pulling phone records for this group. I need to see what each of you were up to leading up to the attack."

"Makes sense, good call," Isaiah says.

* * * * *

Elise and Emily wait at a table for Christian to arrive.

"Your brother, late again, of course."

"Mom, why are you surprised? He's always late. I don't understand why everyone is still surprised about it. It's always been this way."

"Maybe, but for his mother, I would hope that he would be on time for me. More time spent together," Emily explains.

"Well, just make him stay later. I'll leave early, so you two can be alone," Elise offers.

"Don't be a brat," Emily says.

"So how about you? Are you fully recovered from last night?" Elise asks.

"Truth be told, it has been a really, really long time since I had that much to drink. Not sure why, but I just let myself go," she explains.

"Well, it looks like you're continuing the party," Elise points with her eyes.

"Oh, this, mimosas are harmless," Emily tells her.

Elise smiles as she shakes her head. She looks around and makes eye contact with Marvin.

"Mom, why is Marvin sitting alone?" Emily takes a drink of her mimosa.

"Oh, he is fine," she responds.

"Well, no reason to sit alone, just have him join us," she tells her mother as she waves him over.

"Well, what about you, dear, are you dating anyone right now?" Emily asks.

"No, Mother. I really haven't had time, you know. With the halo missing an all."

Marvin gets to the table.

"Yes?" Marvin says.

"Oh, we don't need anything. I was actually just waving over to come sit with us," Elise tells him.

"Oh." He looks at Emily.

"Yeah, sure, that's fine," she says.

"Very well, I will grab my things."

Elise waits for Marvin to go away to tell her mother, "All right, no more talk of my dating life. Don't want to upset Marvin."

Emily looks up at her with a suspicious look.

"I know what you just did, you weasel," Emily tells her.

Elise smiles at her mom. Marvin returns to the table and gets settled in. At the same time, Christian walks into the restaurant.

"Have you ordered?" Marvin asks the ladies.

"No, we haven't," Elise responds.

Christian reaches the table.

"I need to get my order transferred to this table," Marvin says.

"Hey, Marvin," Christian says as he sits.

"Christian," he responds.

"Hey, sis."

"You fucked up," Elise says, holding a butter knife.

"Mom," he says as he grabs her hands, still staring at Elise and her butter knife.

"Why are you always late, son, and actually..." Emily looks around. "Where is Hayley?"

Elise and Christian look at each other. Elise clears her throat.

"Um, Hayley isn't coming, Mother."

"Well, why not?" Emily asks.

"Mom, Hayley and I broke up awhile ago," he tells her.

"WHAT!" Emily shouts out.

"Whattttttttt!" Elise says, surprised.

"You knew," Christian says to Elise.

The server gets to the table. "Is everyone here?" she asks.

Emily looks at her. "We're going to need more time."

"Okay," the server says as she walks away.

"Or we could order, then keep talking," Elise suggests.

"When did this happen? Why? Did you know?" She looks at Elise.

"You?" She looks at Marvin.

"I did not, madam," he says emphatically.

"I mean, yeah, what kind of a best friend I am if I didn't know something like that," Elise expresses as she lowers her volume.

"Oh my, why? How long ago did this happen?" Emily asks.

"I don't know, Ma, two months maybe," he says as he stares at a menu.

"Oh, you don't even care to tell your own mother. That's how unimportant I am." She puts her hand on her forehead.

"Ma, that is not true."

"What happened?" she asks.

"I don't know. It was her. She wanted space, something different," he explains.

"Did you do something wrong?" Emily asks.

Marvin's food arrives.

"The meat lovers' skillet?"

"Ah, right here," Marvin says.

"How did you get food?" Christian asks.

"We have been waiting for you, you shit," Elise tells him.

"What is your problem?" He turns to Elise. "Is that why you want to shank me?" he asks.

"Oh no, a different reason, bruh." He shakes his head at her.

"What did you do?" Emily asks again.

"I didn't do anything, Ma. Geezo, what is going on here. Thought we were supposed to have a meal. This is crazy with you two. Maybe I should just leave," he suggests.

"I'll find you," Elise says in an ominous tone.

"Okay, creep."

"No, don't leave, I'm sorry. I just thought you two were so perfect for each other, and I just wish you were more open with me. That's all," Emily expresses.

"I'm sorry, Mother. There isn't much I can tell you about why she left me. Elise probably knows better than me. I still want her back."

"Well, do you know?" Emily asks Elise.

"We should order. Let's order," Elise suggests.

"Do you?" Emily asks again.

"No, I don't, okay? But he should know, since you keep messing with her," Elise tells Christian.

"What are talking about?" he asks.

"I know what happened the other night. Why would you do that?" she asks.

"Whatever, did you even talk to her about that? Did she tell you that she called me, she came to my place, she called me telling me she missed me."

"You should have been stronger and said no," Elise suggests.

"What? Whatever, you're crazy," he tells his sister.

"Does that mean you're getting back together?" Emily asks.

"No, Ma, but has Elise told you that she is in love with Landon?"

"WHAT!" Marvin shouts out.

* * * * *

Jason returns to the hotel alone. He and Delaney spent much of the day together, and now he sent her away on a shopping spree. Another surprise within the surprise. They plan on reconnecting later in the evening. For now, he wants to relax and figure out what he will have for dinner. He turns on the TV to view the menu. He goes and pours himself a drink then returns to view the menu. He places his order and turns on some music. He positions a seat in front of the window, overseeing the ocean. He relaxes and waits until his dinner arrives. A half an hour passes, and there is a knock at the door.

"Room service."

"Well, hello, young lady."

"I have your dinner, sir," she says in her Spanish accent.

"Ah, yes, come on in," he tells her.

"Where you like this?" she asks.

"There, next to the coffee table is fine," he tells her. She goes over to set up. As she sets up, she notices him checking her out from the rear.

"You eat alone?" she asks.

He smiles at her.

"Well, I was hoping for some company," he tells her.

"Oh, like your work," she asks as she doesn't understand the context.

He laughs. "No, I mean I was hoping for someone like you to join me for my dinner," he explains.

She turns away as she blushes.

"You like me?" she asks.

"Yes, girly, I like you a lot," he tells her.

She continues setting up his meal. As she does, she makes her intentions known that she is interested in him and his offer. She is obvious with her body language and makes it a point to be inviting.

He gets off the couch and walks over to her. He begins to caress her ass. It brings her to smiles. She begins to move her ass in an inviting way. She lifts her skirt with one hand as she rubs his hip with the other. He helps her lift her skirt with both of his hands. She moves her hand from his hip to his crotch and lowers his zipper. She sticks her hand into his pants and begins to stroke his cock. He presses his crotch against her ass.

"You're a hot little piece of ass," he tells her.

She moves them over, close to the bed. She lifts one of her legs onto the bed. With her skirt lifted and her pussy exposed. "You like no panties?" she asks.

"Oh yes," he says as he bends down to kiss her ass. She moans as she leans toward the bed.

"You inside me please," she tells him.

He rises and pulls his cock out. Sticks it in her wet pussy and begins to thrust his hips. She grabs on to the bed with both hands.

* * * * *

The party is in full throttle now, and everyone is enjoying themselves. They have a large turnout, and everyone is feeling great. Matthew has not shown up yet, but Becca and Brodie know it's only a matter of time. They have made a commitment to not concern themselves with his appearance. They figure that at the very least, they got a win by getting friends removed from the invite list, a list they were never on to begin with. Still, they would much rather him not come at all. They see Sherri across the room. Becca approaches her as Brodie goes off to mingle with other friends.

"Fix your face," Becca tells Sherri.

"What?" she asks.

"I know where your head is. You need to be enjoying yourself," Becca says.

"Geez, can't hide anything from you, can I?" Sherri says.

"No, you can't. Now you better get rid of that face before I do it for you," Becca tells her.

Sherri looks at her with a puzzled expression. "You're mean," she tells Becca.

"I just want you to have fun at your own party. That's all," Becca tells her.

"You invited your friends here. Have you even talked to them?" Becca asks.

Becca walks around and away from Sherri while maintaining a stare at her for as long as she can before she must turn her head forward. Sherri knows that her friend makes a great point, but her concern now is Matt's friends. She told her roommates that Matt's friends weren't coming, but the truth is, she doesn't know for sure. Matt never really confirmed that he wasn't going to bring them. If he shows up, it will be with his friends, and she knows it. She takes a deep breath and smiles. She sees some friends across the way and walks in their direction.

* * * * *

Jose walks into the bar to meet with the four devils. He grabs a seat at the table.

"Ty, my guy. It's been a long time, huh."

"Hey, Uncle," he responds.

"Luis."

"Hey, Jose."

"Why you late, Pops? Now you have to catch up," Curt tells his dad.

"Of course. I was just taking care of some business," Jose agrees as Curt waves the bartender over.

"What were you boys talking about?" Jose asks.

"The next season of football, but that's not why we invited you," Robert tells him.

"I love football, but I understand there is something else that might get me really excited," Jose expresses.

"Well, let's get right to it," Robert says.

The bartender comes over to take another order.

"Like I started telling you, Pops, Luis here started this whole thing by telling me that Ty is thinking differently about Jason." He pauses to check with Ty. "You mind if I do, or do you?" he asks.

"Go right ahead," Ty tells him.

"Ty here is not happy with the way Jason is running things. He feels the way we do?" Robert explains.

"Is that right?" Jose asks.

Ty nods.

"Luis figured he would, at least, facilitate a conversation about the possibility of going against Jason," Robert adds.

"So what have you talked about already?" Jose asks.

"Just gauging where Ty is. What it would mean if he were willing to follow through. Some questions are, who would take over? Do they have a plan? Would they be ready to lead?" Curt says.

The bartender arrives with more drinks.

"I see, I see. So what are you thinking, Ty? My boys have been doing all the talking," Jose asks.

"Well, first, like I told them already, I'm not committing to anything right now. We're just talking. But you know I've just been unhappy with how soft he has gotten. And Crystal, I think it's her. Actually, I want to take her out now. Her I'm ready to do. But I just want to go back to the time where we were constantly fucking the angels up," Ty express.

"So if you feel this way now, then what is stopping you from moving forward with replacing him?" Jose asks.

"It has more to do with others around him, not so much him," he says.

"Well, my pops has had a plan in place for a long time. If you're on board, we'd be good to go," Robert tells Ty.

"So you started this his, huh?" Jose looks at Luis.

"Just the conversation," Luis says.

"You've done a good thing, son," Jose tells him.

"Luis is pretty bold. He's on board too. He was telling us that Jason doesn't return to town until Tuesday. What's the possibility of a takeover with that timeline?" Curt asks his dad.

"Not happening. We shouldn't even entertain that idea. In fact, I don't know that I would do anything in the next month, two months. There is a possibility that he may come through and redeem himself," Ty tells the table.

"What does that mean?" Robert asks.

"We just attacked the angels. Shot them out of the sky. We almost had the halo. Right now, the halo is lost, so it's as much as ours as it is theirs now. That was just the beginning. According to Franco, there is more coming. I trust Franco, and Franco trusts Jason. Franco tells me that I will love what's coming next," Ty explains.

"Well, what is it?" Jose asks.

"He doesn't have the details yet. They should be coming down next week," Ty adds.

"So let me get this straight, you're supposed to get excited about something you don't know about?" Curt asks.

"Not excited. What I'm saying is that Jason has launched a plan, and I'm willing to see what it is. This maybe it, if I don't like what we do, maybe I'll be ready then," he tells the group.

"Hmm," Jose mumbles.

"According to Franco, it's going to involve every devil. This is supposed to be large scale," Ty adds.

Jose laughs aloud. "Ty, that sounds like a good, old-fashioned fight on the battlefield. Been there, done that. We have lost most of those. That's what you are waiting for?" Jose asks.

"Well, we will see. Like I said, if I don't like it, then I'll call ya," he tells Jose.

"All right, well, this was a waste of my time," Jose expresses.

"Yeah, maybe ours too," Curt adds.

"Here is something you have to understand. I've been watching my brother for a long time, and you're right. He has gone soft. It's hurt all the devils. He's my brother, but his time is up. We are not on his schedule. We are on mine. When I'm ready to go, I hope you're on our side. I like you. I would hate to have to take you out as well," Jose looks at Ty.

Ty takes a drink as Luis leans back in his chair and grips his beer.

"You do what you got to do," Ty says.

"I will. See, this plan that I've been cooking, it's ready. Having you would just be the second cherry on top," Jose tells him.

"It's that easy to kill your own brother, huh?" Ty asks Jose.

"It wouldn't be the first time it happened. We are devils. It's in our nature to be bad, to be evil. It's in us. We are born this way. Cold-blooded killers, even our own, if it's the means to the end of the angels."

* * * * *

The party is midway through, and Matt finally shows up. He doesn't bother knocking; he just walks in. As he walks in, he finds Sherri already standing next to the door. Brodie sees Matt enter; it is obvious that he is not happy about it. Sherri watches as Matt closes the door. She realizes that his friends aren't with him.

"It worked," she thinks to herself. She is that much happier knowing that his friends didn't show.

Now she and her friends can relax.

"Hey, baby," she says as she leans in for a kiss. He gives her his cheek. Her brows drop as she plants the kiss.

"So this party is cracking," he says with surprise.

"Yeah, it is. It's great, isn't it? I missed you," she tells him. Matt completely disregards her affection.

"Where's the beer?"

"Um, there is some in the kitchen and in the back."

Not the response she was hoping for, but she follows him to the back. On the way there, Becca spots Sherri and her boyfriend. She crunches her face. Matt gets to the cooler and grabs a beer. He cracks it open and takes a drink. Sherri watches as the drink turns into the consumption of the entire beer.

"Geez, you in a hurry or something?" she attempts to joke.

He tosses the empty can over the rail.

"Hey, why did you do that?" she asks.

"We have recycling inside. You have to go pick that up," she instructs him.

"I'll get it on my way out," he tells her.

"No, you have to go get it now. I'll go with you," she offers.

He looks at her as he grabs another beer. He opens it and walks inside. He begins to roam around, not really caring if she is next to him.

"Babe, you have to go down and get that can," she tells him.

He ignores her.

"Babe, I'm trying to talk to you," she says.

"Babe let's just party, huh," he suggests.

"Do you plan on talking to me to me at all tonight?" she asks.

"Yeah, we are going to talk," he tells her.

"Well then, why don't you stop and turn around and talk to me," she commands.

He continues to move around, ignoring her. He stops suddenly; she doesn't notice in time and runs into his back. He turns around.

"What do you want to talk about?" he asks her. He stares at her for a brief second and then begins looking around. She stares up at him as he avoids eye contact. She wants to cry but is holding back. She's hurt by his behavior.

"Why are you acting like this?" she asks him.

"I'm just trying to party," he answers.

They stand in silence. They are in the middle of the crowd, but none are paying attention. Becca, on the other hand, has had her eyes locked on them since she spotted them going outside for beer. She can tell something isn't right.

"You're hurting my feelings," she tells him. He shrugs his shoulders.

"You hurt my feelings by not allowing my friends to come to this party. You got what you wanted. They're not here," he replies.

She offers no response, just a sad expression. She now knows why he is treating her with such a cold attitude. Her emotions get the best of her, and she can't hold her tears in anymore. They begin to run down her face. She struggles to get her next words out.

"But I'm here. We get to spend some time together," she tells him.

"You are selfish," he responds. She walks around him and goes up to her room. Becca, with her eyes locked on them, sees her walk away and goes after her.

* * * *

The party continues with a positive flow, at least for those who are not hosting. Matthew has been lying low, as he doesn't care to talk to anyone at the party, nor do the partyers care to talk to him. Matthew is visibly irritated and bored. Sherri isn't around to witness his misery as she is still up in her room getting consoled by her friend. Matthew had every intention of having his friends attend, so he had them on standby, and when Sherri went upstairs, he texted them to come over. About twenty minutes pass when there is a knock at the door. None of the hosts can hear it, so a random person next to the door answers. A group of males is at the door. The partygoer welcomes them in, not knowing who they are. The group comes in and begins looking for Matthew. It doesn't take long before Matthew finds them.

"What's up, you pussies?" he says to his buddies.

"Hey, cocksucker," one of Matt's friends replies.

"I'm glad you mofos are here. There are plenty of tight hotties here. Let's get some beer," Matthew tells his friends. They all walk over to the cooler in the back.

"We have to catch up. Let's shotgun," Roby tells the group.

They all grab a beer can and prepare. The commotion of the group preparing for a beer shotgun grabs Brodie's attention. He gets himself into position to see a little better. He sees Matthew laughing, which is odd to him, considering earlier he saw him bored and miserable. He moves closer to see why Matthew is laughing. He sees him holding a beer with both hands. As he makes out the scene, he realizes what's happening.

"Son of a bitch," he says softly. He sees Matthew's friends surrounding him. He looks around for Becca and Sherri. He doesn't see them, so he decides to check their rooms. He works his way through the crowd and goes up the stairs. He gets to Sherri's door and knocks as he lets himself in. He finds the girls laughing.

"What are you guys doing?" he asks them.

"Just talking," Sherri tells him.

"We were just about to head back down," Becca tells him.

"Well, Matt's idiots are here," he tells the girls.

The girls look confused for a second.

"Idiots?" Sherri asks.

"His friends are here," Brodie clarifies.

"Matt's friends are here?" Becca asks.

"Yup," he answers with an unhappy smile on his face.

"Oh my god!" Sherri says.

"I thought you told him they couldn't come," Becca checks.

"I did. He obviously didn't listen," she responds.

"Damn it, I just know something bad is going to happen," Becca expresses.

Sherri has a concerned look on her face. "Maybe it won't be that bad," she offers.

"I will bet any amount of money that something is going to happen. You're going to have to tell them to leave, or I will," Becca commands.

"I'll talk to him again," Sherri tells her friends.

"Sherri, he just made you cry and treated you like shit, and then he called his friends over. You need to do more than just talk to him," Becca suggests.

Sherri thinks about it a second. "You know what, you are right. This is bull crap," she says as she stands.

Becca and Brodie laugh at Sherri.

"Bull crap, huh?" Brodie asks, still laughing.

"Yeah, what's wrong with that?" she asks.

"You mean bullshit," Becca asks.

"It's the same thing," Sherri tells them.

"It's just hilarious how you don't like to say bad words," Brodie tells her.

Sherri walks toward him. "I have to go take care of some shit," she says to Brodie's face.

Becca follows her and smiles in Brodie's face as she passes him. Sherri marches out the door and down the stairs. Brodie and Becca follow closely behind. She gets through the crowd and looks around. She finds Matt and his friends outside. By now, they have displaced anyone who was outside, and they are drinking like it is a race. Sherri walks up to Matt and tugs at his shirt.

"Hey, I need to talk to you," she tells him. She motions to him that she wants to talk inside away from his friends.

"Let's go upstairs to talk," she tells him.

"Right now, come on. I'm with the boys," he pleads.

"Yeah, right now," she reiterates.

"I'm only going upstairs for one thing," he tells her.

She grabs him by the arm and pulls him inside. She leads him through the crowd and to the stairs. Matthew pulls his arm away from her.

"Come on, what the hell are we doing?" he asks her.

"Why are they here? I told you not to invite them," she says.

"Ah, fuck, man, don't start with me right now," he replies.

"I told you in advance that they were not invited," she says with an elevated tone.

Matthew walks away to return to his friends.

She follows. "Matthew, I am not done talking to you," she says with his back turned.

Matt reaches his friends.

"You in trouble, bro?" his friend asks.

"Fine, we'll do it right here," she tells Matt.

He turns around. "Do what?" he asks.

"Your friends have to leave right now," she tells him.

Matt stares at her.

"It's cuz of that fuckin' faggot, isn't it?" Jack yells aloud.

Sherri looks at Jack, then she looks right back at Matt.

"It is, isn't it?" Matt verifies.

That was not the response she wanted from Matt. She steps over to Jack. "Don't you ever call him that again, ever, JACK," she says his name with some Moxy. "And it's not him, it's me. So get the fuck out of my house," she says with a strong tone.

Matt looks confused, wondering where the Sherri she knows went. She returns to Matt. "It's me. I want them gone now," she says sternly. She has drawn the attention of those that are nearby. Matt takes a step back. He is surprised at the way she snapped at him. He doesn't know how to react; he has never seen her like this. Sherri turns to face his friends. "All four of you, get the hell out of my home," she says as she takes a beer out of Jack's hand.

"This is my beer. All of this is my beer. You were never invited here, so get your fuckin' asses out of my house," she says with a level of attitude never before witnessed by her boyfriend or her best friends.

She takes a drink of the beer she confiscated. The four friends stand frozen; they too have never seen this side of Sherri. They begin to make their way inside and through the crowd, to the door. Some in the crowd begin to cheer and chant as the friends walk by.

"Well, if they go, then I go," Matt tells her.

Sherri takes a step closer to him, takes a drink, looks him in the eyes. "Well, if you go, then we are over," she responds.

Becca and Brodie hold each other. Matt stands still for a moment to think. She has never threatened their relationship before. He looks over at the door and sees his last friend walk out. He looks down at her.

"I'll call you tomorrow. You better have this attitude gone by then," he instructs her. Matt begins to walk toward the door, through the crowd. Sherri turns to see him leave but doesn't say a word. She is holding strong on the outside but also feels nervous and scared on the inside. Brodie and Becca walk up to Sherri and give her a big hug.

"I am so turned on by you right now," Becca tells Sherri.

"So am I," Brodie adds. Her two friends give her some more praise and reinforcement, that what she did was brave and the right thing to do. She is in deep thought, so she does not hear what they are saying. She is not sure how to feel in that moment. She is also a little surprised about how she reacted. As everyone cheers around her, she wonders how she did it.

It's like I blacked out, she thinks to herself.

"Sher Bear, Sher Bear," she hears coming into focus. Becca is trying to get her attention.

"Are you okay?" Becca asks.

"Yes, yeah, I was just thinking about something," she tells her.

"Okay, let's party, huh," Becca tells her.

They hug one more time and then raise their drinks up and begin to yell and scream in laughter. Becca is super happy and energized by the display she saw from her friend.

"Let's bring this house down!" Sherri yells loud at the crowd.

Sunday

The clock nears 11:30 a.m., and Becca opens one eye. Several seconds later, the second one opens. With both eyes open, she lifts her head just enough to look around. Her head was lying on her friend's shoulder as they both lie on the kitchen floor. She continues to look around until she realizes that she's lying in the kitchen. She continues to look around; she immediately thinks about Sherri.

"Where is she?" She's not ready to move yet, so she drops her head again and closes her eyes.

Moments later, she rolls to her side and gets on her elbow. She squints a little and runs her hand through her hair. She continues to look around as she gets to her knees. She stares into the living room then gets to her feet.

She walks toward the living room, stepping over a male she doesn't know. She gets to the middle of the living room and looks around. Sherri is nowhere to be found. She gets to the stairs and stops. Stairs are the last thing she's in the mood for at that moment. She takes her first step and climbs the stairs like a zombie.

As she reaches the top, she can see two females lying on the ground, right at the top of the stairs. She steps over the bodies. She gets to Sherri's door; it's cracked, so she opens it a little more. She looks around and cannot see Sherri but can see a couple sleeping in Sherri's bed. She goes on to her own room. When she opens her door, she sees Sherri lying under her bed with her top half sticking out from under the bed.

"What was she doing?" she says softly. Having found her, she moves on to look for Brodie. She walks back down the stairs, again stepping over the bodies, this time, managing the stairs a little easier, but not by much. She gets to his room, and the door is closed. She opens it to find two girls in his bed. She looks in his bathroom and finds it empty. She walks back out into the living room. She looks out at the balcony and sees a pair of legs crossed. She walks toward the legs and finds him lying there.

Is he sleeping still or again? she thinks. With her friends accounted for, she goes to the sink for water. She goes to the couch with her water and sits for a minute.

While she sits, the two girls from the top of the stairs come downstairs and make their way out of the apartment without saying a word to her. She hears a noise coming from the outside; she looks over. Brodie walks into her view and stops.

"What are you doing?" he asks.

Becca stares at him and just shrugs her shoulders. He looks around the apartment.

"Where's Sherri?" he asks.

"Oh, my room," she answers.

"Hmmm," he mumbles.

"Well, let's go wake her up," he says.

"We really shouldn't," she says as she gets off the couch and follows Brodie to her room.

Brodie sits down next to Sherri's head. Becca gets onto the bed and lies over Sherri, lying the same direction.

"I am having trouble remembering last night," Becca says.

"Yeah, it got crazy, right?" Brodie responds.

"It was out of control," they both hear.

Sherri's addition to the conversation surprised the two. Brodie looks down at her, but Becca is too weak to react.

"Where am I?" Sherri asks.

"You are halfway under Becca's bed," Brodie tells her.

"Hmm, where did you guys sleep?" she asks.

"I slept in my bed," Brodie tells her.

"But you came in from outside," Becca tells Brodie.

"I moved out there after I woke up, get some fresh air and sun," he tells Becca.

"Well, I woke up on the kitchen floor," Becca says.

"Ew, kinky," Brodie comments.

Both girls find it funny but don't have much strength to laugh.

"We have several people scattered around the place passed out. Oh, and there are two girls sleeping in your bed, Brodie," Becca tells them.

"What! Really?" he asks with excitement.

"Yeah, I saw them," she replies.

"No foolin'?" he checks.

"No foolin'," she confirms.

"I should probably make my way back down there then and make sure they're still naked, know what I'm sayin'?" he tells the girls.

"You're messing with us, right?"

"You knew there were girls in your bed?" Becca asks.

Brodie smiles at her. He slowly gets to his feet, but before he can take a step, he feels a grab at his ankle. He looks down.

"Wait, you have to help me," Sherri asks with a muffled voice.

"I can't," Becca says as she flings her arm over the bed, hovering over Sherri's head.

"Not you, him," he clarifies.

Brodie gets back down on one knee and pulls Sherri's bottom half out from under the bed.

"How did you end up with only your bottom half under the bed?" he asks.

"Never mind, it can't be the only unexplainable thing that happened last night," he adds.

She gets to her feet and gets herself onto the bed. Brodie turns to make his way out of the room.

"Wait! We still need you. You need to help me onto the pillows, please," Becca asks. He grabs her by the armpits to lay her next to Sherri.

"Ooowww," Becca moans.

"What, I just moved you," Brodie says.

"I know, that's what hurt," Becca replies. Both girls cuddle each other and fall asleep again. Having helped his friends into position, Brodie walks out of the room to check on the women he left in his bed.

* * * * *

Nate walks into his living room where Brad is waiting.

"Hey, Bradley."

"Thanks for meeting with me. I know you are busy, sir," Brad says.

"Oh, don't mention it. Meeting with you will always be a priority. Grab yourself a drink. So what kind of updates do you have?"

"In Sisters, over two hundred angels are looking for the halo. Paloma is leading the charge there."

"That's a good number. I wonder if it's enough for those conditions," Nate questions.

"Yeah, I'm monitoring it. We have been adding as Paloma sees fit. I'll touch base with her tomorrow and see where we are at," Brad tells Nate.

"I know you have a great plan in place. I'm just restless about the halo. I don't mean to question you. Don't mind me," Nate says.

"I understand, sir. It's a stressful time for us all."

"Yes, well, I think it would be great for the angels if we went down there to visit. Would you mind setting that up?"

"Great idea, I'll set it up for next week," Brad tells him.

"What else do you have?" he asks.

"So closer to home, I started the investigation into the crash. I had initial meetings with the three survivors. I didn't get much from them. Let me asks you something. What would you think if I told you that on the way home, JR was completely quiet according to the other angels?" Brad asks as he gets up to top off his drink.

"Hmm, not sure what to think about that. Doesn't seem too concerning. Anything else about that?"

"No, just that he didn't talk to any of the others on the return home. He was next to Z the whole time pretty much and didn't even talk to him. Z, on the other hand, was fixated on the halo for a while."

"That isn't abnormal either," Nate says.

"Right, so I didn't get much from them. I'm also going to check the phone records for all eight angels," Brad mentions. "I went through the black box with Becky. It showed that the jet itself wasn't being tracked. That means that something or someone inside was sending a signal."

"That is so disturbing. I can't imagine it being any of those angels," Nate says.

"Yeah, agreed. I'll be talking to folks in Bend as well. When we go next week, I'll spend some extra time down there to talk to folks."

"Very well," Nate says with a deflated tone.

"How are you doing, sir?" The question catches Nate off guard.

"Well, like I said earlier, I am pretty restless and feel helpless. I wish I could do more. So that visit will be good. I'm also waiting for Jason to return to town. I still want to meet with him," Nate responds.

"Good, well, let me know if there is something I can help with," Brad offers.

"Thank you, Bradley, but you are doing so much already. You will let me know if you're getting stretched too thin." Brad smiles.

"Besides, I've got Erin taking care of me. With her around, there is no way I'll need anything," he tells Brad.

"I believe that," Brad says.

"That reminds me, let's set a date for Lupe and Lisa over for dinner. I would really like to see your little one."

"Sure, I'll have Lupe call Erin and set a date." Brad finishes his drink.

"Okay, I'm going to head out. I'll keep you updated," he tells Nate.

* * * * *

A movie is playing as the three friends lie on the sectional recovering from the party. The plan was to clean, but so far, they have only managed to order food and watch movies.

"Where is my water?" Brodie asks himself. He looks around his immediate area and can't find it. He looks over at the girls. "Have you guys seen my water bottle?"

"Oh yeah, here," Becca grabs it and tosses it in his direction.

"It's empty," he points out.

"Yeah, I wanted some, and I didn't want to get up. You dozed off, so I just reached for it."

"So you gonna refill it?" he asks.

"No, I don't want to get up."

"You ain't right," he tells her. About twenty minutes go by, and the current movie finishes.

"I love that movie," Sherri says.

"Yeah, it's a good one," Brodie says as he gets off the couch.

"Oh, get me water too please?" Becca asks.

"Nope," he responds.

"Come on, Brodie," she complains.

"Here, I'll get you some, but I have to pee first," Sherri says as she gets up.

Brodie returns from the kitchen.

"What are we watching next?" he asks.

"When are we going to tell her?" Becca asks in a soft voice.

"I don't know. It's hard to just come out with it," he says.

"Well, we are halfway through the day, and we still have to clean and do other shit. We have to tell her today," she expresses.

"I know, but we also feel like shit, and what if she isn't in the mood for it?"

"Brod, there is no good time to tell anyone this kind of thing, but we have to tell her today."

"Tell me what today?" Sherri asks as she returns to the living room.

Becca looks over at her then looks at Brodie. She raises her eyebrows at him.

"What, guys? Do you guys have something to say to me?" Sherri asks again.

"Brodie does, we both do, but more Brodie," Becca says.

Sherri looks at Brodie. "Brod, what's going on?" she asks as she returns to her seat.

"Fine, I have to tell you something. You're going to want to sit," he starts with a joke.

She puts her hands out and nod. Becca adjusts herself then scoots close to Sherri and wraps her arms around her.

"You two are creeping me out right now. What is going on?" she asks again.

"Okay, so—"

"Wait!" Becca shouts.

"What?" Brodie asks.

"My water, nobody got me water," she says.

Her friends look at her.

"It's gonna have to wait, or you can get it yourself," Brodie tells her.

"I'll wait," she responds.

"All right, here is goes. Sherri, the other day, when Becca and I were at the store, Thursday—I think the same day as our dinner—I saw Matt with another girl."

Sherri stares at him then looks down at her hands. Becca and Brodie look at each other in an awkward silence.

"Sher Bear, honey, talk to us, what are you thinking right now?" Becca asks.

The silence continues. She looks at Brodie.

"Um, how? I mean can you describe it a little more?" she asks.

"Well, Becca was in a different aisle. I saw this chick down the aisle pushing a cart. I stared at her for a moment then saw Matt walk up right behind her and put his hands on her. I quickly turned away, so he wouldn't recognize me. I followed them because I wanted to find Becks. They were pretty affectionate with each other. I wanted to avoid her running into him. I found her, and I made up a story about a girl so that I could get her to the other side of the store. We waited there until I saw them leave together. When I found her, I yelled her name out because they were close. I'm fairly sure he heard it," he explains.

Sherri begins to cry as Becca is holding her.

"I'm so sorry, Sher."

"You have nothing to be sorry about. Thank you for telling me," she says as she wipes away tears.

"Ugh, I feel so stupid. I wonder how long this has been going on. Like, what did I do wrong?" Sherri expresses.

"Honey, you didn't do anything wrong. He's the one that betrayed you, broke your trust. You were good to him, too good," Becca tells her.

"Maybe that was the problem."

"Nope, absolutely not, you're not the problem here. You haven't done anything wrong. Don't even begin to think that way," Brodie tells her.

"This just makes sense. I mean, we don't like him, of course, but there was just shit about him that was telling of this. I'm not saying we knew he was going to cheat on you, but based on the kind of guy he is, it's not surprising," Becca adds.

"Well, it's over, I will not put up with this. Guess you guys are happy, huh."

"Not at your expense. This is awful. I hate that you are hurting like this," Becca tells her.

"Yeah, we will just be happy that he won't be able to continue hurting you," Brodie adds.

"So what are you going to do now?" Becca asks.

She sniffles as she wipes away some more tears.

"I'm going to go break up with him."

"You want me to come with you?" Becca offers.

"No, I have to do this alone. I'll confirm it from him, then it'll be over." She stands up. "I'm going upstairs for a bit first, then I'll go. I need some time to think. Listen, I'll help when I get back. I'm sorry to have to do this right now," Sherri says.

"Don't worry about it. Becca and I will take care of the mess. You do what you got to do," Brodie tells her.

Sherri looks down at her hands and begins to sob. "Thanks, guys."

Becca gives her a big squeeze. "We love you, honey," Becca tells her.

"I love you guys too," she responds.

* * * * *

"Ariah, checking in," Katy radios.

"Copy that," Ariah responds.

A minute passes.

"Ariah, checking in," Katy radios again.

"Copy that. Did you not get my last response? Or is this an unscheduled check-in?" Ariah asks.

"Ariah, checking in," Katy radios again.

"Kate, are you okay?" Ariah asks.

"Ariah, checking in," Katy radios a fourth time.

"Katy, are you okay? What's going on? You are freaking me out. Say something different," Ariah requests. She gets no response. Katy hears something behind her, so she turns around to check. She sees nothing.

"Katy, what are you doing! Come in, over," Ariah requests.

She has paused her search for the moment to focus on her friend. Katy turns back around and continues her search.

"Ariah, checking in," Katy says again as she bursts into laughter.

"Katy, what the hell are you doing? Are you okay?" Ariah asks with great concern.

"Yeah, I'm fine, I'm just fucking with you."

"Goddamn it! Why are you doing that?" Ariah asks as she resumes her search.

"Oh, I'm just bored. But I did want to ask you if you wanted to have dinner together today?" Katy hears more noise behind her, so she turns to look again.

"I shouldn't for making me worry just now," Ariah says.

There is silence between them. Katy doesn't see anything again, but she is sure something or someone is following her. She turns back around.

"Cool then, how about some Chinese?" Katy asks.

"What? Did you just not hear what I said?" Ariah asks.

"Um, yeah, you said yes, right?" Katy asks with uncertainty.

"No, I didn't say yes. What is going on with you? You're not paying attention to me, are you?" Ariah asks.

"Sorry, I thought I saw something," Katy explains. She sets up a little decoy for the follower then takes cover under some brush.

"You better be careful. It might be the devils again. You need me to go your way?" Ariah offers.

"No, no, it's nothing," Katy says very softly.

"Why are you whispering?" Ariah asks.

"Oh, I see a deer. Don't want to scare it. So dinner?" Katy asks again.

"Sure, weirdo. There's one minute until the next check-in, so let's just say that this is it. I'll do the check-ins from now on, no more games," Ariah tells her.

"Cool, got it. I'm out," Katy relays. Katy can she a person come into her line of sight.

"What are you doing?" she asks herself. She stares a little longer to observe their actions. The follower continues toward the decoy. She decides to circle around to get behind them. The follower can see the decoy but stops because they are unsure if it's her or something else. Katy pulls her bow out and an arrow. She sets her arrow as she gets closer to the unsuspecting follower. The follower gets close enough to the decoy to realize that it's just that. Katy is now behind them with her bow drawn.

"Put your hand up slowly," Katy orders.

The follower slowly raises their arms out to their side.

"Now stand up and turn around," she orders.

The follower stands and slowly turns around.

"You. Why are you following me, devil?"

The devil stays silent.

"Get on your knees, and put your hands behind your head. And take your hoodie off," Katy commands.

The devil does all three actions simultaneously.

"Why are you following me? You're the same devil from the other day, right? Near JR's body?" she asks.

The devil nods.

"You had a chance to kill me, and you didn't, why?" she asks.

"Now you have a chance to do the same. What are you going to do?" the devil asks.

Katy stares at him as she remembers their first interaction and the feeling that came over her then. She is having the same feelings now.

"I don't know yet. That depends on what you do, or what you say," she tells him.

He slowly brings his hands out from behind his head.

"I'm going to stand up," he tells her. "Have you made your decision?" he asks.

"About what?" she asks.

"If you're going to kill me," he says as he stands up. He shows her his palms and puts them down.

"You should go," Katy tells the devil.

"I've enjoyed watching you work," the devil tells her.

"What do you mean? How long have you been watching me?" she asks.

"Since you got into town, back at your hotel," he says.

She looks at him with discontent. "Don't think about making any moves," she warns him.

"Listen, if I wanted to harm you or kill you, I would have done that already."

"You had your crossbow aimed at my head," she tells him.

"I did. I wanted to make sure you stayed in place. I wanted to see you. Instead, I helped you find your friend's body. I didn't get a thank-you."

"Is that what you want? Is that why you're following me?"

"You saw me the other day, but I've been watching you for several days now," he tells her.

She doesn't know how to respond; she stays quiet.

"I think you are the most beautiful woman I have ever seen," he tells her.

She fights against a smile.

He is a devil, she thinks.

"Go, you need to leave," she tells him.

He smiles at her as he puts his hands out and bows away. Before he completely turns around, he looks at her. "I'll be seeing you again," he says as he turns around completely and jogs away.

She lowers her bow and looks around as she snaps out of what felt like a spell to her. She takes a deep breath and checks her surroundings again.

"What the fuck just happened?" she says aloud.

* * * * *

Sherri pulls up to Matt's house. She waits in her car, struggles to get out because she is nervous, upset, and nauseous and has a little anxiety. She sees one of his friends peek out the window. Knowing that the friend will inform Matt of her arrival, she finally gets out of the car after taking some deep breaths. She walks up to the door and waits. She closes her eyes then opens the door. She sees Matt in the living room with two of his friends/roommates. The friends don't acknowledge her as they are upset from getting kicked out of the party.

"We need to talk," she says in a soft voice.

"Well, that's going to have to wait," he replies.

She smiles. "Okay, that's how you want to do it. Fine, we will do it right here," she says in an elevated voice. She walks and stands right in front of him, obstructing his view to the TV. The three men look at her.

"Look, I don't care about last night. That was a bogus party, anyways. We throw way better parties than that. We're good," Matt tells Sherri.

"Hell, yeah, we do," his Roby confirms.

She smiles again. "This isn't about the fuckin' party last night." She gets Matt's attention.

"I'm going to ask you some questions. Well, one, really, then there might be some follow-up questions. This question is a simple yes-or-no question. You don't get ask me questions in return."

Matt has a confused look on his face.

"Are you cheating on me?" she asks.

The friends' eyes open wide. Matt remains stone-faced.

"What?" he asks.

"That's a question. You don't get to ask questions. Just answer. This one is a simple yes-or-no question. Are you cheating on me?" she asks again.

"What are you talking about?" he asks.

She clamps her lips and laughs. She leans into his face. "The next word out of our mouth should be yes or no. If it's anything other than one of those two words, I'm going to break this place."

There is a small pause. He begins to muster up a response but holds back and exhales instead.

"You're crazy," he says.

She stands straight up, turns around, and walks over to a trophy. She grabs it and throws it at the large flat-screen TV.

"What the fuck?" Matt shouts.

"Holy shit, man," Roby says.

"What the fuck did you do that for?" Patrick says.

The sounds of a trophy hitting the TV draws the attention of the other two roommates, Jack and Tim.

"What the fuck happened?" Jack asks.

"My TV," Tim says.

"More shit is going to break in the house if Matt can't tell me what I want to know," she tells the group.

"Bro, you need to take your shit somewhere else—your room, outside, I don't care. This ain't our problem," Tim tells Matt.

"It's too late for that. This is happening right here, right now," she tells the group.

"Fuck this," Jack says as he rushes over to grab some of his valuables. This prompts the other three roommates to do the same. All four grab what is important to them to avoid getting damaged.

"Are you cheating on me?" she asks again.

"No!" Matt yells out.

A couple of the roommates look over at him, surprised. Sherri walks over to the kitchen and grabs a deep fryer off the counter, unplugs it, and slams it on the floor.

"Ah, hell no. Bro, get her the fuck out of here. She's fucking all my shit up!" Tim yells.

She grabs a knife on her way out of the kitchen and sticks it in her back pocket.

"What if I told you that you were seen at a Safeway with another girl this past Thursday."

"Who told you that?" he asks.

She walks over to grab a mini wooden bear statue and throws it at the large living-room window, shattering it.

"Holy fuck!" Patrick shouts.

"Dude, I'm calling the fuckin' cops. Damn it, forgot to grab that bear!" Roby shouts.

"You going to let the cops take me?" she asks Matt.

"Dude, don't. I'll take care of this," Matt tells his roommates.

"You're more concerned about who told me and less concerned about telling me if it's true?" she asks him.

"Let's go outside," Matt tells her.

"You haven't answered a single question," she says.

"Store, is it true?" she asks.

"Let's go outside," he says again.

She pulls the knife out of her pocket.

"She has a fuckin' knife!" Patrick yells.

Matt stands up and puts his hands up. Sherri goes to one side of the couch, jabs the arm rest, and tears it down the middle. The roommates are in disbelief.

"Ah, my fucking couch!" Jack yells.

"Tell me the truth," she continues to carve up the couch. Matt goes to her and grabs her wrist with the knife in her hand.

"Stop this shit now," he says. She stands straight up and looks at him.

"Let my wrist go now," she says.

"Drop the knife first," he tells her. She throws it to the couch. He lets her wrist go. She turns to his roommates. "Your boy here isn't particularly good at following instructions. He really has no regard for your possessions."

"You're a crazy fuckin' bitch!" Jack yells at her.

She chuckles. "This is nothing. I'm just getting started."

"Sherri, stop this shit now," Matt tells her.

She turns around and walks up to him.

"Just tell me. I already know. I just need to have it confirmed by you. Are you cheating on me?"

Matt clears his throat and takes a deep breath. "Yes."

"Okay, I'm done here. That is all I needed to know."

She walks toward the door.

"Are we not going to talk about this?" he asks.

She turns around. "There is nothing to talk about. You cheated. I don't need to know the details. We are done. You will never see me again."

On her way to the front door, she grabs an ashtray. She turns and throws it at a fish tank. *Clink!* The sound of broken glass fills the air.

"What the fuck!" Patrick yells.

Fifty gallons of water splash onto the floor and spread around the house. She walks out the front door to her car.

"You motherfucker. You could have said yes ten minutes ago," Jack says.

"No shit, you're paying for all of this shit," Roby says.

She gets to her car and opens her trunk; she pulls out two boxes of Matt's possessions and sets them on the front lawn. Matt watches from the front door. She pulls out a book of matches and lights a match. She tosses it into one of the boxes. It catches fire fast as she had poured lighter fluid on it earlier. She lights a second match and tosses it into the second box. She closes her trunk and walks to the car door.

"Babe, let's talk about this. We can work this out!" he desperately shouts.

She looks up at him. "I'm free from you."

* * * * *

It's midday Sunday, and the halo has been floating for about four and a half days. It now rests inside the lagoon of Ross Island in Portland. Ross Island splits the Willamette and has an opening on the northeast side. As it flowed toward the downtown area, the current—combined with water activity such as boats, kayakers, and other water activities—pushed the halo to the open side of the island where a final wave drove it into the lagoon. Along the way, the halo managed to avoid the waterfalls further back at Willamette falls. Its destiny might be much different if the falls would have caught it.

But instead, it now sits in the calm waters of a lagoon. The halo has floated to the edge and is currently hooked by a rock that lines the island. There isn't a natural current that goes through the lagoon, but boats do enter the area occasionally. So any chance it has to continue its journey is dependent on the activity of people. Most of the island is private, so the public isn't allowed onto the land, and the portion that is not private is owned by the city, and people must meet a specific criterion to gain permission to access that area. Still, it's not uncommon for people to take their watercraft into the lagoon and hang out. For now, it will sit and wait, not too far from its home.

I hope you enjoy this book as much as I enjoyed writing it. I infused many personal elements from my life, which brings me much pride, but I also hope that these elements add a unique tone to this book.

Thank you for your support, and I look forward to bringing you the next part of the story soon.

CPSIA information can be obtained
at www.ICGtesting.com
Printed in the USA
BVHW041310210323
660846BV00005B/106

9 781684 986859